THE LUCK OF THE VAILS

Edward Frederick Benson was born on 24 July 1867 in Berkshire, the son of a future Archbishop of Canterbury, and one of six children. He studied at Kings College, Cambridge and at the British School of Archaeology in Athens. Benson's first book, *Dodo*, was published to popular acclaim in 1893 and was followed by over a hundred books, including novels, histories, biographies and ghost stories. In 1920 Benson became a full-time tenant of Lamb House in Rye, which had once been home to the novelist Henry James. Rye provided the setting for Benson's popular 'Mapp and Lucia' stories and their author served three terms as mayor of Rye in the late 1930s. E. F. Benson died on 29 February 1940.

ALSO BY E. F. BENSON

Queen Lucia
Miss Mapp
Lucia in London
Lucia's Progress
Trouble for Lucia
The Blotting Book

E. F. BENSON

The Luck of the Vails

VINTAGE BOOKS
London

Published by Vintage 2013

2 4 6 8 10 9 7 5 3 1

First published in Great Britain by William Heinemann in 1901

Vintage
Random House, 20 Vauxhall Bridge Road,
London SW1V 2SA

Addresses for companies within The Random House Group Limited can
be found at: www.randomhouse.co.uk/offices.htm

The Random House Group Limited Reg. No. 954009

A CIP catalogue record for this book
is available from the British Library

ISBN 9780099572435

The Random House Group Limited supports the Forest Stewardship
Council® (FSC®), the leading international forest-certification organisation.
Our books carrying the FSC label are printed on FSC®-certified paper.
FSC is the only forest-certification scheme supported by the leading
environmental organisations, including Greenpeace. Our
paper procurement policy can be found at
www.randomhouse.co.uk/environment

Typeset in Meridien by Replika Press Pvt Ltd, India

Printed and bound in Great Britain by Clays Ltd, St Ives plc

To my brother

ARTHUR CHRISTOPHER BENSON

This story of his, not of my invention
is affectionately
dedicated by its admiring scribe.

PART I

Chapter 1

The Shadows Dance

THE short winter's day was drawing to its close, and twilight, the steel and silver twilight of a windless frost, was falling in throbs of gathered dusk over an ice-bound land. The sun, brilliant, but cold as an electric lamp, had not in all its hours of shining been of strength sufficient to melt the rime congealed during the night before, and each blade of grass on the lawns, each spray and sprig on the bare hedgerows, had remained a spear of crystals minute and innumerable. The roofs of house and cottage sparkled and glimmered as with a soft internal lustre in the light of the moon, which had risen an hour before sunset, and the stillness of a great cold—a thing more palpably motionless than even the stricken noonday of the south— gripped all in its vice. Silent, steadfast lights had sprung up and multiplied in the many-windowed village, but not a bird chirped or dog barked. Labourers were home from the iron of the frozen fields, doors were shut, and the huge night was at hand.

The sequestered village of Vail lies in a wrinkle of the great Wiltshire downs, and is traversed by the Bath road. The big inn, the Vail Arms, seems to speak of the more prosperous days of coach and horn, but now its significance to the shrill greyhounds of the railway is of the smallest, and they pass for the most part without salute. About a mile beyond it to the outward-bound traveller stands the big house, screened by some ten furlongs of park, and entering the gate, he will find himself in a noble company of secular trees, beech in the majority, and of stately growth. Shortly before the house becomes visible a spacious piece of meadow-land succeeds to the park; thence the road, passing over a broad stone bridge which spans the chalk stream flowing from the sheet of water above, is bounded on either side by terraced lawns of ancient and close-napped turf, intersected at intervals by gravel walks, and turning sharply to the right, follows a long box hedge, once cut into tall and fantastic shapes. But it seems long to have lacked the shears and pruning hand, for all precision of outline has been lost, and what were once the formal figures of bird and beast have swelled into monstrous masses of deformed shape, wrought, you would think, by the imagination of a night-hag into things inhuman. Here, as seen in the dim light, a thin neck would bulge into some ghastliness of a head, hydrocephalous or tumoured with long-standing disease; here a bird with dwindled body and scarecrow wings stood on the legs of a colossus; here conjecture would vainly seek for a reconstruction.

The end of one of the wings of the house, which was built round three sides of a quadrangle, abutted on to this hedge so closely that a peacock with bloated tail peered into the gun-room window, and in the centre of the gravel sweep rose a bronze Triton fountain, bearded like an old man with long dependence of icicle. A bitter north wind had accompanied the early days of the frost, and this icy fringe had grown out sideways from the lip of the basin, blown aside even as it congealed. Flower-beds, a riband of dark untenanted earth, ran underneath the windows, which rose in three stories, small-paned and Jacobean. As dark fell, light sprang out in the walls, as the stars in the field of heaven, but to right and left of the front-door there came through a row of windows yet uncurtained a redder and less constant gleam than the shining of oil or wax, now growing, now diminishing, leaping out at one moment to a great vividness, at the next suddenly dying down again, so that in the corners of the room there was a continual battle of shadows. Now, as the flames from the wood burning on the great open hearth grew dim, whole battalions of them would collect and gather, again with the kindling of some fresh stuff, they would be routed and disappear. This fitfulness of illumination played also strange tricks with the tapestries that hung on two of the four sides of the hall; figures started suddenly into being, and were blotted out before the eye had clearly visualized them, and in the inconstancy of the light a nervous man might say to himself that stir and movement was going on among them; again they rode to hounds, or took the jesses off the hawk.

The present is the heir of all the achievements of former ages, and while this great house, with its mile-long avenue, its tapestries, its pictures, its air of magnificent English stability, finely represented all that had gone before, all that was going on now was enclosed in the two large armchairs drawn close to this ideal fire, in each of which sat a young man. They talked but in desultory fashion, with frequent but not awkward pauses of some length, for any social duty of keeping the conversation going was to them quite outside a practical call. They had also been shooting all this superb frosty day, and the return to warmth and indoors, though productive of profound content, does not conduce to loquacity.

'Yes, a bath would be a very good thing,' said one, 'but it is, perhaps, a question whether in the absolutely immediate future tea would not be better.'

This was too strong a suggestion to be merely called a hint, and the other rose.

'Sorry, Geoffrey,' he said, 'I never ordered tea. I was thinking—no, I don't think I was thinking. Tea first, bath afterwards,' he added meditatively.

Geoffrey Langham stroked an imperceptible moustache.

'That's what I was thinking,' he said, 'and I'm glad to see you appreciate the importance of little things, Harry. Little things like tea and baths matter far the most.'

'Anyhow, they occur much the oftenest,' said Lord Vail.

'I was beginning to be afraid tea wasn't going to occur at all,' said Geoffrey.

Harry Vail appeared to consider this.

'You were wrong, then,' he said, 'and you are on the way to become a sensuous voluptuary.'

'On the way?' said Geoffrey. 'I have arrived. Ah, and tea is following my excellent example!'

The advent of lamps banished the mustering and dispersal of the leaping shadows, and threw the two figures seated on either side of the tea-table into strong light, and, taken together, into even stronger contrast. The birth-right of a good digestion, you would say, had been given to each, and for no mess of pottage had either bartered the clear eye and firm leanness of perfect health but, apart from this and a certain lithe youthfulness, it would have been hard at first sight even, when resemblances are more obvious than differences, to see a single point of likeness between the two. Geoffrey Langham, that sensuous voluptuary, seemed the seat and being of serene English cheerfulness, and his face, good-looking from its very pleasantness, contrasted strongly with that of the other, which was handsome, in spite of a marked and grave reserve which a stranger might easily have mistaken for sullenness. Indeed, many who might soon have ceased to be strangers had done so; and though Harry Vail had perhaps no enemies, he was in the forlorner condition of having very few friends. In fact, had he been made to enumerate them, his list would have begun with Geoffrey, and it is doubtful whether it would not also have ended with him.

But these agreeable influences of tea and light seemed to produce a briskening effect on the two, and their talk, which, since they came in, had touched a subject only to dismiss it, settled down into a more marked channel.

'Yes, it is a queer sort of coming-of-age party for me,' said Lord Vail, 'and it was really good of you to come, Geoffrey. I wonder whether anyone has ever come of age in so lonely a manner. I have only one relative in the world who can be called even distantly near. He comes this evening. Oh, I told you that.'

'Your uncle,' said Geoffrey.

'Great-uncle, to be accurate. He is my grandfather's youngest brother, and, what is so odd, he is my heir. One always thinks of heirs as being younger than one's self.'

'Cut him off with a shilling,' said Geoffrey.

'Well, there isn't much more, in any case, except this great barrack of a house. What there is, however, goes to him, and it can hardly be expected that he will marry and have children now.'

'How old is he?' asked Geoffrey.

'Something over seventy.'

'And after him?'

'The Lord knows. Anybody; the first person you meet if you walk down Piccadilly perhaps—perhaps you, perhaps the Prime Minister. Honestly, I haven't any idea.'

'Marry, then, at once,' said Geoffrey, 'and disappoint the man in the street and the Prime Minister, your uncle and me.'

Harry Vail got up, and stood with his back to the fire, stretching out his long-fingered hands to the blaze behind him.

'What advice!' he said. 'You might as well advise me to have a Greek nose. Some people have it, some do not; it is fate.'

'Marriage is a remarkably common fate,' remarked Geoffrey; 'commoner than a Greek nose. I have seen many married people without it.'

'It is commoner for certain sorts of people,' said Harry, 'but you know, I——' and he stopped.

'Well?' asked the other.

'I am not of those sorts, the sorts who go smiling through the world, and are smiled on in return. It was always the same with me. I am not truculent, or savage, or sulky, I believe, but somehow I remain friendless. I should be a hermit, if there were any nowadays.'

'Liver,' said Geoffrey decidedly. 'The fellow of twenty-one who says that sort of thing about himself has got liver. "Self-Analysis, or the Sedentary Life", a tract by Geoffrey Langham. Here endeth the gospel.'

Harry smiled.

'I don't think about my character, as a rule,' he said. 'I don't lead a sedentary life, and I haven't got liver; but if one is a recluse it is as well to recognize the fact. I haven't got any real friends like everybody else.'

'Thank you,' said Geoffrey; 'don't apologize.'

'I shall if I like; indeed, I think I will. No one but a friend would have come down here.'

'Oh, I don't know about that,' said the other. 'I would stay with people I positively loathed for shooting no worse than what we had today. In the matter of friends, what you said was inane. You might have heaps of friends if you choose; but you don't find friends by going into a room alone and locking the door behind you.'

'Ah! I do that, do I?' said Harry, with a certain eager interest in his tone.

'Just a shade. You might have heaps of friends.'

'That may be or may not; it is certain that I have not. Oh, well, this is unprofitable. Take a cigarette from the recluse.'

They smoked in silence a minute or two.

'Your uncle!' asked Geoffrey. 'He comes tonight, you said.'

'Yes, I expect him before dinner. You've never seen him?'

'Never. What is he like?'

Harry pointed to a picture that hung above the fireplace.

'Like that,' he said, 'exactly like that.'

Geoffrey looked at it a moment, shading his eyes from the lamp.

'Fancy dress ball, I suppose,' he said.

'No, the costume of the period,' said Harry. 'It is not my uncle at all, but an ancestor of sorts. The picture is by Holbein; but, oddly enough, it is the very image of Uncle Francis.'

'Francis Vail, second Baron,' spelled out Geoffrey, from the faded lettering on the frame.

'Yes, his name was Francis, too.'

'What is that great cup he is holding?' asked the other.

'Ah, I wondered whether you would notice that. I will show it you this evening—at least, I am certain that what I have found is it.'

'It looks rather a neat thing,' said Geoffrey. 'But I can't say as much for the second Baron, Harry. He seems to me a wicked old man.'

'There is no doubt that he was. Among other charming deeds, he almost certainly killed his own father. He was smothered in debt, came down here to try to get his father to pay up for him, and met with a pretty round refusal, it appears. That night the house was broken into, and the old man was found murdered in his bed. The burglar seems to have been a curious man—he took nothing, not a teaspoon.'

'Good Lord! I'm glad I'm not of ancestral family. Which is the room—*the* room?'

Harry laughed.

'The one at the end of the passage upstairs. Shall I tell them to move your things there?'

'That is true hospitality,' said Geoffrey. 'But I won't bother you. Do either of them walk?'

'Francis does; so if you meet that gentleman

about, and find he is insubstantial, you will know that you have seen a ghost.'

'And, if substantial, it will only be your uncle?'

'Exactly, so you needn't faint immediately.'

Geoffrey got up and examined the picture with more attention.

'If your uncle is like that,' he said, 'I'm not so sure that I wouldn't sooner meet the ghost.'

'I'm afraid it is too late to put him off now,' said Harry; 'and unless there is a railway accident, you will certainly meet him at dinner. But I don't understand your objection to my poor old ancestor's portrait. I have always wondered that such an awful old wretch could be made to look so charming.'

'There is hell in his eyes,' said Geoffrey.

Harry left his chair and leaned on the chimneypiece also, looking up at the picture.

'Certainly, if you think he looks wicked,' he said, 'you will see no resemblance between him and my uncle. Uncle Francis is a genial, pink-faced old fellow, with benevolent white hair. When I used to come down here years ago, before my father's death, for the holidays, he always used to be awfully good to me. But he has been abroad for the last three years, and I haven't seen him. But I remember him as the most charming old man.'

'Then in essentials he is not like that portrait,' said Geoffrey, turning away. 'Well, I'm for the bath.'

'After you. Turn on the hot water when you're out, Geoff.'

Harry did not immediately sit down again when his friend left him, but continued for a little while to look at the second Baron, trying to see in it what Geoffrey had seen, what he himself had always failed to see. He moved from where he stood to where Geoffrey had been standing, still looking at it, when suddenly, no doubt by some curious play of light on the canvas, there flitted across the face for a moment some expression indefinably sinister. It was there but for a flash, and vanished again, and by no change in his point of view could he recapture it. Soon he gave up the attempt, and, with only an idle and fleeting wonder at the illusion, he sat down, took up a book, and yawned over a page that conveyed nothing to him. Then frankly and honestly he shut it up, and lay comfortably back in his chair, looking at the fire. He must even have dropped into a doze, for, apparently, without transition, in the strange, unformulated fashion of dreams, he thought that his uncle had come, dressed (and this did not seem remarkable) in the fashion of the Holbein portrait, and having greeted him with his well-remembered hearty manner, had sat down in the other of the two armchairs; and though unconscious of having gone to sleep, he certainly came to himself with a start, to find the chair opposite untenanted, and the sound of his own name ringing in his ears. Immediately afterwards it was repeated, and looking up to the gallery that ran across one side of the hall, and communicated with certain of the bedrooms, he saw Geoffrey leaning over in his dressing-gown.

'Bath's ready,' he said, 'and the portrait is looking at you.'

'Thanks. I've been to sleep, I think. Did you call me more than once, Geoff?'

'No; the other time it was the second Baron.' Harry was still a little startled.

'You really only called once?' he asked again.

'Yes, only once. Why?'

'Nothing. Hullo! I hear wheels. That must be my uncle. Turn the hot water off, there's a good chap. I must just see him before I come upstairs.'

Chapter 2

The Coming of The Luck

THE dining-room of Vail was of the same antique spaciousness as the hall, and as there on the lounger, so here on the diner looked down a serious company of ancestors. For so small a party, it had been thought by the butler that conviviality would be given a better chance if, on this frosty night, he laid them a small table within range of the fire rather than that the three should be cut off, as it were, on a polar island in the centre of that vast sea of floor. And, indeed, though naturally a modest man, Templeton felt a strong self-approval at the success of his kind thought; for from the moment of sitting down a cheerful merriness had held the table, rising sometimes into loud hilarity, and never sinking into the contented slough of repletion which is held in England to be the proper equivalent for joviality. But if it was Templeton in part who was responsible for so desirable an atmosphere, there was credit to be given to at least one of the diners.

Pleasant and pink was Mr Francis's face, his hair, though silver, still crisp and vigorous, his mouth a perpetual smile. In absolute repose even, a sunshine lingered there, as in a bottle of well-matured wine, and its repose left it but to give place to laughter. All dinner through he had been the mouthpiece of delightful anecdote, and of observations shrewd but always kindly, rising sometimes almost to the dry level of wit, and never failing in that genial humour without which all conversation, not directed to a definite end, becomes intolerable. Though talking much, he was no usurper of the inalienable right of the others to wag the tongue, and though his own wagged to vibration, he was never tedious. Even in the matter of riddles, introduced by Geoffrey, he had a contribution or two to make of so extravagant a sort that this dismal species of entertainment was for the moment rendered charming. He unbent to the level of the young men, to the futility of most disconnected conversation, without ever seeming to unbend. You would have said that his narrow, clerically opening shirt, with its large cravat and massive gold studs, covered the heart of a boy; that the brains of a clever youth lay beneath that silver hair, prematurely white indeed, yet not from grief or the conduct of a world long unkind. In person he was somewhat short, 'without the inches of a Vail', as he himself said, and pleasantly inclined to stoutness, but to the stoutness which may come early to a healthy appetite and a serene digestion, for it was not accompanied either by pallid flabbiness or colour unduly high, and by the artificial light scarcely a wrinkle could be scrutinized on his beaming face. His dress was precise and scrupulous, yet with a certain antique touch about it, as of one who had been something of a buck in the sixties, his linen far more than clean and fresh, and of a snowiness which certainly implied special injunctions to the washerwoman. His trouser-pockets were cut, we may elegantly say, not at the side of those indispensable coverings, but towards the front of the bow window, and there dangled from the lip of one a fob of heavy gold seals.

They had now approached the end of dinner, decanters glowed on the table, and a silver cigarette-box, waiting untouched, at Mr Francis's request, till the more manly business of wine was off the palate, stood by Harry's dessert-plate. Already, even in this second hour of their acquaintance, the three felt like old friends, and as the wine was on its first round, the two young men were bent eagerly forward to hear the conclusion of a most exciting little personal anecdote told them by Mr Francis. He had to perfection that great essential of the narrator, intense interest and appreciation of what he was himself saying, and the climax afforded him the most obvious satisfaction. In his right hand he held his first glass of untasted port, and after an interval accorded to laughter he suddenly rose.

'And now,' he said, 'comes the pleasantest moment of our delightful evening. Harry, my dear boy, here is long life and happiness to you, from the most sincere of your well-wishers. And for myself, I pray that a very old man may some time dance your children on his knee. God bless you, my dearest fellow.'

He drank the brimming glass honestly to the last drop, and held out his hand to the young man, with a long and hearty grasp. Then with quick tact, seeing the embarrassment of remark-making in Harry's face, he sat down again, and without pause enticed the subject off the boards.

'How well I remember your dear father coming of age!' he said. 'Dear me! it must be forty years ago, nearly twice as long a time as you have lived. There's a puzzle for Mr Langham, like the one he gave me to do. It was this very port, I should say, in which we drank his health. The yellow seal, is it not, Harry? Yes, yes; your grandfather laid it down in the year '40, and we used to drink it only on very great occasions, for he would say to me that it was a gift he had put in entail for his grandchildren, and was not for us. And so it has turned out. He was very fond of port, too, was dear old Dennis; it was not a gift that cost him nothing. You would scarcely remember your grandfather, Harry?'

'I just remember him, Uncle Francis,' said the lad, 'but only as a very old man. I don't think he liked children, for whenever he saw me he would have no more than a word or two to say, and then he would send for you.'

'Yes, yes, so he would—so he would,' said Mr Francis, 'and we used to have great games together—did we not, Harry? Games did I say? Indeed, we seemed to be real Red Indians in the wilderness and Crusaders with paper lances. Dear me! I could play such games still. Hide-and-seek, too—a grand business. It requires, as poor Antrobus used to say, all the strategy of a general directing a campaign, combined with the unflinching courage of the private, who has to go straight forward, expecting artillery to open on him every minute. Yes, and the old man felt it, too. I have seen him playing it with his grandchildren when he was Prime Minister, and, upon my word, he was more in earnest about it than the young people!'

Coffee had come in, and after a few minutes the three moved for the hall. At the door, however, Harry paused and stayed behind in the dining-room. Mr Francis took Geoffrey's arm in his affectionate way, and the two walked into the hall.

'It has been so pleasant to me to meet you, my dear boy,' he was saying, 'for years ago I knew some of your people well. No, I do not think I ever knew your father. But I must tell you I am bad at surnames; one only calls the tradespeople Mr So-and-so, and I shall call you Geoffrey. You are Harry's best friend; I have a claim upon you. Fine hall—is it not?—and the pictures, well, they are a wonderful set. There is nothing like them for completeness in England, if one excepts the royal collections; and, indeed, I think there is less rubbish here.'

The portraits were lit by small shaded lamps, which stood beneath each, so that the whole light was thrown on to the picture, and the beholder left undazzled. Mr Francis had strolled up to the fireplace, still retaining Geoffrey's arm, and together they looked at the picture of Francis, second Baron.

'A wonderful example of Holbein,' said Mr Francis; 'I do not know a finer. They tried hard to get it for the exhibition a few years ago, but it couldn't leave Vail. I should have been quite uncomfortable at the thought of it out of the house. Now, some people have told me—Ah! I see you have noticed it, too.'

'Surely there is an extraordinary likeness between you and it,' said Geoffrey. 'Harry just pointed to it when I asked him what you were like.'

Mr Francis's eyes pored on the picture with a sort of fascination.

'A wonderful bit of painting,' he said. 'And how clearly you see not only the man's body, but his soul! That is the true art of the portrait-painter.'

'But not always pleasant for the sitter,' remarked Geoffrey.

'I am not so sure. You imply, no doubt, that it was not pleasant for this old fellow?'

'I should not think his soul was much to be proud of,' said Geoffrey.

'You mean he looks wicked?' said Mr Francis, still intent on the canvas. 'Well—God forgive him!—I am afraid he must have been. But, that being so, I expect he was as much in love with his own soul as a good man is. For he does not look to me a weak man, one who is for ever falling and repenting. There is less of Macbeth and more of his good lady in old Francis. Infirm of purpose? No, no, I think not!'

He turned abruptly away from the picture, and broke into a laugh.

'He was a wicked old man, we are afraid,' he said, 'and I am exactly like him.'

'Ah! that is not fair,' cried Geoffrey.

'My dear boy, I was only chaffing. And here is Harry; what has he got?'

Harry had come after them as they spoke thus together, carrying in his hand a square leather case. The thing seemed to be of some weight.

'I wanted to show you and Geoff what I have found, Uncle Francis,' he said. 'I thought perhaps you could tell me about it. It was in one of the attics, of all places in the world—hidden, it seemed, behind some old pictures. Templeton and I found it.'

Mr Francis whisked round with even more than his accustomed vivacity of movement at Harry's words.

'Yes, yes,' he said with some impatience. 'Open it, then, my dear boy, open it.'

An old lock of curious work secured the leather strap which fastened the case, but this dangled loose from it, attached to its hasp.

'We could find no key for it,' explained Harry, 'and had to break it open.'

As he spoke, he drew from the case an object swathed in wash-leather, but the outline was clearly visible beneath its wrappings.

'Ah, it is so,' said Mr Francis below his breath, and as Harry unfolded the covering they all stood silent. This done, he held up to the light what it contained. It was a large golden goblet with two handles, of a size perhaps to hold a couple of quarts of liquor, and even by lamplight it was a thing that dazzled the eye, and made the mouth to water. But, solid gold as it was, and of chaste and exquisite workmanship, there was scarce an inch of it that was not worth more than the whole value of the gold and the craft bestowed thereon, so thickly was it encrusted with large and precious stones. Just below the lip of the cup ran a ring of rubies, of notable size and wonderful depth of colour, and below, at a little interval, six emerald stars, all clear-set in the body of the cup. The lower part was chased with acanthus-leaves, each outlined in pearls, and up the fluted stem climbed lordly sapphires. Sapphires again traced the rim of the foot, and in each handle was clear-set a row of diamonds—no chips and dust, but liquid eyes and lobes of light. Half-way down the bowl of the cup, between the emerald stars and the points of the acanthus-leaves, ran a plain panel of gold, on which was engraved in small Early English characters some text that encircled the whole.

Harry was standing close under the lamp as he took off the covering, and remained there a moment, holding in his hand the gorgeous jewel, and looking at it with a curiously fixed attention, unconscious of the others. Then he handed it to his uncle.

'Tell me about it; what is it, Uncle Francis?' he asked, and involuntarily, as the old man took it, he glanced at the picture of Francis, second Baron, who, in the portrait, held, beyond a doubt, the same treasure that they were now examining.

Mr Francis did not at once reply, but handled the cup for a little while in silence, with awe and solemnity in his attitude and expression. As he turned it this way and that in his grasp, jewel after jewel caught the light and shone refracted in points of brilliant colour on his face. The burnished band, on which was engraved the circle of the text, cut a yellow line of reflection across his nose and cheeks, which remained steady, but over the rest of his face gleams of living colour shone and passed, and now as a ruby, now an emerald, sent their direct rays into his eyes, they would seem lit inside by a gleam of red or green. At length he looked up.

'Hear what the thing says of itself,' he said. 'I will read it you.'

Then, turning the cup till he had found the beginning of the text, he read slowly, the cup revolving to the words:

> 'When the Luck of the Vails is lost,
> Fear not fire nor rain nor frost;
> When the Luck is found again,
> Fear both fire and frost and rain.'

'Very pretty,' said Geoffrey, with a critical air; but Mr Francis made no reply. His eyes were still fixed on the jewel.

'But what is it?' asked Harry.

'This? The cup?' he said. 'It is what I have read to you. It is the Luck of the Vails.'

Geoffrey laughed.

'You've got it, Harry, anyhow,' he said, 'for weal or woe. How does it run? "Fear fire and frost and rain." Take care of yourself, old man, and don't smoke in bed, and don't skate over deep water.'

Mr Francis turned to him quickly, with a sudden recovery of his briskness.

'You and I would risk all that, would we not, Geoffrey,' he said, 'to have found such a beautiful thing? Yes, Harry, I see you have noticed it. There it is in old Francis's hand in the picture. Where else should it be if not there? Whether he made it or not, I can't tell you, but that is its first appearance as far as we know.'

Still holding it, he looked at the portrait, then stretched it out to Harry.

'There, take it,' he said quickly.

'But tell us all about it,' said Harry. 'What happened to it afterwards? How is it I never heard of it?'

'Your father would never speak of it,' said Mr Francis, 'nor your grandfather either. Your father never saw it, your grandfather only once, when he was quite a little boy. Neither could bear to speak of it when it was lost. And so it was in the attic all the time!'

Harry's eyes were sparkling; a sudden animation seemed to possess him.

'Tell us from the beginning,' he said.

He was already wrapping the goblet up again,

and Mr Francis looked greedily at it, till the last jewel had been hidden in the wash-leather.

'Well, it is a strange story, and a short one,' he said, 'for so little is known of it. It has appeared and disappeared several times since Holbein painted it there, as unaccountably as it has appeared again now. In the attic all the time!' he exclaimed again.

'But the legend—what does the legend mean?' asked Harry.

'I have no idea. Perhaps it is some old rhyme, perhaps it is a mere conceit of the goldsmith. But be that as it may, those of your house who have possessed the Luck always seemed to think that it brought them luck. It was in old Francis's time, you know, that coal was found on your Derbyshire estate, which so enriched him for a while. In his son's time certainly the Luck disappeared, for we have a letter of his about it, and as certainly the field of coal came to an end. It appeared again some eighty years later, and again disappeared, and then the grandfather of your grandfather found it. He, you know, married the wealthy Barbara Devereux, and it was he who showed the Luck to your grandfather. Then it was lost for the last time, and with it all his money in the South Sea Bubble.'

Harry looked a shade disappointed at this bald narrative.

'Is that all?' he asked. 'Where does the fire and frost and rain come in?'

Mr Francis laughed.

'Well, oddly enough, old Francis was burned to death in his bed. Mark Vail was drowned. Henry Vail, the last holder of it, was frozen to death in his travelling carriage crossing the St Gothard. But a man must die somehow. Is it not so? Poor, wicked old Francis! he thought, perhaps, to bring a curse on the house, if it was indeed he who made the Luck; but how futile—how futile! Did he think that the elements were in league with some occult power of magic and darkness that he possessed? Ah, no; beneficent Nature is not controlled by such a hand. He knows that well, maybe, now, and perhaps therein is his chastisement, for indeed he was a man of devilish mind.'

PART II

PART I

Chapter 3

The Spell Begins to Work

MR FRANCIS was by choice an early riser, and next morning, before either of the young men was awake, he had been splashing and gasping in his cold tub, had felt with the keenest enjoyment the genial afterglow produced on his braced and invigorated skin by the application of the rough towel, and was now out on the terrace, pacing briskly along the dry gravel walk on this adorable winter morning, waiting cheerfully for his desired breakfast. Now and then he would break into a nimble trot for fifty paces, or even give a little skip in the air as a child does, from the sheer exhilaration of his pulses. His thoughts, too, must have been as sparkling as the morning itself, as brisk and cheery as his own physical economy, for from time to time he would troll out a bar or two of some lusty song, or stop to chirrup with pursed lips to the stiff, half-frozen birds, and his pleasant, close-shaven face was continually wreathed in smiles. Here was one, at least, in whom old age had brought no spell of freezing to laggard blood, no dulling of that zest of life which is so often and so erroneously considered as an attribute of youth only; life was still immensely enjoyable, and all things were delightful to his sympathetic eye.

Such a buoyancy of spirits is a most engaging thing, provided only it be natural and unforced. But too often the old who remain young have the aspect as of grizzly kittens, their spirits are but a parody of youthfulness, their antics broken-winded and spasmodic. In a moment they fall from the heights of irresponsible gaiety to an equally unwarrantable churlishness, they maintain no level way, their capers are those of jerking marionettes, a performance of jointed dolls.

But how different was the joyousness of Mr Francis! Nothing could be more native to him than his morning exhilaration. Authentic was the merriment that sparkled in his light-blue eyes, authentic the lightness of his foot as it tripped along the gravel walk, and none could doubt that his fine spirits were effortless and unaffected.

To reach so ripe an age as that to which Mr Francis had attained means, even to those whose life has lain in the pleasantest lines, to have had to bear certain trials, sorrows, and misunderstandings necessarily incident to the mere passage of years. To bear these bravely and without bitterness is the part of any robust nature, to bear them with unabated cheerfulness and without any loss of the zest for life is a rarer gift; and the silver-haired old gentleman who paced so gaily up and down the terraced walks, while he waited for young men to have their fill of sleep and make a tardy appearance, was a figure not without gallantry. Here were no impatient gestures; he was hungry, but the time of waiting would not be shortened by fretfulness, nor had he any inclination to so unamiable a failing, and for nearly half an hour he pursued his cheery way up and down. At length the welcome booming of the gong sounded distantly, and he tripped towards the house.

Harry was down, the clock pointing to an indulgent half-past nine, but the youthful moroseness of morning sat on his brow. To so old a traveller through life as his uncle the ways of weaning this were manifold, and he broke into speech.

'Splendid morning, my dear boy,' he said, 'and the ice, they tell me, bears. What will you do? What shall we do? Are you shooting today or skating, or will you like to take a tramp round the old place with me as you suggested last night?'

Harry was examining dishes on the side-table with a supercilious air.

'Very cold, is it not?' he said. 'We were thinking of shooting. Do you shoot, Uncle Francis?'

'I will shoot with pleasure, if you will let me,' he said. 'Yes, it is cold—too old for pottering about, as you say. Fish-cakes, eggs and bacon, cold game. Yes, I'll begin with a fish-cake. What a hungry place Vail is! I am famished, literally famished! And where is Geoffrey?'

'Geoffrey was going to his bath when I came

down,' said Harry. 'It is to be hoped he will be more nearly awake after it. He had one eye open only when I saw him.'

'Fine gift to be able to sleep like that,' said Mr Francis. 'I heard you two boys go up to bed last night, and sat an hour reading after that. But I awoke at eight, as I always do, and got up.'

Harry's morose mood was on the thaw.

'And have you been waiting for us since then, Uncle Francis?' he said. 'Really, I am awfully sorry. We'll have breakfast earlier tomorrow. It was stupid of me.'

'Not a bit, not a bit, Harry. I like a bit of a walk before breakfast. Wonderful thing for the circulation after your bath. Ah, here's Geoffrey! Good morning, my dear boy!'

'We'll shoot today, Geoff, as we settled,' said Harry. 'Uncle Francis will come with us. Wake up, you pig!'

Geoffrey yawned.

'How's the Luck?' he said. 'Lord! I had such a nightmare, Harry—you and the Luck and Mr Vail and the picture of the wicked baron all mixed up together somehow. I forget how it went.'

'Very remarkable,' said Harry. 'I dreamed of the Luck, too, now you mention it. We must have dreamed of the same thing, Geoff, because I also have forgotten how it went.'

'And I,' said Mr Francis, 'dreamed about nothing at all very pleasantly all night. And what a morning I awoke to! Just the day for a good tramp in the woods. Dear me, Harry, what a simpleton your dear father used to think me! "What are you going to do?" he would ask me, and I would only want a pocketful of cartridges, a snack of cold lunch, and leave to prowl about by myself without a keeper, no trouble to anybody.'

'Yes, that's good fun,' said Geoffrey. 'Now it's a rabbit, or over the stubble a partridge, then a bit of cover and you put up a pheasant. Let's have a go-as-you-please day, Harry.'

'The poetry of shooting,' said Mr Francis. 'Cold partridge for anyone but me? No? You lads have no appetites.'

The keeper had been given his orders the day before, and very soon after breakfast the three shooters were ready to start. They went out by a garden-door which gave on a flight of some dozen stone steps descending to the lawn, and Mr Francis, leading the way, nearly fell on the topmost of them, for they were masked with ice, and half turned as he recovered himself to give a word of warning to the others. But he was too late, and Harry, who followed him, not looking to his feet, but speaking to Geoffrey over his shoulder, at the same moment almost had slipped on the treacherous stone, and fallen sprawling, dropping his gun and clutching ineffectually at the railing to save himself. Mr Francis gave one exclamation of startled dismay, and ran to his assistance.

'My dear fellow,' he cried, 'I hope you are not hurt?'

Harry lay still a moment, his mouth twisted with pain, then, taking hold of the railing, pulled himself to his feet, and stood with bowed head, gripping hard on the banister.

'All sideways on my ankle,' he said. 'Just see if my gun's all right, Geoff. Yes, I've twisted it, I'm afraid.'

He paused another moment, faint and dizzy, with a feeling of empty sickness, and then hobbled up the steps again.

'An awful wrench,' he said. 'Just give me your arm, Uncle Francis, will you? I can hardly put my foot to the ground.'

Leaning on him, he limped back into the hall and dragged off his boot.

'Yes, it feels pretty bad,' he said; 'I came with my whole weight on to it. I shall be as lame as a tree.'

Mr Francis was on his knees, and in a moment had stripped off Harry's stocking with quick, deft fingers.

'What bad luck! What awfully bad luck!' he said. 'Put a cold water compress on it at once, my dear boy. It is already swelling.'

Harry lifted his leg on to a chair opposite.

'It's just a sprain,' he said. 'Go out, Uncle Francis, you and Geoffrey. I'll put a bandage on.'

Templeton had answered Mr Francis's ringing of the bell, and was dismissed again with orders for cold water and linen.

'Not till I've seen you comfortable; my dear fellow,' said Mr Francis. 'Dear me, what bad luck! Does it hurt you, Harry?'

'No, no, it is nothing,' said he rather impatiently, irritated both by the pain and the fussing. 'Do go out, Uncle Francis, with Geoffrey, and leave me. The men are waiting by the home cover. I can look after myself perfectly.'

Mr Francis still seemed half loath to leave him, and, had he followed his inclinations, he would have instituted himself as sick-nurse, to change the bandage or read to him. But it was the part of wisdom to humour the patient, who quite distinctly wished to be left alone; and as even the most solicitous affection could not find grounds for anxiety in the sprain, with a few more sympathetic words he followed Geoffrey, who was chafing to be gone. The latter, indeed, might have appeared somewhat cold and unsympathetic in contrast with Mr Francis and his repeated lamentations; but his 'Bad luck, Harry', and Harry's grunt in reply had something of telegraphic brevity, not misunderstood.

In spite of his protestations that he was no more than an indifferent shot, it soon appeared that Mr Francis was more than a decently capable performer with the gun, and his keenness and accuracy as a sportsman were charmingly combined with the knowledge and observation of a naturalist. He pointed out to his companion several rare and infrequent birds which they saw during the morning, and implored the keeper that they might not be shot for curiosities.

'Half the time I am shooting,' he said to Geoffrey, 'I am of a divided mind. Is it not a shame to kill these beautiful and innocent things? I often wonder—— Ah!' Up went his gun, and a high pheasant was torn from the sky, leaving a few light neck-feathers floating there. 'And even while the words are in my mouth, I go and contradict my sentiments,' he said, ejecting the smoking cartridge. 'What a bundle of incongruous opposites is a man!'

They shot for not more than a couple of hours after lunch, for the sun set early, and Mr Francis confessed to a certain unreasonable desire to get home quickly, and see how Harry had fared.

'Indeed, I was half minded to stay with him, in spite of his wish,' he said; 'for the hours will have been lonely to him. But he is like all the Vails, self-reliant, and beholden to no one.'

They were crossing the last meadow before they should again reach the garden, and even as he spoke a hare got up from its form in the tussocky grass not more than ten yards from them, and scuttled noiselessly, head down, across the field. Geoffrey had already taken the cartridges from his barrels, and Mr Francis raised his gun to his shoulder, hesitated a moment, and then fired. He hit the beast just as it gained the fence of the cover from which they had come. They saw it bowled over, and drag on a pace or two into the bushes, then suddenly from where it had disappeared there came a screaming horribly human. Mr Francis paused, then turned quite pale, and Geoffrey, seeing his stricken face, imagined he thought that he had wounded a beater.

'It is only the hare,' he said; 'the men were all out two minutes ago.'

Mr Francis turned to him.

'Only the hare!' he cried. 'Yes, only the hare. How dreadful! how dreadful! I have wounded it!' And he started off running to where the beast had been last seen, and disappeared in the cover.

Geoffrey sent a couple of beaters to assist in the search, but himself went on to the house, wondering a little at the inconsistency which would allow a man to shoot at a hare running straight away in a bad light, and yet send him hot-foot after it when wounded. Yet the inconsistency was pleasing: keenness was responsible for the doubtful shot; an indubitable horror of causing an animal pain prompted the pursuit of it. He found Harry lying up, his ankle somewhat severely sprained, but it no longer pained him, and he asked after his uncle.

'Just at the last moment he shot a hare, wounding it,' he said, 'and ran back to try to recover it. He will be in at once, I should think.'

But half an hour passed, yet still he did not come, and Harry was already wondering what could have happened, when he appeared, all smiles again.

'Dear lad, have you had a very tedious day?' he asked. 'The thought of you has been constantly in my mind. I should have been in half an hour ago with Geoffrey, but I wounded a hare, and had to go and look for it. Thank God, I found it. The poor beast was quite dead. But it screamed; it was terrible, terrible!'

There was a good piano by Bechstein standing in the hall, and that evening, after dinner, as Harry lay on the sofa nursing his injury, while his uncle, sitting by him, recalled a hundred little reminiscences of his own young years which he had spent here, Geoffrey, who was an accurate performer of simple tunes, played idly and softly to himself, listening half to his own music, half to the talk of the others. Now he would indicate some graceful inevitable fragment of Bach, now a verse of some Chevalier song, all with a tinkling elementary techique, but with a certain facility of finger and decided aptitude for the right notes. By degrees, as this went on, a kind of restlessness gained on Mr Francis. He would break off in the middle of a story to hum a bar of the tune Geoffrey was playing, beating time to it with a waving hand, or turn round in his chair to say over his shoulder, 'A graceful melody, my dear boy; please play us that again.'

But before long this restlessness grew more emphatic, and at last he jumped nimbly out of his chair.

'I must fetch my flute,' he exclaimed; 'I must positively fetch my flute. I play but indifferently, as you will hear, but it is such a pleasure to me. What a charming instrument is the flute! So pastoral, the nearest thing we know to the song of birds. Be indulgent, my dear Geoffrey, to the whim of an old fellow, and play some easy accompaniments for me. I have a quantity of little pieces for the flute by Corelli and Baptiste.'

He hurried to the door, and they heard his step quickly crossing the gallery above. In a few moments he reappeared again, a little out of breath, but with a beaming face. He fitted his flute together with affectionate alacrity, turned to the piano, and opened a volume of easy minuets and sarabands.

'There, this one,' he said; 'it is a breath of heaven, a real breath of heaven. You have two bars of introduction. Ah! a shade slower, my dear boy; it is an antique measure, you must remember. Graceful, leisurely—yes, that is exactly right.'

He knew the music by heart, and, when once they were fairly started, turned from the piano towards Harry. His cheerful ruddy face composed itself into an expression of beatific content, his eyes were half closed, the eyebrows a little raised, and his body swayed gently to the rhythm of the tune. The formal delicacy of the composition enthralled him. Perhaps it brought with it the aroma of his youth, the minuets he had danced fifty years ago; perhaps it was only the sweet and certain development of the melody which so moved him. At the end, in any case, he could not quite command his voice, and he patted Geoffrey gently on the shoulder by way of thanks.

'The next,' he said; 'we cannot pass by the next. The two are complete only together.'

They played thus some half-dozen little pieces, ending with a quick ripple of a gavotte to put them in good spirits again—so said Mr Francis—and at the last he lovingly packed up his flute and left it on the piano, saying that they must be very indulgent to him and let him play again.

Two or three days after this, Harry was sufficiently recovered to be able to go out again, though still limpingly, and it was arranged that they should shoot certain of the covers near the house which might be expected to furnish them with a good day's sport, and at the same time would entail but little walking. The frost had twenty-four hours ago completely broken before a warm and violent wind from the south-west, and the dead leaves, which had lain in ice-glued and compacted heaps, were once more driven about in scurrying multitudes. The sky was low and ominous, a wrack of torn and flying cloud, and scudding showers fell ever and again; but the sport was excellent, and they little heeded the angry fretfulness of the heavens.

Their beats took them at no time far from the house, and they returned there for lunch; but by this time the weather had grown so vastly more inclement that Mr Francis cried off the resumption of the day, but Harry, eager for out of doors after his two days' imprisonment, persuaded Geoffrey to come out again. The rain was a steady downpour in the slackened wind, but his argument that they were not made of paper carried weight.

They returned drenched indeed, but with a satisfactory report of themselves and the birds, to find Mr Francis performing very contentedly on his flute before the hall fire. But he jumped up briskly as they appeared.

'Dear boys, how wet you are!' he cried. 'Of course, you will change your clothes at once, will you not? And I should recommend a glass of hot whisky-and-water. Shall I ring the bell? I told Templeton to see that there was abundance of hot water for your baths. And you've not overtired yourself, I hope, dear Harry?'

This incessant solicitude of his uncle, however, clearly arising from affection, was on the way to getting on Harry's nerves and rousing opposition. At any rate, the suggestion that he should guard against a chill predisposed him not to be in any hurry to go upstairs.

'Oh, tea first,' he said, not meaning it; 'one can change afterwards. Are you going now, Geoff? Ring the bell as you pass, will you?'

A positive cloud dimmed the brightness of Mr Francis's face.

'Dear boy, you are being horribly imprudent,' he said. 'Do let me persuade you to change at once.'

This drove determination home. Harry was unpleasantly conscious of the clinging flabbiness of soaking clothes; but had their touch shaken him with an ague, it would not have moved him from his chair. He intended to do that which he chose to do.

'Oh, I'm all right, Uncle Francis,' he said; 'I never catch cold.'

Tea came, and Harry ate and drank with studied leisure, and conversed politely to his uncle. Already he felt the premonitory prickling of the skin which precedes a chill, but it was nearly half an hour before he lounged upstairs. He did not intend to be fussed over and treated like a child, and the advice to go and change had been so obviously sensible that it should never have been offered, and to the contrariness of youth was impossible to accept. Thus the well-meant but ill-timed counsel drove him into an opposite course.

Again, after dinner, the evening was melodious with the breathings of Mr Francis's flute; but the child-like pleasure which the performer had taken before in his own performance was sensibly dimmed. He played with a wandering attention and an uncertain finger, without the gusto of the artist, and his eye rested anxiously on Harry, who had more than once complained of the cold, and now sat huddled up by a mountainous fire, bright-eyed, and with a burning skin, which seemed to him to cover an interior of ice. At last Mr Francis could stand it no longer, and laying down his flute, came across to where he sat, and with an extraordinary amenity of voice, yet firmly:

'I insist on your going to bed, Harry,' he said. 'You have caught a chill; it is idle to deny it. Dear lad, do not be foolish. I have troubled and worried you, I am afraid, with my fussy care for you, and I am very sorry for it. But do not make a bad matter worse, and do not punish me, I ask you, as well as yourself for my ill-timed suggestions. I have apologized; be generous.'

Harry got up. It was impossible that a mere superficial boyish obstinacy, of which he was already ashamed, should stand out against this, and, besides, he felt really unwell.

'Yes, I am afraid I have caught a chill,' he said. 'It was foolish of me not to change, as you advised me when I came in. It was even more foolish of me to have been annoyed at your excellent suggestion that I should.'

Mr Francis's face brightened.

'Now get to bed at once, my dear boy,' he said, 'and I have no doubt you will be all right in the morning. You have plenty of blankets? Good night.'

But Harry was by no means all right in the morning, and it seemed that for his uncle the joy of life was dead. There was no brisk, early walk for him today. Vail was no longer a hungry place, and his breakfast was but the parody of a meal. Unreasonably he blamed himself for his nephew's indisposition, and the morning passed for him in blank turnings over of the leaves of undecipherable books, in reiterated visits to the kitchen with suggestions as to a suitable invalid diet, and disconnected laments to Geoffrey over this untoward occurrence.

'Ah, this will teach a foolish old man to hold his tongue,' he said; 'It will teach him also that old fellows cannot understand the young. How excellent were my intentions, but how worse than impotent, how disastrous! It is a cold job to grow old, Geoffrey; it is even colder to grow old and still feel young. Poor Harry simply thought me a meddling old fogey when I wanted him to take precautions against catching a chill, and I ought to have known that he would think me so. I forget my white hairs. How are you, my dear boy, this morning? I hope you have not a chill, too. I am anxious and unsettled today.'

'Oh, Harry was an ass!' said the other. 'But there's nothing at all to be anxious about. He has a chill, rather a sharp one, and with greater wisdom than he showed yesterday, he stops in bed. Is that *Punch* there? Thank you very much.'

Mr Francis walked to the window, lit a cigarette, and threw it away, barely tasted.

'I wonder if Harry would like me to read to him?' he said.

Geoffrey looked up with an arrested smile.

'I think I should leave him quite alone,' he said. 'I've just been up to him. He's as cross as a bear, and wouldn't speak to me, so I came away.'

'But that is so unlike him,' said Mr Francis. 'He must be ill—he must be really ill.'

Geoffrey began to understand Harry's feelings the day before.

'If I were you, I wouldn't fuss either him or myself,' he said; 'people don't die of a cold in the head.'

'Shall I send for a doctor?' asked Mr Francis. 'We might tell Harry that he happened to call about some case of distress in the village, and wished to consult him about it. Then we could get his opinion. I think, under the circumstances, one might venture on so small an equivocation.'

Geoffrey closed his *Punch*.

'I shouldn't do anything of the kind if I were you,' he said. 'What an abominable morning! I'll play some accompaniments for you if you like.'

'Thank you, dear boy,' said Mr Francis, 'but I haven't the heart to play this morning. Besides, Harry might be dozing; we should run the risk of disturbing him.'

PART III

Chapter 4

The Story of Mr Francis

HARRY VAIL owned a plain, gloomy house in Cavendish Square, forbidding to those who looked at it from the street, chilling to those who looked at the street from it. It was furnished in the heavy and expensive early Victorian style, and solid mahogany frowned at its inmates. During his minority it had been let for a term of years, but on his coming of age he had taken it again himself, and here, when the gloom and darkness of February and swollen waters made Vail more suitable for the amphibious than the dry-shod, he came to receive in exchange the more sociable fogs of London. Parliament had assembled, the roadways were no longer depleted, and Harry was beginning to find that, in spite of the friendlessness which he had been afraid was his, there were many houses which willingly opened their doors and welcomed him inside. Friends of his father, acquaintances of his own, were all disposed to be pleasant towards this young man, about whom there lingered a certain vague atmosphere of romance, a thing much valued by a prosaic age. He was young, attractive to the eye, he stood utterly alone in the world, with the burden or glory of a great name on his shoulders, and people found in him a charming youthful modesty, mixed with an independence of the sturdiest, which, while accepting a favour from none, seemed to cry aloud for friendliness and bask therein when it was found with the mute unmistakable gratitude of a dumb animal. His own estimate of his loneliness had probably been accentuated by the year he had spent, just before he came of age, in studying languages in France and Germany; but in the main it was, when he made it, correct. But at his time of life change comes quickly; the young man who does not rapidly expand and enlarge must, it may be taken for certain, be as rapidly closing up. Within a month of his arrival in London it was beyond question that the latter morbid process was not at operation in Harry.

He and Geoffrey were seated one night in the smoking-room in the Cavendish Square house, talking over a glass of whisky-and-soda. They had dined with a friend, and Harry had inveigled Geoffrey out of his way to spend an hour with him before going home.

'No, I certainly am not superstitious,' he was saying, 'but if I was, I really should be very much impressed by what has happened. I never heard of a stranger series of coincidences. You remember the lines engraved round the Luck:

"When the Luck is found again,
    Fear both fire and frost and rain"?

'Well, as you know, two days after I found the
Luck I slipped on the steps as we were going out
shooting, and sprained my ankle. In consequence
of not looking where I was going, say you, and I
also for that matter. The Luck, say the superstitious:
that is the frost. As soon as I get right, I go out
shooting again, get wet through, and catch a pretty
bad chill. Because I didn't go and change, you say.
The Luck, say the superstitious: that is the rain.
Finally, the very day you left, I tripped over the
hearthrug, fell into the fire, and burned half my
hair off. Well, if that isn't fire, I don't know what
is. "Fear both fire and frost and rain", you see.
Certainly I have suffered from all three; but if old
Francis could only give me a cold and a sprained
ankle and a burn, I don't think much of his magic.
But I've paid the price, and now there is the Luck
to look forward to. Dear me, I'm afraid I've been
jawing!'

'I wonder if you believe it at all,' said Geoffrey.
'For myself, I should chuck the beastly pot into
the lake, not because I believe it, but for fear that
I some day might. If you get to believe that sort
of thing, you are done.'

'I am sure I don't believe it,' said the other, 'and
so I shall not chuck the beastly pot into the lake.
Nor would you if it were yours. But if I did believe
it, Geoff, there would be all the more reason for
keeping it. Don't you see, I've been through the

penalties, now let me have the prizes. That's the way to look at it. I don't look at it, I must remind you, in that way; I only say, What a strange series of coincidences! You can hardly deny that that is so.'

'What have you done with it?' asked Geoffrey.

'The beastly pot? It's down at Vail. Uncle Francis is there too. I wanted him to come up to London with me, but he wouldn't. Now, there's a cruel thing, Geoff. My God! it makes my blood boil when I think of it!'

'Think of what?'

'Of the persistent ill-luck which has dogged my uncle throughout his life; of the odious—well, not suspicion, it is not so definite as that—which seems to surround him. I was at Lady Oxted's the other night, and mentioned him casually, but she said nothing, and changed the subject. Oh, it was not a mere chance—the thing has happened before.'

Geoffrey squirted some soda-water into his glass.

'Suspicion? What do you mean?' he asked.

'No; suspicion is the wrong word. Uncle Francis told me all about his life on the last evening that I was at Vail, and I never heard anything so touching, so cruel, or so dignified. All his life he has been the victim of an ill-luck so persistent that it looks as if some malignant power must have been pursuing him. Well, I am going to try to make it up to him. I wonder if a rather long and very private story about his affairs would interest you at all?'

'Rather! I should like to hear it.'

'Well, this is almost exactly as he told it me from the beginning. He was a twin of my grandfather's—there's a piece of bad luck to start with—and being just half a minute late about coming into the world, he is a younger son, which is no fun, I can tell you, in our impoverished family.'

'That may happen to anybody,' said Geoffrey. 'I'm a younger son myself, but I don't scream over that.'

Harry laughed.

'Nor does he. Don't interrupt, Geoff. Then he married a very rich girl, who died three years afterwards, childless, leaving all her money back to her own relatives. It was a most unhappy marriage from the first, but don't aim after cheap cynicism and say that the real tragedy there was not her death but the disposition of her property. I can tell you beforehand that this was not the case. He was devoted to her.'

'Well?'

Harry's voice sank.

'And then, twenty-two years ago, came that awful affair of young Houldsworth's death. Did you ever hear it spoken of?'

Geoffrey was silent a moment.

'Yes, I have heard it spoken of,' he said at length.

Harry flushed.

'Ah! in connection with my uncle, I suppose?' he said.

'Yes, his name was mentioned in connection with it.'

'It is a crying shame!' said Harry hotly. 'And so
people talk of it still, do they? I never heard of it
till he told me all about it the other night. That is
natural; people would not speak of it to me.'

'I only know the barest outline,' said Geoffrey.
'Tell me what Mr Francis told you.'

'Well, it was this way. He was staying down at
our house in Derbyshire, which was subsequently
sold, for my grandfather had made him a sort of
agent there after his wife's death, and he would
be there for months together. Next to our place
was a property belonging to some people called
Houldsworth, and at this time, twenty-two or
twenty-three years ago, young Houldsworth (his
name was George) had only just come into it, having
had a long minority like me. Uncle Francis used
to be awfully good to him, and two years before
he had got him out of a scrape by advancing to
him a large sum of money. It was his own, and it
was this loan which had crippled him so much on
his wife's death. The arrangement had been that it
should be repaid immediately George Houldsworth
came of age. Well, Houldsworth was not able to do
this at once, for his affairs were all upside down,
and he asked for, and received, a renewal of it.
For security he gave Uncle Francis the reversion
of his life insurance policy.'

Again Harry's voice sank to near a whisper.

'Two days after this arrangement had been
made young Houldsworth and Uncle Francis were
pottering about the hedgerows alone, just with a
dog, to get a rabbit or two, or anything that came in

their way, and, getting over a fence, Houldsworth's gun went off, killing him instantly. Think how awful!'

'Why people will get over fences without taking their cartridges out is more than I could ever imagine,' said Geoffrey; 'but they will continue to do so till the end of time. I beg pardon.'

'Well, here comes the most terrible part of the whole affair,' went on the other. 'There was an inquest, and though my uncle was scarcely fit to attend, for he says he was almost off his head with so dreadful a thing happening, he had to go. He gave his account of the matter, and said that he himself was nearly hit by some of the shot. That, he tells me, was his impression, but he is willing to believe that it was not so, for, as he says, your imagination may run riot at so ghastly a time. But it was a most unfortunate thing to have said, for it seemed to be quite incompatible with the other evidence. Then, when it was known about the insurance policy, horrible sinister rumours began to creep about. He was closely questioned as to whether he knew for what purpose young Houldsworth wanted the money he advanced him, and he would not say. Neither would he tell me, but I understand that there was something disgraceful— blackmail, I suppose. He had an awful scene with Mrs Houldsworth, George's mother. His friends, of course, scouted the idea of such a possibility as was being hinted at, but others, acquaintances, cooled towards him, though not exactly believing what was in the air; others cut him direct. It was only the medical evidence at the inquest, which showed that the injury of which Houldsworth died could easily have been inflicted by himself, that saved my uncle, in all probability, from being brought to trial. He said to me that it would have been better if he had, for then he would have been completely cleared, whereas now the matter will never be reopened.'

'What an awful story!' said Geoffrey.

'Yes; and that was not the end of his trouble. Ten years ago he had to declare bankruptcy, and my father gave him an annuity. But since his death it has not been paid. I never knew anything about it, and he would not allow that I should be told, and he has lived in horrible *pensions* abroad. That seems to me such extraordinary delicacy, not letting me know. I never found out till I came of age.'

'You have continued it?'

'Of course. I hope, also, he will live with me for the main part. I have offered him a couple of permanent rooms at Vail, for he would not come to London. Oh, Geoffrey, it was the most pitiful story! And to think of him, bright, cheery, as we saw him down there, and know what an appalling load of misery he has supported so long! Now it seems to me to be a brave man's part to bear misfortune calmly, without whimpering, but one would think it required a courage of a superhuman kind to he able to remain sociable, cheerful—merry even. But oh! how bitter he is when he shows one all his thoughts! He warned me to rely on nobody.

He said there was not a man in the world, even less a woman, who would stick to you if you were in trouble. Trouble comes, they are vanished like melting snow, a heap of dirt is left behind. Then he suddenly burst into tears, and told me to forget all he had said, for he had given me the outpourings of a disappointed, soured man. I was young. Let me trust everyone as long as I could; let me make friends right and left, only, if trouble came, and they fell away, then, if I could find consolation therein, I might remember that the same thing had happened to others also.'

Geoffrey was staring absently into the fire; his cigarette had gone out, and his whisky was untasted.

'By Gad!' he said. 'Poor old beggar!'

And Harry, knowing that the British youth does not express sympathy in verbose paragraphs, or show his emotion by ejaculatory cries, was satisfied that the story had touched his friend.

Day by day, and week by week, Harry moved more at his ease in the world of people of whom hitherto he had known so little. The wall of the castle which he had erected round himself, compacted by his own diffidence and a certain *hauteur* of disposition, fell like the fortifications of Jericho at the blast of the trumpet, and it was a young man, pleasant in body and mind, pleased with little, but much anxious to please, that came forth. His dinner invitation to some new house would be speedily endorsed by the greater intimacy of a Saturday till Monday, and the days were few on which he sat down to a cover for one in Cavendish Square.

Among these more particular friends with whom previous acquaintance soon ripened into intimacy, Lady Oxted, an old friend of Harry's father, stood pre-eminent. He soon became *ami de la maison,* dropping in as he chose, well knowing he was welcome, and such a footing, speedily and unquestionably gained, was to one of a life previously so recluse a pleasure new and altogether delightful; for Lady Oxted had the power of creating the atmosphere of home, and home was one of those excellent things which Harry had hitherto lacked. He had not consciously missed it, because he had never yet known it; but his gradual understanding of it made him see how large an empty room there had been in his heart. To come uninvited, and to linger unconscionably long, to say firmly that he must be going, and yet to linger, he found to be an index to certain domestic and comfortable joys of life not lightly to be placed low in that delightful miscellany. His nature from his very youth was not yet enough formed to be labelled by so harsh an epithet as austere; but hitherto he had not known the quiet monotonies which can be the cause of so much uneventful happiness. Even for those whose bulk of enjoyment is flavoured with the thrill of adventure and the frothier joys of living, who most need excitement and crave for stimulus, there yet are times for the unbending of the bow, when the child within them cries out for mere toys and companionship, and the soul longs to sit by the meditative fire rather than to do battle with winds and stern events. And Harry was not one of those who need home least; simply he had been frozen, but now for the first time the genial warmth of living began to touch him; he was like a plant put in some sunned and watered place, and its appropriate buds began to appear in this time of the singing bird. Here, too, he met romance with tremulous mouth and the things of which poets have sung.

Chapter 5

A Point in Casuistry

ONE evening towards the end of June Lady Oxted was driving home from Victoria Station, where she had gone to meet the arrival of the Continental express. By her side sat a girl of little more than twenty, who, to judge by the eager, questioning glances which she cast at that inimitable kaleidoscope of life as seen in the London streets, must probably have been deprived of this admirable spectacle for some time; for her gaze was quickened to an interest not habitual to Londoners, however deep is their devotion to the town of towns. The streets were at their fullest in this height of the season and the summer, and the time of day being about half-past five, the landau could make but a leisurely progress through the glittering show. The girl's cheek was flushed with the warm, healthy tinge which is the prerogative of those who prefer the air as God made it to the foul gases which men shut up in their houses; and as they drove she poured out a rapid series of questions and comments to Lady Oxted.

'Oh, I just love this stuffy old London!' she said. 'But what have they done with the Duke of Wellington on his horse? The corner looks quite strange without it. Oh, there's a policeman keeping everybody back! Do you think it's the Queen? I hope it is. Why, it's only a little fat man with a beard in a brougham. Who is he, Aunt Violet, and why aren't we as good as he? Just fancy, it is three years since I have been in London—that's not grammar, is it?—and I had the greatest difficulty in making mother let me come; indeed, if it hadn't been for your letter saying that you would have me to stay with you, I never should have come. And then the difficulties about the time I should stop! It wasn't worth while going for a month, and two months was too long, so I made it three.'

'Well, it is delightful to have you, anyhow, dear Evie,' said Lady Oxted. 'And it really was time you should see London again. Your mother is well?'

'Very; as well as I am, and that means a lot. But she won't come to England, Aunt Violet, except for that one day every year, and I am beginning to think she never will now. It is twenty-one, nearly twenty-two, years ago that she settled at Santa Margarita—the year I was born.'

'Yes, dear, yes,' said Lady Oxted a little hurriedly, and she would seemingly have gone on to speak of something else, but the girl interrupted her.

'You know her reason, of course, Aunt Violet?' she said quietly, but with a certain firm resolve to speak. 'No, let me go on. She told me about it the other day only. Of course, poor George's death must have been terrible for her; but it is awful, it is awful, I think, to take it in the way she does. She still thinks that he died by no accident, but that he was intentionally shot by some man with whom he was out shooting. I asked her what his name was, but she would not tell me. And for all this time, once a year on the day of George's death, she comes to England, puts red flowers on his grave, and returns. Oh, it is awful!'

Lady Oxted did not reply at once.

'She still thinks so about it?' she asked at length.

'Yes, she told me herself. But I hope, perhaps, that her refusing to tell me the man's name—I asked only the evening before I left—may mean that she is beginning to wish to forget it. She wished, at any rate, that I should not know. Do you think it may be so?'

'I can't tell, Evie. Your mother——' and she stopped.

'Yes?'

'Only this: Your mother is hard to get at, inaccessible. It is almost impossible to know what she feels on subjects about which she feels deeply. I once tried to talk to her about it, but she would not. She heard what I had to say, but that was all.'

The girl assented, then paused a moment.

'Poor mother! what an awful year for her!' she said. 'She had only married my father, you know, a few months before George's death, and before the year was out, George, her only son, was dead, and she was left twice a widow, and childless. I was not born for six months after my father's death. How strange never to have seen one's father!'

They drove in silence for a space. Then the girl said suddenly:

'Aunt Violet, promise me that you will never tell me the name of the man who was out shooting with George. You see, my mother would not tell me when I asked her; surely that means she wishes that I should not know.'

Lady Oxted felt herself for the moment in great perplexity. She had the rational habit, now growing rare, of thinking what she was saying, and meaning something by what she said, and as her answer was conceivably a matter of some importance, she paused, thinking intently.

'I am not sure that I had better promise you that,' she said at last.

Evie looked surprised.

'Why not?' she asked.

'I can't quite tell you,' she said. 'Give me time, dear. I will either make you the promise you ask, or tell you why I do not make it, this evening. In the meantime, Evie, I ask you as a favour to avoid thinking about it as far as you are able. Ah! here we are.'

Indeed, the sight of Grosvenor Square was very welcome to Lady Oxted, for just now she had no clearness of mind on the question which the girl had put to her, but very great clearness as to the fact that there were delicate though remote issues possibly at stake. Here was she with a three months' charge of Evie Aylwin, the half-sister of poor George Houldsworth, daughter of his mother, whose attitude towards Mr Francis admitted of no dubiety, while the most constant visitor at her house was the nephew of the man to whom so terrible a suspicion attached. That the two should not meet verged on impossibilities, and was it fair either to one or the other that they should run the ordinary chances of an attractive girl and a handsome boy together without knowing in what curious and sombre prenatal ordination of fate they were cast? It would be like indicating summer rain in hard lines of ink to say that Lady Oxted expected them to fall in love with each other, but among the possibilities such a contingency could not be reckoned remote or unlikely. Probably, the most hardened matchmaker could not call it, but where was the celibate who would say it was impossible? The sudden, unexpected demand of the girl, 'Promise me you will never tell me his name,' had been, unknown to her, a request which presupposed the solution of a problem of a most complicated kind. Lady Oxted, it is true, had asked for time, already, she was afraid, unwisely; that, however, was done, and she had until the evening the power of making or refusing to make that premise. If she made it, she shouldered herself with the responsibility of countenancing the free intercourse of the two, the mutual attraction to which it might easily give rise, and of seeing it pursue its course to its possible evolution in love and marriage. The girl was staying with her; Harry Vail was so assiduous in his presence that he could scarcely be called a visitor. Both were supremely eligible. It was clearly idle to overlook the possibility. Given that these things occurred, she foresaw a moment, possibly very unpleasant, and certainly to be laid to her door, when Mrs Aylwin heard of the engagement of her daughter to the man on whose name, in her mind, rested the stain of so intimate a blood-guiltiness.

But this unwelcome conclusion brought with it a sudden reaction of hopefulness. Evie Aylwin had asked her mother the name of George's companion on that fatal morning, and had been denied the information. Did not that argue a loophole of encouraging amplitude? Surely to the weaving feminine mind it meant that the mother, though, perhaps, neither repenting nor regretting the black influence which this suspicion, founded or unfounded, had had on herself, yet wished her daughter to move in absolute freedom, avoiding none, open to all, to conduct her life with perfect liberty, not knowing, more, being prevented by her own mother from knowing, anything with definite label of that tragic affair. Else, how was it conceivable that she should not have said those two words 'Francis Vail'? Mrs Aylwin, so reasoned this acute lady, must have known—for who did not know?—the strange, solitary history of the last and the head of the house, and was not her refusal to mention the uncle's name a silent recognition, if rightly interpreted, that the two might meet?

The thought was a pleasant one, for she was much attached to both Harry and the girl, and for a moment she let her fancy build a fantastic dome in the air. If Mrs Aylwin had recognized this—and the inference was not unreasonable—did not the recognition imply a hope, though of the faintest and most unformulated, that now she saw her long, bitter suspicion to have been a mistake? Then her silence would amount even to a wish that the two might meet, and that one of her blood might in the remote possibilities wipe away by her union that of her blood which had been shed.

To take the other side, if she did not make this promise, she had to refuse, with what softenings and limitations you will, to bind herself. In case, then, of what event, to meet what contingency, would she make the reservation? Under what circumstances, that is to say, did she desire to leave herself free? Clearly in case of the possible happening, of the two falling under the spell of each other. But in that case (clearly also, she was afraid) it would be far better to tell the girl now, at once, and save her the greater shock. To hear the name Vail now, this moment, would be nothing to her; to hear the name Vail in its more sinister connection, when already it had a vital sound to her ear, was a pang that might be saved her now, but not hereafter.

Again, still dealing with these remote possibilities, in which connection alone her decision had any significance, was it conceivably fair to Harry to reveal, though in the most intimate way and the most pain-sparing words, the stain that hung over his name? Long ago Lady Oxted had settled with herself that the affair was dead and buried. At the time, even, it had been no more than an unproven and dark suspicion, though endowed with all the mysterious vitality of evil; but was she, of all women, who held that to repeat an evil tale is only one degree removed from inventing it, to stir for any purpose that coiled worm of suspicion? The thought was an abhorrence to her, and Evie's mother, it seemed, in her own dealings with her own child, had endorsed her unwillingness. But it was certain that if the name had to be told it must be told now, for supposing the two remained strangers to intimacy, there would be no greater harm done now than afterwards; but if intimacy was otherwise to be, it was better to kill it in the womb than to let it live and destroy it afterwards.

A third alternative remained, to write to Mrs Aylwin, saying quite simply that Harry Vail was an intimate friend of hers, that he was attractive, and of unblemished character and reputation—so much she was bound to say for the young man's sake—and what did the mother want done? But such a letter, she felt, would be a thing to blush over, even when alone. How demented a match-maker she would appear!

Back swung the balance. She was in the position of mother to the girl, and the mother, out of her own mouth, had desired that she should not know the name. That desire had reached Lady Oxted casually, not knowing to whom it journeyed, but it had arrived, and she was bound to respect it. The promise was as good as made.

Evie had gone to her room after tea, and these various fences faced Lady Oxted on all sides till the ringing of the dressing-bell. But that sound suggested the dinner-table to her, and at the thought of the dinner-table she suddenly felt the conclusions wrested from her, for she remembered for the first time that Harry dined with them that night. And though she did not expect that, on entering the drawing-room, he would immediately throw himself on his knees at Evie's feet, it seemed to her that, as a controlling power, she was put on the shelf—that the issues of things were in younger and stronger hands than hers.

She found a letter or two for her in the hall, and taking these in her hand, she went upstairs.

'The Luck of the Vails,' she said to herself, and the phrase shaped itself to her steps—a step to a syllable.

Still with her letters in her hand, she looked in at Evie's room, and finding her 'betwixt and between', went on to her own, and as her maid did her hair she opened the letters. The first was from Harry.

'The greatest luck,' it ran. 'The Grimstons have influenza in the house, and have put me off. So I can and will and shall come to you for Sunday at Oxted. I shall see you this evening, but I can't resist writing this.'

'Kismet,' murmured Lady Oxted, 'or something very like it.'

Chapter 6

The Meeting

DINNER was over, and of Lady Oxted's party there only remained by eleven o'clock a couple of her guests. There was a ball at one house, an evening party at another, a concert at a third, and each claimed its grilling quota, leaving even at this hour only Harry Vail and Geoffrey Langham. Lord Oxted, as was his wont, had retired to his study as soon as his duties as host would admit without positively violating decency, but the two young men still lingered, making an intimate party.

During the last few months Harry had continued to so expand that it would have been difficult to recognise in him the hero of that recluse coming-of-age party but half a year ago. But this change was the result of no violent revolution; his nature had in no way been wrested from its normal development—merely that development had been long retarded, and was now proportionately rapid. For years his solitary home had ringed him with frost, the want of kindly fireside interests had led him on the path that conducts to the great unexplored deserts of the recluse, but the impulse given, the plunge into the world taken, he had thriven and grown with marvellous alacrity. Indeed, the stunted habit of his teens remained in him now only as shown in a certain impression he produced of holding himself still somewhat in reserve, in a disposition, notable in an age which loves to expose its internal organism to the gaze of sympathizing friends, to be his own master, to retain if he wished a privacy of his own, and to guard, as a sacred trust, his right to his own opinion in matters which concerned himself.

Lady Oxted, however, on this as on many other occasions, felt herself obliged to find fault with him, and the presence of her niece, it would appear, did not impose bounds on her candour.

'You are getting lazy and self-contented, Harry,' she remarked on this particular evening. 'You are here in London professing to lead the life of the people with whom you associate, and you are shirking it.'

Harry looked up with mild wonder at this assault, and drew his chair a little closer up to the half-circle they made round the open window, for the night was stifling, and the candles had drooped during fish.

'I never professed anything of the kind,' he said, 'and I don't yet understand in the slightest degree what you mean. But no doubt I soon shall.'

'I will try to make it plain to you,' said Lady Oxted.

'You have chosen to come to London and lead the silly, frivolous life we all lead. That, to begin with, is ridiculous of you. There is no need for you to be in London, and why any fairly intelligent young man ever is, unless he has business which takes him there, passes my understanding. You might be down at Vail looking after your property, or you might be travelling.'

'I still don't understand about my professing to lead the life of the people among whom I move,' said Harry.

'I am coming to that. You have chosen to spend these three months in London without any better reason for it than that everybody else does so. That being so, you ought to behave like everybody else. For instance, when Mrs Morris wanted to take you to her sister's dance tonight, you ought to have gone; also Lady Wraysbury asked you to go to the concert at the Hamiltons'. Again you refused.'

'She wanted you to come, too,' said Harry; 'at least, she asked you,' he added, getting in a backhander.

'I'm an old woman, and I choose to sit by my own fire.'

'Won't you have it lit?' asked Harry. 'And I chose to sit there too. But I will go away if you like.'

'And will you go to the dance?'

'No, nor to the concert. If I go away, I shall go to bed.'

'You speak as if you were all six Great Powers sending an ultimatum to Heligoland,' said Lady Oxted.

'Not in the least; if you send me away, I shall go.'

Lady Oxted laughed.

'Heligoland replies that the six Great Powers may wait ten minutes,' she said.

Harry turned to Evie Aylwin.

'Yes, I feel just as you do,' he said eagerly, reverting at once to the conversation which had been interrupted by Lady Oxted's strictures. 'I love the sense of being in the middle of millions of people, all of whom, just like you and me, have their own private paradise and joy of life, which the world probably never guesses.'

Evie looked at him quickly.

'Have you a private joy, Lord Vail?' she asked. 'Do tell me what it is. A thing that is private is always interesting.'

Harry laughed.

'It is called "the Luck",' he said—'"the Luck of the Vails".'

'Are you really beginning to believe in that nonsense, Harry?' asked Lady Oxted.

'I have begun,' said he.

'Oh, Aunt Violet, how horrid you are!' cried Evie. 'Do let Lord Vail tell me about it. It is private; I am dying to know.'

'Shall I? I will make it short, then,' said Harry, 'for Lady Oxted's sake.'

'I would rather that you made it long for mine,' said the girl; 'but that is as you please.'

Lady Oxted gave a loud and quite voluntary sigh.

'Poor dear Harry!' she said. 'Geoffrey, let us talk about something extremely tangible the while. You are on the Stock Exchange. Speak to me of backwardation and contango; that may counteract the weakening effect of Harry's nonsense. Are you a Bear?'

Harry smiled, and drew his chair closer to the girl's. 'I will talk low,' he said, 'so that we shall not offend Lady Oxted, and you must promise to stop me if you get bored. Anyhow, you brought it on yourself, for you asked me about my private joy. This is it.'

Blue eyes, deepened by the shaded light to violet, looked into his as he began his tale; into hers looked brown eyes, which seemed black. He told her of the ancient history of the cup, and she listened with interest to a story that might have claimed attention even from a stranger. Then he came to his own finding of it in an attic upon a winter's day; to the three accidents to himself, each trivial, which had followed the finding; and her eyes, which up till now had been at one time on his, at another had strayed with a certain consciousness and purpose (for he never looked elsewhere than at hers) now this way, now that, had superintended the disentangling of a piece of lace which had caught in her bracelet, or had guided her finger as it traced the intricate ivory of her fan-handle, became absorbed. They saw only Harry's big dark eyes, or at their widest circuit his parted lips from which the words came. Her own mouth, thin, finely-lipped, drooped a little at the centre with interest and expectation, and the even line of teeth showed in the red, a band of ivory set in pomegranate. Once she impatiently swept back a tress of hair which drooped over her ear, but the playing of her fingers with her fan had become unconscious, and her eyes no longer followed them. And it would seem that Harry had forgotten his promise to make the story short for Lady Oxted's sake, and had rather acceded silently to the girl's request to make it long for hers, for the startling revelations about backwardations and Bears had long languished before the tale was done.

At last Harry's voice stopped, and there was silence a moment, though each still looked at the other. Then Evie gave a little sharp involuntary sigh, and her eyebrows met in a frown.

'Throw it away, Lord Vail,' she said sharply, 'throw it away at once, when it will be lost, lost. It is a terrible thing. And yet, and yet, how can one believe it? The thing is gold and gems, that is all. Ah, how I should like to see it! It must be magnificent, this Luck of yours. All the same, it is terrible. How can it be your private joy?'

Harry rose. If he was not earnest, it was an admirable counterfeit.

'Do you not see?' he said. ' "Fear both fire and frost and rain", runs the rhyme. But think what the cup is called: it is the Luck of the Vails, and the Vails are—well, they are I and my uncle. Ah, I forgot one thing. Only two days ago my uncle found the key to its case. It was locked when

I found it, and had to be broken open. Well, I
fell into the fire, I caught a chill in the rain, I
sprained my ankle owing to the frost. I have paid
the penalties of the Luck. Now, don't you see, I
am waiting for the luck itself. Indeed, perhaps it
has begun,' he added.

'How so?' asked the girl, with security, for she
knew he was not the kind of man to pay inane
compliments.

'Since I found it I have begun to become human,'
he said gravely. 'Indeed, six months ago I had no
friend in the world except Geoffrey.'

'What's that about me?' asked Geoffrey, who
was playing picquet with Lady Oxted.

'I was only saying you weren't such a brute
as you appeared,' said Harry, without looking
round. 'I'm a true friend, Geoff.' Then, dropping
his voice again: 'Then, on the finding of the Luck,
I became—oh, I don't know what I became—what
I am, anyhow.' He leaned back again in his chair,
blushing a little at his own unpremeditated burst
of egotism. 'Of course, soberly, and in the light
of nine a.m. earnestness, I don't believe in it,'
he continued; 'but my having those three little
accidents was a very curious coincidence, following
as they did on the heels of my finding the Luck.
Anyhow, it pleases me to think that there may be
one coincidence more—that those three little bits
of bad luck will be followed by a piece of very
good luck. That is my private joy—the thought of
some great good thing happening to me. And then,
oh then, won't I just take the Luck and stamp on

it, and throw the rent pieces to the four winds of heaven!'

There was a moment's silence as his voice, slightly raised, gave out the blindly spoken words, which had yet a certain ring of truth about them. But as soon as they were spoken Evie's mood changed.

'Oh, you mustn't!' she cried. 'You could not bring yourself to destroy such a lovely thing. Those stars of emeralds, those clear-set diamond handles! Oh, it makes my mouth water to think of them! I love jewels!'

Lady Oxted at this point was deep in the heavily swollen waters of Rubicon, and her tone was of ill-suppressed acidity.

'Is the nursery-rhyme nearly finished?' she asked.

Harry advanced to her and held out his hand.

'Make it up, Lady Oxted,' he said. 'My fault entirely.'

Evie followed him.

'Dear Aunt Violet,' she said, 'shake hands with Lord Vail this moment. He has given me the most exciting half-hour, and you may die in the night, and then you'll be sorry you spoke unkindly to him. And now we'll talk about liquidation as much as you please. Oh, you are playing picquet! Really, Lord Vail, your story was one of the most interesting I have ever heard. You see, it isn't over yet; you still have the Luck. That makes all the difference. One is never told a ghost-story till the house is pulled down, or all the people who have seen the ghost are in lunatic asylums. But your story is now only at the beginning. Upon my word, I can't make up my mind what you ought to do with the Luck. But I'll tell you some day, when I feel certain. Oh, I shall never feel certain!' she cried. 'You must act as you please.'

'I have your leave?' he said, quite gravely and naturally.

'Yes.'

At that again their eyes met, but though they had looked at each other so long and so steadily on this first evening of their acquaintance, on this occasion neither of them prolonged the glance.

Presently after the two young men left and strolled back to Geoffrey's rooms in Orchard Street, on the way to Cavendish Square. Both were of the leisurely turn of mind that delights in observation, and makes no use whatever of that which it has observed, and scorning the paltry saving of time and shoe-leather to be secured by a cab, they went on foot, through the night bright with lamps of carriages and jingling with bells of hansoms.

'Well, I've had an awfully nice evening,' said Harry. 'Extra nice, I mean, though it is always jolly at the Oxteds'.'

'I thought you were enjoying yourself,' said the other, 'when you refused to go to the concert, for which, as you remember, only this afternoon you were wishing for an invitation. Afterwards, also, I thought you were enjoying yourself.'

'Oh, for God's sake, don't try to be sly!' exclaimed Harry. 'I wished I was a better hand at telling a story. But, all the same, I think it didn't bore Miss

Aylwin. After all, the Luck is a very curious thing,'
he added.

'You are going to Oxted for the Sunday, are you
not?' asked Geoffrey.

'Yes; the Grimstons have the flu in the house,
bless them! And you go home, don't you? Oh,
I never saw such wonderful eyes in my life!' he
cried.

'You are alluding to mine, apparently?' said
Geoffrey.

'Yes, of course I am. Deep violet by candlelight,
and soft, somehow, like velvet.'

'Very handsome of you. I'll look tonight when
I go to bed. My hair, too, soft and fluffy, and the
colour of the sun shining through a mist.'

Harry laughed.

'The habit of being funny is growing on you,
Geoff,' he said. 'Take it in time, old chap, and see
some good man about it. Oh, it's no good going to
bed now; let's go to the Club; it's only just down
Park Lane. I'm not feeling like bed just yet.'

Meantime, at the house they had just left, Evie
had gone up to bed, leaving Lady Oxted to do what
she called, 'write two notes', a simple diplomatic
method of stating that she did not herself mean
to come upstairs immediately. These written, she
announced, she would come to talk for five minutes,
and they would take, perhaps, a quarter of an hour
to write. In other words, as soon as Evie had gone,
she went downstairs to seek her husband in his
room, where she would be sure to find him sitting
by a green reading-lamp, in mild exasperation at

anything which the Government might happen to have done with regard either to a kindly old President of a South African Republic or the second standard for Board Schools.

'Violet, it is really too bad!' said he, as she entered. 'Have you read the Home Secretary's speech at Manchester? He says—— Let me see; where is it?'

'Dear Bob,' said his wife, 'whatever he said, you would quite certainly disagree with it. But never mind showing it me this minute. I want your advice about another matter.'

A faint smile came over Lord Oxted's thin, sharp face. He usually smiled when his wife came to him for advice. He put down his paper and crossed one leg over the other.

'What sort of advice?' he asked. 'Be far more explicit before you consult me. Do you want to tell me of some decision you have made, and wish me to agree with you, or is it possible that you have not yet made your decision? It is as well to know, Violet, and it may save me from misunderstanding you.'

Lady Oxted laughed.

'I am not yet sure which it is,' she said. 'Let me tell you my story, and by that time, you see, I may have made up my mind; in which case I shall want the first sort of advice, but if I have not, the second.'

'That sounds fair,' he assented.

In a few words she told him all that had passed between her and Evie.

'And now,' she concluded, 'am I to promise or not?'

Lord Oxted was a cynic in a certain mild and kindly fashion.

'Certainly promise,' he said. 'And, being a woman, you will probably, at the very back of your mind—the very back, I say—reserve to yourself the right to break it if it becomes inconvenient to keep it.'

'Don't be rude, Bob. I think I shall promise, but at the same time write to Mrs Aylwin.'

Her husband chuckled quietly.

'That is precisely what I meant,' he said, 'only I did not put the reservation quite so far forward in your mind. Did the two young people get on well together?'

'Too well. Harry has developed an amazing knack of getting on well with people. And he is coming to us for the Sunday.'

'Then most likely you are already too late. You should have thought of these things before, Violet. Your after-thoughts, it is true, are often admirable, but, so to speak, they never catch the train. Bear this also in mind: if anything happens—if the two get engaged, we shall be liable at any moment to a crushing descent from Mrs Aylwin. If she comes, I go. That is all.'

'But she is charming.'

'And completely overpowering. I will not be made to feel like a child in my own house. Dear me, you have probably got into a mess, Violet. Good night, dear.'

'You agree with me, then?' she asked.

'Completely, entirely, fervently. For it is clear to me that you want the first sort of advice.'

Lady Oxted went slowly upstairs and to Evie's room. Her maid had already left her, and the two settled themselves down for a talk. The night was hot, and Evie, in a white dressing-gown, with a touch of blue ribbon, lounged coolly by the open window. The hum of ambient London came up to them like the sound of drowsy innumerable bees, and the girl listened in a sort of ecstasy.

'Hark! hark!' she cried; 'hundreds, and thousands, and millions of people are there! Lord Vail felt just as I do about it. Oh, what a host of pleasant things there are in the world!' she cried, stretching out her arms as if to take the whole swarming town to her breast. Then she turned quickly away into the room again. 'Now, dear aunt,' she said, 'before we settle down to talk—and I have lots to say—let me know that one thing. Do you promise never to tell me the name of that man?'

Lady Oxted did not pause.

'Yes, I promise,' she said.

'Thank you. So that is all right. It would be dreadful, would it not, if I had been obliged to be afraid that every particularly delightful person that I met was the son or the nephew, or the cousin of that man, or even the man himself! But now that is all right. Mother would not tell me, and you, knowing her wish—is it not so?—also will not. Oh, Aunt Violet, I intend to enjoy myself so! What a jolly world it is, to be sure! I am so glad

God thought of it! Is that profane? No, I think not.'

Lady Oxted, it has been said, had anticipated one unpleasant moment. This, she considered, made two. And though it was not her habit to question the decrees of Providence, she wondered what she had done to deserve a position where the converse of candour was so sorely in demand. But she had not much time for thought, for Evie continued:

'Only one evening gone,' she said, 'and that not yet gone, and what pleasure I have already had! Aunt Violet, how could you want Lord Vail not to tell me the story of the Luck? It was the most exciting thing I have ever heard, and, as I told him, he is only at the beginning of it. Italy, the south, is supposed to be the home of romance, but I do not find it there. Then I come to England, and in London, in Grosvenor Square, I hear, within an hour or two of my arrival, that story. I think——' She stopped suddenly, got up, and sat down on the sofa by Lady Oxted.

'Lord Vail, who is he?' she asked. 'What pleasant people you have at your house, Aunt Violet! He is so nice. So is his friend Mr Langton, is he not? So was the man who took me in to dinner. What was his name? I did not catch it.'

There was not much comfort here. The girl had forgotten or not heard the name of the man who took her in to dinner; she had got Geoffrey Langham's name wrong and out of all these 'nice people' there was only one name right.

'Langham, dear; not Langton,' said Lady Oxted.

'And the man who took you in to dinner was Mr Tresham. Surely you must have heard his name. He is in the Cabinet. Really, Evie, you do not appreciate the fine people I provide for your entertainment.'

The girl laughed lazily, but with intense enjoyment.

'Not appreciate?' she said. 'Words fail me to tell you how I appreciate them all. Mr Tresham was simply delightful. We talked about dachshunds, which I love; and what else? Oh, diamonds. I love them also. Aunt Violet, I should like to see the Luck; it must be a wonderful thing. So Mr Tresham is a Conservative?'

'It is supposed so,' said Lady Oxted, with slight asperity. 'When the Conservatives are in power, dear, the Cabinet is rarely composed of Liberals.'

The girl laughed again.

'Dear Aunt Violet, you are a little hard on us poor innocents this evening. You blew up Lord Vail in the most savage manner, and now you are blowing me up. What have we done? Well, now tell me about Mr Langham.'

'Geoffrey is a younger son of Lord Langham,' said the other. 'He is on the Stock Exchange, and is supposed to know nothing whatever about stock-broking.'

'How very good-looking he is!' said Evie. 'If I wanted to exchange stock, I should certainly ask him to do it for me. Somehow, people with nice faces inspire me with much more confidence than those whom I am assured have beautiful minds. One can see their faces—that makes so much difference.'

Lady Oxted assented, and waited with absolute certainty for the next question. This tribute to Geoffrey's good looks did not deceive her for a moment: it was a typical transparency. And when the next question came she only just checked herself from saying, 'I thought so.'

'And now tell me about Lord Vail,' said Evie, after a pause.

'Well, he seemed to be telling you a good deal himself,' said Lady Oxted. 'What can I add? He is not yet twenty-two, he is considered pleasant, he is poor, he is the head of what was once a great family.'

'But his people?' asked Evie.

'He has no father, no mother, no brothers or sisters.'

'Poor fellow!' said Evie thoughtfully. 'But he doesn't look like a person who need be lonely, or who was lonely, for that matter. Has he no relations?'

'Of his name only one,' said Lady Oxted, feeling that Providence was really treating her with coarse brutality, 'that is his uncle—his great-uncle, rather— Francis Vail,' and as she spoke she thought to herself in how widely different a connection she might have had to use those two words.

'Do you know him?'

'I used to, but never intimately. He has not lived in the world lately. For the last six months he has

been down at Harry's place in Wiltshire. The boy
has been exceedingly good to him.'

'Is he fond of him?'

'Very, I believe,' said Lady Oxted. 'He often speaks
of him, and always with affection and a tenderness
that is rather touching.'

'That is nice of him,' said the girl with decision,
'for I suppose he cannot be expected to have much
in common with him. And so the old man lives
with him. He is old, I suppose, as he is Lord Vail's
great-uncle?'

'He is over seventy,' said Lady Oxted, turning
her back to the storm.

'And Harry Vail is poor, you say?'

'Considering what the Vails have been, very
poor,' said Lady Oxted. 'But you probably know
as much about that as I, since Harry took so very
long telling you the story of the Luck. It was lost
once in the reign of Queen Anne, and during the
South Sea Bubble.'

'Yes, he told me about that,' said Evie. 'It is
strange, is it not?'

Suddenly she sat up as if with an effort.

'Oh, tomorrow and tomorrow, and lots more
of them!' she cried. 'Tell me what we shall do
tomorrow, Aunt Violet. I am sure it will all be
delightful, and for that very reason I want to think
about it beforehand. I am a glutton about pleasure.
Will you take me somewhere in the morning, and
will delightful people come to lunch? Then in
the afternoon we go to Oxted, do we not? I love
the English country. Who will be coming? Is it a

beautiful place? What is the house like? Tell me all about everything.'

'Including about going to bed and going to sleep, Evie?' asked the other. 'It is long after twelve; do you know?'

'And you want to go to bed,' she said. 'I am so sorry, Aunt Violet. I ought to have seen you were tired. You look tired.'

'And you, don't you want to go to sleep? You were travelling all last night.'

The girl looked at the smooth pillow, and sheet folded back.

'Ah, it does look nice,' she said. 'But indeed I don't feel either sleepy or tired. Anyhow, Aunt Violet, I am not going to keep you up. Oh, I am so glad you got mother to let me come and stay with you! I shall have a good time. Good night.'

'Good night, dear. You have everything?'

'Everything. More than everything.'

Chapter 7

The Point in Casuistry Solves Itself

LADY OXTED always breakfasted in her own room, and before she appeared next morning she had spent a long hour in wrestling over her letter to Mrs Aylwin. She had been desirous to tell the unvarnished truth and yet to steer clear of a production by a demented matchmaker, and her letter, it must be confessed, was an admirable performance. Evie had told her, so she wrote, of her mother's refusal to let her know the name of the man at whose door she laid, or used to lay her son's death, and taking this to mean that Mrs Aylwin, for any reason, did not wish Evie to know it, the writer had, at Evie's request, promised on her own part not to tell her. The present Lord Vail, she must add, Mr Francis's nephew, was a constant visitor at her house, and he and Evie had already met. Mrs Aylwin, she was bound to understand, put no prohibition on their meeting in the way they were sure to meet during the season. Lord Vail was a young man, pleasant, attractive, and of excellent disposition.

Lady Oxted laid down her pen for a moment at this point, then hurriedly took it up to add an amiable doxology and sign it. She felt convinced she could not do better—convinced also that if she gave the matter further consideration, it would end in her doing much worse. Then she took Evie out with a warm and approving conscience.

That afternoon they left London, as had been originally planned, to spend the Sunday at their country house in Sussex. During the hours of the night Lady Oxted had sternly interrogated herself as to whether she ought on any lame or paltry excuse to put Harry off, but on the strength of her promise given to Evie, and the letter she was about to write to Mrs Aylwin, she felt she could not take any step in the matter until she received her answer. To put him off, argued the inward voice, was to act contrary to the spirit of her promise, which entailed not only silence of the lips, but abstinence from any manoeuvring or outflanking movement of this kind. This reasoning seemed sound, and as it went in harness with her instinct, she obeyed it without question.

The house stood high on a broad ridge of the South Downs, commanding long views of rolling fields alternating with the more sombre green of the woods. To the east lay the heathery heights of Ashdown Forest, peopled with clumps and companies of tall Scotch fir; southwards, the smooth austerity of the hills behind Brighton formed the horizon line. Thatched roofs nestled at cosy intervals beside the double hedgerows which indicated roads, a remote church spire pricked the sky, or an occasional streamer of smoke indicated some train burrowing distantly at the bottom of the valleys before it again plunged with a shriek into the bases of the tunnelled hills; but except for these the evidences of humanity were to be sought in vain. The house itself was partly Elizabethan, in part of Jacobean building, picturesquely chimneyed, and high in the pitch of its outside roofs; inside it was panelled and oaken-beamed, spacious of hearth, and open of fireplace. Round it ran level lawns, fringed with flower-beds, wall-encompassed, which, as they receded further from the house, gradually lost formality, and merged by imperceptible steps into untutored nature. Here, for instance, you would pass from the trim velvet of the nearer lawns into the thick lush grass of an orchard planted with apples and the Japanese cherry, but the grass was thick in spring with the yellow of the classical daffodil, the scarlet of the anemone was spilled thereon, and the dappled heads of the fritillary rose bell-shaped. Here, again, in a different direction, the lawn further from the house was invaded by a band of lilac-bushes, and, to the wanderer here, a Scotch fir would suddenly stand sentinel at a turn of the grassy path; while, if his walk took him but fifty yards more remote, the lilacs would have ceased, and he would be treading the brown, silent needles of the fir grove, exchanging for the sweet, haunting smell of the garden shrubs the clean odour of the pine. In a word, it was a place apt to reflect the moods of the inhabitants: the sombrely-disposed might easily see in the pines a mirror of their thoughts; the lilacs, whose smell is ever a host of memories, would call up a hundred soft images in hearts otherwise disposed; while for the lover of pointed conversation, what *milieu* could be more suitable than the formality of the lawns near the house, which, clean and trim-cut as French furniture, irresistibly gave to those who sat and talked there a certain standard of precision? Beyond, again, the orchard was every evening a singing contest of nightingales, and through the soft foliage of fruitful trees moon and stars cast deep shadows and diapers of veiled light into grassy alleys.

The party was but a small one, for influenza had for the last month been pursuing its pleasant path of decimation through London; and, as Mr Tresham remarked while they drank their coffee in the tent on the lawn after lunch next day:

'Those of us who are not yet dead are not yet out of its clutches.'

Lady Oxted sighed.

'I had it once a week throughout last summer,' she said. 'It is a consolation when it is about to know that the oftener you have it the more liable you become to it.'

Mrs Antrobus finished her coffee and tried to feel her pulse.

'I never can find it,' she said, 'and that is so frightening. It may have stopped for all I know.'

'Dear lady,' said Mr Tresham, 'I will promise to tell you whether it has stopped or not, not more than a minute after it has done so, as it will then be too late!'

'Ah! there it is,' said Mrs Antrobus at length— 'one, two. It has stopped now. Take the time, Mr Tresham, and tell me when a minute has gone.'

'Your mother is the only really healthy person I know,' said Lady Oxted to Evie. 'Whether she is ill or not, she always believes she is perfectly well, and as long as one fully believes that, as she does, it really matters little how ill one is.'

Lord Oxted got slowly out of his chair.

'Some doctor lately analysed a cubic inch of air in what we should call a clean London drawing-room,' he said. 'He found that it contained over two hundred bacilli, each of which, if they lived carefully and married, would, with its family, be soon able to kill the strongest man. I surrendered as soon as I heard it.'

'Quite the best thing to do,' said Mr Tresham, 'for otherwise they would kill you. It is better to give yourself up and be taken alive.'

'It is certainly better to remain alive,' said Mrs Antrobus. 'That is why we all go to bed when we get the influenza. We surrender, like Lord Oxted, and so the bacilli do not kill us, but only send us away to the sea-side. It is the people who will not surrender who die. Personally I should never dream of going about with a high temperature; it sounds so improper.'

Evie was sitting very upright in her chair listening

to this surprising conversation. She had seen Mrs Antrobus for the first time the evening before, and had made Lady Oxted laugh by asking whether she was a little mad. It had been almost more puzzling to be told that she was not than if she had been told that she was. And at this remark about her temperature Evie suddenly looked round for a sympathizing eye. An eye there certainly was, and she felt as if, in character of a hostess, she had looked for and caught Harry Vail's. At any rate he instantly rose, she with him, and together they strolled out of the Syrian tent on the lawn, and down towards the cherry-planted orchard.

For a few paces they went in silence, each feeling as if a preconcerted signal had passed between them. Then Evie stopped.

'I wonder if it is rude to go away!' she said. 'Do you think we ought to go back?'

'It is never any use going back,' said Harry. 'Certainly in this case it would not do. They would think'—and a sudden boldness came over him—'they would think we had quarrelled.'

Evie laughed.

'That would never do,' she said, 'for I feel just now as if you were an ally, my only one. What strange things Mrs Antrobus says! Perhaps they are clever?'

She made the suggestion hopefully, without any touch of sarcasm.

'Most probably,' said Harry. 'That would be an excellent reason, anyhow, for my finding them quite impossible to understand!'

'Don't you understand them? Then we certainly are allies. You know, I asked my aunt last night whether she was at all mad, and she seemed surprised that I should think so. But really, when a woman says that she wishes she had been her own mother, because she would have been so much easier to manage than her daughter, what does it all mean?' she asked.

'Oh, she's not mad,' said Harry. 'It is only a way she has. There are lots of people like her. I don't mind it myself; you only have to laugh; there is no necessity for saying anything.'

'And as little opportunity,' remarked Evie.

She paused, then pulled a long piece of feathery grass from its sheath.

'England is delightful,' she said with decision. 'I find it simply delightful, from Mrs Antrobus upwards or downwards. Just think, Lord Vail, I have not been here for three years. What has happened since then?'

'To whom?'

'To anybody. You, for example.'

'Have I not told you? I have come of age. I have found the Luck.'

Evie threw the grass spearwise down wind. She had not exactly meant to speak so personally.

'Ah, the Luck!' she exclaimed. 'Lord Vail, do promise to show it me!'

Thereat Harry again grew bold.

'Nothing easier,' he said. 'I have to go down to Vail next week. Persuade Lady Oxted to bring you down for a day or two. The Luck is the only inducement, I am afraid—it and some big bare Wiltshire Downs.'

'Big, large, and open?' she asked.

'All that. Does it please you?'

'Immensely. I should love to come. And the Luck is there? You must know that I am horribly inquisitive—perhaps, if you were indulgent, you would say, "interested", and leave out the "horribly"—in other people's concerns. So tell me, what do you hope the Luck will bring you?'

'I don't dare to hope. I am inclined to wait a little.'

Evie frowned.

'That would be all very well for a woman,' she said. 'but it won't do for a man. It is a woman's part to sit at home and wait for the Luck; but it is a man's to go and seek it.'

'I am on the look-out for it. I am always on the look-out for it,' he said.

Some shadow passed across the brightness of Evie's eyes; again the personal note had been a little too distinct in her speech, and she replied quickly:

'That is right. I should go for the highest if I were you. I think I should plot a revolution and make myself King of England—something big of that sort.'

'I had not thought of that,' said Harry, 'and I sometimes wonder—it is all nonsense, you know, about the Luck, and of course I don't really believe in it, but I sometimes wonder——'

He paused a moment.

'I wonder whether you would care to hear some more family history?' he said at length.

'Is it as exciting as the Luck?' asked the girl.

'I don't know if you would find it so. It is certainly more tragic.'

'Do tell me,' she said.

'Promise me to exercise your right of stopping me as before.'

'I never stopped you!' she exclaimed.

Harry laughed.

'No. I meant that you had the right to,' he said. 'Do you really want to hear it? It is intimate stuff.'

'Indeed I do,' she said.

Harry paused a moment, then began his story.

'There lives at Vail,' he said, 'a man whom I honour as much as anyone in the world, my great-uncle, Francis Vail. He is old, he has led the most unhappy life, yet if you met him casually you would say he was a man who had never seen sorrow, so cheerful is he, so full of kindly spirits.'

'He is your only relation, is he not?' asked the girl.

'He is. Who told you?'

'Lady Oxted. I beg your pardon; I did not mean to interrupt.'

'He has led a life of continuous and most unmerited misfortune,' said Harry, 'and when I began just now "I wonder" I was going to say, "I wonder whether the Luck will come to him." You see, it is a family thing. He, one would think, might get the good, not I. And I honestly assure you that I should be more than delighted if he did.'

'It is about him you would tell me?' asked Evie.

'About him. I need not give you the smaller details —his unhappy marriage, his sudden poverty, his bankruptcy even, for there is one thing in his life so terrible that it seems to me to overshadow everything else.'

They had come to a garden seat at the far end of the orchard, and here Evie sat down. Harry stood beside her, one foot on the bench, looking not at her, but out over the dreamy, sleeping landscape.

'It is nearly twenty-two years ago,' he said, 'that my uncle was staying down at an estate we used to have in Derbyshire, which has since been sold. The place next us belonged to some people called Houldsworth. What?'

An involuntary exclamation had come to Evie's lips, but she checked it before it was speech.

'Nothing,' she said quietly. 'Please go on.'

'And young Houldsworth,' continued Harry, 'who had just come of age, was great friends with my uncle, who was as kind to him as he is to all young people, as kind as he always is—and that I hope you will soon know for yourself. Well, one day the two were out shooting together——'

Evie made a sudden, quick movement.

'And George Houldsworth accidentally shot himself,' she said.

Harry paused in utter surprise.

'You know the story?' he said.

'Yes, I know it.'

'You, too!' he cried. 'Good God, the thing is past this more than twenty years, and people still talk of it! Oh, it is monstrous! So I need not tell you the rest?'

'No,' said Evie quietly. 'Your uncle was unjustly—for so I fully believe—unjustly suspected of having shot him. It is monstrous! I quite agree with you. But I am not so monstrous as you think,' she added, rather faintly.

In a moment Harry's heightened colour died from his face.

'Miss Aylwin, I did not say that!' he exclaimed earnestly. 'Forgive me if I have said anything that hurt you. But indeed I did not say that!'

Evie looked at him a moment. She knew the thing she had so much desired not to know, but the knowledge, strangely enough, did not frighten or affect her.

'No, in justice to you, I will say that you did not. But you broke out, "It is monstrous," when I told you I knew the story.'

Again the colour rose to his face, but now not vehement—only ashamed.

'I did,' he said. 'It is quite true. I spoke violently and unjustifiably. But if you knew my poor uncle, Miss Aylwin, I do not think you would find it hard to forgive me; you would see at once why I spoke so hastily. He is the kindest and best of men, and the most soft-hearted. Think what that suspicion must have been to him, the years, so many of them and all so bitter, in which it has never been cleared up.'

'I do think,' she said softly, 'and I like you for your violence, Lord Vail. You are loyal. It is no bad thing to be loyal; but'—and she looked up at him—'but you must not think that I am a willing listener to gossip and old scandal that does not concern me.'

'I do not think that,' cried Harry. 'Indeed, I never thought that.'

His words rang out and died on the hot air, and still the girl made no answer. This way and that was her mind divided. Should she tell him all? should she tell him nothing? The latter was the easier path, for his last words had the ring of truth in them, convincing, unmistakable, and she, so to speak, was acquitted without a stain on her character did she decide not to speak. But something within her, intangible and imperative, urged other counsels. Her reason gave her no account of these, but simple instinct only called to her. What prompted that instinct, from what deep and vital source it rose, she did not pause to consider. Simply it was there, with reason warring on the other side. The battle was brief and momentous. Immediately almost she spoke.

'I am sure you never thought that,' she said; 'but I wish'—and her pulse ticked full and rapid—'I wish to prove to you how it was not through gossip that the knowledge came to me. For this is how I heard it: my mother was George Houldsworth's mother.'

Harry drew a long breath, which hung suspended in his lungs. His eyes were fixed on the eyes of the girl in a long glance of sheer astonishment, and hers were not withdrawn. At last—

'God forgive us all!' he said. 'And do you forgive me?'

Evie looked up quickly, with a glowing face.

'Forgive you? What is there for which I can forgive you, Lord Vail?' she said. 'And I honour you for your championship of your kinsman, who has suffered, as I believe, unmeritedly and most cruelly,' and her heart spoke the words which her lips framed.

They walked back in silence towards the house, for to each the moment was too good to spoil by further speech, and the silence was spontaneous and desired, the distance of the poles away from awkwardness. To Harry, at any rate, it seemed too precious to risk of it the loss of a moment; he would not have opened his lips, except that one word should issue therefrom, for all his Luck could bring him, and that word he dared not utter yet; he scarcely even knew if, so to speak, it was there yet. And in Evie the triumph of her just speech over a more conventional reticence filled her with a deep and secret joy. She ought to have said what she had said; she could have said no less, and she felt it in every beat and leaping pulse of her body. The recognized and proper reserve of a girl to a young man meant to her at that moment less than nothing; her words, she knew, had put her on a new and more intimate footing with him, but she could not have spoken otherwise or not have spoken at all. She had said what was due from one human being, be he boy or girl, or man or woman, to another human being, king or peasant. She had said no more than she need, but, humanly speaking, she could not have said less. The thing had been well done.

But just before they reached the lawn again she spoke.

'My mother, of course, told me the story,' she said. 'I asked her for the name of—for your uncle's name; but she would not tell me. It is better'—and again her blood spoke—'it is better thus.'

Next moment they turned the corner, and found the party as they had left it, for they had been gone scarcely ten minutes. Mrs Antrobus was lighting one cigarette from the stump of the other.

Chapter 8

The Second Return to Vail

IT was the day following Lady Oxted's return to London from the Sunday in the country that she received the expected letter from Mrs Aylwin in answer to her own. The opening of it, it would be idle to deny, was made with an anxious and apprehensive hand. Already it was plain to her with how swift and strong a movement, as of flood-water hastening towards sluice-gates, the first attraction between the two was speeding into intimacy, and had she known what had passed between them in the orchard, she would have guessed that its swiftness had outrun her eye. Already it would have been far better, if the girl was to know the name her mother had refused to tell her, that she should have known it on the night of her arrival. But these things were past prayer, and Lady Oxted drew the sheet of paper from its envelope, and found, at any rate, that the communication was short.

'I leave it entirely to your judgment,' wrote Mrs Aylwin, 'whether you tell Evie or not. You say that you have promised not to; in that case, supposing at some future time you consider it advisable, and you can accept the quibble, tell it her, not in your name, but in mine. My reason for not telling it her you may easily have guessed: the knowledge, or so I thought it, that George was murdered, has poisoned my life, and now I question myself as to whether I have been certainly right about it. But remember this: if there arises between the two—the thing is possible, as evidently you foresee—a friendship which develops, as is natural between a man and a maid, it is certain that some time Evie will know. I leave it to you to decide whether it is better that she should know now or later. I thank you, dear Violet, for your care for her.'

'Dear Violet' heaved a sigh of relief. Mrs Aylwin had been known to stagger those who were dear to her by sending them letters which partook of the nature of an ultimatum. But there was no ultimatum here. She was willing to treat, and this letter, though couched with the precision of an official despatch, was not without amenity.

She hurried downstairs to join Evie—for they were going out to lunch—with the sense of a burden removed. Such being the attitude of Mrs Aylwin, she determined that her own promise to the girl should certainly stand, and she thought with scornful wonder of her husband's diagnosis that, at the very back of her mind, she would reserve to herself the right to break it. Men's ideas of women, she told herself, were incredibly crude and elementary. They reserved for themselves a monopoly of certain qualities, like courage, justice, and honour, and simply took it for granted that such things did not exist for women. Poor dear Bob, and after so many years, too!

Evie was somewhat silent as they drove down Bond Street, and though her gaze at the jostling crowds was not less intent than usual, it seemed to have lost the sparkle of its avidity, and to dwell rather than alight and be gone again. She looked this morning at the seedy toy-sellers and flower-vendors more than at their fragrant or painted wares, and instead of finding fascination in the little tin figures that moved their scythes over the surface of an absolutely smooth pavement with the industry of those who reap the whirlwind, or commenting on the phenomenal cheapness of collar-studs, it was rather the tragic meanness of their exhibitors which today attracted her.

'How do you suppose they live, Aunt Violet?' she asked. 'Look at that man with studs—six a penny. I know, because I bought six on Saturday. Well, supposing he sold sixty a day, which I imagine he does not, and that they cost him absolutely nothing, in the evening he would have tenpence. Yet they are not beggars: they work for their bread. Now, in Italy we have nothing like them; their place is taken by the smiling, picturesque *lazzaroni*, who would not stir a finger to help themselves. They just sit in the sun and smile, and get fed. Oh dear!'

'What is it now, Evie?' asked Lord Oxted.

'Nothing. I suppose I am just realizing that it takes all sorts to make a world, and that extremes meet, and so on. Look at me, now. Here am I in this comfortable victoria, much more like the *lazzaroni* than the toy-sellers, and who shall say how far the toy-sellers are above the *lazzaroni*? I sit in the sun, and if there is no sun I sit by the fire, and to do me justice, I generally smile. Yet, supposing I had to work for my bread, should I do it cheerfully, do you think? Should I maintain even a low average of industry? Supposing there came some great call on me for courage or resolution, should I respond to it? I have no reason whatever for assuring you or myself either that I should.'

Lady Oxted's mind flew back with an inward smirk of satisfaction to her own heroic determination to keep the promise she had made to Evie.

'Probably you would,' she said. 'Probably we are not so bad. When it comes to our having an opportunity for behaving abominably, we do not behave as we thought we were going to. The thought of the dentist poisons my life for days beforehand, yet I go all the same, and ring the dreary bell, and behave, I believe, with average courage under the wheel. Morally, too, I expect we are better, when a thing has to be done, than we were afraid we were going to be. Also, on the whole, one is more honourable than one thinks— more honourable, certainly,' she added, with a sudden irrepressible spurt of indignation against her husband, 'than those who know us best believe us to be.'

Evie laughed.

'Dear aunt, have you been very honourable lately?' she asked, 'or has Uncle Bob been doubting your first qualities?'

'Cynicism always ends in disappointment,' remarked Lady Oxted, leaping a conversational chasm, 'but since it is cynical, I suppose it expects it.'

'Is Uncle Bob a cynic?' asked Evie, dragging her back over the chasm again.

'Well, I made a promise the other day,' said Lady Oxted, 'and asked him his advice about it. He told me I should probably reserve to myself the right to break it.'

Evie sat up suddenly, and toy-maker and *lazzaroni* were swept from her mind.

'A promise?' she said. 'Not the promise you made me?'

Lady Oxted looked up in surprise.

'Yes, the same. Why, dear?'

Evie deliberated with herself for a moment.

'For this reason,' she said slowly: 'because I now know what I asked you not to tell me. Your promise has had the kernel taken out of it.'

'You know? Who told you?'

'Lord Vail,' she replied.

Lady Oxted looked at the girl's heightened colour, wondering what emotion flew that beautiful standard there.

'I will never waste an ounce of resolution again in determining to abide by my word,' she announced.

Evie laughed again, with a great ring of happiness in the note.

'Then you will confirm Uncle Bob in his cynicism,' she replied, 'and disappoint him of all his pleasant little disappointments.'

It was not long before Lady Oxted found that to be chaperon to one of the greatest heiresses in England could not be regarded even by the most negligent as a sinecure, and to fulfil its duties at all adequately cost considerable time and thought. Had the girl been dull, heavy, serious, or plain, her task would have been lighter; but as it was, Lady Oxted became, before a fortnight was past, a really hard-worked woman. Evie's appetite for gaiety was insatiable. She took to London like a bird to the air, found everybody charming, and everybody returned the compliment. Indeed, the girl seemed to bring wherever she went a breath of spring and morning, so utterly sincere and spontaneous was the pleasure that bubbled from her; and since nothing pleases people so much as to find themselves pleasing, London in general was exceedingly glad that Santa Margerita was the poorer for Evie's presence here. With the eager avidity of youth, and with youth's serene digestion, she gathered and devoured the heaped-up feast of daily and nightly gaiety. Self-consciousness for once seemed to have been left out of the composition of a human being, and she played and laughed and enjoyed herself among these crowds as a child may play in the daisies by itself in some spring meadow, not hoarding and reflecting on its happiness, but simply happy. Parsifal with the flower-maidens was not more unreflective than she, surrounded by the well-dressed hosts, her charm in the mouth of all.

It might have been hoped, thought Lady Oxted, that since so large a ring was always assembled to see her smile, the smiles would have been, considering the number and variety of the circle, distributed with moderate evenness. In this she was not disappointed, but—a thing far more disconcerting to the responsible chaperon—Evie's seriousness certainly was not impartial. For all the world but one she seemed to have no seriousness, but about that one there could be no mistake.

Already between her and Harry there existed a relation, dear and indefinable, to be dwelt on with silent wonder; some alchemy, secret and subtle, untraceable as the course of the swallow's flight, was at work; an effervescence already had begun to stir, brightening the dark well of destiny within them by a hundred points of light; a mysterious luminosity was growing in tremulous flame.

Until the receipt of Mrs Aylwin's letter, Lady Oxted had felt a little uncertain as to whether she could accept Harry's invitation for herself and the girl to Vail. In any case, the next two Sundays were impossible, and the matter had been left undecided. But now that all restriction was withdrawn, she arranged to take Evie down in three weeks' time, at the end of the month. Harry himself, however, had business at his house which could not be postponed, and towards the end of the week he went down there, with the intention of clearing

it off as quickly as might be, and returning again
to London.

Mr Francis had been at Vail almost continuously
since the winter, and Harry found him in the
enjoyment of his usual merry spirits. He looked even
better in health and younger to the eye than when
his nephew had seen him last, and the briskness
of his movements, the clear, scarcely wrinkled skin
of his face, were indeed surprising in one of his
years. He had driven to the station to meet Harry,
and the train being stopped on an inside curve
just before reaching the platform, Harry, leaning
out of the window, saw him standing there. Mr
Francis caught sight of his face, and pulling out his
handkerchief, continued to wave it till the train
finally drew up at the platform.

'And here you are, my dearest boy,' he cried
effusively, before Harry was out of the carriage.
'How late your train is! It is scandalous and
abominable! I should have found two sharp words
for the station-master, I expect, if I had not been
so happy to think you were coming. How well you
look, Harry! London seems to suit you as well as
the country suits me.'

'Indeed, that is saying a great deal,' said Harry,
looking at that cheerful, healthy face. 'I have never
seen you looking better, Uncle Francis.'

A smile of great tenderness played round the
old man's mouth.

'And for that I have to thank you, my dear
boy,' he said, 'in that it is to you I owe my quiet
retreat, my days of busy tranquillity. Ah, Harry, it

has been worth while to grow old if at the end you find such peace as is mine.'

They drove briskly up the mile of deep country lane which separated the station from the high-road, and Harry found an unlooked-for pleasure in the wealth of honey-suckle which embowered the hedges in their fragrant curves, and in the clean, vigorous tendrils of the dog-rose, starred with the delicacy of its pink blossom. Something in that young unfolding of simple loveliness which had never really struck him before now smote on his heart with a pang of exquisite pleasure. How wonderful was youth, and the growth of young things! How like in some subtle and intimate way were these springing sprays of blossom to a girl on the verge of womanhood! For instance—and he turned to his uncle again.

'Yes, London suits me,' he said, the thrill and surprise of his thoughts glowing in his handsome face. 'People are so kind, so friendly. Oh, it is a warm, nice world!' and his hand shook the two horses to a swift trot.

'You will always find people kind and friendly to you, Harry,' said Mr Francis, 'if you look at them as you looked at me just now. Men and women know nothing so attractive as happiness. My dear boy, what have you been doing to yourself? You are more radiant than Apollo.'

Harry laughed.

'I would not change places with him,' he said. 'I will take my chance as Harry Vail. I have done nothing to myself, if you ask; but I have found many friends. But I do not forget, Uncle Francis, that the first friend I found was you, and I do not think I shall find a better.'

They turned into the glare of the white highroad, and Mr Francis, who, while they were in the shadow of the deep lane-banks, had carried his hat on his knee, letting the wind blow refreshingly through his thick white hair, put it on again.

'Ah, Harry, I hope you will some time, and soon, find a friend, and dearer than a friend, for life,' he said, 'who will speedily make you forget your old uncle. But give him a seat in the chimney-corner. That he asks, though he asks no more, and let him nurse your children on his knee. He has a way with children; they never cry with him. I pray, I often pray,' he said, lifting his hat as he spoke with a gesture touching and solemn, 'that I may do that. That, dear Harry, would be the crowning happiness of my happy days.'

The words died gently on to the air; no direct reply was needed. For a moment Harry was half determined to tell his uncle of his dream and his hope, longing with the generous warmth of youth for the sympathy which he knew would so fully be his, and the words were even on the threshold of his lips when Mr Francis suddenly straightened himself from his attitude of musing, and plunged into less intimate talk.

'I have not been idle, dear Harry,' he said, 'while you have been away, charging about the world, as youth should. I think you will find—I may say it without undue complacence—that the home-farm is in better order and is more profitable than it has ever been. There is no credit due to me; it is simply the work of a bailiff I had the luck to find, an invaluable man. And in the autumn I can promise you better pheasant-shooting than there has been for many years.'

'I am sure it is so,' said Harry, 'and we will prove it together, Uncle Francis. Really, I cannot thank you enough; it is too good of you to devote yourself as you have been doing to the estate. Dear me, it is four months since I was here. I am an absentee landlord, but a better landlord than I has been on the spot, and I am not afraid that I shall be shot at.'

They turned in at the lodge gates, and bowled swiftly along under the huge trees. The hay was standing high in the fields to the left, on the right the pasturage of the park was grazed by sleek kine, already beginning to leave the mid-day shadows of the trees for their evening feed in the cool, and the sense of smell and scent alike drank deep of the plentiful and luxuriant summer. Rooks held parliament in their debating-houses in the high elms, round the coops of the pheasant-rearing hens chirped innumerable young birds, and the breeze that should blow at sundown was already stirring to try its wings. Extraordinarily pleasant to Harry was the sense that all this was his, yet there was neither vainglory nor selfishness in his delight, for he valued his own, not for the thought of what it was to him, but for the joy another perhaps should take in it. Then, emerging from the mile-long avenue, they came to the shining lake, and the sound of coolness from the splashing sluice. Swan and water-lily reflected themselves on the surface, and as they turned the corner a moor-hen made its water-logged scurry to the cover of the reed-beds. Then, with a hollow note from the wheels, they rolled over the bridge, and turned in under the monstrous shape of the cut-box hedge to the gravel-sweep in front of the house. There it stood, the shadow of one of the wings fallen half across the courtyard, stately and grave, full of dignity and grey repose, surely no unworthy gift to offer to any. And at that thought a sudden pulse leaped within him.

'It is all unworthy,' he said to himself, banishing with an effort that irrepressible thrill of joy, 'and I the unworthiest of all.'

He lingered a moment at the door, and then followed Mr Francis into the house. Again the joy of possession seized him. His were the tall faint tapestries of armoured knights and garlanded lovers, his the rows of serious portraits which seemed today to his eye to have a freshness and welcome for him which had never been there before. He contrasted, with keen relish of the change, his last home-coming and this. What a curious dreamlike month that had been which he had spent here at his coming-of-age! How grey and colourless life seemed then, if looked at in the light of all that had passed since! He had pictured himself, he remembered, slowly putting spadeful after spadeful of time, heaped gradually from month to year, on the grave of his youth, spending a quiet, often solitary, existence here in the home of his fathers. Uncle Francis, so he had planned it in those days when he had been alone here before his arrival and Geoffrey's, no doubt would be glad to come here sometimes. Geoffrey, too, would very likely spend a week with him now and again in the shooting-season. Otherwise, it would be natural for him to be much alone, and the prospect had called up in him no emotion even so lively as dislike. He would be out of doors a good deal, pottering and poking about the woods, he would read a good deal, and no doubt the year would slip away not unpleasantly. In course of time the portrait of Henry Vail, twelfth Baron, and of seemingly morose tendencies, would gloom from the wall, for that series must not be broken. A little longer, and moss would be green in the lettering of his tombstone.

But now he could scarcely believe that the lad who had meditated thus six months ago, not dismally, but without joy, could be the same as he who stood with a kindled eye beneath old Francis's picture. He looked at his own hand as he raised his teacup, he looked at his boots and his trousers. Yes, they were certainly his, and he it had been who had drunk tea here before. What, then, had happened? he asked himself. He had discovered the world, that was all, and Columbus had only discovered America. And the world was quite full of charming things, and people in particular; to descend to details, or to generalize on the whole—he hardly knew which was which—it was full of one person.

Chapter 9

Cardiac

MR FRANCIS soon joined him for tea, and, after proposing a stroll in ten minutes' time, had gone to his room to answer an urgent letter. Harry was well content to wait, for nothing could come amiss to so harmonious a mood as his, and, lighting a cigarette, he strolled round the walls beholding his forbears. Opposite the portrait of old Francis, second Baron, he stood long, and his eye sought and dwelt on the Luck as a familiar object. The sun streaming through the western windows fell full on to the picture, and the jewels, so cunning and exact was their portrayal, sparkled with an extraordinary vividness in the gleam. The Luck! Was it the Luck which had given him these days of wonderful happiness, with so great and unspeakable a hope for the days to come? Was this the huge reward it granted him, for which he had paid but with a cold in the head, a burn on the hand, a sprain of the foot? How curious, at the least, those three coincidences following so immediately on the finding of the Luck had been! How curious also this awakening of his (dating from the same time) from the solitary lethargy of his first twenty-one years! For the awakening had come with the coming of Uncle Francis, and his own instant attachment to him. It was indeed he—he and Geoffrey, at any rate, between them, on their visit here—who had started him on the voyage which had already resulted in the discovery of the world. It was then that his potential self had begun to rustle and stir in the chrysalis of isolation which had grown up round it, very feebly and tentatively indeed at first, but by degrees cracking and bursting its brown bark, then standing with quivering and momentarily-expanding wings, which gradually unfolded and grew strong for flight. The Luck! Was it indeed the gems and the gold which had done this for him? It was much, it was very much; but to him now how infinitely more than he had did he desire! Six months ago he had desired nothing, for he was dead; but now, being alive, how he yearned for more—one thing more!

A sudden idea seized him, and he rang the bell, and until it was answered looked again at the picture. Old Francis's face, he thought, and old Francis's hands, did not fare so well in the sunlight as the glorious jewel which he held. The hands clutched rather than held the cup; the lines of them were greedy and grasping; they gripped the treasure with nervous tension; and in the face there were ugly lines which he had never noticed before, but which bore out the evidence of the hands. Avarice sat on that throne, and cunning as deep as the sea, and cruelty, and evil mastery. Still looking and wondering, he suddenly saw the face in a different light: it was no longer a vile soul that looked from those eyes, but the kind, cheerful spirit of his own uncle. He started, for the change had the vividness of actuality, and at the moment the bell was answered by the old butler.

'Ah, Templeton,' he cried, 'I am glad to see you. All well? That's right. I rang to say that I wanted you to get out the Luck—the big cup, you know, which you and I found in the attic last Christmas— and put it on the table tonight as a centre-piece.'

'Mr Francis has the key, my lord,' said Templeton; 'it is on his private bunch.'

'Ask him to give it to you, then. Say it was by my order. Oh, here he is! Uncle Francis, I want the key of the case in which is the Luck. I want to have it on the table tonight.'

'Dear boy, is it wise?' said Mr Francis. 'Supposing the house was broken into; you know the thing is priceless.'

'But burglars cannot take it from before our noses while we sit at dinner,' said Harry; 'and as soon as dinner is over, even before we leave the room, it shall be put back again. See to that, Templeton! That is the key, is it Why, it is gold, too! Old Francis knew how to do things thoroughly.'

Uncle and nephew strolled out together—Harry with his head high and leading the way. An extraordinary elation was on him.

'I have a feeling that the Luck is bringing me luck,' he said. 'Oh, I don't seriously believe it, but think how strange the coincidences have been. Fire and frost and rain! I had a turn with all of them. And you know, Uncle Francis, since I found it, I have had more happiness than in the whole of my life before.'

'What happiness, Harry?'

'Friends—you the first; the joy of life; the conscious feeling that one is alive, which I suppose is the same thing. All, all,' he cried—'the world, men, women, things, all!'

Mr Francis did not reply at once, but went forward a few steps, his eyes on the ground.

'Don't believe it, Harry,' he said. 'I would never have told you about the foolish old story if I had thought that there was the slightest chance of your paying more attention to it than one gives to a fairy tale. My dear boy, you are really quite silly. You caught cold because you would not listen to my excellent advice and change your clothes when you got in from shooting; you sprained your ankle because you did not look where you were going, and see that the steps were covered with ice; you burned yourself because a careless housemaid had forgotten to tack down the carpet. I do not believe in magic at all; there is, I assert, no such thing; but even if one did, it would be a very childish, weak kind of spell that could only bring curses of that sort.'

'That is just what I think,' said Harry, 'the evil, perhaps, has run down, so to speak; it is nearly

impotent. Oh, I am only joking. But if that is
the price I have paid for my present happiness,
I consider it dirt-cheap. And if the Luck can give
me more happiness, I hereby declare to the powers
that work it that I will take any amount more on
the same scale of charges.'

Mr Francis laughed, and took Harry's arm
affectionately.

'Dear lad, you were only jesting, I know,' he said.
'But it is not well to dwell on such fantastic things
too much, though we constantly remind ourselves
that they are nonsense. The human mind is a
very wonderful and delicate piece of mechanism,
and if once we begin playing experiments with a
thing of which we understand so little, it may get
out of order and strike the wrong hour, and fail
to keep time. Lead your wholesome, honourable
life, dear boy, and take gratefully what happiness
comes in your way, and do not forget whence it
comes. Then you will have nothing to fear from the
Luck.'

'No, and nothing to gain from it,' said Harry,
'for I expect magic cannot touch those who do
not believe in it.'

'Dear boy, enough,' said Mr Francis, with a certain
earnestness. 'You have told me you do not believe
in it. Ah, what a wonderful evening! Look at those
pink fleeces of cloud in the west, softer than sleep,
softer than sleep, as Theocritus says. How I wish I
was a painter! Think of the privilege of being able
to show those sunset glories—to show, too, as the
true artist can, the feelings, infinite and subtle,

which those rose clouds against the pale blue of
the sky produce in one, to show them to the toiler
of the London streets. Ah, Harry, what a wealth
of senses has been given us, what diverse-facing
windows to our souls, and how little we trouble to
look out of any, or to keep bright and clean even
one! The gourmet even, the man who eats his
dinner, using his palate with intelligence, is a step
above most people. He has trained a sense. And
what exquisite pleasure that sense, even though
it be the most animal of all, gives him! And who
can say that each sense was not given us in order
that we should cultivate it to the fullest?'

Suddenly he raised his hat, and in a low, clear
voice he cried:

' "Oh, world, as God has made it, all in
  beauty!
And knowing this is love, and love is duty,
What further can be sought for or
  declared?" '

For a long moment he stood there, his face
irradiated by the fires of sunset, his eyes soft with
gentle unshed tears, his hair stirred by the caress
of the evening breeze, with who knows what early
dreams and cool reveries of boyhood reminiscent
within him? His harsh, untoward past had gone
from him; he had lived backwards in that moment
to the days before troubles and darkness came
about his path. Aspirations seemed to have taken
the place of memory—he was a youth again, and

Harry's face as he looked at him was loving and reverent.

It was already deep dusk when they turned back, and only the faint reflections of the fires of sunset lingered in the sky. The green of grass and tree had faded to a sombre grey, and the green of the fantastically cut box-hedge had deepened to black when they again passed under its misshapen shapes and monstrous prodigies. Somehow the look of it cut out against the unspeakable softness and distance of the sky struck Harry with something of an ominous touch.

'That must be seen to,' he said, pointing to it; 'look at the horror of its shapes; it is like a collection of feverish dreams.'

'The old box-hedge?' asked Mr Francis. 'If I were you I should not have it touched. See how Nature is striving to obliterate the intruding hand of man. How grotesque and quaint it appears in this light! How delightfully horrible!'

'Horrible, certainly,' said Harry; 'but I do not find delight there. Come, Uncle Francis, let us go in. It is already close upon dinner-time, and one has to dress.'

But the box-hedge seemed to have a strange fascination for Mr Francis, and he still lingered there, standing in that road, with his eye wandering down the lines of that nightmare silhouette.

'Indeed I would not touch it, dear Harry,' he said. 'It is so grotesque and Gothic. What a thickness the hedge must be! eight feet at the least.'

'But it is hideous,' replied the lad. 'It is enough to frighten anybody.'

'But it does not frighten you or me, or the gardeners either, we may suppose. At least, I have heard of no hysterics.'

'That is probably true, but—— Well, come in, Uncle Francis. We shall be so late for dinner, and I am dying for it.'

An hour later the two had finished dinner, and were waiting for coffee to be brought. Harry, after finishing his wine, had lit a cigarette, which had been the occasion of some playful strictures from his uncle, who still held his unkindled in his soft, plump fingers.

'One sip, only one sip of coffee first, Harry,' he said. 'It is almost wicked to light your cigarette till you have had one sip of coffee. That is the psychological moment. Ah, that dazzling thing! How it sparkles! It was a good idea of yours to have it on the table, Harry. It makes a noonday in the room. How the Luck welcomes you home, my dear boy! But though I cannot sparkle like that, not less do I welcome you.'

Indeed, that winking splendour in the centre of the table was enough to strike sight into blind eyeballs. The candles that lit the table, though shaded from the eye of the diner, poured their unobtruded rays on to it from fifty angles, and each stone glowed with an inward and ever-varying light. The slightest movement of the head was sufficient to turn the blue lights of the diamonds into an incandescent red; again a movement and the burning danger signals were changed to a living green. The pearls shone with a steady lustre, like moons through mist, but even the sober emeralds caught something of the madness of the diamond-studded handles, and glowed with colours not their own. The thing had fascinated Harry all dinner-time, and the spell seemed to grow, for suddenly he filled his glass again.

'The Luck,' he said, 'I drink to the Luck,' and he put down an empty glass.

An affectionate remonstrance with his folly was on Mr Francis's lips when the servants entered with coffee. Behind the footman who carried it walked a man with liqueurs whom Harry could not remember having seen before. He looked at him a moment, wondering who he was, when he recollected that his uncle had spoken to him about his own man, who, he proposed, should wait on him at Vail. Last came Templeton, carrying the leather case of the Luck.

Harry took coffee and liqueur, and had another look at his uncle's valet. The man wore the immovable mask of the well-trained servant; he was no more than a machine for handing things.

'Yes, take the cup, Templeton,' said Harry; 'have you the key of it?'

'No, my lord; it is on Mr Francis's bunch.'

'Would you give me the key, Uncle Francis? I will lock it myself and keep the key.'

Mr Francis did not at once answer, but continued sipping his coffee, and Harry, thinking he had not heard, repeated his request. On the repetition Mr Francis instantly took the key off his bunch.

'By all means, dear boy,' he said; 'it is much better so, that you should have it.'

Templeton packed the jewel in its case, and Harry turned the key on it.

'Lock it up yourself, Templeton,' he said, 'in one of the chests. I must have a new case made for it, I think. This is very old, and it would be much too easily carried away—eh, Uncle Francis?' and he swung the locked case lightly in his hand.

'It is the original case, Harry,' he said. 'I should be sorry to change it.'

The men left the room, Templeton going last, with the case containing the Luck. The candles still burned brightly, but half the light seemed to have been withdrawn from the room now that the great jewel no longer gleamed on the table; it was as if a cloud had hidden the sun. Harry still held the key in his hand, looking curiously at its chased and intricate wards, and for a few moments neither spoke. Then he put it into his pocket, and pushing his chair a little further from the table, flung one leg over the other.

'I propose to stop here four or five days, Uncle Francis,' he said, 'but not more, unless we cannot get through our business. But indeed I cannot see what there is to do. The place looks in admirable order, thanks to you. There is the box-hedge; that is positively all I can see that wants looking to.'

Mr Francis laughed gaily.

'Dear Harry,' he said, 'if you are not careful

you will become as absurd on the subject of this box-hedge as you are in danger of becoming about the Luck. The dear, quaint, picturesque thing! How can you want it trimmed and cut!'

Harry laughed.

'As you say, it does not frighten you or me or the gardeners,' he said; 'but, as I was about to tell you as we drove from the station, when something put it out of my head, I shall have to consider others as well.'

Suddenly he stopped. In the intense pleasure with which he had looked forward to the visit of Evie and Lady Oxted, which should be, so he had figured it, hardly less welcome to his uncle, as a sign, visible and pertinent, of how utterly dead and discredited was the lying rumour which at one time had so blackened him, he had not consciously reckoned with the moment of telling him. But he went on, almost without a pause:

'At the end of the month Lady Oxted has promised to come and spend a Sunday here, and with her will come—oh, Uncle Francis, how long this or something of the sort has been delayed and how patiently you have waited for it!—with her will come her niece, Miss Aylwin, who has just come to England from Italy.'

He looked not at his uncle as he spoke, but, with a delicacy unconscious and instinctive, kept his eyes on the ground. Such an announcement as the visit of George Houldsworth's sister must, he knew, be momentous to the old man, and perhaps would give rise to an emotion which it was not fit that other eyes should see. His uncle would know that in the mind of one at least most intimately connected with the tragedy suspicion was not. This visit would be a reconciliation, formal though silent. It was right that the hearer should have as great a privacy as might be, and so, both when he spoke and after he had finished speaking, Harry kept his eyes on the ground.

There was a moment's silence, broken by the crash of breaking china, and, looking quickly up, Harry saw the coffee-cup fallen from his uncle's hand, and the brown stains leaping over the white tablecloth. The spoon clattered metallic in the shattered saucer, and jumped to the floor, and Mr Francis's hand dropped like lead on the edge of the table. The candles were between Harry and his uncle; he could see no more, and he sprang up with a sudden pang of horror rising up within him.

There, with his head fallen over the back of the chair, lay Mr Francis, sprawling and inert. His face was of a deadly, strangled white; the wholesome colour had fled his cheeks, and only on the lips and below the eyes lingered a mottled purple. His breathing was heavy and stertorous—you would have said he snored—and from the corner of the slack mouth lolled the protruding tongue. His hands lay limp upon his lap, grey and purple.

Harry made one step of it to the bell, and rang peal after violent peal, scarce daring to look, yet scarce able not to look, at that mask-like horror of a face at the end of the table. 'What had he done?

What if he had killed him? Death could not be more ghastly,' ran the shrill voice of terror-stricken thought through his head. His instinct was to go to him, though his flesh shrank and shivered at the thought of approaching *that*, to do something, but he knew not what; yet meddling might only cause damage irreparable, instead of giving relief. Still, he did not cease ringing, and it seemed to him that the muffled clanging of the bell he rang had sounded for years, when steps came along the passage and burst into the room.

'There, there, look to him! What is the matter?' cried Harry, still working on the bell like a man demented. 'Send for the doctor—send for his servant; perhaps he knows what to do. Ah, there he is!' and he dropped the bell-handle.

Mr Francis's valet of the mask-like face had gone straight to his master, and, lifting him bodily from the chair, laid him flat on the floor. Then, with deft fingers, he untied his cravat and collar, and told them to open all doors and windows wide. He tore open his shirt and vest, so as to leave his breathing absolutely free, and then paused. The great rush of warm summer air that poured in gently stirred the hair on Mr Francis's head, and rustled the folds of the tablecloth; yet in spite of this, and the heavy, stertorous breathing of the stricken man, it seemed to Harry that an intense silence reigned everywhere. Maid-servants had gathered in the doorway; but Templeton, with a guttural word, sent them scurrying down the passages, and the three watched and waited round the one.

Then by blessed degrees the breathing grew less drawn and laboured, and by the light of the candles which Mr Francis's man had placed on the floor near the body it was possible to see that the colour of the face was less patched. Then the valet turned to Harry, who, white-faced and awestruck, stood at his shoulder.

'He will do well now, my lord,' said Sanders. 'It was lucky you did not touch him. Mr Francis has had these fits before—cardiac, the doctors say—but the right thing is to lay him flat.'

'He is not dead? He will not die?' cried Harry, shaking the man by the shoulder, as if to make him hear.

'Lord bless you, no, my lord!' he said. 'As like as not he'll be dressed tomorrow before you are awake. Cardiac weakness,' he repeated, as if the words were a prescription, 'and all agitation to be avoided.'

'Oh, my God, I never meant to agitate him!' cried Harry. 'I told him something which I should have thought he would have given his right hand to hear.'

The man smiled.

'Just the sort of thing which would agitate him, my lord,' he said, 'if you'll excuse my saying so. And now, Mr Templeton, if you'll be so kind as to get a shutter or something, we'll move him up to bed, keeping him flat. I'll sit up with him tonight.'

'You're a good fellow—an awfully good fellow!' cried Harry. 'And there is no further anxiety? Shall I not send for the doctor?'

'Quite unnecessary, my lord. See how quiet his breathing has become. As like as not he will sleep like a child. He's had these attacks before, and I know well when the danger is over. Cardiac. You can go to sleep yourself, my lord, as if nothing had happened.'

Chapter 10

Mr Francis is Better

THE cheerful optimism of Sanders was borne out by events, if not in letter, at any rate in spirit, and Harry on waking received the most encouraging reports from the sick-room. Mr Francis had slept well for the greater part of the night, and though he would take his breakfast in bed, he expected to be down by the middle of the morning. He particularly desired that Harry should be told, as soon as he woke, how completely he had recovered from his attack, and sent him his dear love.

Here, at any rate, was great good news. Again and again during the night Harry had woke from anxious feverish dreams of that ghastly mask-like face and sonorous breathing; all the earlier hours seemed a constant succession of agonized awakenings. Now it would be the white mottled face, which grew ever larger and nearer to his own, that tore him almost with a shriek from his uneasy slumber, after long paralysed attempts to move; now it would be the breathing, that got louder and yet more guttural till the air reverberated with it. Again and again he had sat up in bed with flying pulse and damp forehead, and lit a match to see how much more of the night there was still to run; or, looking for any sound of movement from his uncle's room at the end of the passage, he would think he heard steps along the corridor, and a stealthy opening or shutting of midnight doors. Once it was a spray of jasmine tapping at his window which woke him with a start, and, thinking that some evil news was knocking at his door, it was with an effort that he controlled his throat sufficiently to bid the knocker enter. But about the time of the first hint of the midsummer dawn, when the birds were beginning to tune their notes for the day, and the bushes and eaves grew merry with chirrupings, he fell into a more peaceful sleep, and woke only on the rattle of his blinds being rolled up.

His heart leaped as he received his uncle's message, and he got up immediately, and, putting on only a dressing-gown and slippers, went out with a rough towel over his arm for a dip in the lake before breakfast. The sluice at the lower end of it, where a cool ten feet of water invited him, lay not more than a couple of hundred yards from the house across a stretch of nearly level lawn, and was hidden from both road and house by a screen of bushes. Sleep still lingered like cobwebs in drowsy corners of his brain, but all the horror of the evening and its almost more horrible repetitions

during the earlier hours of the night, had been
swept away by the news at awakening, and it was
with a thrill of pleasure, as indescribable as the
scent itself of the clear morning, that he drank
deep of the freshness of the young day. The sun
was already high, but the grass that lay in the
shadow of house and bush was still not dry of its
night dews, and a thousand liquid gems brushed
his bare ankles. The gentle thunder of the sluice
made a soft, low bass to the treble of birds and the
hum of country sounds—that summer symphony
which pauses only for the solo of the nightingale
during the short dark hours. The lightest of breezes
ruffled the lake, scarcely shattering the mirrored
trees and sky that leaned over it. And Harry stood
for a moment white and bare to the soft wind, with
the sun warm on his shoulders, wondering at the
beauty of his bath. Then, with arms shot out above
his head and his body braced to a line, he sprang
off the stone slab of the sluice, and disappeared in
a soda-water of bubbles and flying spray.

Surely that moment, he thought, as he rose
again to the surface, was the crown and acme of
bodily sensation. The sleep had been swept from
him—house, bed, pillows, darkness had gone. He
was renewed, starting fresh again, cool and clean,
with all the beautiful round world waiting for
him. Expectancy and hope of happiness, interest,
awakening love, were all strung to their highest
pitch in this completeness of bodily well-being; his
soul was moulded in every part to its environment,
freed of its bodily burden, and with a song in his

mouth he stepped out of the water for the glow of the towel.

He sauntered leisurely back to the house, purring to himself at the delight which the moment gave him. How could there be men who found their pleasure in eating and drinking, in the life of crowded rooms, and smoky towns, when in half the acres of all England, and round all its coasts, were such possibilities? How, above all, was it possible to exist for a moment if one had not the privilege of being violently in love? Then, with a laugh at himself, he suddenly found that he was hungry, ravenous, and his step quickened.

Half an hour later he was seated at breakfast, but already the first mood of the day was past. He had for an hour gone free, untrammelled by all the obligations which events and circumstances entail, but now he was captured again. One thing in particular wove a heavy chain round him. He had seen with amazed horror the effect on his uncle of that news that he had thought would be so welcome. Was it reasonable to suppose, then, if a name alone produced so ill-starred a result, that he could bear the sight of the girl? After the catastrophe of the night before, it would be cruelty of a kind not to be contemplated to return again to the subject. The disappointment was grievous. That visit of Lady Oxted's and Evie's, so bright in anticipation that his mind's eye could scarcely look on it undazzled, must be given up. Plain, simple duty, the ordinary incontrovertible demands of blood and kinship, compelled him to it. His own happiness could not be purchased at the cost of suffering to that kindly old man; and who knew how much he might be suffering even now?

Then, with the mercurial fluctuation of those in love, he fell from the sky-scraping summits into a black, bottomless gulf of despondency. Evie could not come here, she could never come here, he told himself. And at that, and all which that implied, he pushed his chair quickly back from the table, and left a half-eaten breakfast. His reasonable mind could not make itself heard; it told him that he was pushing things comically far, that he was imagining an inconceivable situation when he concluded that a young man must not marry because of the feelings of his great-uncle on the subject; but his mood was not amenable to reason. The world had gone as black as an east wind, and all the flowers were withered.

He heaved a lover's sigh, and, going out of the glass-door into the garden, walked moodily up and down the lawn for a space, consumed with pity, half for himself, half for his uncle. Directly above were the windows of his own bedroom, wide open, and a housemaid within was singing at her work. Further on were the two rooms in which his uncle chiefly lived, a big-sized dressing-room in which he slept, and next door the bedroom which he had turned into a sitting-room. These windows were also open, and Harry, even on the noiseless grass, trod gently as he passed them, with that instinct for hushed quiet which all feel in the presence of suffering.

'Poor old fellow! poor dear old fellow!' he thought
to himself, with a pang of compunction at the
shock he had so unwittingly caused that cheerful
suffering spirit.

Then suddenly, as he passed softly below, there
came from the windows, mingling in unspeakable
discord with the housemaid's song, a quick shower
of notes from a flute.

Harry paused; the player was evidently feeling his
fingers in the execution of a run, and a moment
afterwards the dainty tripping air of 'La donna
è mobile' came dancing out into the sunlight
like a summer gnat. Twice the delicate tune was
played with great precision and admirable light-
heartedness, which contrasted vividly with the
listener's mood, and was instantly succeeded by
some other Italian air, unknown to the lad, but
as gay as a French farce.

Harry had paused open-mouthed with
astonishment. His own thoughts about his kinsman,
sombre and full of tenderness, were all sent flying
by the cheerful measure which the kinsman was
executing so delightfully. A smile began to dawn in
the corners of his mouth, enlightenment returned
to his eye, and, standing out on the gravel path,
he shouted up:

'Uncle Francis! Uncle Francis!'

The notes of the flute wobbled and ceased.

'Yes, my dearest fellow,' came cheerfully from
above.

'I am so glad you are so much better. May I
come up and see you?'

'By all means, by all means. I was just on the point of sending Sanders down to see if you would.'

Harry went up the stairs three at a time, and fairly danced down the corridor. Sanders, faithful and fox-like, was outside, his hand on the latch.

'You will be very careful, my lord?' he said. 'We mustn't have Mr Francis agitated again.'

'Of course not,' said Harry, and was admitted.

Mr Francis was lying high in bed, propped up on pillows. The remains of his breakfast, including a hot dish of which no part remained, stood on a side-table; on his bed lay the case of the beloved flute.

'Ah, my dear boy,' he cried, 'I owe you a thousand and one apologies for my conduct last night. Sanders tells me I gave you a terrible fright. You must think no more of it; you must promise me to think no more of it, Harry. I have had such seizures many times before, and of late, thank God, they have become much rarer. I had not told you about them on purpose. I did not see the use of telling you.'

'Dear Uncle Francis, it is a relief to find you so well,' said Harry. 'Sanders told me last night that he knew how to deal with these attacks, which was a little comfort. But I insist on your seeing a really first-rate doctor from town.'

Mr Francis shook his head.

'Quite useless, dear Harry,' he said, 'though it is like you to suggest it. Before now I have seen an excellent man on the subject. It is true that the attack itself is dangerous, but when it passes off it passes off altogether, and during it Sanders knows very well what to do. Besides, in all probability it will not recur. But now, my dear boy, as you are here, I will say something I have got to say at once, and get it off my mind.'

Harry held up his hand.

'If it will agitate you in the least degree, Uncle Francis,' he said, 'I will not hear it. Unless you can promise me that it will not, you open your mouth and I leave the room.'

'It will not, it will not,' said the old man. 'I give you my word upon it. It is this: That moment last night when you told me what you told me was the happiest moment I have had for years. What induced my wretched old cab-horse of a constitution to play that trick I cannot imagine. The news was a shock to me, I suppose. Ah! certainly it was a shock, but of pure joy. And I wanted to tell you this at once, because I was afraid, you foolish, unselfish fellow, that you might blame yourself for having told me, that you might think it would pain or injure me to speak of it again. You might even have been intending to tell Miss Aylwin that you must revoke your invitation. Was it not so, Harry?' and he waited for an answer.

Harry was sitting on the window-sill, playing with a tendril of intruding rose, and his profile was dark against the radiance of the sky outside. But when on the pause he turned and went across to the bedside, Mr Francis was amazed; for his face seemed, like Moses', to have drunk of some splendour, and to be visibly giving it out. He bent over to the bed, leaning on it with both hands.

'Ah, how could I do anything else?' he cried. 'I could not bear to be so happy at the cost of your suffering. But now, oh, now——'

And he stopped, for he saw that he had told his secret, and there was no more to say.

Mr Francis, seeing that the lad did not go on with the sentence, the gist of which was so clear, said nothing to press him, for he understood, and turned from the seriousness of the subject.

'So that is settled,' he said, 'and they are coming, you tell me, at the end of the month. That is why you want the box-hedge cut, you rascal! You are afraid of the ladies being frightened. I almost suspected something of the kind. And now, my dear boy, you must leave me. I shall get up at once, and be down in half an hour. Ah, my dear Harry, my dear Harry!' and he grasped his hand long and firmly.

Harry left him without more words, and strolled out again into the sunlight, which had recaptured all its early brilliance. Had ever a man been so ready and eager to spoil his own happiness? he wondered. Half an hour ago he had blackened the world by his utterly unfounded fears, all built on a fabric of nothingness, and in a moment reared to such a height that they had blotted the very sun from the sky, and, like a vampire, sucked the beauty from all that was fair. A thought had built them, a word now had dispelled them.

He went round to the front of the house, where he found a gardener busy among the flower-beds, and they went together to examine the great hedge.

It would be a week's work, the man said, to restore
it to its proper shape, and, Harry answering that it
must therefore be begun without delay, he went off
after ladder and pruning tools. Then, poking idly
at its compacted wall with his stick as he walked
along it, Harry found that after overcoming the
first resistance the stick seemed to penetrate into
emptiness, though the whole hedge could not have
been less than six or eight feet thick. This presented
points of interest, and he walked up to the end
far away from the house, and, pushing through a
belt of trees into which the hedge ran, proceeded
to examine it from the other side. Here at once
he found the key to this strange thing, for, half
overgrown with young shoots, stood an opening
some five feet high, leading into the centre of
the hedge, down which ran a long passage. More
correctly speaking, indeed, the hedge was not one,
but two, planted some three feet apart, and this
corridor of gloomy green lights led straight down
it towards the house. At the far end, again, was a
similar half-overgrown door, coming out of which
one turned the corner of the hedge and emerged on
to the gravel sweep close by the house, immediately
below the windows of the gun-room.

To Harry there was something mysterious and
delightful about this discovery, which gave him a
keen, child-like sense of pleasure. To judge from the
growth over the entrances to the passage it must
have been long undiscovered, and he determined
to ask his uncle whether he remembered it. Then
suddenly and unreasonably he changed his mind;

the charm of this mystery would be gone if he shared it with another, even if he suspected that another already knew it, and, smiling at himself for his childish secrecy and reserve, he strolled back again to meet the gardener to whom he had given orders to clip it. There must be no possibility of his discovery of the secret doors; the box-hedge should be clipped only with a view to the road; the other side should not be touched, a whited sepulchre. These orders given, he went back to the house to wait for the appearance of Mr Francis.

The latter soon came downstairs, with a great Panama hat on his head, round which was tacked a gaudy riband; he hummed a cheerful little tune as he came.

'Ah, Harry,' he said, 'I did not mean you to wait in for me on this glorious morning, for I think I will not go fast or far. Long-limbed, lazy fellow,' he said, looking at him as he sat in the low chair.

Harry got up, stretching his long limbs.

'Lazy I am not,' he said; 'I have done a worldful of things this morning. I have bathed; I have breakfasted; I have listened to your music; I have given a hundred orders to the gardeners—at least, I gave one; I have read the papers. Where shall we go, Uncle Francis?'

'Where you please, as long as we go together, and you will consent to go slowly and talk to me. I am a little shaky still, I find, now that I try my legs; but, Harry, there is a lightness about my heart from your news of last night.'

'It is good to hear you say that, for I cannot convey

to you how I looked forward to telling you. And you feel, you really feel, all you said to me?'

Mr Francis paused.

'All, all,' he said earnestly. 'The past has been expunged with a word. That burden which so long I have carried about is gone, like the burden of Christian. Ah, you do not know what it was! But now, if she—Miss Aylwin—believed it, she would not come within a mile of me; if her mother still believed it, she would not let her, and Lady Oxted would not let her. A hard, strange woman was Mrs Aylwin, Harry; I told you, I remember, what passed between us. But it is over, over. Yes, yes, the healing comes late and the recompense, but it comes, it has come.'

'I do not know Mrs Alywin,' said Harry. 'I have never even seen her. But I can answer for it that Miss Aylwin believes utterly and entirely in your innocence.'

'How is that—how is that?' asked Mr Francis.

'She told me so herself,' said Harry. 'How strange it all is, and how it all works together! I told her, you must know, the first evening I met her, about the Luck, and last week, when I was down with the Oxteds, I told her, Uncle Francis, about the awful troubles you had been through—particularly, particularly that one. At the moment I did not know that she was in any way connected with the Houldsworths; I knew of her only what I had seen of her. And then in the middle she stopped me, saying she knew all, saying also that she entirely believed in you.'

Mr Francis walked on a few steps in silence, and Harry spoke again.

'Perhaps I ought not to have told her,' he said, 'but the Luck held. She was the right person, you see; and somehow—you will agree with me, I think, when you see her—she is a person to whom it is natural to tell things. She is so sympathetic—I have no words—so eager to know what interests and is important to her friends. Yes, already I count myself a friend of hers.'

'Then her mother had not told her all?' asked Mr Francis, with the air of one deliberating.

'Not all, not your name. She had no idea that she was talking to the nephew of the man about whom she had heard from her mother.'

Mr Francis briskened his pace, like a man who has made up his mind.

'You did quite right to tell her, Harry,' he said—'quite right. It would come to her better from you than from anyone else; also it is far better that she should know before she came here, and before you get to know each other better. I have always a dread of the chance word, so dear to novelists, which leads to suspicion or revelations. How intolerable the fear of that would have been! We should all have been in a false position. But now she knows, we have no longer any fear as to how she may take the knowledge; and thank you, dear Harry, for telling her.'

The next two or three days passed quietly and busily. There were many questions of farm and sport to be gone into, many balancings of expenditure and income to be adjusted, and their talk, at any rate, if not their more secret thoughts, was spread over a hundred necessary but superficial channels. Among such topics were a host of businesses for which Mr Francis required Harry's sanction before he put them in hand—a long section of park paling required repair, some design of planting must be constructed in order to replace the older trees in the park against the time that decay and rending should threaten them. All these things and many more, so submitted Mr Francis, were desirable, but it would be well if Harry looked at certain tables of estimates which he had caused to be drawn up before he decided, as he was inclined to do, that everything his uncle recommended should be done without delay. Items, inconsiderable singly, he would find ran to a surprising total when taken together, and he must mention a definite sum which he was prepared to spend, say, before the end of the year, on outdoor improvement. Things in the house, too, required careful consideration; the installation of the electric light, for instance, would run away with no negligible sum. How did Harry rank the urgency of indoor luxuries with regard to outdoor improvements? If he intended to entertain at all extensively during the next winter, he would no doubt be inclined to give precedence to affairs under the roof; if not, there were things out of doors which could be mended now at a lesser cost than their completer repair six months hence would require.

Mr Francis put these things to his nephew with

great lucidity and patient impartiality, and Harry, heavily frowning, would wrestle with figures that continually tripped and threw him, and in his mind label all these things as sordid. But the money which he could immediately afford to spend on the house and place was limited, and he had the sense to apply himself to the balancing. At length, after an ink-stained and arithmetical morning, he threw down his pen.

'Electric light throughout, Uncle Francis,' he said, 'and hot water laid on upstairs. There is the ultimatum. The house is more behind than the park, therefore the house first.'

'You see exactly what that will come to?' asked Mr Francis.

'Yes, according to the estimates you have given me I can afford so much, and the park palings may go to the deuce. One does not live in the park palings, and since you mention it, I dare say I shall ask people here a good deal next winter. Let's see; this is mid June—let them begin as soon as Lady Oxted and Miss Aylwin have been, and they should be out of the house again by October, though the British workman always takes a longer lease than one expects. I shall want to be here in October. Oh, I wish it was October. Pheasant-shooting, you know,' he added, in a tone of apology.

He tore up some sheets of figures, then looked up at his uncle.

'You will like to have people here, will you not, Uncle Francis?' he asked. 'There shall be young people for you to play with, and old people for me to talk to. And we'll shoot, and oh, lots of things!'

He got off his chair, stretching himself slowly and luxuriously.

'Thank goodness I have made up my mind!' he said. 'I thought I was never going to. Come out for a stroll before lunch.'

Whether it was that the multiplicity of the arithmetical concerns came between the two, or, as Harry sometimes fancied, his uncle was not disposed to return to that intimacy of talk which had followed his strange seizure on the first night, did not certainly appear. The upshot, however, was plain enough, and, busy as a committee of ways and means, the two did not renew their conversation about Miss Aylwin and all that bordered there. As far as concerned his own part, Harry did not care to speak of what was so sacred to him, and so near and far; she was the subject for tremulous solitary visions, to discuss was impossible, and to trespass near that ground was to make him silent and awkward. No great deal of intuition was necessary on Mr Francis's part to understand this, and he also gave a wide berth to possible embarrassments.

The Sunday afternoon following Harry left again for London, for he was dining out that night. He said good-bye to his uncle immediately after lunch, for at the country church there was a children's service which Mr Francis had to attend, since he was in charge of a certain section of the congregation—those children, in fact, who attended his class in the village Sunday school.

Chapter 11

Mr Francis Sees His Doctor

HARRY had held long sessions in his mind as to whether he should or should not ask other people to Vail, to meet Lady Oxted and Miss Aylwin at the end of the month. It was but a thin hospitality, he was afraid, to bring two ladies down to Wiltshire to spend a country Sunday, and provide for their entertainment only the society of himself and his uncle; and this fear gradually deepening to certainty, he hurriedly asked four or five other guests only two days before the projected visit, in revolt all the time at the obligations of a host. All of these, however—as was not unnatural at this fullest time in the year—were otherwise engaged, and he opened each letter of regret with increasing satisfaction. He had been baulked in the prosecution of his duty; it was no use at this late hour trying again.

There were also other reasons against having a party; his uncle's health, for instance, so he wrote

to him, had not been very good since his attack.
He had been left rather weak and shattered by
it, and though his letter was full of that zest and
cheerfulness which was so habitual a characteristic
with him, Harry felt that it might be better,
particularly since his first meeting with Miss Aylwin
would of necessity be somewhat of an emotional
strain to him, not to tax him further either with the
arrangements incidental to a larger party, or with
their entertainment. These dutiful considerations,
it must be confessed, though perfectly genuine,
all led down the paths of his own desires; for it
was just the enforced intimacy of a *partie carrée* in
the country from which he promised himself such
an exquisite pleasure. With a dozen people in the
house, his time would not be his own; he would
have to look after people, make himself agreeable
to everybody, and be continually burdened with the
hundred petty cares of a host. But the way things
were, all that Sunday they would be together, if
not in foursome then in pairs; and the number of
possible combinations of four people in pairs he
could see at once was charmingly limited.

But though to him, personally, the refusal of
others to come to his feast was not an occasion
for regret, an excuse to the two ladies as to the
meagreness of the entertainment he was providing
for them, however faltering and insincere, was
still required. This he made with a marvellously
radiant face a few evenings before their visit, as he
sat with them in Lady Oxted's box at the opera.

'I have to make a confession,' he said, drawing his

chair up at the end of the second act of 'Lohengrin', 'and as you are both so delighted with the music, I will do so now, in the hope that you may let me off easily, There is absolutely no one coming to meet you at Vail; there will be my Uncle Francis and myself, and that is all.'

Evie turned to him.

'That is charming of you,' she said, 'and you have paid us a compliment. It is nothing to be asked as merely one of a crowd, but your asking us alone shows that you don't expect to get bored with us. Make your curtsey, Aunt Violet.'

'But there's the Luck,' said Lady Oxted. 'I gathered that the Luck was the main object of our expedition, though how it was going to amuse us I don't know any more than I know how Dr Nansen expected the North Pole to amuse him. And why, if you wanted to see it, Evie, Harry could not send for it by parcel post I never quite grasped.'

'Or luggage train, unregistered,' said Evie. 'Why did you not give it to the first tramp you met, Lord Vail, and ask him to take it carefully to London, for it was of some value, and leave it at a house in Grosvenor Square, the number of which you had forgotten? How stupid of you not to think of that! And did you see the Luck when you were down last week?'

'Yes, it came to dinner every night. I used to drink its health.'

'Good gracious, I shall have to take my very smartest things!' cried Evie. 'Fancy having to dress up to the Luck every evening!'

'Give it up, dear, give it up,' said Lady Oxted. 'The Luck will certainly make you look shabby, whatever you wear. Oh those nursery rhymes! Ah, here's Bob! Bob, what can have made you come to the opera?'

Lord Oxted took his seat, and gazed round the house before replying.

'I think it was your absolute certainty that I should not,' he replied. 'I delight in confuting the infallible. For you are an infallible, Violet. It is not your fault; you cannot help it.'

Lady Oxted laughed.

'My poor man,' she said, 'how shallow you must be not to have seen that I only said that in order to make you come!'

'I thought of that,' he said, 'but rejected the suspicion as unworthy. You laid claim, very unconvincingly I allow, the other day to a passion for truth and honour. Indeed, I gave you the benefit of a doubt which never existed. And you all go down to Vail on Saturday? I should like to come, only I have not been asked.'

'No, dear,' said Lady Oxted. 'I forbade Harry to ask you.'

'Oh, you didn't!' began Harry.

'I quite understand,' said Lord Oxted. 'You refrained from asking me on your own account, and if you had suggested such a thing, my wife would have forbidden you. One grows more and more popular, I find, as the years pass.'

'Dear Uncle Bob, you are awfully popular with

me,' said Evie. 'Shall I stop and keep you company in London?'

'Yes, please do,' said he.

'But won't it be rather rude to Lord Vail?'

'Yes, but he will forgive you,' said Lord Oxted.

'Indeed I shan't, Miss Aylwin,' said Harry. 'Don't think it. But will you, then, come to Vail, Lord Oxted? I thought it would be no use asking you.'

'I may not be popular,' said he, 'but I have still a certain pride.'

Here the orchestra poised and plunged headlong into the splendid overture of the third act, and Lady Oxted, whose secret joy was the hope that she might in the fullness of time grow to tolerate Wagner by incessant listening to him, glared furiously at the talkers and closed her eyes. Lord Oxted, it was observed by the others, thereupon stole quietly out of the box.

The curtain rose with the 'Wedding March', and that done, and the lovers alone, that exquisite duet began, rising like the voices of two larks, from height to infinite height of passion as clear and pure as summer heavens. Then into the soul of that feeblest of heroines began to enter doubt and hesitation; the desire to know what she had promised not to ask grew in the brain until it made itself words, undermining and unbuilding all that on which love rests. Thereafter, the woman having failed, came tumult and death; the hopeless lovers were left face to face with the ruin that want of trust will bring upon all that is highest, and with the drums and the slow, measured rhythm of despair, the act ended.

'The hopeless, idiotic fool of a girl!' remarked Evie, with extreme precision, weighing her words. 'Oh, I lose my patience with her!'

'I thought your tone sounded a little impatient,' said Lady Oxted.

'A little! Why, if Lohengrin had said he wanted to write a letter, she could have looked round the corner to see that he was not flirting with one of the chorus, and have opened his letter afterwards. If there is one thing I despise, it is a suspicious woman.'

'You must find a great many despicable things in this world,' remarked Lady Oxted.

'Dear aunt, if you attempt to be cynical, I shall go home in a hansom by myself,' said Evie.

'Do, dear, and Harry and I will follow in the brougham. Do you want to stay for the last act?'

'No; I would sooner go away. I am rather tired, and Elsa has put me in a bad temper. Good-bye, Lord Vail, and expect us on Sunday afternoon; please order fine weather. It will be enchanting; I am so looking forward to it.'

Harry himself went down to Vail on Friday afternoon, for he wished both to satisfy himself that everything was arranged for the comfort of his visitors, and also to meet them himself when they came. The only train he could conveniently catch did not stop at his nearest station, and he telegraphed home that they should meet him at Didcot. This implied a ten-mile drive, and his train being late on arrival, he put the cobs to their best pace in order to reach Vail in time for dinner. Turning quickly and rather recklessly into the lodge gates, he had to pull up sharply in order to avoid collision with one of his own carriages which was driving away from the house. A stable-helper, not in livery, held the reins, and by his side sat a man of dark, spare aspect, a stranger to him. As soon as they had passed he turned round to the groom who sat behind.

'Who was that?' he asked.

'I don't know his name, my lord,' said he, 'but I drove him from the station last Monday. He has been staying with Mr Francis since then.'

Harry was conscious of a slight feeling of vexation, arising from several causes. In the first place—and here a sense of dignity spoke—any guest either of his or his uncle's ought to be driven to the station properly, not by a man in a cap and a brown coat. In the second place, though he was delighted that Uncle Francis should ask any friend he choose to stay with him, Harry considered that he ought to have been told. He had received a long letter from his uncle two days ago, in which he went at some length into the details of his days, but made no mention of a guest. In the third place, the appearance of the man was somehow grossly and uncomfortably displeasing to him.

These things simmered in his mind as he drove up the long avenue, and every now and then a little bubble of resentment, as it were, would break on the surface. He half wondered at himself for the pertinacity with which his mind dwelt on them, and he determined, with a touch of that reserve and secrecy which still lingered in corners and angles of his nature, that if his uncle did not choose of his own initiative to tell him about this man, he would ask no questions, but merely not forget the circumstance. This reticence on his own part, so he told himself, was in no way to be put down to secretiveness, but rather to decency of manners. His uncle might have the Czar of all the Russias, if he chose, to stay with him; and if he did not think fit to mention that autocrat's visit, even though it was in all the daily papers, it would be rude even for his nephew to ask him about it. But he knew, if he faced himself quite honestly, that though good manners were sufficient excuse for his reticence, he preferred to employ secretiveness, and nothing else was the reason for silence. Certainly he wished that the man had not been so disrelishing to the eye; there was something even sinister about the glance he had got of him.

Mr Francis was in the most cheery and excellent spirits, and delighted to see him. He was employed in spudding plantains from the lawn as the carriage drove up. But, abandoning this homely but useful performance as soon as he heard the wheels on the road, he almost ran to meet him.

'Ages, it seems literally ages, since you were here, dear boy!' he said. 'And see, Harry, I have not been idle in preparing for our charming visitors. Croquet!' and he pointed to a large deal box that lay underneath the clipped yew-hedge.

'Templeton and I found the box in a gardener's shed,' he said, 'and we have been washing and cleaning it up. Ah! what a fascinating game, and how it sets off the ingenuity of the feminine mind! I was a great hand at it once, and I think I can strike the ball still. Come, dear boy, let us get in; it is already dinner-time. Ah! my flute—it would never do to leave that;' and he tripped gaily off to a garden-seat near, on which lay the case containing that favourite instrument.

It happened that at dinner the same night Mr Francis passed Harry through a sort of affectionate catechism, asking him to give exhaustive account of the manner in which he had spent the hours since he left Vail a fortnight ago. Harry complied with his humour, half shy, half proud of the number that had to be laid inside Lady Oxted's door, and when this was finished, 'Now it is my turn, Uncle Francis,' he said. 'Begin at the beginning, and tell me all as fully as I have to you.'

'Well, dear Harry, if I have not galloped about like you, taking ditch and fence, I have trotted along a very pleasant road,' he said. 'All the week after you left me I was much employed in writing about estimates and details with regard to the electric light. You must look at those tomorrow. They will be rather more expensive than we had anticipated, unless you have fewer lights of higher power. However, that business was finished, I remember, on Saturday. On Sunday I had my class, and dawdled very contentedly through the day. All this week I have been busy in little ways. One day will serve for another. At the books all morning, and in the afternoon pottering about alone, doing a bit of gardener's work here, feeding the pheasants there— and they are getting on capitally—or down at the farm. Then very often a nap before dinner and a blow on the flute afterwards. A sweet, happy, solitary time.'

The servants had left the room, and as Mr Francis said these words he looked closely at Harry, and saw his face, as he thought, harden. The lips were a little compressed, the arch of the eyebrows raised ever so little; something between surprise and a frown contracted them. He had already thought it more than possible that Harry might have met the other trap driving away from the house, and he thought he saw confirmation of it in his face. He sighed.

'Ah, Harry,' he said, 'can you not trust me?'

Mr Francis's voice was soft, almost broken; his blue eyes glistened in the candlelight, but still looked intently at his nephew. And at the amenity and affection in his tone the boy's reserve and secretiveness, which he had labelled good manners, utterly broke down.

'You have read my thoughts,' he said, 'and I apologize. But why—why not have told me, Uncle Francis? You would not have thought I should mind you having whom you liked here.'

Mr Francis sighed again.

'I will tell you now,' he said, slightly accentuating the last word. 'I did not tell you before; I purposely concealed it now; yes, I even used the word "solitary" about my life during the last week in order to save you anxiety.'

'Anxiety?' asked Harry.

'Yes. You met, probably, somewhere near the lodge gates, one of your carriages going to the station. A man out of livery drove it, a man of middle age sat by him. He was my doctor, Harry, and he came here on Monday last. I wished'—and his tone was frankness to the core—'I wished to get him out of the house before you came. I did not know you were coming till this afternoon, and I saw he could just catch the train to town. I ordered the carriage to take him instantly, and the man had not time to get into livery. That is all.'

At once Harry was all compunction and anxiety. He left his chair at the end of the table, and drew up close beside his uncle.

'Dear Uncle Francis,' he said, 'what was his opinion of your health? He was satisfied?'

'Fairly well satisfied,' said Mr Francis. 'The upshot was that I must live very quietly, and take no great exertion, and guard against quick movements. I might then hope—I might certainly hope—to live several more years yet. At my age, he said, one must not go hurdle-racing. Seventy-three—well, well, I am getting on for seventy-three.'

Harry was tongue-tied with a sort of vague contrition, for what he could hardly tell. He had been put in the wrong, but so generously and kindly that he could not resent it. He had had no suspicions of any kind, and his uncle's simple frankness had made him wear the aspect of the suspector. Indeed, where could suspicion look in? Suspicions what of? The gist of his feeling had been that he should have been told, and here was the considerate reason why he had not, a reason sensible, conclusive, and dictated by thoughtful affection. Yet he felt, somehow, ashamed of himself, and his shame was too ill-defined for speech. But there was no long pause, for Mr Francis almost immediately got up from his chair, with a nimbleness of movement which perhaps his doctor would not have liked.

'Well, a truce to these sombrenesses, Harry,' he said. 'Indeed, I am brisk enough yet. Ah! what a pleasure to have you here instead of that excellent, kind, unsociable fellow! I have such a good story for you. Let us go to the billiard-room; I could not tell you before the servants, though I have had it on the tip of my tongue all evening. The doctor recommended me billiards after dinner; gentle, slow exercise like that was just the thing, he said. Well, the story——'

Harry rose too.

'One word more,' he said. 'Is your doctor a really first-rate man? You remember I wanted you to see a good man. What is his name?'

'Dr Godfrey,' said Mr Francis, '32, Half Moon Street. He is a first-rate man. I have known him since he was a boy.'

Chapter 12

The Meeting In The Wood

THE two ladies were to arrive about tea-time next day, and as the hour drew on a lively restlessness got hold of Harry. He could neither sit, nor stand, nor read; but after a paragraph of a page, the meaning of which slipped from his mind even as his eyes hurried over the lines, he would be off on an aimless excursion to the dining-room, forget what he had gone about, and return with the same haste to his book. Then he would remember that he wanted the table tonight in the centre of the room, not pushed, as they had been having it, into the window, and there must be a place left for the Luck in the middle of the table. Again he would be off to the dining-room. There was the table in the centre of the room, and in the centre of the table a place for the Luck, for he had given twenty repetitions of the order to Templeton, which was exactly twenty repetitions more than was necessary. Harry, in fact, was behaving exactly like the cock sparrow in mating time, strutting before its lady, an instinct in all young males. But there were not enough flowers. There must be more flowers and less silver. How could Dutch silver be ornamental in the neighbourhood of that gorgeous centrepiece, and how, said his heart to him, could the Luck be ornamental, considering who should sit at his table?

After giving these directions, he went back again to the hall where tea was laid. Mr Francis was out on the lawn. He could see his yellow Panama hat, like a large pale flower, under the trees. The windows were all open, and the gentle hum of the warm afternoon came languidly in. Suddenly a fuller note began to overscore these noises in gradual crescendo. The crisp gravel grated underneath swift wheels, and next moment he was at the door. And at sight of the girl, all his Martha-like cares, the Dutch silver, the position of the table, slipped from him. Here was the better part.

'Welcome,' he said, 'and welcome and welcome,' and held the girl's hand for longer than a stranger would, and it was not withdrawn. A little added colour shone in her cheeks, and her eyes met his, then fell before them. 'So you have not stayed to keep Lord Oxted company,' he said. 'I can spare him pity. How are you, Lady Oxted?'

'Did you think I should?' asked Evie.

'No, I felt quite certain you would not,' said Harry, with the assurance which women love. 'Do come in. Tea is ready.'

'And I am ready,' said Evie.

'And this is the hall,' continued Harry, as they entered, 'where everyone does everything. Oh, there is a drawing-room. If you wish, we will be grand and go to the drawing-room. I had it made ready. But let us stop here. Will you pour out tea, Lady Oxted?'

Lady Oxted took a rapid inventory of the tapestry and portraits.

'I rather like drinking tea in a cowshed,' she remarked.

In a few moments Mr Francis entered with his usual gay step, and in his hand he carried his large hat.

'How long since we met last, Lady Oxted!' he said. 'And what a delight to see you here!'

'Miss Aylwin—Uncle Francis,' said Harry unceremoniously.

The old man turned quickly.

'Ah, my dear Miss Aylwin,' he said—'my dear Miss Aylwin.' And they shook hands.

Harry gave a little sigh of relief. Ever since his uncle's attack a fortnight ago he had felt in the back of his mind a little uneasiness about this meeting. It seemed he might have spared himself the pains. Nothing could have been simpler or more natural than Mr Francis's manner; yet the warmth of his hand-shake, the form of words, more intimate than a man would use to a stranger, were admirably chosen—if choice were not a word too full of purpose for so spontaneous a greeting—to at once recognise and obliterate the past. The meeting was, as it were, a scene of reconciliation between two who had never set eyes on each other before, and between whom the horror of their vicarious estrangement would never be mentioned or even be allowed to be present in the mind; and Mr Francis's words seemed to Harry to meet the situation with peculiar felicity.

The old man seated himself near Lady Oxted.

'This is an occasion,' he said, 'and both Harry and I have been greatly occupied with his house-warming. But the weather—there was little warming there to be done; surely we have ordered delightful weather for you. Harry told me that Miss Aylwin wished for a warm day. Indeed, his choice does not seem to me, a poor northerner, a bad one; but Miss Aylwin has perhaps had too much Italian weather to care for our poor imitation.'

'Lord Vail refused to promise,' said Evie; 'at least, he did not promise anything about the weather. I was afraid he would forget.'

'Ah, but I told my uncle,' said Harry. 'He saw about it; you must thank him.'

Evie was sitting opposite the fireplace, and her eye had been on the picture of old Francis which hung above it. At these words of Harry's she turned to Mr Francis with a smile, and her mouth half opened for speech. But something arrested the words, and she was silent, and Harry, who had been following every movement of hers, tracing it with the infallible minute intuition of a lover to its deriving thought, guessed that the curious resemblance between the two had struck with a force that for the moment had taken away speech. But before that pause was prolonged, she answered.

'I do thank you very much,' she said. 'And have you arranged another day like this for tomorrow?'

She looked, as she spoke, out of the open windows and into the glorious sunshine, and Harry rose.

'Shall we not go out?' he said. 'Uncle Francis will think that we do not appreciate his weather if we stop in.'

Evie rose, too.

'Yes, let us go out at once,' she said, 'but let me put on another hat. I am not in London, and my present hat simply *is* London. Oh, Lord Vail, I long to look at that picture again, but I won't; I will be very self-denying, for I am sure—I am sure it is the Luck in the corner of it.'

She put up her hand so as to shield the picture from even an accidental glance.

'Will you show me my way?' she asked. 'I will be down again in a minute.'

Harry took her up the big staircase, lit by a skylight, and lying in many angles.

'Yes, you have guessed,' he said. 'It is the Luck; you will see the original tonight at dinner. Did anything else strike you in the picture? Oh, I saw it did!'

'Yes, a curious false resemblance. I feel sure it is false, for I think that portrait represents not a very pleasant old gentleman. But your uncle, Lord Vail—I never saw such a dear, kind face!'

Harry flushed with pleasure.

'So now you understand,' he said, 'what your coming here must mean to him. Ah, this is your maid, is she not? I will wait in the hall for you.'

The two elder folk had already strolled out when Harry returned to the hall, a privation which he supported with perfect equanimity, and in a few minutes he and his companion followed. As they crossed the lawn, Harry swept the points of the compass slowly with his stick.

'Flower garden, kitchen garden, woods, lake, farm, stables,' he said.

Evie's eyes brightened.

'Stables, please,' she said. 'I am of low, horsey tastes, you must know, and I was afraid you were not going to mention them. We had the two most heavenly cobs I ever saw to take us from the station.'

'Yes, Jack and Jill,' said Harry, 'but not cobs— angels. Did you drive them?'

'No, but I longed to. May I when we go back on Monday?'

'Tuesday is their best day,' said Harry, 'except Wednesday.'

They chattered their way to the stables, where the two angels were even then at their toilets.

'There is not much to show you,' said Harry. 'There are the cobs that brought you. Good evening, Jim.'

The man who was grooming them looked up, touched his bare head, and without delay went on with the hissing toilet, as a groom should. Evie looked at him keenly, then back to her companion, and at the man again.

'Yes, they are beautiful,' she said; and as they turned, 'Is Vail entirely full of doubles?' she asked.

Harry smiled, and followed her into the stables of the riding horses.

'Jim is more like me than that picture of old Francis is like my uncle,' he said. 'I really think I shall have to get rid of him. The likeness might be embarrassing.'

'I wouldn't do that,' said Evie. 'Our Italian peasants say it is good luck to have a double about.'

'Good luck for which?'

'For both. Really I never saw such an extraordinary likeness.'

They spent some quarter of an hour looking over the horses, and returned leisurely towards the house, passing it, and going on to the lake. The sun was still not yet set, and the glory of the summer evening a thing to wonder at. Earth and sky seemed ready to burst with life and colour; it was as if a new world was imminent to be born, and from the great austere downs drew a breeze that was the breath of life—fresh, dry, unbreathed. Evie appropriated it in open draughts, with head thrown back.

'Aunt Violet was quite right, Lord Vail, when she said you should never come to London,' she exclaimed. 'How rude she was to you that night, and how little you minded! Even now, when I have

been here only an hour, I can no longer imagine
how one manages to breathe in that stuffy, shut-in
air. Winter, too; winter must be delicious here,
crisp and bracing.'

'So it would seem this evening,' said Harry; 'but
you must see it first under a genuine November
day. A mist sometimes spreads slowly from the
lake, so thick that even I could almost lose my
way between it and the house. It does not rise
high, and I have often looked from the windows
of the second story into perfectly clear air, while if
you went out at the front-door you would be half
drowned in it. Higher up the road again you will
be completely above it, and I have seen it lying
below as sharply defined as the lake itself, and if
you walk down from that wood up there it is like
stepping deeper and deeper into water. A bad mist
will rise as high as the steps of those two buildings
you see to the right of the house, like kiosques,
standing on a knoll, under which the road winds,
in front of the trees.'

'And the house is all surrounded, like an island?
What odd buildings! What are they?'

'One is a summer-house; I couldn't now tell
you which. We used to have tea in it sometimes,
I remember, when I was quite little. The other is
the ice-house, a horrible place; it used to haunt
me! I remember shrieking with terror once when
my nurse took me in. It was almost completely
dark, and I can hear now the echo one's step
made, and there was a great black chasm in the
middle of the floor with steps leading down, as I

thought, to the uttermost pit. Two chasms I think there were; one was a well. But the big one was that which terrified me, though I dare say it was only ten or twelve feet deep. Things dwindle so amazingly as one grows up. I wish I could see this lake, for instance, as I saw it when I was a child. It used to appear to me as large as the sea seems now, and as for the sluice, it might have been the iron gates of the Danube.'

'I know, things do get smaller,' said Evie; 'but after all, this lake and the sluice are not quite insignificant yet. What a splendid rush of water! And I dare say the ice-house chasm is still sufficient to kill anyone who falls in. That, after all, is enough for practical purposes. But then, even if things grow smaller, how much more beautiful they become. When you were little, you never saw half the colour or half the shape you see now. The trees were green, the sky was blue; but they gave one very surface impressions to what they give now.'

'Oh, I rather believe in the trailing clouds of glory,' said Harry.

'Then make an effort to disbelieve in them every day,' said Evie. 'Shades of the prison-house begin to grow around the growing boy, do they? What prison-house does the man mean, if you please? Why, the world—this beautiful, delightful world. Indeed, we are fortunate convicts! And Wordsworth called himself a lover of Nature!' she added with deep scorn.

'Certainly the world has been growing more beautiful to me lately,' said Harry.

'Of course it has. Please remind me that I have to cut my throat without delay if ever you hear me say that the world is growing less beautiful. But just imagine a person who loved Nature talking of the world as a prison-house. Who was it said that Wordsworth only found in stones the sermons he had himself tucked under them to prevent the wind blowing them away?'

'I don't know. It sounds like the remark of an indolent reviewer.'

Evie laughed.

'Fancy talking about reviewers on an evening like this!' she said. 'Oh, there's a Canadian canoe! May we go in it?'

The far end of the lake was studded with little islands, only a few yards in circumference for the most part, but, as Evie explained, large enough for the purpose. And then, like two children together, they played at Red Indians and lay in wait for a swan, and attempted to stalk a moorhen with quite phenomenal ill-success. No word of any tender kind was spoken between them, they but laughed over the nonsense of their own creating; but each felt as they landed that in the last hour their intimacy had shot up like the spike of the aloe-flower. For when a man and a maid can win back to childhood again, and play like children together, it is certain that no long road lies yet to traverse before they really meet.

Lady Oxted was doomed that night to a very considerable dose—a dose for an adult, in fact—of what she had alluded to as nursery rhymes, for the

Luck seemed absolutely to fascinate the girl, and Harry, seeing how exclusively it claimed her eyes, more than once reconsidered the promise he had made her to have it to dinner the next evening as well. She would hardly consent to touch it, and Harry had positively to put it into her hands, so that she might read for herself its legend of the elements. They drank their coffee while still at table, and Evie's eyes followed the jewel till Templeton had put it into its case. Then as the last gleam vanished, 'I am like the Queen of Sheba,' she said, 'and there is no more spirit left in me. If you lose the Luck, Lord Vail, you may be quite sure that it is I who have stolen it, and when I am told that two men in plain clothes are waiting in the drawing-room, I shall know what they have come about. Now for some improving conversation about facts and actualities, for Aunt Violet's sake.'

Sunday afternoon was very hot, and Lady Oxted, Evie, and Harry lounged it away under the shade of the trees on the lawn. Mr Francis had not been seen since lunch-time, but it was clear that he was busy with his favourite diversion, for brisk and mellow blowings on the flute came from the open window of his sitting-room. Harry had mentioned this taste of his to the others, and it had been received by Lady Oxted with a short and rather unkind laugh, which had been quite involuntary, and of which she was now slightly ashamed. But Evie had thought the thing pleasant and touching rather than absurd, and had expressed a hope that he would allow her to play some accompaniments for him after dinner. If Aunt Violet, she added incisively, found the sound disagreeable, no doubt she would go to her own room.

Harry was in the normal Sunday afternoon mood, feeble and easily pleased, and the extreme and designed offensiveness of the girl's tone made him begin to giggle hopelessly. Evie thereupon caught the infection, for laughter is more contagious than typhus, and her aunt followed. The hysterical sounds apparently reached Mr Francis's ears, in some interval between tunes, for in a moment his rosy face and white hair appeared framed in the window, and shortly afterwards he came briskly across the grass to them.

'It is getting cooler,' he said gaily, 'and I am going to be very selfish, and ask Miss Aylwin to come for a stroll with me. My lazy nephew, I find, has not taken her through the woods, and I insist on her seeing them. Will you be very indulgent to me, Miss Evie, and accept a devoted though an aged companion?'

Evie rose with alacrity.

'With the greatest pleasure,' she said. 'Are you coming, too, Aunt Violet?'

'Not for the wide, wide world,' said Lady Oxted, 'will I walk one yard. Harry, stop where you are, and keep me company.'

The two walkers went up under the knoll on which stood the ice-house, talking and laughing in diminuendo. Harry saw Mr Francis offer the girl his arm for the steep ascent, and it pleased him in some secret fashion to see that, though her light step was clearly in no need of exterior aid, she accepted it. With this in his mind he turned to Lady Oxted.

'It is a great success,' he said. 'They are delighted with each other. Think what it must mean to my uncle!'

Lady Oxted stifled a yawn.

'Who are delighted?' she asked.

Harry pointed at the two figures half-way up the slope.

'You knew whom I meant perfectly,' he remarked.

'I did. I really don't know why I asked. By the way, Harry, I apologize for laughing just now. Your uncle is the most courteous and charming old gentleman, and he is devoted to you. In fact, I got just a little tired of your name yesterday evening before dinner.'

Harry did not reply; he was still watching the two. They had surmounted the knoll, and in another moment the iron gate leading into the ride through the wood closed behind them, and they passed out of sight among the trees.

Mr Francis was, as has been indicated, very fond of young people, and those who had the pleasure of his acquaintance always found him a delightful companion. He had an intimate knowledge of natural history, and this afternoon, as he walked with the girl, he would now pick some insignificant herb from the grass, with a sentence or two on its notable medicinal qualities, now, with a face full of a happy radiance, hold up his hand while a bird trilled in the bushes, in rapt and happy attention.

'A goldfinch, Miss Evie,' he whispered; 'there is no mistaking that note. Let us come very quietly, and perhaps we shall catch sight of the beauty. That lazy nephew of mine,' he went on, when they had seen the gleam of the vanishing bird, 'was saying the other day that there were no goldfinches in Wiltshire. I dare say he will join us here soon. He almost always comes up here on Sunday afternoon. It used to be his father's invariable Sunday walk.'

They strolled quietly along for some half-hour, up winding and zigzag paths which would lead them presently to the brae above the wood, and disclose to them, so Mr Francis said, a most glorious prospect. Below them, down the steep hillside up which they had circuitously made their way, lay the blue slate roof of the stables. In the yard they could see a retriever sleeping, and the sound of a man whistling came up very clear through the stillness of the afternoon. Then they turned a corner—the last, so Mr Francis said—and the path, which had hitherto been all loops and turns, straightened itself out as it gained the end of the ridge up which the wood climbed. But here they were no longer alone, for not fifty yards in front of them they saw a girl in a pink dress, and with her a young man in straw hat and dark-blue serge, of strangely familiar figure; his arm was about her waist. On the instant the man turned, and Evie, to her indescribable amazement, saw that it was Lord Vail. He said a word hurriedly to the girl, and turned off down a side-path, while the girl walked quickly on. The glance had been momentary.

A short, stifled exclamation arose from Mr Francis.

'Ah! the foolish fellow!' he cried; and then, without a pause: 'Yes, as I told you, there are only beeches up here, Miss Evie. Those oaks which you were admiring so much seem to stop as suddenly as if you had drawn a line of demarcation half-way up the hill. Now, why is that, I wonder? The oak is the hardier of the two, yet it is the beeches that prefer the colder situation. Strange, is it not? There used to be oaks here, but they have all died.'

They soon came out at the top of the hill, where the glorious prospect which Mr Francis had promised Evie spread largely round them. But he had grown silent and *distrait*, quite unlike himself, and instead of rhapsodizing over the magnificence of the rolling hills, he gazed for a moment but sadly at them, pointed out to his companion various distant landmarks, as if he did not expect her to be interested, and remarked that it was time for them to turn. Nor was Evie much more talkative; the sight of Harry with that girl had strangely wounded her. Little had she thought, when Mr Francis said he often spent his Sunday afternoon here, that she would see him thus. She told herself that he was perfectly at liberty to walk in his own woods with anyone he pleased, but that he had availed himself of that liberty she felt like an insult offered to her. Her quick eye had taken in the girl in a moment;

her dress, the way she put her feet down when she walked, all spoke of a certain class. Ten to one she was the daughter of the gamekeeper or butler. Ah! how disgusting men were!

Mr Francis walked by her in silence, with a frown on his usually serene brow, and, it would seem, some matter in debate. Suddenly he turned to her.

'Dear Miss Evie,' he said, 'will you allow a very old man to take a very great liberty? Do not think too hardly of Harry, poor fellow, I beg of you. He has been much alone, without companions, and young men will be young men, you know. And I would stake—yes, I would stake all I have—that what you and I have seen was a mere harmless little flirtation, a few words said on either side, not meant by either, a kiss or two, perhaps, changing owner. Harry is young, but he is a good fellow, and an honest one. You are disgusted, naturally; but I have never known—believe me, I have never known—these little foolishnesses of his mean anything; they are altogether superficial and innocent.'

He spoke with a very kind and serious voice, and with much of entreaty in his tone. But Evie's eyes were still hard and angry; she thought she had never heard so tame a defence.

'This sort of thing has gone on before, then?' she asked.

'Ah! do not force me,' pleaded Mr Francis. 'I will go bail, I tell you, on Harry's honesty.'

'Certainly I will not force you,' she said. 'Come, Mr Francis, this is not a nice subject; let us have

no more of it. That was really Oxford we saw just
now, was it? How wonderfully clear the air must
be here!'

They passed down through the wood and to
the house, where they both turned in. But in a
minute or two Evie found she had left a book on
the lawn, and went out to fetch it. Tea was laying
there, and under the trees where she had left them
an hour ago were Lady Oxted and Harry at full
length in their garden-chairs, both, it would seem,
fast asleep. And at that sight a sudden question
asked itself in the girl's mind. How could it possibly
be Harry they had seen in the wood? And before
the question was asked the answer came, and she
said softly to herself, 'Jim.'

Her book was lying close to the sleepers, but
she had already forgotten about it, and she turned
quietly away, casting one glance at Harry, whose
straw-hat was lying on the grass, and noticing
with a faint, unconvincing sense of justification
that his clothes were also of dark-blue serge. But,
habitually honest, even with herself, she knew that
her self-judged case would be summed up against
her, and she set her teeth for a lonely and most
humiliating ten minutes. Without definite purpose
in her mind, except that association should be an
added penance, she went to the lake, and sat down
in the Canadian canoe in which they had played
Red Indians the evening before.

How could she, she asked herself, have been
so distrustful, so malicious, so ready to blacken?
She had seen a young man walking with a girl,

and she had been knave enough, and also fool enough (which was bitter), to accept the shallow evidence of her eyes when they told her that he was Harry. Had she not been warned against such wicked credulity, even as Elsa had been warned by Lohengrin, by the sight of that slim, handsome groom last night in the stable-yard? Had she not said to Harry, 'Is Vail full of doubles?' Out of her own mouth should she be judged. A worse than Elsa was sitting in the Canadian canoe. For half an hour at least she had believed that Harry was flirting with a servant-girl, that he was capable of leaving her to suppose that he was going to keep Lady Oxted company under the trees, and as soon as her back was turned set off to meet his village beauty. Loyalty! a feeling she professed to admire! How would any girl in her position who had an ash of what had once been loyalty have acted? She would have flatly refused to believe any evidence; sight, hearing, every sense, would have been powerless to touch her. Harry could not do such a thing. How did she know that? For the present that was beside the point; she knew it, and that was enough. Perhaps—and the warm colour came to her face—perhaps she would come to that presently.

She sat up and beat the water with the flat of the paddle. 'Fool, fool—base little fool!' she whispered, a syllable to a stroke.

Suddenly she stopped, the paddle poised.

'I have never known these little foolishnesses of his mean anything' rang in her ears. So! This sort of thing had happened before. . . . What? Was she again skulking and suspecting, even after the lesson she had received! She had believed, though only for half an hour, the evidence of her own eyes, and she had suffered for it. Was she now to believe the evidence of somebody else's tongue? Yet Mr Francis had said it, that dear old fellow who was evidently so devoted to Harry, so pained at what they had seen. No; it did not matter if the four major prophets had said it. She knew better than all the stained glass in Christendom, and again she belaboured the water to the rhythm of 'Fool, fool—base little fool!'

For a few moments her thoughts flew off to Mr Francis. He must have known that Harry's twin brother was a groom in the stables, yet he had been as certain as she that it was Harry they had surprised in the wood. He had been at pains to persuade her that the fault was venial, to remind her that young men would be young men, that Harry was honest. Why had he felt so certain on so slight a glance that it was Harry? What did it mean? Then she whisked Mr Francis from her mind. He was as despicable as she, neither more nor less. He was as great a fool as she.

Was he? Was he? Did he know Harry as well as she, he who had known him all his life, she who had known him a month, no more? Certainly he did not, could not. She, who knew him so well, had rightly accused herself of disloyalty to him, compared herself to Elsa, and him. . . . Did she, then, owe him loyalty? Ah, a big word!

She put the dripping paddle back into the boat, for she was in wider fields than self-reproach has ever hedged about, and leaned forward, hearing the ripples lap and cluck on the sides. Supposing anyone else, Geoffrey Langham, for instance, had chosen to walk in a wood with a dairymaid, would she have cared, would it have stung her? Not a jot. Then why——

At this she rose, stepped out of the boat, and for a moment looked at the wavering outline of her reflection in the lake. Then she stood upright, her arms fallen by her sides, and a little voice spoke within her, which she tried to tell herself was not she.

'I surrender,' it said.

She walked back to the lawn, proud and shy of the revelation she had made to herself, and with a mind once more unshadowed. Lady Oxted apparently had just awoke, and was looking distractedly round, as if she found herself in a strange bedroom; Harry, with one arm behind his head, still slumbered.

'Unconscious innocent—tea!' said Lady Oxted, truculently poking him in the ribs with her parasol.

Harry opened both his eyes wide like a mechanical doll awakening.

'Why did you do that?' he said. 'I have been lying here quietly, thinking. Have they come back from their walk?'

'No,' said Lady Oxted; 'they are lost. A search-party went out about three hours ago to look for them. Rockets and other signals of distress have been seen intermittently from the downs.'

Harry sat up and saw Evie, and instantly turned his back on Lady Oxted.

'Did you have a nice walk?' he asked. 'I wish I had come with you. I'—and he looked round to see whether the parasol was within range—'I have been terribly bored this afternoon. Lady Oxted has positively no conversation.'

Evie looked first at him, then at her aunt.

'Well, you both look all the better for your—your silence,' she said. 'Yes, Lord Vail, we had a charming walk. And we surprised your double love-making in the wood.'

'Oh yes, the dairymaid,' said Harry. 'She's as pretty as a picture.'

'I always wonder where the lower orders get their good looks from,' said Lady Oxted parenthetically.

Harry picked up his straw hat.

'Probably from the lower orders,' he remarked. 'Let's have tea. Sleeping is such hungry work, is it not, Lady Oxted? I am sure you must be famished.'

'Elephantine wit,' sighed that lady. 'When Harry is so kind as to make a joke, which is, unfortunately, not so rare as one might wish, I always feel as if heavy feet were tramping about directly overhead.'

'And when Lady Oxted makes a joke,' said the lad, 'which is not so often as her enemies would wish, she always reminds me of a sucking spring directly underfoot. I give one waterlogged cry, and am swallowed up. Do pour out tea for us, Lady Oxted. You are such an excellent tea-maker.'

'The score is fifteen all,' remarked Evie.

'When did Harry score?' demanded Lady Oxted, seating herself at the urn.

'Just now, dear aunt. And so Jim is to marry the dairymaid, Lord Vail?'

'And who is Jim?' asked Lady Oxted.

'My double. I wish I knew as much about horses as he. Yes, Jim is walking out with the dairymaid.'

'I have heard enough about Jim,' said Lady Oxted decisively. 'Here is Mr Francis. Mr Francis, take my side; there is a league against me.'

'A charming one,' said Mr Francis, directing his gay glance to Evie. But the girl did not meet it; she looked quite gravely and deliberately away.

Chapter 13

Harry Asks a Question

HARRY was leaving next morning with the two women, being unable to induce Lady Oxted to stop another day; and, in consequence, he sat up late that night, after they had gone to bed, looking over the details of the expense of putting in the electric light. The cheapest plan, it appeared, would be to utilize the power supplied by the fall of water from the lake, for this would save the cost of engines to drive the dynamos. In that case it would be necessary to build the house for them over the sluice, but this, so wrote the engineer, would not interfere with the landscape, for the roof would only just be seen above the belt of trees; or, if Lord Vail did not mind a little extra expense, a tasteful erection might be made, which instead of diminishing, would positively add to the beauty of the view from the house. Then followed a horrific sketch of Gothic style.

Harry's thoughts were disposed to go wandering

that night, and he gave but a veiled and fugitive attention to the figures. The lake suggested other things to him brighter than all the thirty-two-power lamps of the electric light. The latter, it appeared, could be in the house by September, but the other was in the house now. In any case there should be no horrors ornamental or otherwise over the sluice, and he turned to the second estimate, which included engines, with a great determination to think of nothing else.

The scene of this distracted vigil was his uncle's sitting-room, where all the papers were to hand. Mr Francis had sat up with him for half an hour or so, but Harry had then persuaded him to go to bed; for all the evening he had appeared somewhat tired and worried. Then from next door there came for some half-hour the faint sounds of brushings and splashings, that private orchestra of bedtime, and after that the house was still.

Harry settled down again to his work, and before long his mind was made up. He would have, he saw, to screw and pinch a little, but on no account should anything, Gothic or not, spoil the lower end of the lake; then, pouring himself out some whisky-and-soda, he took a last cigarette.

The table where he worked was fully occupied, but orderly. A row of reference-books—Bradshaw, the Peerage, Whitaker's Almanack, and others— stood in a green morocco case to the left of the inkstand; to the right, in a silver frame, a large photograph of himself. Among other books he was amused to see a Zadkiel's Almanack, and he drew it from its place, and turned idly over a leaf or two. There was a cross in red ink opposite the date of January 3, on which day, so said this irresponsible seer, a discovery of gold would be made. Harry thought vaguely for a moment of South Africa and Klondyke, then suddenly gave a little gasp of surprise. That had been the day on which he had found the Luck.

The coincidence was strange, but stranger was the fact that his uncle, who had so often remonstrated with him on his half-laughing, half-serious notice of the coincidences which had followed its discovery, should have a Zadkiel at all, strangest that he should have noted this date. Then suddenly a wave of superstitious fear came over him, and he shut Zadkiel hastily up, for fear of seeing other dates marked. Two minutes later he was already laughing at himself, though he did not reopen Zadkiel; and, as he took his candle to go to bed, his eye fell on a red morocco 'Where Is It?' which lay on the table. He knew that there was some address he wanted to verify, but it was a few moments before he turned to G. There was the name, 'Dr Godfrey, 32, Wimpole Street,' and on each side of the name minute inverted commas. He looked at it in some astonishment, for he would have been ready to swear that his uncle had told him 32, Half Moon Street.

He went straight to his room, however, without wasting conjecture or surmise over this, undressed, and blew out his candle. Outside a great moon was swung high in heaven; no leaf trembled on the trees, but through the summer night the songs of many nightingales bubbled liquidly.

A few nights afterwards he and Geoffrey were sitting alone in the house in Cavendish Square. Harry had been full of figures, wondering what was the least sum on which this London house could be made decently habitable. One room wanted fresh paper, distemper was essential to another, most required fresh carpets, and stamped leather was imperatively indicated for the hall. Geoffrey listened with quiet amusement, for Harry was talking with such pellucid transparency that it was difficult not to smile. Then the question of electric light at Vail was touched upon; and suddenly he stopped, rose, and beat the ashes of his pipe out into the grate.

'By the way, Geoff,' he said, 'supposing you looked out the name of a man whom you did not know, and had only once heard of, in a "Where Is It?" belonging to a friend, and found the name in inverted commas, what inference, if any, would you draw? No, it is not a riddle—purely a matter of curiosity.'

Geoffrey yawned.

'Even Sherlock Holmes would not infer there,' he said; 'and even his friend Watson could not fail in such a perfectly certain conclusion.'

'What conclusion?'

'Wait a moment; let us be an obtuse detective. Is the person from whom you have heard the name the same as the person to whom the "Where Is It?" belongs? Lord! I give points to Watson.'

'It happens that it is so. Does that influence your conclusion?'

'It only makes it even surer; no, it can't do that, but it leaves it as sure as it was. Of course, the name in the "Where Is It?" is not the man's real name—not the name he goes by, anyhow.'

'So it seemed possible to me.'

'Then you were wrong. There is no question of possibility. It is dealing with absolute certainties. Now, satisfy my curiosity. I have not much, but I have some.'

'Bit by bit,' said Harry. 'Have you ever heard of a Dr Godfrey—heart specialist, I take it—who lives at 32, Wimpole Street?'

'Never. But Wimpole Street is just round the corner. I imagine he will have a plate on his door. I thought your heart was in a parlous state.'

'Oh, don't be funny,' said Harry, 'but come along.'

Geoffrey got up.

'Shall I have to hold your hand?' he asked.

'No, I am not going to consult him. Indeed, there is no mystery about the whole matter. Simply Dr Godfrey is my uncle's doctor, and he consulted him the other day about his heart. I happened to look out the doctor's address in his "Where Is It?" and found the name in inverted commas. Oh, by the way, there is a red book by you. Look out 32, Half Moon Street. Does Dr Godfrey live there?'

Geoffrey turned up the street.

'Certainly not,' he said. 'But why?'

'Nothing,' said Harry, unwilling to mention the

different address, which might have been a mistake
of his own.

'Come, Geoff.'

They were there in less than a couple of minutes:
Harry had not even put on a hat for the traversing
of so few paving-stones. An incandescent gas-lamp
stood just opposite the door, and both number and
plate were plainly visible. On the plate in large
square capitals was 'Dr G. Armytage.'

They read it in silence, and turned home again.
Geoffrey had pursed up his lips for a whistle, but
refrained.

'We spell it Armytage, and pronounce it Godfrey,'
he said at length. 'Sometimes we even spell it
Godfrey, or perhaps G. stands for Godfrey. Not that
it makes any difference.'

Harry laughed, but he was both puzzled and a
little troubled. Then the remembrance of the evening
when he had seen the strange and distasteful man,
Dr Armytage it must now be supposed, driving
away from the house, came to his mind. How
excellent and kindly on that occasion had been the
reasons for which his uncle had desired that the
visit should remain unknown to Harry! And after
that lesson, should not the pupil give him credit
for some motive, unguessable even as that had
been, but equally thoughtful? He had given him
a wrong name and he felt sure a wrong address;
in his own reference-book that same wrong name,
but with inverted commas, appeared. Harry being
human and of discreet years, did not relish being
misled in this manner, but he told himself that

there might be admirable reason for it, which he could not conjecture. He had intended, it is true, to see Dr Godfrey privately, so as to get his first-hand opinion on his uncle's condition, but he was not at all sure that he would ring at Dr Armytage's door-bell

Lady Oxted, a few days after this, fell a victim to influenza, and after a decent interval, Geoffrey, who, for the remainder of the summer, had let his own rooms in Orchard Street, and lived with Harry, called on the parts of both to ask how she was, was admitted, and taken upstairs to her sitting-room. Her voice was very hoarse, a temperature thermometer lay on the table by her, and he felt himself a very foolhardy young man.

'It is no use your being afraid of it,' said that lady to him by way of greeting, 'because on the one hand the certain way to get it is to be afraid of it, and on the other you have to stop and talk to me. I have seen no one all day, not even Bob, as I don't want fresh cases in the house, and of course I haven't allowed Evie near me. Oh, I am reeking of infection; make up your mind to that.'

'But I don't matter,' said Geoffrey.

'Not the least scrap. Really it is too provoking, getting it again. I believe every doctor in Wimpole Street has seen me through at least one attack. I shall begin on Cavendish Square soon. Now talk.'

The thought of Dr Armytage and the strange confusion of names and addresses had often been present in Geoffrey's mind since he and Harry had made that short and inconclusive expedition to No. 32, Wimpole Street, and here perhaps was an opportunity for adding a brick to that vague structure that was in outline only in his mind.

'Have you tried Dr Godfrey?' he asked.

'I never heard of him. Otherwise I should have tried him. Where does he live?'

'It is not quite certain,' said Geoffrey. 'Personally, I believe at 32, Wimpole Street.'

'Is this supposed to be bright and engaging conversation,' asked Lady Oxted, 'which will interest a depressed influenza patient?'

'It may interest you in time,' said Geoffrey. 'To continue—have you ever heard of a Dr G. Armytage, heart specialist, of 32, Wimpole Street?'

The effect of this was instantaneous. Lady Oxted sat up on her sofa, and her shawl whisked the temperature thermometer to the ground, smashing the bulb.

'Yes, of course I have,' she said. 'So have you, I imagine. Or perhaps you were not born. How detestably young, young men are.'

'They get over it,' said Geoffrey.

'Yes, and become middle-aged, which is worse. Now tell me all you know, categorically, about Dr Armytage.'

'I don't know that there is one for certain,' said Geoffrey. 'True, his plate is on the door. I don't know if I have a right to tell you. In any case, really I know nothing.'

Lady Oxted made an impatient gesture.

'It concerns Francis Vail, of course,' she said.

Geoffrey stared.

'How did you know that?' he asked.

'I will tell you when you have finished your story,' she said, 'which, I may remind you, you have not yet begun.'

Harry had told his friend about his chance encounter at the lodge gates with the doctor, and Geoffrey could pass on the story complete: Mr Francis's silence about his visit there, his excellent reason for silence, the false name given to Harry, and, so he thought, the false address, the false name in his reference-book with the Wimpole Street address, and finally their visit to the door. Lady Oxted heard him with gathering interest, it would appear, and long before the end she was off her sofa, and walking up and down the room.

'And now for your story,' said he. 'How did you know that it concerned Mr Francis?'

Lady Oxted sat down again.

'G. Armytage is Godfrey Armytage,' she said, 'a side-point only. You have told your tale very clearly, Geoffrey. But there is one weak point in the evidence.'

'Evidence? What evidence?' asked Geoffrey.

'Yes, evidence is the wrong word—chain of circumstance, if you will. The weak point is that there is no certain proof of the identity of Dr Godfrey with Dr Armytage. It is certain to you and me, I grant you, but still— Did Harry say what this man he met driving to the station was like?'

'"Not a canny man," were his words,' said Geoffrey— '"dark, clean-shaven, forty, and distasteful."'

'That is on all fours,' said Lady Oxted.

'You haven't answered my question,' Geoffrey reminded her.

'No; I will. Did you ever hear of the Houldsworth case—the death of George Houldsworth?'

'Yes; Harry told me about it.'

'All? The evidence of the doctors?'

'No, not that.'

'George Houldsworth was shot, you will remember. At the coroner's inquest the whole question naturally turned on the distance from his head at which the gun which killed him was fired. This, you will easily understand, was of the utmost importance, for if the muzzle of the gun was not more than, say, a yard or four feet off, it was certainly possible that he had shot himself accidentally. But imagine the gun to have been ten feet off, it becomes certain that some gun not his own shot him. Now, his head was shattered; it looked to the ordinary mind as if the injury must have been done by shot that had already begun to spread—I cannot speak technically. But the doctor who maintained that the shot might easily have been fired within the shorter distance, who was responsible, in fact, for the case not going beyond the coroner, was Dr Godfrey Armytage.'

Geoffrey was silent a moment.

'Well, it is all natural enough,' he said at length. 'Mr Francis, on your own showing, has probably known the man for a long time; it is natural also that he did not wish to tell Harry his real name, for it was connected with that dreadful tragedy. It is also natural, if Dr Armytage is an eminent man, that he should wish to consult a doctor he knew about his condition. Why not?'

'For this reason,' said Lady Oxted: 'Dr Armytage is not a heart specialist any more than you or I. He is a surgeon, and not a very reputable one. I needn't go into details. But it would be as sensible to go to him, if you suffered from heart, as to go to a cabinet-maker.'

Geoffrey frowned.

'What does it all mean?' he asked sharply.

'I have no idea at all,' said Lady Oxted. 'Probably it means nothing. Things seldom do. In any case say nothing to Harry.'

Tea came in at this moment, and they talked of other matters till the man had left the room. Then—

'One thing more,' said Lady Oxted, 'and the last. I hardly like to say to you that I suspect nothing and nobody, because that sounds as if there was possibly something to suspect. There is nothing. But this is a curious circumstance, and it has interested me.'

Geoffrey walked back to Cavendish Square feeling vaguely sombre and depressed. A tepid drizzle of rain was falling, making the pavement slippery; the air was hot and thundery, suggestive of expectancy and unrest, and this accentuated his mood. He had no clue of any kind as to what these secret dealings could possibly mean, and nothing that his ingenuity could suggest was even a faintly satisfactory solution.

Every moment the sky seemed to be pressing more heavily on to the earth, and it was as if the very tightness of the air prevented the breaking of the storm. By the time he had reached Cavendish Square a faint thick twilight showed overhead, the drizzle of rain had ceased, and only a few large drops fell sparingly. He let himself in with his latchkey, and found himself immediately face to face with Harry, who was just coming out. And at the sight of him he suddenly felt that his vague fear was going to be at once realized, for in his eyes sat a miserable despair.

'Harry, Harry! what is the matter?' he cried.

Harry did not look at him.

'Nothing,' he said. 'Where have you been?'

'Sitting with Lady Oxted.'

'Then perhaps she will see me. She is better, I suppose. Tell me, Geoff,' and he fidgeted with the door-handle, 'did you see Miss Aylwin?'

'No. Lady Oxted does not allow her to come to her room for fear of her getting the influenza.'

'Thanks. I shall be back for dinner, I expect. But don't wait,' and he opened the door.

Geoffrey laid his hand on his arm.

'You are not going to do anything foolish, Harry?' he asked in a sudden, vague spasm of alarm.

'No, you idiot. Let me go.'

'Is there nothing I can do?' he asked.

'Nothing, thanks.'

Geoffrey went into the smoking-room, and sat down in a bewilderment of distress and anxiety.

What could possibly have happened? he asked himself. If anything had gone wrong—if Mr Francis, to imagine the worst, had even died suddenly—surely Harry would have told him. Then why did he wish to see Lady Oxted, but apparently did not wish to see Miss Aylwin? For the moment he thought there might be a light here; it was conceivable that he had proposed to her and been refused. But when? where? For Geoffrey had left him not two hours ago in his accustomed good spirits. Again, if he had ever felt certain of anything, it was that, unless the girl was the most infernal and finished flirt ever made for the undoing of man, the attraction between the two was deep and mutual. And no girl had ever seemed to him less of a flirt than Evie. Even if this was so, why should Harry at once wish to go to Lady Oxted? These things had no answer; there was nothing to do but wait—wait drearily and listen to the hiss of the faster-falling rain.

Harry drove to Grosvenor Square through the blinks of lightning, and was shown up. Like Geoffrey, Lady Oxted was appalled at that drawn and haggard face; like Geoffrey, too, the question whether Evie had refused him suggested itself to her, but was instantly rejected.

'My dear boy, what is the matter?' she cried. 'Have you bad news from Vail?'

Harry took a letter from his pocket, and folded it down so as to leave some ten lines of large, legible hand for her to read.

'Will you read that?' he said, giving it to her.

She took it from him, and he sat down in the window.

' . . . must prepare yourself,' it ran, 'for a great shock. I saw with such pleasure your intimacy with Miss Aylwin, and I know, I am afraid I know, what you hoped. Harry, dear boy, you must not allow yourself any fond feelings there. She is already engaged, so I heard this morning from a friend near Santa Margarita, to a young Italian Marchese. So make a great effort, and cut her out of your life with a brave and unfaltering hand. She has treated you . . ' and the exposed page ended.

Lady Oxted read it through and tossed it back to Harry.

'There is not a word of truth in it,' she said, 'though it is true enough that a certain Italian Marchese, not very young, fell in love with her last winter, and was refused. I suppose your correspondent has got hold of some muddled version of that.'

Harry was white to the lips, but a gleam had returned to his eye.

'Are you sure?' he asked tremulously. 'Are you quite sure? I trust very deeply the person who wrote this letter.'

I don't pretend not to guess who it is from,' said Lady Oxted, 'but I am quite sure. If you don't believe me, ask Evie herself. Indeed,' she added, looking suddenly at him, 'I think that would be a most excellent plan, Harry.'

Harry got up; there was no mistaking this, and Lady Oxted had not meant that there should be.

Only last night she had told her husband that the two had been philandering quite long enough, and announced her intention of pushing Harry over the edge as quickly as possible. Her opportunity had not delayed its coming, and she meant to use it.

'Where is she?' asked Harry almost in a whisper. 'Perhaps—perhaps——'

'She has just come in,' said Lady Oxted, feeling a violent desire to take Harry by the scruff of the neck and hurl him into Evie's presence, 'she is in the drawing-room.'

'Alone?' asked Harry.

'I don't know. Go and see.'

Harry hesitated no longer, but left the room. Lady Oxted heard his step first of all slow on the stairs, then gradually quickening, and it would seem that he took the last six steps in a jump.

Evie was alone when he entered, seated at the far end of the room, ten miles away it seemed to him. He felt his head swim, his knees were unloosed, his mouth was dry, and his heart hammered creakily in his throat. Then he raised his eyes again and met her glance. And at that his courage coursed back like wine in his veins; she flooded and overflowed his heart; he was lost in an amazement of love, a man again. In two steps he covered those ten miles.

'You told me to aim at being the King of England,' he said; 'I have aimed far higher. And I have come to you for the crown.'

Thus no word was said at all about the Italian Marchese, no longer young.

Chapter 14

Lady Oxted's Idea

LADY OXTED, in spite of her husband's general reflections upon her character, could not reasonably be called an ungenerous woman, and when, ten days after these last occurrences, it was her painful duty to visit the convalescent sofa of Geoffrey Langham, she said, without circumlocution or any attempt to shirk due responsibility, that she supposed it was she from whom he had caught the influenza. Geoffrey, on his side, did not regard this as anything but a certain conclusion, but added, with the irritable resignation which accompanies convalescence, that he did not suppose she had done it on purpose.

The effect of this was to make Lady Oxted wonder whether she had really given it him at all.

'You speak as if it were quite certain,' she said. '*But* when one comes to think of it, Harry came to see me the same day, in great depression, which predisposes you to catch it, and he hasn't, so to speak, blown his nose since.'

'Very well, then, you did not give it me,' said Geoffrey. 'Please have it your own way. It was my own idea. I evolved influenza for myself. Besides, Harry was deeply in love. You can't do two things at once.'

'Hush-a-by, baby,' said Lady Oxted. 'Geoffrey, I didn't come here to be contradict—'

'No, to contradict, it appears.'

'Primarily, not even that, but to propose that you and I and Bob should go down to Oxted tomorrow; or, rather, to tell you that Bob and I are going, and propose that you should join us; we shall get well in half the time down there.'

'Are you not well?' asked Geoffrey. 'You look a picture!'

'A picture of a boiled rag,' said Lady Oxted, 'treated with extreme realism. Well, will you come?'

'Of course I will, with pleasure. I long to get out of this frowsy town. What does Miss Aylwin do?'

'She will go to the Arbuthnots while I am away, poor dear!'

'She might do worse. And Harry?'

'Harry will probably go to the Arbuthnots, too, a good deal,' remarked Lady Oxted.

She got up.

'I am glad you have promised to come without any hesitation,' she said, 'because otherwise I should have had to press you, which is degrading. Harry's engagement has given me a lot to think about, and I want to express my thoughts to some very slow, ordinary person like you, in the same way as Molière used to read his plays to his housekeeper. I have got a sort of idea in my head, and I wish to see how it impresses the completely average mind.'

'I hope it is a nice idea,' said Geoffrey. 'But one can't tell with you. You have such an inconvenient sort of mind.'

'It isn't nice,' said Lady Oxted; 'in fact, it is just the opposite. However, you will hear more of it tomorrow evening. Here's Harry. I shall go. Dear me, I wonder whether Bob looked as idiotic as that when we were engaged? I don't think he can have, or I should have broken it off.'

Harry's face, in fact, wore a smile of intensely inane radiance, but his desire to score off his aunt, as he now called her, caused it to fade off like the breath off a razor.

'No, dear aunt,' he replied, 'but, you see, he wasn't engaged to a person of—well, to Evie.'

Lady Oxted put her nose in the air, as if she had caught the whiff of a bad smell.

'Can you explain the idiocy of your smile when you entered?' she asked.

'Rather; I was just going to, when you began to be personal. Three Sundays ago, when Evie was down at Vail, she went out walking after lunch with Uncle Francis. Do you remember, dear aunt, and you snored loud and long under the trees on the lawn all that blessed afternoon? Yes, I see you remember. Well, they met—oh, Lord! you can't beat this—they met Jim and the dairymaid walking out all properly in the wood, and Evie thought, until she came back and found me on the lawn—she seriously thought—that Jim was me. She was furious—I got her to confess that she was furious. Great Scot! she thought I was flirting with the dairymaid. I know a maid worth two of her.'

Lady Oxted began to attend suddenly in the middle of this.

'And what did Mr Francis say?' she asked. 'Did he also think it was you?'

'I don't know; Evie didn't mention him. And, then, we began talking about something else. Poor old Geoff, how goes it? If you give me the flu, I'll poison your beef-tea, and you may lay to that. It's all the Luck.'

Lady Oxted sighed.

'"Jack and Jill went up the hill,"' she remarked.

'Yes, you may laugh if you like,' said Harry, 'but I'm beginning to believe in the Luck. I paid my penalty, and now I'm getting the reward. Oh, a big one! Did anybody ever hear of such luck?' he demanded.

'Laugh!' cried Lady Oxted. 'Who talked of laughing? Of course, if Evie chooses to marry a man with unmistakable signs of incipient mania, and Mrs Aylwin doesn't object, it's her own affair. But I wish I was her mother.'

'Yes, that would be something,' said Harry, in a tone of extreme indulgence. 'It would be

charming for you, as you can't be her husband.
Poor aunt!'

'Thirty—love,' said Geoffrey.

Lady Oxted gathered up a card-case and
parasol.

'You just wait, my boy, till I get you to Oxted,'
she said truculently.

'Is Geoff going to Oxted?' asked Harry, throwing
himself extravagantly on the sofa by him. 'Geoff,
Geoff, would you leave me alone—alone in London,
like Jessica's first prayer? I will follow you, if it
be on foot and begging my bread. I cannot live
without you. See Wilson Barrett,' he explained,
sitting upright again, and smoothing his tumbled
hair.

Lady Oxted shrugged her shoulders and shook
a despairing head.

'Poor Evie!' she said—'poor dear Evie!'

Harry sprang up, and stood with his back to
the door.

'Now, why "poor Evie"?' he asked. 'Explain
precisely why. You don't leave the room until you
have explained.'

'If you don't come away from that door and let
me out,' said Lady Oxted, 'I shall ring the bell,
Harry, continuously. This sort of ballyragging is
so good for a man with a splitting headache, and
shattered by influenza. I always tell everybody how
considerate you are.'

'Geoff, have you got a headache?' asked Harry.

'No; fight it out.'

Lady Oxted cast one baleful glance at him,

advanced to the bell, and made an awkward, unconvincing movement to indicate that she was pressing it. Harry burst into loud, rude laughter.

'Try again,' he said. 'You have to press the button in the centre of the bell, not a spot on the wall-paper. More to your left.'

'Forty—love,' said Geoffrey.

Lady Oxted turned away from the bell with dignity.

'I don't understand the difficulty some people feel about apologizing,' she said. 'I apologize fully for all J have said.'

'Explain it,' said Harry.

'There is no explanation known to me. I spoke at random; I have not the slightest idea what I meant. Let me out, Harry.'

At this he granted her liberty, saw her to the door, and ran upstairs again.

'Oh, Geoff,' he said, 'she had on a big broad-brimmed hat and little yellow shoes. I saw them.'

'That all?' said Geoffrey. 'Rather South Sea Islander for the park.'

Harry sighed.

'Yes, I once used to think that sort of thing funny, too,' he said. 'Never mind; you can't know. However, there was the hat, and her face was underneath it.'

'Now, that is really extraordinary,' said Geoffrey.

'The face? I should just think it was. It's the most extraordinary thing in the world. And it's mine, and mine is hers. Lord, whatever can she do with such an ugly mug?'

'Is that the end?' asked Geoffrey, without any show of impatience.

'No, you blamed idiot, that's only the beginning. She was walking, do you understand, with Mrs Arbuthnot. So I thought, "None of that, now, woman!" and I just said so flat; at least, I didn't say so, but they understood what I meant, and so we sat down on two little green chairs, and I paid twopence for them—dirt cheap!'

'You and Mrs Arbuthnot and she. I quite follow.'

'Of course. Oh, I'm not sure what happened to Mrs Arbuthnot. She didn't go to heaven—at least, I didn't see her there; so I suppose—oh, well, I suppose she stopped where she was. I dare say she's there now. So I said, "Evie."'

'And she said, "Harry,"' remarked Geoffrey.

Long brown fingers stole round his neck.

'Now, tell me the truth, like G. Washington,' said Harry. 'Were you listening?'

'No; I guessed. Take your hand away.'

'Devilish smart of you, then. She did say, "Harry," and I won't deny it. My name, I tell you, you malingering skunk! She meant me! She called me Harry. Oh, Lord!'

'Well, it's altogether the most remarkable thing I ever heard,' said Geoffrey; 'and as the bell for lunch sounded ten minutes ago, I propose that you should tell me the rest afterwards.'

It was Geoffrey's first attempt at stairs since he

had gone to bed, and he threw an arm round Harry's neck and leaned his weight on him.

'And ten days ago,' he said, 'I met death and despair in the hall, and that was you. "This is what comes of the Luck," thought I. Oh, Harry, if I wasn't so shaky I'd fetch you such a whack in the ribs!'

And after the manner of the British youth, they quite understood each other.

The influenza party left London next day after lunch. Lord Oxted had brought a whole library of Blue-books with him, out of which he hoped to establish an array of damaging facts against the Government, and his red pencil, as they sped out of London, had no sinecure. Mile after mile of the inconceivable meanness of house-backs fell behind them, and at last Lady Oxted consented to the partial opening of one of the carriage-windows.

'There, that is a proper breath of air,' she said. 'Sniff it in, Geoffrey. But I will have no suburban microbes flying into my face. Oh, we are wrecks, we are wrecks, but we will stop at Oxted till we are refloated.'

Lord Oxted frowned heavily, and scored the offending page.

'Is the man Colonial Secretary,' he asked, 'or is he the autocrat of all the Englands? And it never occurred to any of them, apparently, that there might be something in those grand pianos. I should have thought that somebody might have guessed that this immense importation of huge cases implied something. But I am wrong; nobody guessed it. They said they could not be expected to see through stone walls. Stone walls, indeed! They couldn't see through plate-glass windows.'

'So the pianos turned out to be stone walls,' said his wife.

'Yes; they were put up round Pretoria.'

The heat in London had been intense, and perhaps it was not less at Oxted, but there was a difference in its quality unnoticed by the thermometer, and after tea the two wrecks made themselves exceedingly comfortable on the lawn, and Lady Oxted, without warning, began the statement of her idea to the very ordinary person.

'Harry's marriage is fixed for the middle of November,' she said; 'Evie will have to go back to Santa Margarita first, and I hope she may persuade her mother to come over for it. It is now the middle of July; there are four months before he will be married. Much may happen in four months.'

'As a rule very little does,' remarked Geoffrey.

'In this case I sincerely hope that very little will,' said she. 'Geoffrey, I am not altogether happy about it.'

'Why not?' he asked. 'You told me you pushed Harry till he went and asked her. Did you mean him to be refused? Or are you afraid that either of them will think they have made a mistake? Of course, they are both young.'

Lady Oxted laughed.

'You funny old maid,' she said. 'No, I am not afraid of that.'

'Never mind me,' he said. 'What are you afraid of, then?'

Lady Oxted was silent so long that Geoffrey would have repeated his question had he not felt quite certain that she had heard it. As it was, it was a full half-minute, an aeon of a pause in conversation, before she replied. Then, 'Of Mr Francis,' she said.

Geoffrey had just lit a match for his cigarette, but he held it so long that it burned down, and he threw it hastily away as the flame scorched his finger-tips. The cigarette he put very carefully and absently back in his case.

'What on earth do you mean?' he asked.

'It was to tell you that—that I particularly wanted you to come down here. Listen!'

Lady Oxted felt herself suddenly nervous, even when her only audience was the very ordinary person. She had thought the matter over in her own mind so constantly that she hoped she was familiarized with it; but when it came to speaking of it she found she was not. Thus it was that she began very haltingly, and with frequent pauses.

'I feel sure that he is essentially opposed to the marriage,' she said, 'for reasons which I will soon tell you, and when he professes to be so much delighted with it, I conclude he is acting a part. Now, one has always to be cautious in dealing with a man who is acting, until you know both what his part is and what he himself is. As regards Mr Francis, I know neither. I feel sure, however, that he is a very clever old man. Well?'

'But is it not pure assumption that he is acting a part?' asked Geoffrey.

'No, it is reasoned truth. I will tell you how I know it. The Sunday that Evie and I were down at Vail, Mr Francis and Evie (Evie told me this, and Harry, as you heard yesterday, corroborated a part of it) walked in the afternoon in the wood just above the house, and suddenly came on one of the grooms, Jim—yes, his name was Jim—walking out with his young woman, who is dairymaid. Now, Jim in appearance—you have seen him many times, probably—is the very spit and image of Harry, Evie (they only had the most momentary glance of him) thought it actually was Harry, till she saw him half an hour later, sleeping under a tree on the lawn. But it appears that Mr Francis also thought it was Harry, for he said to himself, half aloud, "Ah, the foolish boy!" Now, you, Geoffrey, have known Harry some time, and well, have you ever known him behave as many young men do behave: talk to barmaids, flirt with waitresses, all that kind of thing?'

'Never. He never did such a thing. At Oxford we used to call him the "womanthrope".'

'Then explain to me what follows. Mr Francis begged Evie not to be too hard on him. He said that Harry was honest, that his "previous foolishnesses"—the exact expression, Evie tells me—had never been anything serious. Now you say there never were any.'

'No, never,' said Geoffrey—'not to my knowledge, at least. Oh, I can go much further than that: I know there cannot have been. Harry simply is not that kind of fellow.'

'Then it appears to me that Mr Francis only alluded to the harmless nature of Harry's "previous foolishnesses" in order to set Evie against him. A nice girl, you know, does not like that sort of thing. And how was it that it never occurred to Mr Francis that the two figures they saw were Jim and his young woman? It is impossible that it should not, it seems to me. The two are engaged, Harry tells me; they often walk out together. Mr Francis must have known that; he must also have known of Jim's extraordinary likeness to Harry.'

'But the likeness deceived Miss Aylwin. By the way, had she ever seen Jim?'

'Yes, the evening before only.'

'Yet she was deceived. Why not Mr Francis also?'

Lady Oxted paused.

'It is very unlikely, but I grant you that it is possible. Take what I have told you alone, and it proves nothing. But there is more.'

She was speaking less lamely now—the words had begun to come.

'You met Harry in the hall when you went back from having tea with me a fortnight ago,' she said. 'How did his face strike you? Was it very happy? And do you know the cause of it?'

'No; Harry did not tell me, though I asked him.'

'Then I shall tell you,' said Lady Oxted. 'I know how his face struck me, for he came to see me immediately afterwards. I thought all was over between him and Evie. Harry thought so too, and his reason for it was a letter he had just received, of which he showed me a piece. In it Mr Francis—I know it was he: Harry told me so afterwards—said that Evie was engaged to an Italian Marchese. Here again there was a certain foundation for his thinking so. It was true, at any rate, that last winter an Italian in Rome fell very violently in love with her, that he proposed to her; but Evie refused him point-blank. The thing was talked about, for it was a very good match; but Mr Francis tells Harry she is engaged. He may have been told so—again, it is just possible, though not more than possible. Now, take these two incidents together. In each Mr Francis made, let us say, a mistake; on one occasion he mistook the groom for Harry, on the other he says that Evie is engaged to an Italian, whereas that was never true; she refused him. Now, does a common motive seem to lie behind these two mistakes? Supposing for a moment that these mistakes were, well, deliberate mistakes—very cleverly founded on fact, I grant—can you account for both of them by supposing one desire in Mr Francis's mind?'

'I see what you mean,' said Geoffrey.

'Say it then; I want it said.'

'You mean that Mr Francis wished to prevent their engagement. Is that bald enough?'

'Yes, that will do. It is a possibility which must not be overlooked. He has failed, but I see no reason to suppose that anything has since happened which reconciles him to their marriage. His letter to Harry in answer to the announcement of his engagement was charming, perfectly charming. But so was his letter in which he urged him to be brave and cut Evie out of his life with a firm hand. So also, no doubt, was his manner when he begged Evie to overlook Harry's platonic little walk with a dairymaid.'

Geoffrey felt vaguely uneasy. Now that these things were said to him, he knew that somewhere in the very inmost recesses of his brain there had lurked for some time a feeling of which he was ashamed—a secret, unaccountable distrust of this kind old man. It had been emphasized by the curious adventure of Dr Armytage's door, and since then it had grown more alert, more ready to put up its head.

'Now, why,' continued Lady Oxted, speaking rapidly, 'should he wish to separate the two? You would have thought—Harry thought, and still thinks that by this marriage Mr Francis would feel that the old stain of suspicion that for so long had been on his name ever since the Houldsworth affair will be removed. And Harry has good reason for thinking so. Mr Francis himself told him that Evie's coming to Vail was the happiest thing that had happened to him for years. Why, then, should they not marry?'

'Perhaps Mr Francis finds that the continued revival of those memories which Miss Aylwin calls up is too painful,' said Geoffrey.

'Does that seem to you reasonable?' asked Lady

Oxted, 'and, if reasonable, can mortal mind invent a more awful piece of selfishness?'

Geoffrey considered a moment.

'No, it does not seem to me reasonable,' he said. 'I recant that.'

'Can you, then, think of any other motive?'

'Ah, you are monstrous,' said Geoffrey suddenly. 'You suggest monstrous things.'

'I have suggested nothing. I want to hear your suggestion. What is it, Geoffrey?'

'You mean that Mr Francis does not want Harry to marry at all. You remember that he is Harry's heir. Do you not see how absurd such an idea is? Whoever heard of an old man over seventy trying to make his grand-nephew celibate? You might as well hope to rear a child who should never see a fire or a book.'

'Ah, you are shocked,' said Lady Oxted; 'but wait a moment. Do you remember what you told me about Dr Godfrey and Dr Armytage? Geoffrey, what is that sinister man doing at Vail? He is appalling, I tell you. He is one of the black spots on the medical profession. Heart specialist! He is a surgeon of terrible dexterity—unscrupulous, venal. What does Mr Francis want with him?'

Geoffrey got up in great excitement.

'I will hear no more,' he said in a tremulous voice. 'It is you who suggest things that I have to put into words. Tell me what you mean—say straight out what you suspect.'

Lady Oxted rose, too.

'If I knew what I suspected I would tell you,' she

said. 'But I can't make out what it is. At any rate, we have talked long enough for the present.'

She paused a moment, then broke out again, her own anxiety—how deep she had never known till this minute—breaking all bounds.

'Promise me this,' she cried. 'Promise me you will be a good friend to Harry. Be much with him, be observant—not suspicious, but observant. Remember that I am afraid, though I do not know what of. See if you cannot find out what it is that I fear. There, that is enough. You promise me that, Geoffrey?'

'I will not play detective,' said he. 'I both like and honour that old man.'

'I do not ask you to play detective,' she said. 'And I pray that your liking and honour for Mr Francis may never be diminished. But be much with Harry, and be full of common sense. Come.'

'Yes, I will promise that,' said he.

PART IV

Chapter 15

Frost

Harry left London at the end of the month, paid a couple of visits in England, went to Scotland for the remainder of August and loitered there, since he was at the same two houses as Evie, till September had reached its second decade of days, and then travelled south again with her. She was on her way straight to Santa Margarita, to spend the remainder of the month of months with her mother, and Harry saw her off by the boat express from Victoria, she having sternly and absolutely refused to let him do anything so foolish as to travel to Dover with her.

'You would propose coming to Calais next,' she said; 'and Calais is but a step to Paris. I know you, Harry. And—and how I hate the journey, and how I should love it if you were with me!'

'Oh, let me come!' said he.

'Not even to Herne Hill,' and the train slid out of the vaulted gloom of the station.

Geoffrey joined him late on the same day, and next afternoon they set off together down to Vail. Stockbroking, it appeared, was, like pheasants, quite impossible in September, and he was going to spend the remainder of the month with Harry, unless some unforeseen urgency called him back. This, he considered, was not in the least degree likely to happen, for the unforeseen so seldom occurs.

'The house is all upside down, Geoff,' said Harry to him as they drove from the station, 'and all the time which you do not employ in getting severe electric shocks over unprotected wires you will probably spend in falling into hot and cold water alternately upstairs. The housemaids' closets seem to me just now the only really important thing in England. I thought it better not to tell you all this before we started, for fear of your not coming.'

'Oh, I can always go back,' said Geoffrey. 'Is Mr Francis there?'

'Just now he is, but he is going away in a few days,' said Harry. 'In fact, he is only waiting till I come, to put the unprotected wires into my hands.'

'Is he well?'

'Yes, extraordinarily well, and he asked after you in his last letter to me. Also he seems wonderfully happy at the thought of my marriage. So we are both pleased. Well, I'm sure I don't wonder; it will be a sort of death-blow to that tragedy twenty years old and more now—a sort of seal and attestation of the vileness of the suspicion. Besides, you know, it's pretty nice for anyone to have Evie in the house always.'

'Is he going to continue being with you, then?' asked Geoffrey.

'Certainly, as much as he will. Evie and I settled all that without any disagreement, thank you. He also is thinking of having a little *ventre à terre*, as somebody said, in town—a sort of little independence of his own. I am delighted that he will. Six months ago he couldn't bear the thought of going about among people again; but now it is all changed. He will begin to live again, after all these years. Dear old fellow, what a good friend he has been to me! Fancy caring about people of twenty or so when you are over seventy. What wonderful vitality!'

Whatever shadow of approaching cloud—so thought Geoffrey—might darken Lady Oxted's view of the future, it was clear that to Harry there could not have been a more serene horizon. Since that first afternoon down at Oxted he had not exchanged a further word with her or anyone else on the subject, and by degrees that ghastly conversation had grown gradually fainter in his mind, and it was to him now more of the texture of a remembered nightmare than an actual experience. For several days afterwards, it is true, it had remained very unpleasantly vivid to him; she had been so ingenious in her presentation of undeniable facts that at the time, and perhaps for a fortnight afterwards, it had nearly seemed to him that Mr Francis had been plotting with diabolical ingenuity against this match.

If such were the case, his apparent delight at it assumed an aspect infinitely grave and portentous, his smiles would have been creditable to a fiend. But as the sharper edge of memory grew dulled, these thoughts, which had never been quite sufficiently solid to be called sober suspicions, became gradually nebulous again. Two circumstances had been the foundation of Lady Oxted's theory, each separately capable of explanation, and in making a judgment so serious it was the acme of unfairness, so it seemed to him now, to put the two together and judge. Each must be weighed and considered on its separate merits, and if neither had weight alone, then neither had weight together. There had been darker insinuations to follow; at these Geoffrey now laughed, so baseless appeared their fabric. Dr Armytage might or might not be a reputable man, but the idea of connecting his visit to Vail, when one remembered how long he had known Mr Francis, with something sinister and unspoken with regard to Harry, was really a triumph for the diseased imagination which is one of the sequelae of influenza.

Oddly enough, as if by thought transference, Harry's next words bore some relation to this train of ideas which had been passing through Geoffrey's mind.

'Do you remember that evening when we went to find Dr Godfrey, Geoff?' he said. 'Well, I have so often thought about it since, that I have determined to tell Uncle Francis about it, and ask him to explain it all.'

This appeared an excellent plan to Geoffrey, for, little as he believed in the solidity of Lady Oxted's bubbles of imagination, it would still be a good thing to have them pricked.

'Do,' he said; 'ask him some time when I am there. I should like to see his face when his little ruse is exposed. It might be a useful lesson. Personally, I never know how to look when my little ruses are discovered.'

Harry laughed.

'There's an excellent explanation behind, you may be sure of that,' he said.

Accordingly at dinner that night, in a pause in the conversation, Harry suddenly asked:

'Seen Dr Godfrey again, Uncle Francis?'

'No, I have had no occasion to send for him, I am thankful to say,' he answered. 'I have been wonderfully well these last two months.'

'Geoff and I went to see him one night at 32, Wimpole Street,' continued Harry. 'Oh, we were not going to consult him. But we just went to his house.'

It would have been hard to say whether a pause followed this speech. In any case it was but a moment before Mr Francis broke out into his hearty cheerful laugh.

'And I'll be bound you didn't go in!' he cried. 'Dear Godfrey! he would have been delighted to see you, though. Ah, Harry, what a good thing you and I are friends! We are always finding each other out. So you actually went to 32, Wimpole Street, and found not Dr Godfrey's name on the plate, but Dr Armytage's. How did you get his address, you rascal?'

'Your "Where Is It?" was lying on your table the last night I was here, when I worked at the electric light estimates. I turned to G.'

'Simple,' said Mr Francis. 'Everything is simple when you know all about it. And my explanation is simple too. I didn't want you to go to Armytage, and fuss yourself about me, so when you asked me for his name, I told you, if you remember, his Christian name, Godfrey, and I am afraid I gave you the wrong address. He is a dear fellow, a dear good fellow, but the sort of man who warns you against tetanus, if you cut yourself shaving. He would certainly have alarmed you, how unnecessarily look at me now and judge. He knows too much; I am always telling him so. He knows how many things may go wrong, and he bears them all in mind. Yes, my dear boy, I deceived you purposely. Do you acquit me? I throw myself on your mercy, but I beg you to bear in mind how kindly were my intentions.'

'Without a stain on your character,' said Harry.

Coffee was brought in at this moment, Templeton, as usual, bearing the case of the Luck, which had been the centrepiece at dinner.

'Ah! they are going to put the Luck to bed,' said Harry. 'I drink to the Luck. Get up, Geoff.'

Geoffrey rose in obedience to the toast-master, and, looking across at Mr Francis, saw that his hand trembled a little. His genial smile was there, but it seemed to Geoffrey, in that momentary glance he had of him over the flowers, that it was a smile rather of habit than happiness. His glass was full, and a few drops were spilled as he raised it to his mouth. The thing, trivial as it was, struck him with a curious sense of double consciousness; it seemed to him that this was a repetition of some previous experience, exact in every particular. But it passed off immediately, and the vague, rather uncomfortable impression it made upon him sank below the surface of his mind. It was already dim as soon as it was made.

'So we are together again, we three,' said Mr Francis, when he had drunk to the Luck, and carefully watched its stowage in its case. 'It is like those jolly times we had last Christmas, when this dear fellow came of age. What a chapter of little misfortunes he had, too! When he was not slipping on the steps he was falling into the fire, when he was not falling into the fire he was catching a severe chill.'

'Not my fault,' said Harry; 'it was all the Luck.'

'Dear boy, you are always jesting about the Luck. Do be careful, Harry. If you do not take care, some day you will find that you have fancied yourself into believing it. Six, eight months have passed since then. What have you suffered since at the hands of fire and frost and rain?'

'Ah! don't you see?' cried Harry. 'The curse came first, then the Luck itself—I met Evie. Is not that stupendous? Perhaps the curse will wake up again, and I shall sprain my ankle worse than before, and burn my hand more seriously, before the middle of November. I don't care; it's cheap, and I wonder they can turn out happiness at such a trifling cost. I expect there's no sweating commission at the place where the old scoundrel who made the Luck has gone.'

Mr Francis looked really pained.

'Come, come, Harry!' he said gravely. 'Let us go, boys; they will be wanting to clear away.'

This implication of rebuke nettled Harry. He was a little excited, a little intoxicated with his joy of life, a little headstrong with youth and health, and he did not quite relish being pulled up like this, even though only before Geoffrey. But he did not reply, and with a scarcely perceptible shrug of his shoulders followed Mr Francis out. Shortly after his uncle got out his flute, and melodies of Corelli and Baptiste tinkled merrily under the portraits of the race.

Next day uncle and nephew had estate business to occupy them. 'Their work,' Mr Francis gaily declared, 'would, like topmost Gargarus, take the morning'; and Geoffrey was given a dog and a keeper and a gun to amuse himself till lunchtime. He wanted nothing better, and soon after breakfast he was off and away for all he could find in wood and hedgerow. The stubbles only and the small brown bird were dedicated for tomorrow.

Mr Francis and Harry worked on till one, but on the striking of that hour the latter revolted.

'I can't go on any more,' he said—'I simply can't.

Come out till lunch, Uncle Francis; it is only an hour.'

Mr Francis smiled and shook his head.

'Not today, dear boy,' he replied; 'there is this packet of letters I have to get through before the post. But do you get out, Harry, and sweep the cobwebs away.'

Harry stood up, stretching himself after the long session.

'Cobwebs! what cobwebs?' he asked.

'Those in your curly head.'

'There are no cobwebs. Oh, Uncle Francis, as we are taking of cobwebs, I want to get that summer-house on the knoll put in order—the one close to the ice-house, mean. Have you the keys! By the way, which is which?'

Mr Francis was writing, and, as Harry spoke, though he did not look up, his pen ceased travelling.

'Yes, a very good idea,' he said after a moment. 'The keys are in the cabinet there—two of the same; the same key fits both. Indeed'—and his pen began slowly moving again—'indeed, you will find plenty of cobwebs there. The summer-house is the one on the left as you ascend the knoll going from the house. Don't go plunging into the ice-house by mistake. They are both shuttered on the inside; it would be a good thing if you were to open all the windows and let them get a good blow out. Shall I—— Oh no, I must stick to my work.'

Harry had found the keys, and as he turned to

leave the room, 'The one on the left is the summer-house?' he asked again.

'Yes, the one on the left,' said Mr Francis, again fully absorbed in his writing.

Harry, key in hand, went out whistling and hatless. The morning was a page out of heaven, and as he strolled slowly up the steep grassy bank where the two outhouses stood, with the scents and sounds of life and summer vivid in eye and nostril, he felt that his useful occupation of the hours since breakfast had been a terrible waste, when he might have been going quietly and alert with Geoffrey through cover and up hedgerow, to the tapping of sticks and the nosing of the spaniels. However, he had been through the farm accounts with minute care; there would be no call for such another morning till the closing of the next quarter.

The two buildings towards which he went were exactly alike, of a hybrid kiosque sort of appearance, fantastic and ridiculous, yet vaguely pleasing. Each was octagonal, with three blank sides, four windows, and a door. Still whistling, and full of pleasant thoughts, he fitted the key in the lock of the one to the left hand, and, turning it, walked in. The interior was dark, for, as Mr Francis had told him, all the windows were shuttered inside, and coming out of the bright sunlight, for a moment or two he saw nothing. For the same reason, no doubt, it struck him as being very cold.

He had taken three or four rather shuffling steps across the paved floor, when suddenly he stopped. Somehow, though he saw nothing, his ear instinctively, hardly consciously, warned him that the sound of his steps was not normal. There should have been—the whole feeling was not reasoned, but purely automatic and instinctive—no echo to them in so circumscribed a building, but an echo there was, faint, hollow and remote, but audible. At this his whistling stopped, his steps also, and, drawing a loose match from his trouser pocket, he struck a light. Less than another pace in front of him was a black space, on which the match cast no illumination: it remained black.

He felt a little beady dew break out on his forehead and on the short down of his upper lip, but his nerves did not tell him that he was afraid. He waited exactly where he was till the match had burned more bravely, and then he chucked it forwards over the blackness. It went through it, and for two or three seconds no sound whatever reached his ears. Then he heard a little expiring hiss.

Still not conscious of fright, he went back, with the light of another match, for the door had swung shut behind him, and in another moment was out again, with the sweet, soft sunshine round him, and the firm grass beneath his feet. He looked round. Yes, he had gone to the left-hand building, the one his uncle had told him was the summer-house. He had nearly, also, not come out again.

At this sobering reflection a belated spasm of fear—for he had felt none at the moment of danger—seized him, but laying violent hold of himself, he marched up to the other door, unlocked it, and, throwing it open, waited on the threshold till his eyes had got accustomed to the darkness; then, seeing a couple of wicker tables and some garden-chairs peep through the gloom, he went in turn to each window, unshuttered it, and threw it open.

At this moment the iron gate leading into the woods close behind him clanged suddenly, and with a jump that testified to his jangled nerves, he looked out. It was Geoffrey, gun on shoulder, coming back to the house. Harry leaned out of the window.

'Come in here, Geoff,' he said.

Geoffrey looked round.

'Hullo! have you been opening the old summer-house?' he asked.

'Yes,' said Harry, very deliberately, 'I've been opening the old summer-house.'

Geoffrey handed his gun to the keeper, who was close behind him, and vaulted in through one of the open windows.

'Rare good morning we've had,' he said. 'You should have come, Harry. Why, you look queer. What's the matter?'

Harry had sat down in one of the garden-chairs, and was leaning back, feeling suddenly faint.

'I've had the devil of a fright!' he said. 'I went gaily marching into the ice-house by mistake, and only just stopped on the lip of the ice-tank or the well—I don't know which it was. Either would probably have done.'

'Lord! how can you be such an ass?' cried Geoffrey. 'You knew that one of the two was an ice-house, and yet you go whistling along out of the sunshine into pit-murk, and never reflect that the chances are exactly even that the next moment you will be in kingdom come.'

'Give me a cigarette and don't jaw,' said Harry, and he smoked a minute or two without speaking. 'Say nothing about this to my uncle,' he said at length. 'I believe it would frighten him to death. I asked him just before I came out which was the summer-house, and he told me the left hand of the two as you go up from the house. Well, he made a mistake. It turns out that the left-hand one is the ice-house.'

'What!' shouted Geoffrey, his whole talk with Lady Oxted suddenly springing into his mind like an opened jack-in-the-box.

'Can't you hear what I say?' asked Harry, rather irritable from his fright. 'Uncle Francis had forgotten which was which, and I nearly went, as you put it, to kingdom come in consequence. There's nothing to shout about. For God's sake, don't let him know what happened! I really believe it might be the death of him.'

'It was nearly the death of you,' said Geoffrey.

'Well, it wasn't quite, and so there's the end of it. Anyhow, don't tell him; I insist on your not telling him. Come, let's go down to the house. I'm steadier now; I don't remember being frightened at the moment, but when there was no longer any reason to be frightened, my knees dithered under me.'

As they approached the house across the upper lawn they saw Mr Francis, some distance off, in one of the shady alleys going down to the lake, walking away from them. The Panama hat, with its bright riband, was on his head, at his mouth was the flute, and quick trills and runs of some light-hearted southern dance floated towards them. Suddenly, it would seem, the gaiety of his own music took irresistible hold on him, for, with a preliminary pirouette, and a little cut in the air, his feet were taken by the infection, and the two lads lost sight of him round a bend in the path, performing brisk impromptu steps to his melody.

They looked at him, then at each other a moment in silence, Harry with a dawning smile, Geoffrey with a deepening frown.

'I wouldn't tell him about the ice-house affair for ten thousand pounds,' said Harry. 'Geoff, I wonder if you and I will be as gay as that when we are over seventy years old.'

'It is highly improbable,' said Geoffrey.

It still wanted a quarter of an hour to lunch-time, and Harry went indoors to finish up. Geoffrey, however, remained outside, and as soon as Harry was gone began playing a very curious and original game by himself. This consisted in stalking Mr Francis, and was played in the following manner. He hurried over the grass to the entrance of the path where they had last seen him, and followed cautiously from bush to bush. Soon he had the sound of the flute again to guide him, but after a little, hearing that it was getting louder, he retired on his own steps, and from the shade of certain rhododendrons observed the cheery old gentleman coming back again along the path he had taken. Mr Francis passed not thirty yards from the stalker; then the music ceased, and he crossed the lawn in the direction of the two kiosques. At that a sudden nameless thrill of horror took hold of Geoffrey, and creeping after him till both kiosques had cleared the angle of the house, he observed his doings with a fascinated attention.

Mr Francis went first to the ice-house, and turned the handle of the door, but apparently found it locked. He stood there a few seconds flute in hand, and, taking off his Panama hat, passed a handkerchief over his forehead, for the day was very warm. Then it would seem that the open windows of the summer-house caught his eye, and in turn trying that door, he found it open. He did not, however, enter, but merely held the door open, standing on the threshold. Then he turned, and rather slowly—for the grass, maybe, was slippery from along drought—began to descend again towards the house. Geoffrey, on his part, made a wide circuit through the shrubbery, and emerged on to the gravel in front of the house just as Mr Francis entered. The latter saw him, but apparently had no word for him, and on the moment the bell for lunch rang.

Their meals usually were merry and talkative; lunch today, perhaps, only proved the rule, for it was eminently silent. Geoffrey was gloomy and preoccupied, his mind in an endless tangle of indecision, shocked, horrified, yet ever telling him that this nightmare of a morning could not be true. Harry also, his nerves still on edge with the experience of the last hour, was inclined to brevity of question and answer, while the brisk cheerfulness of Mr Francis, which, as a rule, would cover the paucity of two, seemed replaced by a kind of dreamy tenderness: he sighed, ate little; it was as if his mind dwelt on some regret of what might have been. Perhaps the weather was in part responsible for this marked decay of elasticity, for the clear warmth of the morning had given place to a dead sultriness of heat; the atmosphere had grown heavy and full of thunder. At last, as they rose from a very silent meal, 'I went up to the summer-house this morning, Uncle Francis,' said Harry, with the air of a man who had carefully thought over what he was going to say. 'It wants putting in order, for it is damp and very cobwebby, as you warned me. But it would be worth while to do it; there is a charming view from the windows. I shall send a couple of servants up to clean it and make it a bit more habitable.'

'Do, dear boy—do' said Mr Francis. 'Dear old place—dear old place! Your father used to be so fond of it.'

The threatening of a storm grew every moment more imminent, and the two young men, who had intended to ride over the downs, decided to postpone their expedition. They stood together at the window of the smoking-room watching the awful and mysterious mobilization of cloud, the hard, black edges of thunder, ragged, as if bitten off some immense pall, coming up against what wind there was, and rising higher every moment towards the zenith, ready to topple and break. Once a scribble of flight, some illegible, gigantic autograph, was traced against the blackness, and the gongs of thunder, as yet remote, testified its authenticity. Before long a few large drops of rain jumped like frogs on the gravel path below the windows, and a hot local eddy of unaccountable wind, like a grappling-iron let down from the moving vapours above, scoured across the lawn, stirring and rattling the dry-leaved laurels in the shrubbery, and expunging, as it passed, the reflections on the lake. It died away; the little breeze there had been drooped like a broken wing; the willows by the water were motionless as in a picture; a candle on the lawn would have burned with as steady a flame as in a glass shade within a sealed room. The fast-fading light was coppery in colour, and the darkness came on apace as the great bank of congested cloud shouldered its way over the sky, but, despite the gloom, there was a great precision of outline in hill and tree.

Harry turned from the window.

'We shall have to light the lamps,' he said. 'It is impossible to see indoors. Really, it looks like the Day of Judgment. Shall we have a game of billiards, Geoff?'

As he spoke, the door was opened with hurried

stealth, and Mr Francis, pale, and strangely shrunken to the appearance, came in.

'Ah, here you are,' he said. 'I was afraid you had gone out, and that I was alone. Is it not horrible? We are going to have a terrific storm. What a relief to find you here! I—I should have been so anxious if you had been out in this.'

'We were just going to the billiard-room,' said Harry. 'Come with us, Uncle Francis; we will play pool, or cut in and out.'

'Thank you, dear Harry, but I could not possibly play with the storm coming on,' he said. 'Thunder always affects me horribly. But if you will let me, I will come with you, and perhaps mark for you. I cannot bear being alone in a thunderstorm.'

They went to the billiard-room, and Harry lit the lamps, while Mr Francis, creeping like a mouse round the walls, and taking advantage of the cover of the curtains, began hurriedly closing the shutters.

'Oh, why do you do that?' said Harry. 'We shall not see the lightning.'

Even as he spoke a swift streamer of violet light shot down, bisecting the square of window where Mr Francis was nervously tugging at the shutter, and for a moment showing vividly the dark and stagnant shapes of the drooping trees. Mr Francis's hand fell from the shutter as if it had been struck, and with a little moaning sigh he covered his face with his hands. Almost simultaneously a reverberating crash, not booming or rumbling, but short and sharp, answered the lightning, and

Mr Francis hurried with crouching steps to the sofa.

'Put up all the shutters, I implore you, Harry,' he said in a stifled voice. 'Shut them quickly, and draw the curtains over them. Ah!' he cried, with a whistling intake of breath, 'there it is again!'

His terror was too evident and deep-seated not to be pitied, and the two young men hastily closed all the shutters, drawing the curtains over them as Mr Francis had requested.

'Is it done—is it done?' he asked in a muffed voice, his face half buried in a sofa cushion. 'Be quick; oh, be quick!'

For an hour he sat there with closed eyes and finger-muffled ears while the storm exploded overhead, the picture of cowering terror, while the other two played a couple of games. From time to time, if there had been a comparatively long interval of quiet, he would begin to take a little interest in the play, and once even, when for some five minutes the steady tattoo of the rain on the leads overhead had continued unbroken by any more violent sound, he went to the marking-board. But next moment a dirling peal made the rest drop from his hand, and at a shuffling run he went back to the sofa and again muffled ears and eyes.

The storm passed gradually away, the sharp crack of the overhead thunder gave place to distant and yet more distant rumblings, and the afternoon was not over when Mr Francis, cautiously opening a chink of shutter, let in a long, dusty ray of sunshine. The heavens were clear again, washed

by the rain, and of a most pellucid blue, and Mr
Francis, recovering with mercurial rapidity, went
gaily from window to window unshuttering.

'What a relief, what a blessed relief!' he cried.
'How delicious is this freshness after the storm! Ah,
the beauty of the world! I drink it in; it is meat
and drink to me.'

He nodded to the others.

'I must go out,' he said. 'I must go out and see
if this horrible storm that has passed has done any
damage. I am afraid some trees may have been
struck by that cruel lightning, in all their strength
and beauty. It is terrible to think of, that exquisite
delicate life, rent, shattered in a moment by the
flame.'

He went out, and the two others looked at each
other like augurs.

'Nerves,' said Harry.

'Bad conscience,' said Geoffrey, and these were
all the comments made by either on Mr Francis's
hour of purgatory.

It was too late when the storm was over to go for
the intended ride, and after tea Harry and Geoffrey
sauntered aimlessly out, played Red Indians again
among the islands of the lake (a game which on
the present occasion was far less delightful to Harry
than when he had played it last), and finally came
homewards as dusk fell. As they passed down
the box-hedge, it suddenly occurred to Harry (so
imaginative had been the realism with which his
friend had played Red Indians) that Geoffrey was
perhaps capable of seeing the secret of the inside

passage in a suitably romantic light, and he took him round to the back of the hedge.

'A mystery, Geoff, a deep dark mystery,' he said, and shutting his eyes against the springing twigs which had overgrown the door jumped into the hedge. Tho elastic fibres of the box flew back like a spring into their normal position, and Geoffrey, who for the moment had been intent, with back turned, on the lighting of a cigarette, looked up when that operation was over, and found that Harry had vanished as suddenly and as completely as any lady in the cabinet-trick. In the dusk it was impossible, except to anyone who knew where to look, to see any difference of uniformity in the texture of the hedge, and the illusion of his vanishing was complete.

'Here, Geoff, come in,' said Harry, still invisible, 'and don't put out that match. It is darker than the plague of Egypt.'

'Come where? How? Where are you?'

Harry laughed, and held back thc twigs.

'That was a great success,' he said. 'And oh, Geoffrey, if you have a spark of the romantic left in you—and I think you have, for you were a masterly Red Indian—this ought to make it blaze. Look! a tunnel right down the hedge. Isn't that secret and heavenly? Think how many plots we might overhear if people were only kind enough to make them as they went down the road. Think of the stirring rescues you could make, hiding here till the pursuit went by.'

Geoffrey was quite suitably impressed.

'I call this really ancestral,' he said. 'Talk low, Harry; we may be overheard. Where does it lead to?'

'Right down to the house, and comes out by another door, like the one we went in by, just opposite the gun-room window. Geoff, if you'll conceal yourself here all tomorrow, I'll bring your meals when I can slip away without attracting attention. You mustn't smoke, I'm afraid.'

'Oh, if only there was the smallest cause for doing so!' said Geoff. 'Does no one know it except you and me?'

'I don't think so. I daren't ask Uncle Francis if he does for fear he does. I shall tell Evie, but no one else. Lord, what a baby one is! Why does this give me pleasure? There, just peep out at the end, Geoffrey, so that if you are pursued from the house you will know where the door is; but be cautious. Now we'll walk up again inside, and steal softly out where we came in, else someone from the house might see us. No, I think not another match. It's too risky.'

'I should like to give one low whistle,' said Geoffrey.

'Just as a signal? All right.'

Even as the whistle was on his lips, there came from somewhere close at hand a sudden gush of notes from a flute, and the two stood there huddled against each other in the narrow passage, petrified into sudden silence and immobility, but shaken with inward laughter. Peering on tiptoe, as it were, through the hedge, they could just make out the figure of Mr Francis, walking airily along the grass border by the edge of the drive, on his way to the house. Soon his feet sounded crisp and distant on the gravel, and the two idiots breathed again.

'A near thing,' said Harry. 'Let us go back, Geoff; if you had lit that match, we should almost certainly have been discovered.'

Mr Francis left early the next morning for London to see two or three little flats, one of which he thought might perhaps be compassable with the modest sum he was prepared to give for a *pied á terre* in town. None of them were in very fashionable districts; the one which seemed to him most promising was in Wigmore Street, and this held forth the additional advantage of being near Cavendish Square. Harry had telegraphed to the caretaker there to get a couple of rooms ready for his uncle, and without his knowledge (for he would certainly have deprecated such a step) he had sent up from Vail a kitchenmaid, who was also a decent cook, in order to make him more comfortable. Mr Francis had breakfasted, and the trap to take him to the station was already at the door when the two young men came down, and he hailed them genially from the threshold, as his luggage was put up.

'Good morning, dear boys,' he cried. 'You will have a lovely day for your shoot. It is perfect after yesterday's storm. Yes, I am just off, I am sorry to say. I shall stop at least a week in town, I expect, Harry, but I will let you know when I am thinking of coming back.'

Harry went out, just as his uncle climbed nimbly up into the dog-cart. Geoffrey had stayed in the hall, and was glancing at the paper.

'Uncle Francis,' he said, 'do take that more expensive flat in De Vere Gardens, if you find it suits you better. Don't consider the extra expense at all; I can manage that for you perfectly.'

'You are too generous to me, dear Harry,' said the other, stretching down and grasping his hand. 'But no, dear boy; I could not think of it. I shall be immensely comfortable in that one in Wigmore Street. But thank you, thank you. Luggage all in? Drive on, Jim,' he said abruptly.

Harry turned indoors, and went across the hall to the dining-room. But Mr Francis, after having driven not more than a couple of hundred yards, stopped the cart, and, descending, began to walk back towards the house. Half-way there he stopped, and stood for a moment lost in thought, then, with an air of a taken decision, went on more quickly. On the threshold again he stopped, biting his lip and frowning heavily.

At that moment Geoffrey got up from his paper, and, crossing the door into the entrance hall on his way to join Harry in the dining-room, saw him through the glass-door standing like this, and went to see why he had come back. And the face that met him was the face of old Francis, a wicked, malignant mask, even as Harry had seen it that day when the sun shone brightly on the picture. But next moment it changed and melted.

'I thought you had gone,' said Geoffrey. 'Have you forgotten something?'

'Yes, my flute,' said Mr Francis, not looking at him, and, picking it up from where it lay on the piano, he went out again, and walked quickly up the drive to where the dog-cart was waiting.

'That was not what he came for,' thought Geoffrey to himself.

Chapter 16

Fire

HARRY was in the most extravagantly high spirits that morning, and at breakfast the two laughed over the most indifferent trivialities like schoolboys. Stories without wit, and of the bluntest kind of point, rude personal remarks, repartees of the most obvious and futile kind, were enough to make one or other, and usually both, fit to choke with meaningless laughter. To Geoffrey, at least, there was great and conspicuous cause for a mounting spiritual barometer in the departure of Mr Francis. All yesterday, since he had seen him tripping up to the ice-house after Harry's escape, he had grown increasingly aware of a creepiness of the flesh which his neighbourhood, or the thought of him, had produced. He had not slept well during the night, and had kept awaking from snatches of nightmare-dozing, in which sometimes Mr Francis, sometimes the figure of the portrait of old Francis, would be enticing Harry on to some dim but violent doom.

Now, like some infernal Piper of Hamelin, Mr Francis
would precede Harry, playing on his flute, and
drawing him ever nearer to a bank of lurid cloud
out of which from time to time leaped crooked
lightning; now he would have him affectionately by
the arm, and walk with him chatting and laughing
towards a little house that stood on rising ground.
The house, to the tongue-tied dreamer who longed
to warn his friend but could not, kept changing
in form; now it would stand alone, now it would
be but one in a countless row of houses all alike,
stretching to left and right from horizon to horizon;
but whether solitary or among a hundred identical
with it, he knew that there lurked there a danger of
vague and fatal kind. Sometimes it was the beams
and very stones of it that were ready to fall as soon
as the door was opened; sometimes every window
of it, he knew, would bristle with shooting flames
as soon as Harry set foot within it; sometimes he
could see that it was in reality no house at all, but
a black pit, infinite in depth, from which rose an icy
miasma. Yet in whatever form Harry's companion
appeared, and in whatever form the house, when
they were quite close to it, Mr Francis would push
Harry suddenly forward with an animal cry of
gratified hate, and Geoffrey would start from his
dream in a sweat of terror. Then there was another
shocking point: the man who walked with Harry
was indefinite and changeable; he would start with
him in the image of Mr Francis, and they would
yet be but a stone's-throw on their walk when it
was Mr Francis no more, but the old baron of the

Holbein picture. Sometimes Evie's face would look out in panic terror from an upper window, and the dreamer could see her wave her hands and scream a warning; but the two apparently could neither see nor hear her, and drew steadily nearer that house of death.

But the sanity of the morning sun, the crisp chill of his bath, above all the departure of Mr Francis, restored Geoffrey to his normal level, and, the normal once reached, the pendulum swung over to the other side by as much as it had fallen short during those nervous terrors of the night, and he ate with a zest and appetite more than ordinary, and a keen and conscious relish for the day. Even at the end of this ridiculous meal, when he had already laughed to exhaustion, a fresh spasm suddenly seized him, and Harry paused, teacup in hand, to know the worst.

'Oh, it is nothing,' said Geoffrey; 'indeed, it didn't strike me as at all funny at the time. But as I came across the hall, there was Mr Francis at the door, though I had heard the dogcart start. He had come back for something, he had forgotten. Guess what it was; I only give you one guess.'

Harry's hand began to tremble, and the corners of his mouth to break down.

'His fl—flute,' he said in quivering tones.

'Right!' shouted Gooffrey. 'And I wonder—oh, how I hurt!—I wonder whether he will do steps round Cavendish Square tonight, playing on it!'

Harry had begun to drink his tea a moment too soon.

They smoked a cigarette in the hall, Geoffrey eager to be off, Harry, contrary to his habit, strangely inclined to loiter. Their talk had veered to the more serious subject of shooting, and Harry was expressing an old-fashioned preference for a gun with hammers to the more usual hammerless.

'I can't think why I do prefer it,' he said; 'but there it is. I put a gun at half-cock instinctively if I have to jump a ditch, but I do not feel quite at home with that little disc uncovering "safe". Supposing it shouldn't be? Come along, Geoff, we'll start, as you are in such a hurry. The men meet us at the lodge; we'll just get our guns and go.'

They went down the stone-flagged passage to the gun-room, which looked out on the box-hedge. There were two guns lying on the table, and Geoffrey, after looking at the other, took up his own.

'You're a consistent chap,' he said to Harry. 'After all you tell me of your preference for hammers, you shoot, apparently, with a hammerless.'

Harry picked up the gun, and looked at it.

'Not mine,' he said—'Uncle Francis's. Ah, there's mine!'

Another gun with hammers was leaning nearly upright in a rough gun-stand, more like a stand for sticks, in the corner. Harry took hold of it some half-way up the barrels, and then, it seemed to Geoffrey to give a little jerk as if it had stuck. On the moment there was a loud explosion, a horrible raking scratch was torn in the wooden panelling of the wall, and an irregular hole opened in the ceiling. The charge could not have missed Harry by more than three inches, but he stood there, the smoking gun in his hand, without a tremor. Then he turned to Geoffrey.

'The Luck is waking up,' he said. 'Frost yesterday—that was the ice-house—and this looks awfully like fire.'

Several panes of glass in the window had been shattered by the concussion, and Harry pointed the gun out.

'Now for the second barrel,' he said; and the click of the falling trigger was the only answer.

He opened the breech, and took out the smoking cartridge-case.

'One cartridge only,' he said; then, looking down the barrels: 'And the left barrel is clean. It looks rather as if the gun had been cleaned and a cartridge put in afterwards. Odd thing to happen. Now we'll go shooting, Geoff.'

But Geoffrey was holding on to the table, trembling violently.

'You're not hurt?' he said.

'No; I shouldn't go shooting if I was. Come, old chap, pull yourself together; there's no harm done. I shall make enquiries about this. Don't you say anything, Geoff. I am going to look into it thoroughly, detective fashion.'

'But—but aren't you frightened?' asked Geoffrey feebly.

'No, funnily enough, I'm not. It's the Luck; I firmly believe it's the Luck, and the poor old devil who put the curse in it is doing things in a thoroughly futile manner. I am ashamed of him.'

'Ah, destroy the beastly thing!' cried Geoffrey. 'Burn it, smash it, chuck it away!'

'Not I. Oh, it's cheap—it's awfully cheap! A hole in the ceiling, and a penny for the cartridge, and November coming closer.'

'Do you mean to say you believe in it all?' asked Geoffrey.

'Yes; I believe in it all.'

'But, good God, man, somebody put the cartridge there! Somebody told you that the summer-house was on the left——'and he stopped suddenly.

'Yes, Uncle Francis told me that,' said Harry. 'And who made him forget which was which of the two houses? Why, the Luck, the blessed Luck!' he cried almost exultantly.

At this all the nightmares of the last twelve hours swarmed round Geoffrey, flapping about his head.

'And who put the cartridge in that gun?' he cried, not thinking how direct an accusation he was making.

Harry's face grew suddenly grave; the smile was struck from it. A flash of anger and intense surprise flamed in his eyes, and his upper lip curled back in an ugly way. Then, seeing Geoffrey holding on to the table, still dazed and white, he recovered himself.

'Come, old boy,' he said, 'don't be so much upset. Yet, Geoff, you shouldn't say that sort of thing even in jest. Have a whisky-and-soda before going out; you're all shaky. Believe in the Luck, like me, and you'll take things more calmly. Yes, I mean it; at last I really mean it. I am the inheritor of a curse and a blessing, so I take the good with the bad, and, oh, how much the one outweighs the other! By the way, the painters are in the house; they must patch up the paper here, and mend that hole in the ceiling. Shall I order a whisky for you at the same time?'

'No, I'm all right,' said Geoffrey; and he followed the other out.

Harry was at all times a good shot; today he verged on brilliancy. Geoffrey, on the other hand, who as a rule was more than good, today was worse than bad. His gun was a laggard; he shot behind crossing game, below anything that was flying straight away from him; he was not certain about the easiest shots, and he was only certain to miss the more difficult ones. It seemed, indeed, that the two had divided between them the accident in the gun-room; the infinitely short moment in which Harry had felt the hot breath of the fire, sharp and agonizing like a pulled tooth, was his, but the reaction, the retarded fear, the subsequent effect on nerve and brain, were entered to Geoffrey. He was utterly unstrung by this double escape; twice during the last twenty-four hours, in this peaceful country house, had Harry looked in the very face of death—yesterday stepping gaily towards the lip of the ice-tank; today, by as little a margin, escaping this shattering extinction. A foot more, a foot less—and as he thought of it Geoffrey bit his lip for fear of screaming—and brain and bone would have been shredded over the gun-room floor. Accidents would happen; there had always been accidents, and there always would be, but, unlike misfortunes, they nearly always came singly. What was this malignancy that haunted Harry, dogging his steps? What dim figure, deadly and full of hate, hovered on the wing by him, ready to strike? Cartridges do not automatically find their way to guns that are cleaned and put in the stand, as dust collects in corners. They have to be placed there; a human hand has to open the breech, stuff it with death, close it, and put the gun down again. These things must inevitably happen before a gun goes off. Who in this case did them?

They came by one o'clock to one of the prettiest pieces of rough shooting on the ground, a long very narrow strip of moorland country bounded on both sides by reclaimed fields, tufted thickly with heather, diversified by young clumps of fir and dense low-growing bushes, and honey-combed with rabbit-burrows. It was scarcely more than sixty yards across, but full half a mile in length, and the sport it afforded was most varied and unconjecturable. On warm days partridges would be here, covey after covey, sunning in the sandy little hollows bare of growth, or busy among the heather, and from the thickness of the cover and the undulations of the ground a big covey would seldom take the air together, but rise one by one or in couples, without general alarm being given, to right or left of the guns, or even behind them, so close had the birds lain in the long grasses. Here and there attempts had at one time been made to bring the land into cultivation, and as you tramped through heather, you would suddenly come on a vague-edged square of potato-planting, the vegetables run riot with great wealth of thick leaf; or a strip of corn already half wild, and with a predominant ingredient of tares, would make you go slowly on the certainty of the break of brown wings, or the delayed and head-down scurry of a hare.

To those happily old-fashioned enough to care for the sober joys of walking up, it was the very poetry of sport, but today it appeared to Geoffrey a barren and unprofitable place. For the last hour the questions that tormented him had been volleying even more insistently; horrible doubts and suspicions no longer quite vague, flocked round his head like a flight of unclean birds, and he desired one thing, only, to get to the gun-room alone, and clear up a certain point.

They had to walk over a bare and depopulated stubble to get to this delectable ground, and Harry, as they neared it, looked first at Geoffrey's lack-lustre face, then at his watch.

'I had no idea it was so late, Geoff,' he said; 'I think we'll take the rough after lunch. We're only half a mile from the house, and you look as if lunch would do you good.'

He took the cartridges carefully out of his gun.

'No mistake this time,' he said. 'We'll start over the rough at two, Kimber; meet us here. Oh, by the way, come up to the house; I want to ask you something.'

Geoffrey gave up his gun with a sigh of relief.

'Yes, let's do that piece afterwards,' he said; 'I can't hit a sitting haystack this morning, Harry.'

'There's one; have a shot at it,' said Harry. 'Oh, Geoff, don't look so awful! What has happened? There is a hole in the gun-room ceiling. You didn't do it, and I'm not going to send the bill to you.'

'But aren't you frightened?' asked Geoffrey. 'Are you made of flesh and blood?'

'I believe so. But haven't you ever had a shave of being shot? I'll bet you didn't give it a thought half an hour afterwards.'

'I know; but it's more cold-blooded indoors, happening the way it did. And coming on top of your ice-house affair yesterday!'

'It's the Luck,' cried Harry. 'That's the explanation of it and it's proved to the hilt. Fire and frost; they are done; scratch them out, and now there remains the rain. I'm afraid we shall not get the rain today, though. If one has to go through a thing—and I certainly have—it is better to get it over quick, and I, to do me justice, am getting it over. And, oh, Geoff, there's a good time coming!'

Harry had to see the foreman who was in charge of the electric light, as well as the keeper, when he got in; and Geoffrey, after seeing him go upstairs, went quickly through the baize door at the end of the passage from the hall, and down to the gun-room. He wanted to find out what had caused Harry to give a jerk to the gun when he took it up.

He had consciously seen him, the moment before
it went off, put his hand to it to lift it out of the
stand, then give an additional effort, as if it had
stuck. All the morning he had been wondering
about that. The obstacle, whatever it was, must,
he felt certain, have been in connection with the
trigger, for it was that jerk which had caused the
gun to go off.

The men had already been at work over the
damage, but they had gone to their dinner, and
the room was empty. He went to the rack where
the gun had stood, and next moment he gave a
sudden little gasp, though not of surprise; for he
had found only what he expected he should find,
or something like it. Round the post at the corner
of the rack was tied a piece of cotton. Two ends,
each some six inches long, came out from it; the
extremities were ragged, as if the piece had been
broken.

Another gun with hammers stood in a glazed
cupboard at the other side of the room; Geoffrey
took it out, and leaned it in the rack as nearly as
possible in the position in which he remembered
Harry's gun to have stood. Then, kneeling down,
he stretched the two broken ends of cotton in its
direction. They just went round the right trigger.

He had a momentary impulse to call Harry, and
show him this, but decided not to. Harry, as he
had said, was going to investigate the mysterious
presence of a cartridge in a cleaned gun, and, if
he could, trace how it got there. Then would be
the time to throw on this fresh evidence. Till then

it was far better that he should not know, for at present he was inclined to treat the affair as an accident, due, no doubt, to some gross negligence, but nothing worse. This matter of the looped cotton, however, gave a far more sinister aspect to the affair, and the knowledge that there was foul work here was a burden that could be spared him, at any rate, till further light was cast. So very carefully he untwisted the cotton from the post of the rack, and put it in his pocket. The knot, he noticed, was the ordinary reef so familiar to the fly-fisher.

Somehow the certainty of what he had feared and suspected, even though the worst of his suspicions was confirmed, served to steady him. He knew now exactly what was to be faced—a deliberate and very cunningly-devised attempt on Harry's life. Look at it which way you would, this could not conceivably be an accident. Taken alone, the presence of a cartridge in a cleaned gun had been a difficult mouthful, even for an imagination in favour of accidents, to swallow; taken in conjunction with the piece of looped cotton, it could not be tackled. He went over all the circumstances slowly and carefully, as he put the piece of cotton in his cigarette-case. There had been two guns on the table—his, and, as it turned out, not Harry's, but Mr Francis's; Harry's gun, loaded, a trap of nearly certain death to any who took it up, was leaning in the gun-rack. Here were the thoughts of the brain which had contrived these things.

The bell for lunch made him hurry out of the room, and in the hall he found Harry.

'Our reporter has been visiting the scene of the dastardly attempt,' he said. 'Something spicy for the evening papers, Geoff? Oh, by the way, I asked Kimber what he could tell me about that gun of mine. He could tell me a lot. Come in to lunch.'

'And what could he tell you?' asked Geoffrey.

Harry looked at the servants a moment.

'Later,' he said. 'Oh, how I bless the man who invented lunch! Do you remember saying to me once that little things like baths and tea were much more important than anything else?'

'Yes; you called me a sensuous voluptuary,' said Geoffrey.

'I believe I did. So you are. So am I.'

The sensuous voluptuaries went out again as soon as lunch was over, to shoot the rough; and as they walked, Harry told his friend what he had learned from the keeper.

'I asked him first,' he said, 'without telling him what had happened, who put those two guns, yours and my uncle's, on the table, and he didn't know. He had come in early to get cartridges and put the guns out, and found them there. So he took the cartridges and went. Now, until this morning, I haven't shot here since last February, and I didn't take the gun that behaved so—so prematurely today to Scotland. So I asked whether anyone had used it since I went away, and it appeared that Uncle Francis had several times; for his own gun, the hammerless one which we found on the table, had gone to the maker's to have a rust-hole taken out. Do you follow?'

'Perfectly.'

'Well, two days ago, the day we came down here, Kimber was feeding the pheasants, and he heard a shot near at hand; and a moment afterwards a wounded hare ran across the clearing, followed immediately by Uncle Francis. He was almost crying, said Kimber. Do you remember how he wounded a hare last Christmas, and was out for an hour trying to recover it? Well, the same thing had happened, and it was his first shot—remember that. Kimber was certain there had been only one. But this time the hare had run into thick cover, and there was really no chance of getting it, for it had been hit, Kimber saw, only in one leg. Now attend, Geoff, very closely; it's quite a detective story. As they stood there, Kimber saw Uncle Francis take the discharged cartridge-case out of the right barrel, and slip the unused cartridge from the left into it. Now, that bears all the stamp of truth on it. I have seen Uncle Francis do just that a dozen times, when he has killed with his first barrel, and does not immediately expect another shot. To continue: then he drew another cartridge from his pocket, but suddenly said, "I can shoot no more with that poor wounded thing unfound." And he snapped the breech to, and went home. Now do you see?'

'But didn't Kimber clean the gun afterwards?'

'No,' said Harry; 'Uncle Francis's man always cleans his gun, and he, probably, seeing him return to the house almost immediately after he had set out, and go into the garden, naturally thought that he had decided not to shoot, and did not clean the gun. That was why the second barrel was clean; no shot had been fired from it, and Uncle Francis simply forgot that he had left one cartridge in. The whole thing hangs completely together. Then came I, picked up the gun quickly, no doubt hitting the trigger against something, and there is a hole in the ceiling.'

Once again Geoffrey thought of the looped cotton, and once again decided not to tell Harry. There was no use at present, especially since Mr Francis was not here, in giving him so sinister a piece of information.

'That certainly clears up a lot,' he said, conscious of the deadly double meaning of his words.

'It clears it all up,' said Harry; 'and I'll tell you now that I felt immensely uncomfortable about it all morning, though I was not frightened. Of course, it was horribly careless of Uncle Francis to leave that cartridge in, and awfully careless of his man not to look to the gun. He thought Uncle Francis had not been shooting, for he must have returned to the house not more than a quarter of an hour after he set out; but it would have saved some lath and plaster if he had made sure. Here we are; now for the rough.'

Mr Francis, Geoffrey now believed beyond doubt in his secret mind, was no less accountable for this gun-room explosion than for the mistake about the ice-house; and Harry's story, proof to the other of his direct hand, was in a way a relief to him. All morning he had feared and dreaded indications of a second hand—of a gamekeeper privy to the deed, of a servant suborned; and, in particular, his fancy had fixed on that dark man of Mr Francis's, him with the fox-like face and tread of a cat. About him there was something secret and stealthy, so said his imagination, heated by the horrid occurrences of these two days; yet his secrecy and stealth were less abominable than the smiles of his master, his sunny cheerfulness, his playings on the flute. So lately as this morning Geoffrey had laughed when he thought of that flute; flutes in connection with white hairs and old age had seemed to him amusing, ridiculous. But now the memory of his own merriment amazed him; no tears were bitter enough for the contemplation of this deadliness of hypocrisy and hate, and he thought of the Italian airs and the tripping step of the performer with a bewilderment of horror. He did not know how finished an article could be turned out of the workshops of Satan.

But at this the full relief occasioned by Mr Francis's absence came upon him with a great taste of sweetness. True, this last attempt had been made when the old man was not actually in the house; but so long as he was away, Geoffrey did not fear another trap. It would not be like a man of that infernal cunning to leave lying about, as it were, a series of nooses into which anyone might step; his desire would not so far outstrip his prudence. It had been by the merest chance that Geoffrey had noticed that slight check to the lifting of the gun from the rack—by the merest chance that he had found the looped cotton; but apart from this, had either attempt succeeded, no evidence of any kind, or to implicate anybody, would have remained. And not the least of his cunning was shown in the way that he took advantage of Harry's credulity in the power of the Luck. By frost and by fire he had schemed his death, and Geoffrey would have laid long odds that if either by the arrow by day or the terror by night Harry's life again stood in jeopardy, in some manner—vague, perhaps, but simple to trace—rain would be the agent. Here, then, he told himself, was a clue of a kind. To guard against rain, it is true, was a vast and ill-defined project, for such an agency might be held to include many forms of death, from drowning to pneumonia; but it was, he felt sure, through the supposed potency of the Luck that Mr Francis was striking.

They spent a most rewarding hour that afternoon over the rough, and the evening passed, as is the privilege of shooters, in lazy, dozing content. One game of billiards had been succeeded by a nominal reading of the evening papers, and Harry had gone upstairs to bed at eleven, yawning fit to wrench off a jaw not firmly muscle-knit; but Geoffrey, on the excuse of being too comfortable in his big chair to move just yet, had sat on in the hall, not ill-pleased to be alone, for he had many things to ponder, and he had not yet made up his mind what he ought to do. Conclusive as the evidence seemed to him, Harry, he well knew, would not possibly listen to it; to tell Harry what he believed meant simply that he left the house. Something far more conclusive must occur before he told

Harry, and Geoffrey prayed silently that nothing more conclusive should ever be on foot; he was quite satisfied with the demonstration as it stood. And he curled himself more closely in his chair, and began to think.

What, after all, if this series of events was due to the Luck? Certainly, immediately after its finding three accidents by fire and frost and rain had happened to Harry, for none of which could Mr Francis be held remotely responsible. What if now these more serious accidents were to be referred to the same agency? Geoffrey found himself smiling at the absurdity of the thought, yet he still continued to consider it. He did not believe it, so he told himself; his reasonable mind entirely rejected the possibility that a thing inanimate, the work of men's hands, be it made of wood and stone, or gold and precious stones, could control destiny. It mattered not, as far as the Luck was concerned, how one thought of destiny; it was the laws of Nature, if you will, unalterable, of an inexorable logic; or to refer the matter one step back, it was the will of God, who had set these natural laws at work. Yet were not the sins of the fathers visited on the children? Was it not possible, though ever so dimly and unconjecturably, that some subtle law of this hereditary kind governed the destinies of the Vails, and that without supposing that a cup of gold could be responsible for danger, sudden death, and, on the other hand, for the meting out of great happiness and prosperity, yet that the belief in some man's mind as he watched the chasing of the legend on that plaque of gold was true? He had observed, let us suppose—and correctly observed—some tide in the affairs of Vails; he had embodied it allegorically in that rune on the cup, and the allegory was true, because that which it illustrated was true.

Indeed, he had put his allegory into a form extraordinarily vivid. Night after night that gorgeous goblet had stood before the diners in the light of the candles, and night after night it had seemed to grow more and more alive. What if some occult force lurked there—if some unsleeping presence dwelt in those diamonds? From immemorial time men had believed that certain powers and qualities dwelt in precious stones. There was danger in opals, and warning; they turned stale and dim in the presence of an enemy; no opal, he remarked, was set in bowl or handle or foot of the cup, else—here his thought was confused, for the Luck was the potency—it might have sickened and paled when Mr Francis ate his dinner near it. The amethyst drove away the fumes of wine; in diamonds there was sovereignty; sapphires conferred judgment deep and clear as themselves on the possessor. What if there was truth, however small a residuum, in these tales? and how might the potency of the stones be increased if they were put in their appointed settings with a blessing and a curse?

He sat up in his chair conscious that he had been half dozing, for the chime of a clock lingered on the vibrating air; yet he had not heard the hour strike, and, still sleepy, he leaned back again with a strong determination to go to bed instantly.

Suddenly and without cause, so far as he knew, he became broad and staring awake; his eye might unconsciously have seen something, or his ear unconsciously heard a movement, yet not have forwarded it in full to the brain. But every sense told him that he was not alone.

He sat up hurriedly and looked around. Peering cautiously into the room, barely visible in the shadow, was the face of Mr Francis.

Chapter 17

A Bird of Night

FOR a moment neither spoke.

'Dear boy, how late you sit up!' said Mr Francis, coming into the room. 'It has already struck one. You were asleep, I think, when I came in, and I was unwilling to awake you. But now, tell me, is Harry all right?'

Geoffrey by this time had every sense alert; he felt perfectly cool and collected, and saw his policy stretching away in front of him, like a level, well-defined road.

'Yes, Harry, by a miracle almost, is alive and unhurt,' he said.

'Ah, I knew it! I knew it!' said Mr Francis below his breath.

Geoffrey paused a moment.

'You knew what?' he asked very deliberately.

'I knew he had been in great danger,' said the other. 'I had the strongest premonition of it. You remember seeing me this morning come back after

I had started? I came back to warn Harry. Yet how absurd he would think it? I was deliberating about that when you saw me at the door, and wondering what I could say to him. Then I told myself it was a ridiculous fancy of mine, which would pass off. But all day it has clung to me. Do what I would, I could not shake it off, and this evening I came down here to see if all was well. You spoke of Harry having been in great danger. Tell me what happened, my dear boy.'

'He nearly shot himself in the gun-room this morning,' said Geoffrey. 'He took up his gun, which was standing in a rack close to the window, and it went off, narrowly missing him.'

'But it missed him completely?' asked Mr Francis. 'He was not touched?'

'If he had been touched he would not be alive,' said Geoffrey, lighting a cigarette, and looking at Mr Francis very intently. 'The velocity of shot at such very short range is considerable.'

Mr Francis made a very slight movement in his chair, more of a tremor than a voluntary motion.

'Terrible, terrible!' he said. 'What awful fate is it that dogs poor Harry?'

Geoffrey paused with mouth half open, a little breath of smoke curling from the corner of it.

'In what other way has an awful fate dogged Harry?' he asked.

Mr Francis replied almost immediately.

'Those three accidents he had last spring,' he said. 'How strange they were! they quite unnerved me.'

'He was thinking of the ice-house,' said Geoffrey to himself, with absolute certainty. 'That was a mistake.' Then aloud, 'They were not so very serious,' he said.

'No, but uncomfortable. And, then, today.'

'Yesterday, you mean,' said Geoffrey, trying to trap him.

Mr Francis looked up enquiringly.

'True—yesterday. How exact you are, my dear fellow! I had forgotten that it was, as the Irish say, tomorrow already. But how awful! how awful! That was what my strange premonition meant.'

'It is odd that your premonition should have lasted all day,' said Geoffrey, 'when the danger was over by half-past ten this morning.'

For half a second Mr Francis's face altered. The perturbed, anxious look which he had worn throughout the interview gave place, though but for a moment, to a trouble of a different type, annoyance, you would have said, keener and more poignant than his anxiety.

'Yes, the whole feeling I had was unaccountable,' he said. 'But poor Harry! What an awful moment for the dear lad! But how could a cartridge have been in the gun? What frightful carelessness on Kimber's part! He cannot have cleaned it after Harry used it last.'

Again Geoffrey paused with his mouth slightly open. Mr Francis, he considered, was on dangerous ground.

'That was in February,' he said—'eight months

ago. I cannot imagine, somehow, the cartridge being there all this time.'

'He was shooting in Scotland, was he not?' asked Mr Francis.

'Yes, but a man would not carry a loaded gun in the parcel rack,' said Geoffrey. 'It is more usual for a gun to be taken to bits, and put in its case when one goes by train. Besides, as a matter of fact, Harry did not take that gun to Scotland. There are other circumstances as well which lead me, at any rate, to a different conclusion—a different way of accounting for the accident,' he corrected himself.

'What circumstances?' asked Mr Francis. 'Do get on, my dear boy. I am in dreadful anxiety to learn all about this awful thing. Oh, thank God, there was no harm done!'

Before the words were out of his mouth, Geoffrey, who for the moment had hesitated what to tell him, made up his mind. He stifled a yawn, and splashed some whisky-and-soda into his glass.

'Oh, various circumstances,' he said, in a slow, well-balanced tone of indifference, as if the subject were wearisome. 'One, of course, must be well known to you. You had used Harry's gun yourself two days ago—the day we came down here. You wounded a hare—do you not remember?—close to the pheasant-field, and returned home after firing only one shot. You, also, unconsciously, no doubt, transferred the second cartridge from the left barrel to the right. You will hardly remember that? But it explains at least why the left barrel was clean. Then your idle rascal of a man, who, I am told, always cleans your gun, omitted to do it, and there remained a cartridge in it. That, at least, is how Harry and I put the thing together.'

Mr Francis's hands went suddenly to his head, as if they had been on wires, and he clutched despairingly at his hair.

'It is true—it is all too true!' he moaned. 'I did use Harry's gun. I did fire one shot only two days ago. Can I have left the other cartridge in? It is possible—it is terribly possible! Ah, my God, what an awful punishment for a little piece of carelessness! Ah, what a lesson! what a lesson! Supposing he had shot himself, oh, supposing——'

Geoffrey watched him for some few moments in silence, as he rocked himself backwards and forwards in his chair.

'Well, well,' he said at length, 'there is no harm done. A few shillingsworth of lath and plaster will pay for the damage. Oh yes, and an extra penny for the cartridge, as Harry said. But it nearly filled the bag and something more at one shot, like Mr Winkle.'

This very cold and unsympathetic consolation had an astonishing effect on Mr Francis. His rockings ceased, his hands left his head, and by degrees his face again assumed a sad smile.

'Dear lad,' he said, 'you have such invaluable common sense. There is certainly no use in crying over milk which is not spilt. What you said was like a douche of cold water over an aching head—yes, and an aching heart. But, tell me, is Harry very angry with me? does he blame me, as he has every right to, very severely?'

'No, he is inclined to laugh at the whole thing,' said Geoffrey. 'He knows, of course, what a simple, and, in a way, a natural accident it all was. He is no more angry than he was yesterday, when——'And he stopped suddenly, remembering his promise to Harry not to tell Mr Francis of the ice-house occurrence. But dearly would he have liked to have broken his word.

Again a remarkable change took place in Mr Francis's face, and Geoffrey, even in the middle of this midnight fencing-match, thought what a marvellous quick-change artist he would have made, if only he had decided to devote his undeniable talents to that innocuous branch of art. His smile was not; a frightened man sat there, moving his lips as if his mouth were dry.

'Yesterday! What of yesterday?' he asked.

'Nothing,' said the other. 'I, like yourself just now, had forgotten that it was already tomorrow. Do you know, I am very sleepy.'

This was not ill done, for Mr Francis could scarcely refuse to accept an excuse which he had himself offered, and Geoffrey could scarcely prevent smiling. But as soon as Mr Francis spoke again, he was again absolutely intent on their conversation.

'It is too bad to keep you up,' said he; 'but, positively, you must tell me more about this dreadful accident. What else? What else?'

'There is nothing more—to tell,' said Geoffrey, pausing designedly; for his immediate object was now to frighten Mr Francis, and he meant to do it slowly and thoroughly. 'What more, indeed, could there be? It was over in a moment. Partly, I am afraid, by your fault, partly by your man's, a cartridge was left in Harry's gun. Oh, by the way, since you are anxious for minutiae, there is one more tiny point that might conceivably interest you. There seemed to me—I happened to be looking at Harry—some slight resistance somewhere when he took the gun up. He took hold of it, you understand, and then gave it a jerk. It has occurred to me very forcibly, in fact, that this resistance, whatever it was, was the cause of the gun going off.'

'The trigger, perhaps, caught in the edge of something,' suggested Mr Francis.

'I don't think so,' said Geoffrey carelessly.

'Well, something of the kind,' said Mr Francis. 'Or, again, it may have been pure imagination on your part.'

'I don't think that either,' said Geoffrey. 'A gun, even when loaded and at full-cock—as this one must have been—does not naturally go off when loaded. Besides, I found, when I examined the place——'

He stopped suddenly, and looked up at Mr Francis. Quick as a lizard, fear unmistakable and shaking leaped there for a moment, and was as quickly gone.

'You found——?' he asked, under his breath.

'Ah, you remind me. I found a little thing—a very little thing—which may turn out to be important.

Oh, it is ridiculous! I cannot really tell you. I will keep it to myself, please.'

'Really, my dear Geoffrey,' said Mr Francis, 'you tell a story, and stop when you come to the point.'

'I do,' said Geoffrey, 'and I apologize. Anyhow, I have made a scrupulous examination of the place, and have taken note of a small circumstance. Again I apologize.'

Suddenly this nocturnal visit began to show in a different light in Geoffrey's mind. Mr Francis had come here, it is true, at an hour when he might reasonably expect the house to be in bed, but it was still unlikely that he had taken this trouble, and run even so small a risk of detection, simply to learn the result of the morning's accident. What if he had come here for something more reasonable—to destroy, perhaps, some little piece of evidence—the evidence, it might be, which lay even now in Geoffrey's cigarette-case?

'Of course, I will not press you, my dear Geoffrey,' he replied. 'But consider whether it would not be better to tell me.'

Geoffrey paused, this time because he really wanted to think.

'Why?' he said at length. 'Either this occurrence was pure accident, or it was a foul attempt on Harry's life. Yes, that sounds horrible, does it not? But certainly it was either the one or the other. Now, carelessness seems to account very largely for it. You left a cartridge in the gun, your servant did not clean it. But, supposing one had reason to think that there was foul play, I should take this evidence to the police. And, you may be sure, at whatever cost to Harry's feelings, and, of course, yours, at making the affair public, I will do so at once—the moment I can form, or that I think they can form, a conclusive series of evidence.' He got up on these last words, and turned to light a bedroom candle. 'Well, good night,' he said. 'I shall see you at breakfast?'

'No, my dear boy, you will not,' said Mr Francis. 'And, Geoffrey, you must not tell Harry I have been here. I am almost ashamed of my foolishness in coming, but that presentiment of evil which was so strong in me all day drove me. No, I shall be gone again before anyone is stirring, and breakfasting in town while you lazy fellows are still dressing, I dare say.'

Geoffrey thought a moment.

'As you will,' he said. 'By the way, how did you get in?'

'I got in by the front-door,' said Mr Francis. 'It was left unlocked. Very careless of the servants.'

'Very indeed. Did you lock it?'

'Yes, and I was just stealing upstairs when you awoke. I had meant to go very quietly to Harry's room, and just look at the dear lad, to satisfy myself he was all right. If I had not had the good fortune to find the door open, I should have passed the night in the summer-house, and just seen that all was well in the morning. I hope Harry will speak to Templeton about the door.'

'But how will Harry know, unless he knows of your coming?'

'Ah!' Mr Francis paused a moment. 'I will leave it unlocked; indeed I must when I go out. You can then call his attention to it. Good night, my dear boy. I shall go to my room, too. I will sleep on the sofa; the bed must not be slept in.'

Geoffrey turned into his room with slow and sleepy steps, shut the door, and locked it. Then he undressed very quickly, and over his nightshirt put on a dark coat. He was too full of this appearance of Mr Francis, and of wonder what it really meant, to waste time in mere idle contemplation of it, and he sat on his bed, following out end after end of tangled conjecture.

Harry's safety during the hours which had to pass before morning was his first thought, but that he speedily dismissed.

'I have frightened the old man,' he said to himself with strong satisfaction. 'I have made him tremble in his wicked shoes. No, he dare do nothing tonight. There is a witness that he is here, that he arrived secretly after dark, and left before morning. No, Harry is all safe for tonight, but I am glad I woke.'

Geoffrey lay back on his bed, keenly interested in what lay before him, but astounded by the possibly imminent issues. Hitherto his life had always run very easily—a pleasant, light business; but now suddenly there were thrust into his young and inexperienced hands the red reins of life and death— reins that governed, or governed not, horses that he could but indistinctly conjecture. But the reins were in his hands; it was his business, and now, to steer as well as he could between God knew what devils and deep seas. A thousand directions were open to him; in all but one, as far as he could forecast the future, lay disaster. A solution and a rescue he felt there must be, but in what direction did it lie? To go now to Harry's room, what risk was there, what fear of eyes behind curtains, and, once there, what sort of reception would he meet? Harry had gone to bed near three hours ago, and must he be plucked from his sleep to hear this wild tale—a tale so full of conjecture, so scant in certainties? And if he heard it, what, to judge by Geoffrey's previous knowledge of him—his only guide in this lonely hour—would be his manner of taking it? One only; he knew it well: bewildered surprise, and scorn that one whom he had accounted friend should bring him so monstrous a tale; that he must certainly expect indignant speech, or silence even more indignant, and a rupture that would not easily be healed. No, to go to Harry now would in all probability mean to sever himself from him, and this in the hour of dark need and danger.

Geoffrey got up from where he was lying, and walked silently with bare feet up and down the room. Then he stripped off coat and nightshirt, and sluiced head and neck with cold water. He felt awake enough, but stupid from sheer perplexity, and he was determined to give his faculties, such as they were, every opportunity for lively and wise decision. There had been, for instance, some train of instinctive thought in his mind when he had shut the door, but dressed himself for possible action. His brain had told him that he did not mean to go to bed yet. Had it not told him something more? His action in putting on dark coverings had been, perhaps, involuntary; it was his business now to account for it.

Ah! the door by which Mr Francis had entered— that was it. He did not believe that he had come in, as he said, by the front-door, for the noise of its opening and shutting, the noise, too, of the lock which he said he had turned after he had come in, must have awoke him from a sleep that had never quite become unconsciousness. A clock had struck, it is true, the moment before he was completely roused, and he had not heard it; but how often, he reflected, do one's ears hear the clock strike, yet never convey the message to the brain? It was far more likely that the slight stir of movement made by Mr Francis as he peeped round the inner door leading to the staircase had awoke him. How, then, was it possible that he should have opened, shut, and locked a door—the heavy front-door—have crossed the hall, and yet never have broken in upon his doze? Besides, the face that looked at him was that of a man peeping into a room, not of one leaving it. It seemed, then, very likely that Mr Francis had not entered by the front-door; it was also hardly possible that it should not have been locked at nightfall by the servant who put up the shutters.

Then another difficulty occurred. Since Mr Francis

had, by his own account, locked the front-door when he came in, it would be locked now; but he intended to leave the house before the servants were up, and would unlock it then, leaving it unlocked when he left. On the other hand, supposing that Geoffrey's suspicions were correct, and he had not come in by the front-door, nor intended to leave the house that way, he would certainly unlock it before anyone was about in the morning. This, then, was the first point: Would Mr Francis unlock the front-door before morning, and would he leave the house that way? If not, how had he got in, and how would he get out? It was likely, also—more than likely—that, if Geoffrey's darker suspicions were founded, Mr Francis would pay a visit to the gun-room, for there was no question that 'the little circumstance' which he had hinted at had been of more than common interest to the other.

At this time, in his soft pacings and thoughts, there came a little gentle tap at his door. He stood exactly where he was, frozen to immobility, a step half taken, in his hand the towel with which he had been mopping his hair. A second or two later the tap was repeated very slowly.

Geoffrey was in two minds what to do. It was possible that this small-hour intruder was Harry, some nameless terror at his heart; it was possible, again, that Mr Francis was outside, ascertaining whether he was asleep, with some specious excuse on his lips in case he was awake. But if it was Harry, whatever he needed, some louder and more urgent summons was sure to follow—a rattling of his door-handle, his own name called. But after the second tap there was silence.

Geoffrey knew how long a waiting minute seems to the watcher, and deliberately he looked at the hands of the clock on his mantelpiece till two full minutes had passed.

Then he slipped on his coat again, little runnels of water still streaming from the short hair above the neck, put the matches in his pocket, blew out the candle, and with one turn of each hand held his door unlatched and unlocked.

The wards were well oiled, the noise less than a scratching mouse, and he stood on the rug of the threshold warm and curly to his bare feet. Next moment he had closed the door behind him, though without latching it, and was in the long dark corridor running from the top of the main stairs by the hall to the far end of the house, where were Mr Francis's two rooms.

Geoffrey's bedroom was close to the head of the stairs, and the faint glimmer of the starry night filtering through the skylight by which they were lit made it easily possible to find his way down. These stairs lay in short flights, with many angles, sufficiently luminous, but on getting to the first corner he stopped suddenly, for on the wall in front of him was a pattern of strong light and shade; the many-knobbed banister was imprinted there, cast by a candle. But in a moment the shadow began to march from left to right. The light, therefore, was moving from right to left. Someone else, and well he knew who, was also going downstairs at this dead hour, three turns of the staircase ahead of him. Silently moved the shadow, no sound of the candle-bearer reached him, and he might reasonably hope that his own barefooted step was as inaudible to the night-walker as was the night-walker's to him. Then the shadow of the banister was suddenly turned off, another corner had been passed by the other stealthy tread—and Geoffrey moved on again and down.

This staircase at its lower end gave on to a corridor parallel and similar to the one upstairs from which the row of bedrooms opened. Immediately on the right was the door into the hall, round which, but an hour ago, Mr Francis's face had peered; to the left were drawing-room and dining-room, and at the far end the baize door leading into the flagged passage to the servants' stairs and gun-room. Two panes of glass formed the upper panels of this door, and Geoffrey, having reached the bottom of the stairs, saw two squares of light cast through these on to the ceiling of the corridor. They lengthened to oblongs, diminished again to vanishing-point, and disappeared, leaving him once more in the dim filter of starlight. Mr Francis, it was clear, had gone to the gun-room.

Opposite the foot of the stairs, but on the other side of this corridor, stood a tall verde-antique pedestal, on the top of which was a bust of Harry's father. A dark curtain hung behind this, setting off the whiteness of the Carrara bust, and Geoffrey was just considering the value of this curtain as a hiding-place in case Mr Francis (the other point) went through the hall to arrange the front-door, when the square of light through the glass panels again reappeared, silent as a dream, but growing very rapidly brighter. In two steps he was across the corridor, but he had not yet got behind the curtain when the baize door opened again, and Mr Francis reappeared. But now his step was quick and careless of noise, and Geoffrey, casting one glance at him before he stepped behind the curtain, saw rage and hunted fear in his face. And at that the thrill of the tracker awoke in him, and he hugged himself to think of the little piece of cotton in his cigarette-case; its value, to judge by the baffled hate that came up the passage, was immeasurably increased. Then he slid behind the curtain.

The steps came nearer very quickly, muffled but audible, and paused opposite Geoffrey's hiding place. Then for a moment his heart stood still, for they did not turn towards the hall, but pattered swiftly upstairs. He had thought Harry safe for the night, at any rate, but what could be safe from that mask of rage and hatred he had just seen?

In another moment he would have followed at all costs, when a light again shone round the corner of his curtain, and the unseen steps passed where he stood and into the hall. Instantly Geoffrey slipped from his hiding-place, stepped silently across the corridor, and mounted a few stairs. From there he could see Mr Francis's movements in the hall; from there, also, he had a good start of him to the upper floor again. The snap of a lock, the grating jar of a bolt, drawn or withdrawn, followed, and, having heard that, he waited no more, but went swiftly up again to his room, and closed the door behind him quickly, but with elaborate noiselessness. Soon light footsteps came along the passage outside; they went by his door, by Harry's, and grew fainter. The closing of a distant latch was just audible, then all was darkness and silence. The first part of the night's work was over.

Geoffrey lit his candle again, smiling with a certain grimness to himself. His next move, evolved during this last half-hour of waiting and listening, had a simple ingenuity about it which pleased him. It meant another journey to the hall, after a precautionary pause, and the only apparatus required was a little piece of stamp-paper. So at the end of a quarter of an hour he went downstairs again and examined the front-door. Bolt and lock were drawn; Mr Francis's visit, then, had been to undo them, so that they should be found unlocked in the morning. This was on all fours with his private theory, and after a little consideration he secured the door again, partly for the safety of the house, partly for the sake of giving Mr Francis something to think about if he did leave the house that way. Then, standing on a chair and reaching up to his full height, he stuck the piece of stamp-paper across the meeting of the door and jamb; thus no one could open it without tearing the paper.

One thing more remained, and that for the sake of his own peace of mind. At risk of waking him, he went to Harry's room and looked in. Harry was lying on his side fast asleep, and shading his candle, Geoffrey waited till he heard two evenly taken breaths. So far, then, all was well.

He slept but lightly and in broken snatches after the excitements of these hours, and it required no great deed of violence on his inclinations to enable him to get up early. In the cool accustomed daylight the things of the night seemed to have more of the texture of dream than reality, but proof of them awaited him when he went to the front-door, for the little piece of stamp-paper was whole and unbroken, the door still locked and bolted. Then, to make doubly sure of the reliability of his experiment, he himself undid the door and opened it and the stamp-paper was torn in half. It was not by this exit, then, that Mr Francis had left the house.

Harry made his appearance at an hour not unusually late, with a perfectly normal face and manner; no sound of last night's excursions had reached him. They talked in their usual desultory fashion, but Geoffrey's mind was preoccupied with the yet unsolved problem. He felt certain that Mr Francis had some secret way in and out of the house, and it should be the next piece of business to discover what that was. Had he come in by some back-door, or through an unbolted window, he would have told him so last night; but he had said he came through the front-door, a thing impossible. But the subject of a secret door was easy to approach.

'I'm working all morning, Geoff,' said Harry, 'what will you do with yourself? Poke and potter with a gun, if you like; we'll ride this afternoon.'

'I'll poke and potter,' said he, 'but without a gun, I think. I feel box-hedgy this morning.'

'I thought you did,' said Harry cordially, 'but I have no idea what you mean.'

'That is just a little slow of you,' said Geoffrey. 'It means that I shall look behind tapestry and tap panelling, and find a secret staircase.'

'Do. I'll give you a shilling for every secret stair you find.'

'Done. Anything extra for a secret door?'

'Door is two,' said Harry; 'concealed will ten, skeleton fifteen. Other objects will be valued by arbitration. Baron von Vail has kindly consented to be arbitrator,' he added, in a burst of futility.

'Fifteen is a little too low for a skeleton,' said Geoffrey. 'It would fetch more than that at a medical shop.'

'Well, twenty, if you like, but you don't raise me again. Well, I'm off.'

'Where to?'

'To work, you lazy hog.'

'Yes, but where?'

'Smoking-room. If you want to do any panel-knocking there, come and do it at once. What a baby you are!'

Geoffrey rose.

'The search is going to be exhaustive,' he said: 'I'll begin with the smoking-room.'

There ensued a couple of hope-deferred hours. From the smoking-room, which yielded no results at all, he went to Mr Francis's room, which he had fixed upon as being the most likely place for the conjectured passage to communicate with, but the strictest scrutiny of the panelling revealed nothing. He tapped every foot of it, and every foot sounded promisingly hollow, yet nothing of any sort could he discover which should yield him even a sixpence. There were cupboards of the most alluring probability: all wore the aspect of concealment, yet all declined to yield their secret.

Geoffrey had never been in this room before, and after a fruitless search he took a look round before leaving it. Orderly and industrious were the indications of its master; docketed papers lay neatly in little heaps, and the appurtenances of its stationery were finished and complete. Each set of papers had its elastic band, each its note of contents in red ink; two sets of penholders lay in separate trays, and examination of the nibs showed that Mr Francis was of that rare type of man who dedicated without violation certain pens to black ink, certain others to red. The pencils were all well sharpened, ink-eraser was there as well as india-rubber, a taper of green wax was ready for the sealing of important envelopes. All this had a curdling fascination for Geoffrey, but at present he was on the hunt for shillings, and a detailed examination of a writing-table brought him no nearer them.

The whole of the second floor he searched without success, except in so far as the discovery of gaunt, chilly bedrooms, in which a lively imagination might conjure up a pleasing thrill, could be reckoned a reward to his labours. Over most was the trail of the plumber, electric bells and light had been newly introduced, and these modern improvements jostled strangely with the faded mediaeval discomfort of large gloomy beds and tapestried hangings. Like the poor lion with no early Christian, these seemed to mourn the absence of murderous deeds; a suitable stage was set, but no actor trod the boards.

It was a somewhat disheartened adventurer who began his search on the ground-floor, for the ground-floor, he could not but remember, would bring but a small bill of steps to swell his revenues, unless, indeed, the yet undiscovered staircase proved to lead into the basement, and that possibility lent him fresh vigour. But dining-room, billiard-room, and both drawing-rooms were searched without result, and the hall was practically the last cover. Here indeed something might be expected; tapestry covered two sides, the other two carried portraits, and again his search became minute. But half an hour was fruitlessly spent, and there remained only the fireplace side, where hung the portrait of old Francis.

Geoffrey looked at this a moment for inspiration.

'He knew all about it, I'll be bound,' he said to himself. 'Why can't the old brute speak?'

Looking at it thus, he noticed for the first time that the panel in which this picture hung was different to the panelling over the rest of the hall, which was all of linen pattern. But this one panel was plain except for a row of small circular bosses, which ran round it at wide intervals, and Geoffrey, goaded by the thought of his last good chance, mounted a chair and handled each of these in turn. The second he tried moved to the touch, and, as with a sudden upleap of hope he turned it, something clicked within, and the whole panel, portrait and all, swung slowly out on a hinge. There seemed to be a narrow passage in the wall, continuing to right and left of the picture.

Geoffrey stood a moment on the chair, holding the panel from swinging further, puzzled.

'He can't have jumped down from here,' he said to himself. 'Perhaps there is another door somewhere else. Anyhow, he has his exits and his entrances,' and the quotation seemed to him extraordinarily apt.

He got down, after securing the panel again, and started to tell Harry. But after a few paces his legs literally refused to carry him in that direction. The secret was his by right of trove; he must make the first joyful exploration alone. Again he turned the knob, and from his chair vaulted easily into the panel. The passage led right and left into darkness, and he would have jumped down again to get matches, when he saw in a little recess in the wall a candle with matches by it. This was eminently convenient, and due no doubt to Mr Francis's thoughtfulness; and after lighting up, he pulled the panel ajar, and, after satisfying himself that the catch was of the simplest kind, latched it back into its place.

Two thoughts were in his mind as he waited for the red wick of the candle to grow black

again—the one the further tracking of the game
he had definitely roused during the night, the other
sheer childish pleasure in a story of adventure
come true. Alas! for the stockbroker, he cared no
more for the shillings. There was a dark passage
in the wall, and the imperishable child within him
trembled and smiled. Mr Francis, the man felt sure,
had used this passage last night. Here was double
cause for excitement and joy. The candle burned
more bravely, and two ways were open. Like all
right-handed folk, his impulse was to turn to the
left, and, obeying it, he traversed six yards or so
of a level, rough-floored passage. On his right ran
the courses of bricks in the main wall, a little dank
and mildewy; on his left the panelling of the hall
A turn at right-angles—at the corner, no doubt,
of the hall—disclosed a flight of wooden steps
leading downwards. Here the stockbroker awoke;
he greedily counted them, and ten shillings were
his. But the stockbroker, it seemed, was a gentleman
of second-rate vitality; he awoke from his torpor
but to count, and slumbered again, leaving the
child and the hunter to go their way.

At the bottom of these steps Geoffrey paused a
moment to recollect his bearings. He had entered
the secret way on the short side of the hall; the
steps, therefore, were on the long side of it, and
on the garden side of the house. But inasmuch
as the passage, when he entered it, was some six
feet above the ground-level of the hall, these ten
downward steps would bring him back to ground-
level again. He was therefore walking in the outer

wall of the hall, on a level with the floor. This clear, he went slowly on.

Suddenly he was confronted by a blank brick wall straight in front. But on the right hand the regular courses of the brick were interrupted by a panelled wooden oblong, some five feet high; beyond this, up to the wall that ended the passage, the courses went on again. In the middle of it was a round wooden handle, straight below it on the floor ran two flanged metal lines. Laying hold of this handle, he pulled at it, and on each side of the wooden panel opened a jagged edge of light, irregular and full of angles. It drew inwards some three feet till it reached the end of the metal lines, running smoothly, but with a sense of great weight. Sunlight poured in, and Geoffrey stepped on to the lawn outside, and regarded his discovery. Indeed, it had been a cunning brain and hand that had devised this. The house wall outside here ran in courses of small brick, and the opening of this door drew these inwards irregularly. The top of the door, for instance, was four bricks in length, but the second row of bricks detached numbered six; below that, again, was a course of four withdrawn, then one of five, then one of six again. The joining was fitted with extreme accuracy. Here the interspace of mortar between the bricks would move with the withdrawn piece of wall, here it would remain on the wall in place. Detection of the line of the door to one who did not know where to look, even to one who did, would be nearly impossible.

Regarding it more closely, another thing struck

him. Half-way down the withdrawn portion was a broken edge of brick, and, taking hold of this, he drew the door back into its place again. Seen thus, as part of the whole wall, detection appeared impossible. There was no line to follow, and though he had closed it but a moment before, he could not trace the junctures; the thing fitted as well as a jawful of good teeth.

But he surveyed it only for a moment, then, with an effort pushing it back again, he re-entered, closed it behind him, and took up his candle to explore the branch of the passage that led to the right of the picture. He again mounted the ten steps, again came opposite the hinged panel, and passed on. Ten similar steps again led down to the ground-level of the hall, and at the bottom of these the passage ended in a wooden panel, by the side of which was a latch exactly resembling that by which the picture-panel was shut and opened. He turned it, and the hinged woodwork swung wide, giving on the short space between the stairs where he had watched last night, and the door into the hall round which Mr Francis's face had first appeared to him when he awoke from his doze. This, then, explained all. It was here, not from behind the picture, that the old man had entered; from here, seeing a light in the hall, he had peeped round the corner.

Geoffrey stepped out into the corridor, and examined the hinged panel from outside. It was in deep shadow, but round it ran bossed circles, similar to those in that which held the portrait over the mantelpiece. The second on the right in the same manner raised and lowered the latch.

He blew out the candle, leaving it on the bottom step of the secret way, closed the door, and went to the smoking-room. Harry was still at work, ill at ease with figures.

'And seven,' he observed truculently, as Geoffrey entered.

'Twenty,' said the other, 'and two secret doors. I beg your pardon, three. Twenty-six bob, Harry. Stump up.'

Harry raised a malevolent face for a moment, and finished his column.

'Any skeleton?' he asked with pungency.

'No; no skeletons. Will you come and see it now?'

Harry sprang up.

'Look here, Geoff, are you playing the fool?' he said. 'If so, are you prepared to die?'

'Neither,' said Geoffrey, 'but don't let me interrupt you. Better get on with your work; the passage won't run away.'

'Nor will the work. I wish it would. Do you really mean it, Geoff? There is a holy awe about your face.'

'Come and see,' said Geoffrey.

They went together to the panel by the staircase, and entered. Geoffrey lit the candle he had left there, and preceding Harry, who made no comment beyond unintelligible mutterings, stopped opposite the back of old Francis's portrait.

'The second secret door,' he said, opening it; 'the

door I discovered first. I'll show you afterwards
how to get in from the outside. And here,' he said,
pointing to the recess—'here I found this candle
and the matches. Convenient.'

'That candle!' said Harry. 'Why it is nearly new!
It is not dusty. And the matches, too. Used they
to use matches?' And he stopped suddenly. 'Give
me the candle a minute, Geoff,' he said. He looked
at the crest and monogram on it, and returned it.
'Come on,' he said, with something of an effort;
'let's see where the passage leads.'

'What's the matter?' asked the other.

'Nothing; get on.'

They went down to the outer door, and looked
at it again from the outside. Though he had been
through it twice that morning, yet, when it was
closed, Geoffrey could not see where it was, so
perfect was the joining of it.

'And the bit of broken brick is the handle to pull
it to,' said Harry with interest.

But he was visibly preoccupied, and his delight
was clouded; there was no childish joy in him.
Geoffrey guessed the reason for it, and at lunch
afterwards Harry spoke.

'That was a candle of Uncle Francis's, Geoff,' he
said. 'It was his monogram,' and he looked up as
if expecting that his information was surprising.

But Geoffrey went on eating quite calmly.

'So I supposed,' he said.

'Then you think that he knows of the secret
passage?'

'I feel sure he does.'

Harry's face clouded a little more; it was dark already.

'Are you weighing your words?' he asked. 'Do you mean exactly what you say?'

'Exactly. Is not the new candle and the matches proof enough for you?'

'It ought to be. Yet I don't know. I suppose you mean that you have further proof?'

'I don't suppose anything would convince you if that candle doesn't,' said Geoffrey, not yet wishing to tell Harry of Mr Francis's nocturnal visit.

Harry pondered this awhile.

'No, I don't suppose it would,' he observed at length. 'Anyhow, Geoff, if he didn't tell us he knew of the passage, we won't tell him that we do. You used to call me secretive, I remember. I dare say you are right.'

'It seems to run in the family,' said the other.

'You mean that Uncle Francis is secretive too? Well, I think he might have told me of the passage. Hullo, there are the horses! Just wait; I must go through it again. The candle spoiled all my pleasure this morning, and it is heavenly, simply heavenly. Twenty-six bob, you say? Dirt cheap, too.'

Chapter 18

Rain

Two mornings after this discovery of the passage, as they were sitting at breakfast, a telegram was brought in for Harry.

'Brougham to meet the evening train,' he said to the man after reading it; 'and tell them to get Mr Francis's rooms ready.'

'He comes tonight?' asked Geoffrey.

'Yes; I did not expect him so soon. But he is only coming for a couple of days, he says. He has taken the flat in Wimpole Street; I suppose he means to go back there.'

'What is he coming here for?'

'Can't say; to get some furniture and things, I expect. Then the passage is a secret, eh, Geoff?'

'Why, surely,' said Geoffrey, 'like the box-hedge. I shouldn't take the slightest pleasure in it if I thought other people knew——'

'But you said you were sure that Uncle Francis did know,' interrupted Harry.

'Let me finish my sentence, if you don't mind. I was about to say that I shouldn't take the slightest pleasure in it if I thought that other people knew that I knew.'

Harry broke a piece of toast meditatively.

'I'm not sure about it,' he said. 'Personally, I felt rather aggrieved that Uncle Francis had not told me anything about it. Well, wouldn't he as naturally feel aggrieved if I don't tell him?'

'It is superfluous to tell him,' said Geoffrey, 'because he knows already. Secondly, it will spoil all my pleasure if he knows we know, and I shall wish I hadn't found the thing at all. Fifthly and lastly, you never paid me that twenty-six bob, and thirdly, it is your house, after all.'

Harry was silent. Then suddenly:

'Geoffrey,' he said, 'tell me what further proof you have, apart from the candle, that Uncle Francis does know about it. I'll draw you a cheque after breakfast. Haven't got any money.'

'Is that a bribe?' asked Geoffrey.

'Yes.'

'And you really wish to know?'

'Yes; I ask you,' said Harry. 'No, it is not a bribe. If, soberly, you would rather not tell me, don't.'

For a moment Geoffrey could not make up his mind whether he wished Harry to know or not. If only the tale would have put him on his guard, he would have had no hesitation about telling him all—his conversation with Lady Oxted, the looped cotton, the midnight visit. But he felt the right time had not come, though it might come any day. On the other hand, it was difficult to speak merely of Mr Francis's visit without betraying some hint of his suspicions, and this he did not want to do. But the balance of advantage seemed to incline towards telling him; for if he did not, in answer to so direct an invitation, Harry would not unnaturally accuse him, though silently, no doubt, of unfounded suspicions against a man whom he himself honoured very highly. So he determined to speak.

'Three nights ago,' he said, 'on the evening of the gun-room affair, you went to bed early, and I sat in the hall and dozed. I awoke suddenly, and saw Mr Francis's face looking round the corner by the staircase.'

Harry pushed back his chair.

'What!' he said.

'Oh, I was not dozing then. We talked for some time, and he told me why he had come with this secrecy. He also asked me not to tell you, but I don't mind.'

'And why had he come?' asked Harry.

'All day,' he said, 'he had been haunted by a strong premonition of evil, and he had come to make sure you were safe.'

'That's odd,' said Harry. 'On the day of the gun-room affair—well?'

'For one reason and another,' continued Geoffrey, 'I felt sure he had not come in by the front-door. At any rate, I proved that he did not leave by it, for I put some stamp-paper over the joining, and in the morning it was still untorn. And then, if you remember, I said I felt box-hedgy, and found the passage.'

Harry got up, and began pacing up and down the dining-room.

'But how ridiculous!' he said. 'Why couldn't he have told me? Was he ashamed of his premonition?'

'He told me he was.'

Harry felt unreasonably annoyed.

'I won't have my house burglariously entered by anybody,' he said—'Uncle Francis or another. I shall tell him so.'

'As you will,' said Geoffrey, inwardly anxious that he should not.

'Then I shall not tell him so,' said Harry; 'and I shan't tell him that I know about the secret passage. But next time he tries to use it, he shall find no candle there. I've a good mind to block the place up, Geoff.'

'Oh, don't do that. 'Tisn't fair on me.'

'I shall do exactly as I please,' said Harry. 'We'll be finding it full of kitchenmaids next. No, I can't block it up before I've shown it to Evie. But I shall go there every day, and take away his candle, if he puts fresh ones. Lord! I got quite heated about it.'

'That's right,' said Geoffrey; 'don't be sat upon by anybody.'

'Anyhow, you'd better not try,' said Harry viciously.

He continued quarter-decking about the room for a few times in silence, and his annoyance subsided.

'And the old fellow really came down because he had a presentiment about me,' he went on. 'Geoff, that's an odd thing now. It looks as if the Luck touched more than me. It gave Uncle Francis a hint of what it was doing. You know the Luck's getting on. It is making more reasonable attempts on me. Do you think I've been encouraging it too much? Perhaps I have. We won't drink its health tonight.'

'I would if I were you,' said Geoffrey. 'Perhaps in that way you have put the old thing in a good temper. Well, keep it up. It can't avoid having shots at you, but it always manages to miss.'

'Ah, you are beginning to believe in it too.'

'Not a bit. All the effect the Luck has is to make you talk arrant nonsense about it. I believe in it, indeed! I was just humouring you.'

'Your notions of the humorous are obscure,' observed Harry.

Mr Francis arrived late that night, full of little anecdotes about his house-hunting, and loud in praises of his flat. He had only come, as he had said, for a couple of days, to collect some books and sticks of furniture, and by the end of the month at the outside he hoped to have it completely habitable. His pleasure in it was that of a child with a new toy, delightful to hear, and they sat up late, listening to his fresh, cheerful talk, and hearkening between whiles to an extraordinary heavy rain which had come on before sunset, and was beating at the windows.

This downpour was continuous all night, and

next morning they woke to the same streaming heavens: the sky was a lowering arch of deluge, the rain relentless. Harry and Geoffrey, who regarded the sky and the open heavens as the proper roof for man, and houses merely as a shelter for unusual inclemency, had felt not the smallest inclination to stir abroad, but Mr Francis at lunch announced his intention of walking, rain or no rain.

'It doesn't hurt me,' he said; 'a brisk walk, whatever the weather. So neither of you will come?'

Harry looked out into the soupy splashing gravel.

'Geoff, shall we go for a swim?' he said.

'Thank you, no. I'm too old for mud-pies.'

Mr Francis laughed heartily.

'So am not I,' he said. 'Well, Harry?'

'It certainly is raining,' said the lad.

'Not a doubt of it,' assented Mr Francis.

Geoffrey turned to Harry suddenly.

'Fear both fire and frost and rain,' he said, in a low tone.

Harry went briskly towards the door.

'Thanks, Geoff; that settles it,' he said. 'An excellent reason for going, and getting it over today, if possible. Yes, Uncle Francis, I'll put on my boots and come. I'm not made of paper, any more than you.'

Geoffrey followed him into the hall, a sudden vague foreboding filling him.

'Don't go, Harry,' he said.

'You are beginning to believe in it, you know,' said Harry.

'Indeed, I am not.'

'Looks like it,' and, Mr Francis joining them, he went off whistling.

Very much rain must have fallen during the night, for yesterday the lake was not notably higher than its normal limits, whereas now, so few hours afterwards, it had swollen so as to overtop the stonework of the sluice, and a steady rush of water fell over the ledge into the outlet below. This, ordinarily a smooth-flowing chalk stream, was now a riotous race of headlong water, sufficient to carry a man off his feet, and as they paused a minute or two to watch the grand lush of it, they could see that even in so short a space the flow of water over the stonework was increasing in volume, showing that the lake was rising every minute. The gate walls of the sluice were not very thick, and seemed hardly built for such a press of water; in one or two places Mr Francis observed that there seemed to be cracks right through them, for water spurted out as from a hose. The sluice itself seemed to have got somewhat choked with the debris of branches and leaves with which the storm had covered the surface of the lake, and a Sargasso-sea of drift stretched out to a considerable radius from it.

Adjoining the main lock was a small wooden water-gate, designed, no doubt, for relief in time of flood; but this was shut down, and Harry, splashing through the water, tried to pull it up, in order to give an additional outlet, but the wood was swollen with the wet, and he could not stir it. Mr Francis observed his actions with some attention. His feet firmly planted on the stone slab that covered the sluice, and the water rose like a frill over his boots, as with bent and straining figure he exerted his utmost force to raise the gate. Once, as, for firmer purchase, he wedged his right foot against the side of the water channel and bowed to a final effort, the block of stone on which he stood seemed to tremble. A cry of warning rose to Mr Francis's lips, but it remained unuttered; only his face wore an expression of intense conflicting expectation. But Harry's endeavours were fruitless, and, soon desisting, he splashed his way back. Elsewhere the lake was rapidly encroaching on the outskirts of the lawn; pools of rain lay in the lower undulations of it, and these, joining with its swollen waters, formed long liquid tongues and bays. Here a clump of bushes stood out like an island in a lagoon; here an outlying flower-bed was altogether submerged, and the dark soil was floated by the water in a spreading stain over the adjoining grass.

'This will never do,' said Harry; 'the place will be in a mess for months if we don't get the water off somehow. It is that choked sluice which is doing all the mischief. We had better go up to the farm, Uncle Francis, and send some men to clear it. Lord! how it rains!'

'Yes, that will be the best plan,' said he. 'Stay, Harry, I will go, and do you run back to the sluice, my dear fellow, and see if it is raised quite to the top; we never looked at that. You might get a big stick also, and begin clearing away the stuff that chokes it. And have another pull at the wooden gate. If you can get that open it is all right. Go and break your back over it, my dear boy; it seemed to yield a little that last pull you gave. What muscles! what muscles!' he said, feeling his arm. 'Try again at the wooden sluice, and be quick. There is no time to lose; we shall have the water up to the house in less than an hour if this goes on.'

Mr Francis went off at a rapid amble in the direction of the farm, and Harry returned to wrestle with the wooden sluice. Even in the few minutes that they had been away the water had risen beyond belief, and when again he splashed across the stone slab of the sluice to the smaller gate, the swift-flowing stream over the top of it was half-knee deep, and pressed against him like a strong man. It was no longer possible to see the spouting escape beneath, for the arch of turbid water was continuous and unbroken from side to side.

He wrapped his handkerchief round the ring which raised the gate, and again, putting shoulder and straining back into it, bent to his task. One foot he had braced against the stone coping of the side, the other he pressed to the ironwork of the main sluice, and, pulling firmly and strongly, till he felt the muscles of his spine stand out like woven cords, he knew that something stirred. At that he paused a moment, the strong flood pouring steadily round him, and, collecting himself, bent down again, and called on every sinew for one sudden effort. On the instant he felt the stone slab on which he stood reel under his left foot, and half guessing—for the moment was too brief for conscious conclusion—that the sluice had given way bodily, sprang for all he was worth from the overturning mass. But the effort was an effort made in air; his right foot slipped from the edge of the coping, and the whole sluice wall turned under him, throwing him, as luck would have it, clear of the toppling mass, but full into the stream below. As he fell, he caught at the masonry of the sides of the channel to prevent himself being carried down.

For one half-second his grasp was firm; at the next, with an incredible roar of water, the released flood poured down from the lake, brushing his hand from its grasp as lightly as a man whisks a settling fly from sugar, and rolled him over and over among the screaming debris, now tossing him into mid-stream, now burying him in the yellow, turbulent flood, now throwing him up on the top of a wave like chaff in a high wind, as helpless as a sucking child in the grip of some wild beast. Impotently, and without purpose, he snatched at hurrying wreckage, even at the twisted ropes of water that hurled him along. conscious only of the wild excitement of this foregone battle without leisure to be afraid. He seemed to himself to be motionless, while the banks and lawns shot by him with inconceivable swiftness, but bearing towards him as he suddenly remembered, with the same giddy speed, the bridge over which the road to the lodge passed. How often had he stood there watching the trout poise and dart in the clear flowing water!

A turn in the stream-bed, and he saw it rushing up towards him like an approaching train, the water already nearly on a level with its arch, and soon to be how vastly higher with the wave of the flood that carried him in the van of the torrent from the broken sluice. His first instinct was to resolve to clutch at it, in order to stop himself; but in a moment realizing that if he wished to make death certain this was the way of it, he huddled himself together, burying his head in the water. He just saw the first of the flood strike against the bridge in a huge feather of broken turbulence, and then came a darkness full of loud chucklings and suckings, as if the water laughed inwardly with an evil merriment. Once in that blind moment his shoulder was banged against the gorged arch; once he felt his coat catch against some projecting stone, and it was as if the weight of the whole world was pressed against him, as for a half-second he checked the stream; the next he was torn free again, and out into daylight once more.

Not till then did the chance of his ultimate escape strike him with a sense that he might possibly have a share in that matter. Hitherto the wild pace had given a certain bewilderment to his thoughts not unpleasant in itself. All reasoning power, all remembrance of what had gone before, all realization of what might follow after, had been choked; his consciousness, a mere pin-point, did not do more than receive the sensation of the passing moment. But after the bridge had been passed it sprouted and grew; he became Harry Vail again, a man with wits and limbs that were meant to be used, and therewith the will to use them. But the power to use them was a thing arbitrarily directed by the flood. Breath was the prime necessity, and it was a matter requiring both effort and an ebb of the encircling wave to fling his face free from that surging and broken race of water and get air. Only with this returning increase of consciousness was he aware that he was out of breath with his prolonged ducking; for, broadly speaking, he had not decently breathed once since he had tumbled with the tumbling sluice. So with a downward and backward kick, the instinct of treading water, he raised his head from the yellow race, and felt the air sweet and essential. Three long breaths he took, throat-filling, lung-filling, like a man half dead with drought; and as he struggled to overlook the water for the fourth time it was for the purpose of using eyes as well as lungs, and what he saw caused hope to leap high in his heart, though he had not known he had been hopeless. For here the stream had already widely overflowed its banks, now no longer held in by the masonry of the first stretch below the sluice, and every gallon of water that came down spread itself over a widely-increased area; speed and the concentrated volume were even now diminishing. The sense that he was bound and helpless, a swathed child, passed from him, and, pushing with arms and feet (so random a stroke could scarcely be called swimming), he soon saw that he was appreciably leaving the main rush of the stream. Before long he was brought up with a violent jerk; his foot had struck the ground, and the water stood up over his head like a yellow frill. But that was no more than a playful buffet after the grimness of his struggle. He staggered to his feet again, now no longer swimming, after a few more splashing efforts stood firm and upright in waist-high water, leaning with all his weight against the press of the flood. Then step by plunging step he got to land, and at last stood utterly free on the good safe earth.

He stood and dripped for a moment, the water running from all points of himself and his clothes, as if off the ribs of an umbrella; then wringing out the baggier folds with his hands, he tried to start running towards the house. But twenty paces told him he was dead-beat, and dropping to a soberer pace, he made his splashing way across the fields. Suddenly he stopped.

'The Luck,' he cried aloud to the weeping sky. 'It was the rain that did it! Blooming old futile old Luck! It couldn't kill a blue-bottle.'

This was an inspiring thought, and he went the more lightly for it, taking note, with a delightful sense of danger past, of the distance of his water-journey. And what was that spouting column of yellowness and foam three hundred yards further up, standing like a fountain in mid-stream? And with a sudden gasp of reasoned recognition he knew it to be the bridge over which the road passed, under which so few minutes ago he had himself been whirled. Cold and shivering as he was, he could not resist a moment's pause when he came opposite it, and he turned again with a sense of respect for the Luck which his last words, shouted to the streaming heavens, had lacked. Under that he had blindly burrowed, helpless as a baby in an express to stop his headlong course.

'Not such a bad attempt of the Luck, after all,' he said to himself.

Five minutes later he had cast his water-trail over the gravel and into the hall. Geoffrey was deep in an armchair reading.

'Geoffrey, old chap, the Luck's been having another go,' he cried, almost triumphantly. 'But it can't pull it off; it simply can't. Get me some hot whisky and water, will you? and come to my room. I'm going to get between blankets a bit. Nothing like taking care of one's self, and running no risks. I'll tell you all about it. Can't stop now.'

Geoffrey's book flew on to the floor as he sprang out of his chair.

'Oh, Harry, what has happened?' he cried. 'What has he done now?'

'Old Francis?' asked Harry, pointing at the picture. 'He's used the rain this time. Penny squirt, you know. Hurry up and come to my room. Whisky— rather strong, please.'

Harry was out of his clinging clothes in a couple of minutes, and dropping them into an empty hip-bath where they could drip innocuous to carpets, got into blankets, and, sipping his whisky, told Geoffrey all his story, from the moment of the dismemberment of the sluice to his staggering landing half a mile down stream.

'And if ever you want to travel expeditiously by water,' he said in conclusion, 'I recommend you a six-foot flood in a narrow channel. But avoid a water-choked bridge ahead of you; man, it gives you a wambling inside, and no mistake. All the same, it makes you feel an A1 hero afterwards, I can tell you that. Why, I'm choking with pride, just choking, though what the particular achievement is, I can't tell you. I had to go underneath it and there were no two words to it. Well, I went.'

'But what happened to Mr Francis?' asked Geoffrey. 'Couldn't he see that the sluice was groggy?'

'No, of course not, you dolt; he'd gone trotting off to the farm. Oh, I didn't tell you that part, so you're not a dolt. We went out together, as you saw, and I took a haul on that old stricken sluice, but I couldn't make it budge. So we began walking away to get men from the farm, but the water was rising so fast that he went on there alone, and I went back to have another pull at it, which I did, with this blessed result. And oh, Geoffrey, how dry and warm the rain felt when I got out of that flood-race. Lord, I thought I was done. No, I didn't think it, I only knew I was. But not till I got out did the blessed solution strike me: it was the Luck having another shot. And again it has failed. Fire and frost and rain—we've had the whole trio again, and be blowed to them! But there's a hitch somewhere; old Francis can't pull it off. Really, I am almost sorry for him!'

Harry's voice was resonant with conviction and triumph. It was as if he had won a battle that was inevitable between him and a subtle foe. The danger he had been through was swallowed up in the victory he had gained. But this lightness of heart found no echo in Geoffrey.

'I don't like it, Harry,' he said. 'I don't like it one bit. I do not believe in the Luck—it is childish—and you do not believe in the Luck. We have played at make-believe like children, as we played with the discovery of the passage in the box-hedge. And the passage in the box-hedge is far the more real of the two. But it is time to stop all that. Why should these things come to you in such continuity? Why, within a few days, should you nearly fall into an ice-house, then go within an ace of blowing your head off, and finally be carried down in that mill-race of death? There is no use also in saying it is coincidence. Things do not happen like that.'

'No, you are right, not by mere coincidence,' said Harry. 'But they do happen; they have happened to me.'

The windows of the room looked out straight over the lawn on to the lower end of the lake, where the sluice lay, and Geoffrey, as Harry divested himself of the blankets he had swathed round him, and rubbed himself down with a rough towel, went and sat in the window-seat, looking out.

'And it's no use saying that I don't believe in the Luck,' he went on. 'I do believe in it; at least, I think I do, which, as far as I am concerned, comes to exactly the same thing. Oh, it is nonsense!' he cried suddenly. 'I don't think I really believe in it, but I like to think I do. There is the truth as near as I can get it. And yet, perhaps, that isn't the truth; perhaps I do believe in it. Oh, who knows whether I believe in it or not? I'm sure I don't.'

Geoffrey did not reply for a moment. He had felt morally certain after the gun-room accident that, if danger of death again looked into Harry's face, it would be Mr Francis who brought it there; he had even said to himself that it would be by rain that danger would come. By rain indeed it had been; but where, taxing ingenuity to the utmost, did Mr Francis come in? Harry had been alone, Mr Francis half-way to the farm. What if Harry was right? And the thought challenged his reasonable self.

'How can you talk such utter nonsense?' he said angrily. 'How can that pewter-pot break down a sluice and put a cartridge in your gun, and make you go to the ice-house instead of the summer-house?'

' 'Tain't pewter,' said Harry's voice, muffled, in the shirt he was putting on.

At that moment Geoffrey's eye caught sight of the figure of Mr Francis trotting gaily through the rain down the side of the lake from the direction of the farm, and he disappeared behind the bushes that screened the sluice from the house. Almost immediately he reappeared again, this time coming towards the house, with the same lightness of step. He must have seen, thought Geoffrey, that the flood had carried away the sluice. Harry, he must have known, was probably there when it was carried away.

What reconstruction of facts would fit these factors? At present, none; but perhaps Mr Francis could supply them. He rose.

'Mr Francis is just coming in,' he said; 'but I do not see the farm men.'

Harry came across to the window.

'They are probably following,' he said. 'Go down to him, Geoff, and tell him I'm all right.'

'You will be down soon?'

'Yes, in a couple of minutes. You might order tea, too.'

Chapter 19

Geoffrey Leaves Vail

GEOFFREY went slowly downstairs, reciting to himself exactly all he knew. One point was salient: Mr Francis had certainly seen the broken sluice. And he entered the hall.

Mr Francis had taken off his waterproof, and was sitting comfortably in a chair. He looked up with his cheery smile when Geoffrey came in.

'Ah, my dear boy,' he said, 'you were quite right not to come out. The weather was odious. I have never seen such rain. But one feels better, after all, for a breath of air.'

'I preferred the house,' said Geoffrey. 'Was the water in the lake very high?'

'Yes, it was a good deal swollen. In fact, it has carried away a considerable portion of the sluice. It must be seen to.'

'A dangerous moment,' observed Geoffrey, picking up a magazine and turning over the pages.

'Yes, I wish I had seen it go. A fine sight it

must have been, six feet of water in that narrow channel. But we were on the way to the farm, I suppose, when it happened. I must talk—I must talk to Harry about it this evening. It will want mending at once.'

At this moment Geoffrey heard Harry's foot on the stairs just outside the hall. Though he knew nothing of psychology, he believed this to be a psychological moment.

'Is he out still?' he asked, seeing out of the corner of his eye that he was even now entering the hall.

'I suppose so,' said Mr Francis. 'He left me on the way up to the farm.'

Harry had now entered the hall, and his step was noiseless on the thick carpet. Mr Francis, with his chair facing the fire, could not see him, but another half-dozen paces would bring him close.

'You are wrong,' said Geoffrey slowly, 'for he seems to have come in. This is he, is it not, or his ghost?'

Mr Francis, contrary to the doctor's orders, made an exceedingly brisk movement, springing to his feet and facing about. He saw Harry. He cast one brief look at Geoffrey, to which fear and a devilish enmity contributed largely, and turned to his nephew again, in perfect control of himself, and without further hesitation—Geoffrey had scarce time to tell himself that there was an awkward choice he had to make—

'Ah, my dear boy!' he cried, 'so you are all right. I felt sure you would be; but for a moment, for one moment, I was anxious, when I came back from the farm with the men and we found the sluice broken.'

Geoffrey stared in sheer astonishment at the man's glibness.

'With the men?' he asked. 'Surely not!'

'Dear fellow,' said Mr Francis, with the most natural manner, 'how pedantically exact you are! I must be exact, too, it seems. I was a little ahead of them, for I ran back from the farm, being just a little uneasy about the weight of water that I knew must be pressing on the sluice. I thought, indeed, that when Harry made his first attempt to pull it up it was a little unsafe for anyone to stand there.'

Suddenly all his doubts and certainties surged up in Geoffrey's mind.

'Did you warn him?' he asked.

Geoffrey saw Harry's eyebrows knot themselves together in a frown of perplexity which he could not decipher. But Mr Francis turned to him with the eagerness of a boy anxious to confess.

'I did not,' he said, 'and all the time that I was going to the farm the thing weighed on me. I ought to have—I ought to have given way to my old-maid feeling of insecurity. But I was afraid—yes, dear lad, I was afraid Harry would laugh at me. Ah! how I repented my silence when I came back and found the sluice gone— gone!'

'Yes, it went,' said Harry. 'I went too.'

Mr Francis looked at him a moment with eyes

of horror, diminishing to pin-points; then he gave a little cry and sank down in his chair again.

'What do you say? what do you say?' he murmured. 'You were there; you were——'

'Oh, the sluice broke as I was standing on it, having another pull at the wooden gate, as you suggested, and down I went,' said Harry. 'The flood took me right under the bridge—rather a difficult matter, and a quarter of a mile further down. Then I got out.'

Mr Francis lifted up his hands in a weary, uncertain manner.

'Under the bridge! under the bridge!' he said hoarsely.

'It would not take him over,' remarked Geoffrey.

Mr Francis seemed not to hear this comment.

'What can I say?' he cried, 'what can I say or do? And to think that it was my fault! I ought to have warned you. I ought to have been on the safe side. I did not, with my reasonable mind, think that there was any danger; but I was uneasy. Harry, do not blame me too much. I remember advising you one day last winter, when you came in wet from shooting, to go and change, and indeed, my dear boy, you did not receive my advice very patiently. I thought of that. I thought I would not weary you with my meddling misgivings.'

'I don't blame you in the least, Uncle Francis,' said Harry. 'You didn't think the sluice looked sufficiently unsafe to make it better that you should warn me. I also did not realize that it was in a dangerous condition. There is no harm done.'

'I cannot forgive myself,' said Mr Francis.

Harry laughed.

'Ah! there I cannot help you,' he said. 'For my own part, I can only assure you that there is nothing to forgive. There, that's all right,' he added, rather gruffly, desiring to have no scene.

Geoffrey had listened to this with a look of pleased attention, as a man may regard a little scene in a play which he knows well. Mr Francis had been through his part with great dexterity; here another actor, himself, should appear.

'And now for your story, Mr Francis,' he said, very cheerfully, 'as Harry will not give us curdling details. Let me see, you went to the farm, and ran back again, and I saw you go to the sluice. You found it gone. Dear, dear, how terrible for you! So you came quietly back to the house and sat yourself down in front of the fire, where I found you ten minutes ago.'

Mr Francis looked up with a scared eye.

'I hoped and trusted no accident had happened to him,' he said. 'I came to the house to make sure that he was safe. Ah! I cannot talk of it! I cannot talk of it!' he cried suddenly.

'But ten minutes ago you told me that you supposed that Harry was still out,' persisted Geoffrey. 'What a strange thing is the human mind! Here, for instance, I do not follow your thoughts at all. You were uneasy for Harry's safety, for fear of the sluice giving way, and, as soon as you saw for certain that it had given way, you felt no further anxiety. You sat here in front of the fire, though, as you told me, you supposed Harry was out still.'

Mr Francis rose from his chair in great agitation.

'What do you mean? what are you saying?' he cried, in a high, tremulous voice. 'Do you know what your words mean?'

'My words mean exactly what they appear to mean,' said Geoffrey quietly, feeling that the signal had been given and the time was come. 'Hear me: How curious a thing, I said, is the human mind! The sluice, you thought, looked a little unsafe, and you were uneasy for Harry's safety as you went to the farm, for he was making, at your suggestion, an attempt to raise the wooden gate. You come back and find symptoms of the confirmation of your fears. The sluice is broken, Harry is not there. Then you walk quietly back to the house and tell me you suppose that Harry is out still. I repeat that I do not follow your train of thought. It is curious. Harry, does not this seem to you also to be curious?'

Harry looked from one to the other a moment, puzzled and bewildered. Geoffrey spoke so quietly and collectedly that it was impossible not to listen calmly to what he said, impossible, also, not to understand what he meant. On the other hand, he was saying things that were absolutely incredible. From Geoffrey he looked to Mr Francis, who was standing between them. The old man's mouth quivered, his agitation was momentarily increasing.

Then suddenly he recollected the doctor's warning, that all agitation was bad for him, and he was his uncle, his friend, and an old man.

'Stop, Geoffrey!' he cried; 'don't speak. Uncle Francis, don't listen to him. He doesn't mean what you think he means. There is some ghastly misunderstanding. Geoff, you idiot!'

Mr Francis's face grew paler and more mottled. His breathing was growing short and laboured, and Harry was in an agony of terror that another of those awful seizures would come upon him. But in a moment he spoke, slowly, and with little pauses for breath.

'Harry,' he said, 'either your friend—apologizes—unreservedly for—what he has said—or, one of us—leaves the house—now, this evening. It will be for you—to decide—which of us leaves it.'

At these words another terror seized Harry, the terror of the precipice at the edge of which all three of them stood. Whatever happened now, it seemed to him, a catastrophe must be—one friend or the other (and as he thought of the two his mind veered backwards and forwards like a shifting weather-cock) must go. But the primary necessity was, by any means in his power, to stop further words just now, for he feared each moment that Mr Francis would be seized as he stood.

'Uncle Francis, come away,' he said, taking his arm. 'You are agitated; so is Geoffrey; so am I. It is no use talking about a thing in a heat. Wait, just wait. Geoffrey, if you say another word, I'll knock your silly head off.'

But Mr Francis regarded his nephew no more than he regarded the fly that buzzed on the pane.

'What do you mean?' he said, coming closer to Geoffrey, and shaking off Harry's hand. 'What do you mean by what you have just said? Apologize for it instantly! Do you hear? Indeed, it seems to me that I am very good-natured to be willing to accept an apology.'

Harry put in a word he knew to be hopeless.

'Go on, Geoff,' he said impatiently, anxious for the moment only about his uncle. 'Uncle Francis has understood what you said in some different way to what you meant. I don't know what it's all about, but let's have no more nonsense.'

Geoffrey turned on that eager face but an absent and staring eye, hardly hearing his words, for they called up nothing whatever in his mind which answered to them, only collecting himself to speak fully and without excitement. He hardly gave a thought to how Harry might take it, so large and immediate was the need of speaking, so tremendous the part in this horrible nightmare inevitably his.

'I do not apologize,' he said, 'not only because I do not wish to, but because I am simply unable. I endorse every word I have said. I have also more to say. Will you hear it, Harry? I should prefer to tell you alone, but I suppose that is impossible.'

'Quite impossible, I assure you, you young viper,' said Mr Francis, in a voice so cool and self-contained that Harry looked at him in utter surprise. The bursting agitation of a few minutes ago had passed;

his voice, horrid and cold, was the faithful index of his face, and at his words Harry suddenly saw the futility of trying to interfere. The thing was gone beyond his reach. It was as impossible now to stop what was coming as it would have been to stop that hustling flood from the lake by a word to it. He waited, frozen almost to numbness with dread and nauseous misgivings for what should follow, till Geoffrey, in response to Mr Francis's assurance, spoke.

'Your uncle,' he said, 'has for months past been plotting and scheming against you, your happiness, your life. He tried, in the first place, by every means in his power, to prevent your marriage with Miss Aylwin. On the Sunday last June when she was down here they walked in the wood together, and saw——'

'I know all about that,' said Harry.

'I doubt it. Do you know, for instance, that Mr Francis tried to persuade Miss Aylwin to overlook the fact that she had seen you walking with a dairymaid? Do you know that he never suggested to her that the supposed "you" might be Jim, that he told her that all "your previous little foolishnesses"—the exact phrase—had been quite innocent? I think you did not know that.'

The whole scene still seemed utterly unreal to Harry; he could not believe that it was going on. He turned to his uncle.

'Well?' he said.

'Ah, I am on my trial, then?' said Mr Francis

very evilly. 'Harry, my dear boy, it is only because this fellow has been your friend that I stop and listen to these monstrous insinuations. I am asked, I believe, what I have to say to this. Well, what has been said is literally true. I mistook the groom for you. So did Miss Aylwin. We both made a mistake. As for "previous little foolishnesses", that, of course, is a pure invention on the part of some imaginative person.'

'Miss Aylwin told Lady Oxted, Lady Oxted told me,' said Geoffrey, as quietly as if he were giving a reference to some small point of business.

Mr Francis just shrugged his shoulders.

'I remember last winter,' he said, 'that we used to play a very diverting game called Russian scandal.'

'The next move you know, Harry,' continued Geoffrey, still taking not the slightest notice of Mr Francis, 'he wrote to tell you that Miss Aylwin was already engaged.'

Harry wore an inscrutable face.

'Go on,' he said.

'That also did not—did not come off,' said Geoffrey, 'and you were engaged. Ten days ago we came down here. On the first morning you asked Mr Francis which of the two houses on the knoll was the ice-house, and which the summer-house——'

'Ah, you have broken your word to me!' cried Harry. 'You promised to keep that secret from my uncle.'

A violent trembling had seized Mr Francis.

'What? What?' he murmured, half rising from his chair.

'I have broken my word to you,' said Geoffrey, still seemingly unconscious of the presence of a third person. 'I am sorry, but I cannot help it. You followed the directions he gave you, and nearly met your death. We came back together, and found him playing the flute in the garden, dancing to it as he played. Then you went into the house. I remained outside and watched him. He went up the knoll to the two houses, and tried the door of the ice-house. He found it locked, opened the summer-house and looked in. Try to reconstruct what was in his mind. He made no allusion to his mistake. Had he already forgotten that he had given you a direction that nearly sent you to your death? Or was the mistake yours? He told you to go to the left hand of the two houses, so you said to me. Is that the case?'

Harry did not at once reply: he looked eagerly, imploringly at his friend, but he could find no words to express a feeling he could not comprehend; he did not know ever so vaguely what he thought. In despair and utter perplexity, he faced quickly round to his uncle. Mr Francis was sitting with half-closed eyes; his hands, like the hands of a blind man, groped and picked at the buttons in the arm of his chair, stricken helpless. Suddenly, as if with a drowning effort, he threw his head back, and saw Harry.

'No, no,' he said, 'not the left hand, not the left hand. I never said that. Oh, the Luck, the cursed, cursed Luck! I could not—indeed, I could not—have said the left hand. "Do not go to the left hand by mistake"; I can hear myself saying the words now. Oh, weary, weary day! But you went there, you went to the ice-house instead of the summer-house, you went from the brightness of God's sunshine into the dark, to that edge, to the edge of the well. Oh, my God, my God!' and the cry was wrung from him like water from a twisted cloth.

The old man buried his face in his hands, collapsing like a broken doll. He regarded neither Harry nor his accuser, the anguish of his spirit covered him like a choking wave, and into it he went down without a struggle, but only that moaning sob, a sight and a sound to stagger the unbelief of an infidel. And Harry—no infidel, but a lad of kindly heart and generous impulse, quick to believe good, a laggard to impute harm—could not but be moved.

Geoffrey neither looked at the bowed figure nor wavered, and his face was flint. But though that moaning cry, that passionate incoherence did not move him, yet the sight of Harry's face, with its bewilderment of perplexity and compassionate trouble, filled him with a sudden fear. To himself that bent and venerable head was a mockery of grief, a fraud finished and exquisite, and he was more afraid of Harry's divided mind, on which Mr Francis played as on an instrument of music, than he had been of the evil and hunted face that had come down from the gun-room, as he stood behind the curtain, in those dead hours ten days ago.

Mr Francis sat huddled in his chair, his face invisible, his fingers clasped in his white head, and long dry sobs lifted and relaxed his figure like the pulsation of a wave. And though Geoffrey, so few minutes ago, had turned himself to steel, he could not go on speaking with that silent stricken figure in front of him. The low, heart-broken murmuring, the silent sobs—filched resolution from him. Once or twice he began to speak, but no sentence would come. As many times he told himself that he must go on, that he knew that this feigned anguish was a thing to awake horror or laughter, but never pity. Yet it affected him as a scene in the play affects the stalls. It was all unreal, he knew it was unreal, yet he could not immediately speak. Suddenly, and before long, it seemed, while he was still cursing his infirmity of purpose, Harry came to his side.

'Go away, Geoff, go away,' he whispered. 'Leave me with him. Whatever you have to say, you cannot and must not say it now. Look there and judge. It may kill him. Go away, there's a good fellow!'

He got up at once; that was enough. Harry was still willing to hear him; now or at another time, it did not matter. All he wanted was that Harry should hear him to the end, and then his part was done. Exposure! there was no pleasure in the act of it; he only wanted that it should be there. Truly, the man was vile, and an enemy, but he did not covet the post of executioner as such. By him, it is true, justice was done; the murderer was put out of a world with the welfare of which his presence was incompatible, and a man to do it there must be; but who did not shudder at the shadow of the hangman? That dry, inarticulate sobbing, which he had no need to tell himself was but a counterfeit grief, yet wore the respectable semblance of woe. What, again, if remorse had at length touched Mr Francis? What if the imminence of his exposure had at last revealed to him his immeasurable enormity? If such a possibility was within the range of the most distant horizon, how contemptible would be his own part in trampling in a truth that was realized! All that was generous within him—and there was nothing that was not—revolted from so despicable a role.

But against that possibility, how large and near loomed the probability that these grovelling pangs were but of the same texture as the rest! No, he was not taken in. He registered privately the unalterable conviction that Mr Francis was Mr Francis still, for no opprobrious word conveyed to him half the horror of all which that canonized name implied. Yet Harry was by him, asking him, not bidding him, to go. That was sufficient, and even as he told himself it was sufficient, back swung the balance again. What duty could be more obvious, more staring, than to finish now at once with that ineffable old man! Yet he sat there sobbing. And without another word Geoffrey turned and went, leaving uncle and nephew together.

It was not long before Harry joined him in the smoking-room.

'Uncle Francis has gone to his room,' he said. 'He is quieter now; I could leave him safely. But I have telegraphed for the doctor; I daren't take the responsibility of not sending for him. He kept asking me one question, Geoff; he kept repeating and repeating it—Which of you two is to go? He says he will not stop here another night if you remain here. God knows whether I have decided right.'

'It is I who go, you mean?' said Geoffrey.

'Yes, it is you.'

Harry sat down wearily, as if tired out. That, too, was his prevailing feeling: body and mind were dead-beat. Geoffrey rose.

'Since that is so,' he said, 'I ask you before I go to hear the rest of my story; indeed, I must tell it you. Then I shall have done all I can. Oh, it will not take long,' he added, with a sudden inexpressible bitterness. 'In half an hour I shall be gone.'

Harry sprang up as if he had been stung.

'I do not deserve that from you, Geoff,' he said. 'Do you think I want to get rid of you? Do you think it is fine fun for me to tell you to go? I am not conscious of any great pleasure in it.'

'No; I am sorry,' said Geoffrey. 'I had no business to say that or think that. But oh, Harry, before I go, for the dear Lord's sake, hear me! I have not been speaking idly. Do you think, in turn, that it is fine fun for me to get up and bring these awful accusations against Mr Francis?'

'Of course I don't. But the whole thing I have to put on one side for the present. Uncle Francis will not stop in the house while you are here, Geoff, and I cannot let him go, whatever the truth may be, while he is like this. I dreaded every moment that a seizure might come on him again. Besides, he is an old man; he is my uncle. For the present, then, I am like this: I neither believe what you have told me, nor do I disbelieve it. I put it aside, though before long, when my uncle is recovered, I shall have to do one or the other. Either I shall believe, be convinced you are right—and then God knows what I shall do!——or I shall think your accusations wild and incredible, and, I warn you, too infinitely base for words. And then, too,' he added suddenly, 'God knows what I shall do. But at present, as I tell you, there is no question of that. My certain and immediate duty is to look after Uncle Francis.'

'I ask you, then, before I go,' said Geoffrey, 'to hear the remainder of what I have to say.'

'Certainly; but, whatever you tell me, I shall not attempt to judge of it now. You had just spoken about the confusion which came in somewhere between the ice-house and the summer-house.'

So Geoffrey told him of the loop of cotton he had found round the post of the gun-rack, of Mr Francis's visit to the gun-room, and finally of his own finding him in the afternoon, after the breaking of the sluice, sitting before the fire in the hall, 'supposing' that Harry had not yet come in. And Harry heard in silence and without comment.

'That is all?' he asked, when Geoffrey had finished. 'You are sure there is nothing more? You are sure, also, you have been exact throughout?'

'That is all,' said Geoffrey, 'and I have been exact.'

'Then, dear old boy,' said Harry, 'let us for the present put it from our minds. Your carriage will be round in ten minutes; I told them to pack for you. And tell me that you agree with me when I have to ask you to go. I feel, I know, that I cannot do otherwise.'

'Yes, you are right, and God guard you,' said Geoffrey.

Then suddenly the whole flood of fears and suspicions and certainties surged in his mind together and over-flowed it. He was leaving Harry alone with that hellish man. Who knew what he might not attempt next? Every fibre in his being cried aloud to him that danger of subtle and deadly sort hung suspended over Harry, imminent to fall so long as that white-haired old man was under the same roof. But what could he do? He could not force Harry to see the clearness of that which was so clear to him. He could not even make him exercise his judgment upon it. And his anxiety for him broke bounds.

'Yes, you are right,' he said. 'But I cannot persuade myself that I am right to go. Oh, Harry, I ask you once again, do you tell me to go?'

Harry go up and leaned his head on the chimney-piece.

'Don't make it harder for me, Geoff,' he said.

Here was a ray of hope.

'I will make it as hard as I can,' said Geoffrey.

'I appeal to anything that will move you. We are old friends, Harry. Wiser and better friends you will find, but none more faithful. You are doing a cruel thing.'

Harry turned round suddenly.

'Stop!' he said. 'I tell you to go. Oh, Geoff, who is doing the cruel thing? You know. Oh, my God, won't this nightmare cease?'

Geoffrey saw his lips quivering; his own also were not steady. He came close to him, and laid his hands on his shoulders.

'What have we done, Harry,' he said, 'that this should happen to us? You have answered me. But promise me one thing; I insist on that.'

'I will promise you anything you think right to ask me, Geoff,' said he, 'and you know it, provided only it does not make me cancel what I have said and what I have decided to do.'

'It does not. It is simply this: Three times within the last ten days you have been in imminent danger. God knows what it all means, but it is certain that many dangers surround you on all sides. I ask you to promise to be careful. I don't ask you to consider all I have told you now; you must do that when you feel that you can. You promise me this?'

'Willingly.'

'And let it be soon that you consider what I have said. Judge the thing as you would judge for another, and God send you the right judgment. That is all I want.'

'Amen to that,' said Harry.

Chapter 20

Dr Armytage Arrives

DR ARMYTAGE, for whom Harry had telegraphed, arrived about nine that night. He had left London immediately on receipt of the summons, without dining, and, having seen his patient, came downstairs to join Harry in a belated meal. In appearance he was a dark man, and spare, his chin and upper lip blue-black from a strong crop of hair close-shaven; heavy eyebrows nearly met over his aquiline nose; his mouth had a certain secrecy and tightness about it. But his manner was that of a man reserved but competent; his thin, delicate hands were neat and firm in their movements, and Harry, torn and distracted by a world of bewilderment, found it an unutterable relief to have put one out of all his perplexities—the care of his uncle—into such adequate hands.

For the moment, at least, the boon of the doctor's arrival quite overscored that sinister impression he had formed of him when in the summer he had passed him driving to the station.

With regard to the patient, he was grave, but not alarming. Grave, however, one felt he would always be, and Harry remembered Mr Francis's criticism of him—that he knew too much, and had always in his mind the most remote consequences of any lesion, however insignificant.

'I can give you no certain account of him tonight, Lord Vail,' he said. 'I found Mr Francis in a lethargic state, the natural reaction from, so I understand, an agitating scene that took place this afternoon. I did not even speak to him, for I thought it better not to rouse him, as he seemed in a fair way to get a good night's rest. But I spoke to his man, who told me that he thought something agitating and painful had taken place. May I ask you if that is the case?'

'Yes,' said Harry. 'A friend of mine, Mr Francis, and I had a terrible scene this afternoon.'

'Can you tell me about it—the merest outline only? You see, if Mr Francis experiences any return of this agitation, which is, to put it frankly, so dangerous, it might be very likely useful that I should know about it, and be able to soothe him with something more specific than wide generalities.'

Harry paused. They were alone over dessert.

'It is all very horrible,' he said at length, 'and I can hardly speak of it. But I can tell you this: within the last ten days I have had three narrow escapes from a violent and sudden death.'

Dr Armytage put down with neat haste the glass he was raising to his lips, and gave Harry one quick glance from below his bushy eyebrows. Startling though the words were, you would hardly have expected such sudden alertness and interest from so self-contained a man.

'Yes?' he said.

'Well, for one at least of these my uncle blames himself,' said Harry. 'That certainly was one of the causes of his agitation, though perhaps not the greatest immediate cause. Oh, it is awful to speak of it!' he cried. 'Tell me what you advise. Had I better tell you everything?'

'I repeat, it may possibly be of use to me,' said the doctor. 'All you say, of course, will be under the seal of my profession.'

The servants had entered the room with coffee, and Harry did not immediately reply. Templeton, as usual, carried the case of the Luck, and even as he took the jewel into his hand Harry hurriedly filled a wineglass.

'The Luck,' he said, in no very cordial tone. Then, turning to the doctor, 'Please excuse me,' he said; 'it is a custom I have got into. Yes, that is the Luck; my uncle may have spoken to you about it. You would like to look at it?'

The doctor waved it away.

'Another time—another time,' he said, and waited till the servants had left the room. Then, 'Yes,' he continued, 'I have heard Mr Francis speak of it. An extraordinary delusion in so clear-headed a man, is it not? He thinks—I hope I am not intruding into family secrets, Lord Vail—he soberly thinks that the Luck brings blessings and curses on your house. I may say that the idea almost possesses him.'

'Surely you are mistaken,' said Harry. 'He is always laughing, sometimes even he is distressed, at my believing—ah, not believing, but thinking I believe in it. But very curious things have happened,' he added.

'There is doubtless some mistake,' said the doctor. 'But to return: all you tell me will be under the seal of my profession.'

'You mean that I speak to one who is necessarily as silent as the grave,' said Harry. 'You will pardon my insistence on this.'

'I give you my word on it,' said the doctor.

'Well, it is a strange, dark story,' said Harry, 'and if I speak a little incoherently, you will know by the end what perplexities I am in. Now, there are two kiosque sort of places near the house—one is a summer-house, one an ice-house. I got the keys one morning, and asked my uncle which was which. He told me quite distinctly that the left hand one was the summer-house. He made a mistake, and I went whistling into the ice-house—they were both shuttered and quite dark inside—and came within an ace of falling into the big tank. I am quite sure I went to the one he told me was the summer-house.'

'Number one,' said the doctor.

'Next morning he went up to London,' continued Harry, 'and I and Geoffrey Langham (this friend of mine who left today) were going out for a day's shooting. My gun was standing in the rack, and as I took it up, it went off, narrowly missing me. The last person who had used that gun, and who had left the cartridge in it, was my uncle.'

'Number two,' said the doctor.

'Today he and I went out together and looked at the flooded lake. I tried to raise an extra sluice that we have, and, finding that I could not make it move, we went up towards the farm to get men to help. But, again at his suggestion, he went on to the farm and I went back to have another try at it. As I was standing on the main sluice, pulling, the whole thing gave way, and I went down with the flood-water, as near to being drowned as anyone can wish to be. My uncle had thought the sluice not very safe, but he had not thought it worth mentioning.'

The doctor was silent awhile.

'You bear a charmed life, Lord Vail,' he said at length; 'but I think you have more to tell me.'

Harry gave him one dumb, appealing glance, and met eyes which were grave but not unkind, firm and deeply interested. He had the impression that they had long been watching him.

'Yes, I have more, I have more,' he said with agitation, 'and it is horribly painful. Dr Armytage, I have two great friends—or so I think—my uncle and this Geoffrey Langham, a fellow of my own age or thereabouts. This afternoon, to my uncle's face, though I am bound to say he would have preferred to tell me privately, Geoffrey made horrible insinuations, accusations. He said that Uncle Francis had long been my enemy; that he had tried to prevent my engagement to Miss Aylwin; that he had failed there, and that in this affair, for instance, my uncle had intentionally—had intentionally——' And a strangling knot tied itself in his throat, choking utterance.

The doctor pushed the water-bottle gently a little closer to Harry, and he poured himself out a wineglassful and drank it, unconscious that any suggestion had been made to him.

'Then there was an awful scene,' he went on. 'My uncle was nearly off his head, I believe, with remorse and horror for those words which had so nearly sent me to my death, and this was aggravated, I must suppose, by black, ungovernable rage against Geoffrey. I felt that I had never seen an angry man before. He refused to stay another night in the house with him; he asked me continually which of them it was who should go. He could not go—of that I was convinced—in that state, and I sent Geoff off. Besides, I cannot, simply I cannot, believe in Geoff's accusations. It is flatly impossible that Uncle Francis should be guilty of the least intention which Geoff attributed to him. Do I not know him? There must be some other explanation. And if you want to know what my other explanation is, it has stood in front of you all dinner. It was the Luck; fire and frost and rain—the ice-house, the gun, the sluice. Oh, it has happened once before like that.'

'Yes, Mr Francis told me,' said the doctor, still looking very intently at him.

Harry flicked the ash off his cigarette.

'Here am I, then,' he said; 'of my two best friends, one lies upstairs, the other—God knows if I shall ever see the other again. I have to tell him whether I believe what he said, and I cannot believe it. It is monstrous; he is monstrous to have thought it. Yet I see why he thought it; to anyone not believing in the Luck there was no other explanation. There are other things too; I need not trouble you with them. He came to the conclusion, for instance, that my uncle wished to stop my engagement—prevent it, rather, for I was not engaged then. They were specious; good Lord! they were specious enough. But I have been considering them all, and I simply cannot believe them. It is not that I wilfully shut my eyes; I hold them open with pincers and chisels, so to speak, but I am unable—that is clear—to believe anything of this. How could it be possible? God does not allow such things, I tell you.'

'That is your verdict, then? You believe nothing against your uncle?' said the other, with an intonation absolutely colourless.

'I cannot.'

'May I tell your uncle this, Lord Vail?' asked the doctor presently. 'If his agitation returns, I can think of nothing which would so much tend to soothe it as the assurance that these accusations are to you absolutely void and empty—these vile accusations,' he added in a moment.

'Yes, they are vile,' said Harry, half to himself.

'May I, then, use my discretion to tell him so, if I think it desirable?' asked the doctor, pressing his point. 'It would be better, I think, for me to tell him than you. That would be agitating work for both of you,' he said, watching the lad closely.

'Oh, you may tell him whatever you please!' cried Harry, with the sudden petulance of nerves utterly over-wrought.

Instantly the doctor's face changed. The symptom for which he had been waiting had come.

'Now, then, Lord Vail,' he said, with a peremptoriness which startled Harry, 'I do not want two patients instead of one. You were on the verge of hysterics, let me tell you. We will have none of that, please.'

This treatment was shrewd and prompt. Judging rapidly and correctly, he saw that any word of sympathy or kindness would be likely to throw Harry altogether off the balance, and he was justified when, in answer to this rough speech, he saw an angry flush spring to his face. 'I am not accustomed to be spoken to like that,' he said hotly.

'No, it was a liberty on my part,' said the doctor. 'Please excuse it. But I think you will acknowledge that I was right. You are your own man again now.'

Harry considered this a moment, then smiled.

'Yes, you were perfectly right,' he said candidly. 'But I have had rather a trying time today.'

'Indeed you have, and I may say now that I am very sorry for you. I recommend you therefore to go to bed, and not to write to your friend tonight, nor to think what you will say to him when you do.'

'And to go to sleep very quietly and soundly till morning,' said Harry. 'Excellent advice, Dr Armytage.'

'Oh, you will do all these things if you follow my directions,' said the doctor.

'I should like to hear them, then.'

'To drink the dose I will send you up to your room,' he said quietly.

At that moment, as if by a flashlight suddenly turned on, Harry saw himself again meeting at the lodge gates this man for whom, at first sight, he had conceived so violent and instinctive an antipathy, and simultaneously the curious adventure in the search for Dr Godfrey shone in his mind. What if, after all, Geoffrey was right, and he himself was alone in this house with a man such as his friend had pictured Mr Francis to be, and his mysterious confederate physician, whose ways were so dark? The suspicions which had seemed to him so utterly beyond the horizon of credibility leaped suddenly nearer; and when he spoke, though he tried to make no alteration in his tone, even to himself his voice sounded unusual.

'I don't think I shall require any doses,' he said. 'I dare say I shall sleep all right. Thanks, all the same.'

'Ah! you don't trust me,' said the doctor in the same quiet tone.

This exceeding frankness both pleased and offended Harry.

'Is it not a pity to say a thing like that,' he asked, 'when you really have no warrant for it?

To show you how wrong you are, I will take your dose with pleasure.'

The doctor's grave face relaxed.

'That is right, Lord Vail,' he said. 'But do you think your now consenting to take it proves that I was wrong? Might not a man consider that it showed I was right?'

Harry smiled also.

'A man of sufficient ingenuity can make plausible the most extravagant conclusions,' he said, rather enjoying this tiny fencing-match.

'True; we will not draw any at all, since there is no need,' he said. 'And now, with your leave, I will go up and see Mr Francis again. I hope and trust I shall find him asleep.'

'I shall be in the hall,' said Harry; 'please give me your report as soon as you have seen him.'

Dr Armytage went upstairs, and Harry lit a cigarette and waited his return. Dinner and the presence of this capable man had to a large extent quieted his jangled nerves, and he was conscious, more than anything, of a great weariness. The acuteness of his perplexities had for the moment worn off a little, and though their aching weight was no less, they pressed on him, so it seemed, without the fret of sharp edges. He resolutely set himself not to think of them, but rather of that exquisite point of happiness which was day by day coming nearer to him. Evie would be in England in less than a fortnight now; five weeks brought him to that day to which his whole life hitherto seemed to have been leading up. But suddenly the claws and teeth again recaptured him: Geoffrey was to have been his best man, and now—and with that his feverish mill-race of bewildering possibilities began again, and it was a relief when the doctor reappeared.

'Mr Francis is sleeping, I am glad to tell you,' he said. 'Thanks, I will smoke one cigarette before I go upstairs, and when I go, you go, too, if you please, Lord Vail. I have put your dose in your bedroom.'

'Thanks, I will take it. I am tired.'

The doctor settled himself in a chair.

'Yes, that tiredness is exactly what my dose will give a chance to,' he said. 'You are tired and excited—a horrible combination!—and your excitement would certainly keep you awake. That I hope to remove by this sedative draught, and let your tiredness act naturally. But I must really congratulate you on your nerves. In the last ten days you have had enough escapes to last a lifetime, and upon my word you don't look used up. A very fine nervous constitution. Mr Francis also used to have the same power of going through things that would have caused most men to break down utterly.'

'Yes; he has been through awful trouble,' said Harry; 'and really he does not seem more than a man of sixty.'

'Trouble of the most horrible kind!' said the doctor. 'May I ask you, Lord Vail, if Miss Alywin is any relation to—'

'Yes,' interrupted Harry; 'her mother was Mrs Houldsworth.'

'I see you know the story; I was associated somewhat closely with it. I was, in fact, the doctor who gave evidence at the coroner's inquest.'

Again Harry forgot his own perplexities.

'Ah! tell me about that,' he said.

'There is little to tell. The conclusion I arrived at was that the death of Mr Houldsworth might easily have been accidental or self-inflicted—that it was, in fact, the gun he carried which killed him. That of course, was the crucial point. The nature of the wound appeared to me compatible with that interpretation.'

'I knew that you were an old friend of my uncle's,' said Harry, 'but I did not know that your association with him was so intimate as that.'

The doctor was silent a moment, then threw his smoked-out cigarette away.

'I tell you this,' he said at last, 'as a sort of testimony or recommendation, what you will. I came here as a stranger to you; you have received me with very cordial hospitality, and I present,' he added, 'my credentials.'

Harry rose, and held out his hand.

'They are extremely satisfactory,' he said; 'and now for my dose and bed. You sleep in my uncle's sitting-room, I think you said? I hope they have made you comfortable?'

'I have everything,' said the doctor. 'By the way, speaking of your friend Mr Langham, I may tell Mr Francis that he has left, if I think it wise?'

'Certainly, if you wish.'

'That he has gone to London?' suggested the doctor casually.

'As a matter of fact, he has gone to his father's house for a few days, down near Sevenoaks—Lord Langham, you know.'

'Ah, yes,' said Dr Armytage. 'Good night, my dear Lord Vail; I am convinced you will sleep well.'

Half an hour afterwards the house was dark and quiet. Harry had drained his dose, and was sleeping deeply and dreamlessly; Mr Francis was not more wakeful. The night was warm and mellow after the heavy rain, and Dr Armytage sat long at his window looking out with fixed, undeviating eyes into the blackness. At intervals some real or fancied stir from the sick-room would make him rise mechanically, and, crossing the floor, look in on his patient. Once Mr Francis in his sleep called out, 'Harry, Harry, take care!' in a strangling, agonized voice. But even then he did not wake, and the doctor returned again to his seat in the window, and still gazed out into the night. The rain had ceased soon after sunset, and now the sky was nearly clear, and star-inwrought; in the east the moon would soon be rising. But he regarded not, nor saw either stars or the climbing crescent.

At length a striking clock aroused him, and he got up. 'No, no—a thousand times no!' he said to himself.

Chapter 21

Geoffrey Meets the Doctor

DR ARMYTAGE, despite Lady Oxted's round and uncompromising definition of him as a dexterous surgeon of sinister repute, proved himself during the next day or two to be far more intimately acquainted with the vital structure of the animal called man than is at all necessary for one who only concerns himself with the dissection of artery and muscle and the severing of bones. Under his wise and beneficent care, Mr Francis rapidly rose again to his accustomed surface, and, no less testimony to his skill, Harry once more looked the world squarely and courageously in the face. These inner and spiritual lesions require for their healing, not only a skilful diagnosis, but a mind of delicate and certain touch; and of his two patients, the doctor was inclined to think that Harry made the more flattering recovery. During these days he kept uncle and nephew studiously apart. He would allow no visits to the sick-room, and communication was limited to messages passed to and fro by the doctor himself. Mr Francis, on the one hand, was bidden to keep his bed for three days, and quiet was insisted on; quiet, on the other hand, was sternly forbidden to Harry. For him the prescription was to go out as much as possible, and busy himself with any employment—all were good—which he found congenial, and when indoors to apply himself slavishly to all the businesses which Mr Francis had hitherto managed for him.

'Oh, you have plenty to do,' said the doctor to this harassed young gentleman; 'go and do some of it.' But among these things which had to be done was an affair of difficulty—the letter which must be written to Geoffrey.

This, when he put his hand to it, Harry found to be a black, bitter business, and sheet after sheet was begun and abandoned. Had he realized it, he was attempting the impossible; for he had set himself to write a letter which should at once be thoroughly friendly, and yet spit on the allegations which his friend had made. The writer alone did not see that such a letter could not be written even by Solomon, Shakespeare, and the original serpent in conjunction. Thus for a couple of hours one evening Harry wrote and tore, reducing wooden penholders to matchwood, and quires of fair white paper to grist for the housemaid in her fire-lighting, yet still the envelope was no nearer to its postage-stamp, and the dressing bell, indeed, showed him only a brimming wastepaper basket. He could not write this letter; here was the flat truth.

At this juncture the doctor entered the smoking-room, which Harry had chosen to be the arena of these futile endeavours, and a glance at his clouded face seemed enough for him.

'It is difficult, I admit,' he said. 'Ah, you must not be offended with me, Lord Vail. I have guessed right, I know; we doctors have to be thought-readers. You have been making'—and his eye fell on the paper-basket —'many unsuccessful attempts to write to your friend. Perhape I ought to have saved you that trouble.'

Harry turned a dark face on his.

'I am sure there is no secret about it,' he said. 'As like as not I should have told you. I can't write this letter—I just can't write it. Yet I must. But when I begin to tell Geoff the truth, that he has done a dastardly thing, and that I can never see him again, and that I love him just as much as ever, well, the whole thing becomes unreal at once.'

'Yes, those are hard words to a friend,' said the doctor.

'I know, and I am not hard. I love that chap, I tell you. You don't know him; so much the worse for you, for you don't know the best old fool God ever made. I'm just hungry to see him, and I've got to tell him that he is a base cad. Oh, confound the whole round world! By the way, you said you should have spared me this trouble. What do you mean!'

Dr Armytage took a chair close to the table where Harry was failing to write.

'Three days ago, Lord Vail, when I first arrived,'
he said, 'I offered you a sleeping-draught, which
you refused. I suggested that you refused it because
you distrusted me. Tell me, now, was I right in
suggesting that?'

Harry looked straight, as his wont was, at the
dark, secret face he had once thought so sinister.
To him now it appeared only sad.

'What has that got to do with it?' he asked.

'Was that suggestion right?' repeated the
doctor.

'Yes, quite,' said the other frankly.

'Just so. Eventually you did trust me, or at any
rate behaved as if you did, and you found your
confidence not misplaced. You awoke, in fact, after
a good night's rest. And now, if you grant that,
you owe me the benefit of a doubt.'

'Well?'

'I ask you to trust me again,' said the doctor; 'for
the fact is, I have already written to your friend
myself, telling him not to expect a letter from you
yet. I knew that you would find it impossible to
write to him, and it seemed to me that if I wrote
at once, as I did, it would save him some anxious
hours. That is my confession.'

Again Harry tried to feel what he told himself
was a just resentment, but the sentiment that he
raised in his mind was but a phantom. He ought,
so he considered, to feel that his liberty was being
tampered with; but this curiously self-possessed man
appeared to have the gift of impeccable meddling.
Then he laughed outright.

'I simply do not know what to say to you,' he said. 'You take it upon yourself to interfere with affairs of mine that do not in the least concern you, and yet I don't really resent it.'

'In that you are quite wise,' said the doctor.

Harry threw down his pen.

'And not content with that, you patronize me and pat me on the back,' he said. 'I am not at all sure that I intend to stand it. Pray if I may so far interfere in your concerns, what did you say to Geoffrey?' he asked, with a show of spirit.

'I told him not to expect a letter from you yet,' said the doctor. 'I told him not to be impatient and wish for knots to be cut, as long as there was the faintest hope of their being unravelled.'

'Ah, there is not the faintest,' broke in Harry.

'You too, then acquiesce in the cutting? I hope your friend is more reasonable. You have no right to say, while the thing is yet so recent, that a reconciliation of your friend and Mr Francis is impossible. And if that were possible it would comprehend, I take it, a reconciliation with you.'

'Oh, you don't know Geoff, I tell you,' said Harry. 'He will never apologize. He is not given to rush at conclusions, but when he has concluded, he is more obstinate than all the beasts that perish. You waste your trouble if you expect him to recant.'

The doctor rose.

'I repeat, it is too early to expect anything,' he said. 'A difficult situation takes time; if it does not take time, it is not difficult. One thing alone I was certain of, that any letter from you, believing as you do so utterly in your uncle's absolute innocence—if I could put your feeling more strongly, I would—could not tend to mend matters. It would only accentuate your estrangement, temporary, I hope, with your friend. And now, have I your pardon for doing what I have done?'

'Not yet,' said Harry. 'What else did you say?'

'I said that you were as safe here as in the Bank of England. I asked him to be reasonable. Supposing his wild surmise was true, and that you had a very bitter enemy of your own blood in this house, how could he be so foolhardy as to make another attempt on you just now, when three had so conspicuously miscarried, and such suspicious circumstances were in Mr Langham's knowledge? For the circumstances,' he said, looking gravely at Harry, 'were suspicious.'

'I know they were,' said Harry. 'Poor old Geoff! Well, I couldn't have written that letter if I had tried till midnight.'

He got up also, as the dinner-gong sounded.

'That's dinner, and we are not yet dressed,' he said. 'But you were quite right to do it for me, Dr Armytage,' and frankness became him infinitely better than reserve, 'and you might have added that I have a very good friend here who looks after both my uncle and myself.'

Dr Armytage smiled rather grimly.

'I came to the conclusion that such a statement would not have increased his confidence,' he said, 'either in me or in your safety. There is no sense in gushing, particularly if one gushes about one's self.'

That night, when the doctor had made his last visit to Mr Francis, he brought him as usual some small affectionate message from Harry, and Mr Francis yawned, for he was sleepy, and made no immediate reply. But in a moment or two he roused himself.

'My love—my very best love,' he said, 'and add some amiable doxology. By the way, how do you and he get on together? Is it very trying? I am afraid so. But it is of the utmost importance that you should gain Harry's confidence—that you should make him trust you.'

'So you told me, and without boasting I think I may say I have been fairly successful. I made a good beginning, you know, the first night I was here.'

'Ah, yes, that sleeping-draught?' said Mr Francis appreciatively. 'A little bromide of potassium, you told me; quite simple and harmless. A charming drug, and an ingenious idea. Yes, Harry's consenting to take a sleeping-draught from your hands certainly showed that, if he was disposed not to trust you, he was fighting that inclination. And you have improved your advantage, dear Godfrey?'

'Yes, we are on excellent terms. And to tell you the truth, I do not find it trying at all. Your nephew is both amiable and intelligent.'

'Poor Harry!' said Mr Francis softly. 'Yes, his very simplicity has a certain charm, has it not? It is also a very convenient quality. Well, I am to go to sleep,

I suppose: I sleep so well now. And you intend to take me to London at the end of this week?'

'That was the proposal,' said the doctor.

'And you, being an autocrat—for indeed doctors are the only autocrats we have left—insist on it. I assure you it will be the best plan. That young cub who left the other day has wits of a kind: he is rather sharp. It will quiet his outrageous suspicions, I think, if I leave Vail soon. I hope Harry will not be very dull alone,' he added.

'He may not choose to stop here,' said the doctor.

'It does not matter,' said Mr Francis. 'He is certain to come back here before his marriage, to see that the house is quite ready to receive them after their honeymoon. I count on that. By the way, do you call him "Harry" yet?'

'No.'

'Dear Godfrey, how short and glum you are! I never make monosyllabic replies; they are so unnecessarily curt. Try to call him by his Christian name; it produces an admirable effect, and so cheaply. Practise saying "Harry, Harry", when you are alone. You will find it makes it easier. Ah, well, I must go to sleep. Good night, my dear man.'

It was therefore definitely settled and announced to Harry that Mr Francis and the doctor should leave for London at the end of the week. He would be the better, so said the doctor, for a change; for the very dark and autumnal weather which had settled down on Vail during the last day or two was of depressing influence, and he strongly recommended a week or so in London, where the little arrangements and excitements incidental to settling in a flat would keep him agreeably occupied.

Mr Francis dined downstairs on the last night before he left, and seemed his buoyant self again. During the afternoon incessant bubblings from the flute had come from his room, and that sound had been to Harry like the voice of some familiar friend returned. His uncle, indeed, had playfully prefaced his own entry into the hall, after the gong had sounded, with the tune of 'See the conquering hero comes', a little thin on this solo instrument, but he had marched in time to it with an incomparable gaiety, with foot high lifted and a pointed toe.

'And you, dear Harry,' he said, as they had seated themselves after Mr Francis's 'grace', 'what are your plans? I was half inclined to rebel when our dear autocrat gave me my marching orders, and I heard that you perhaps would be left here alone, but my disaffection was quelled by a look. Has Godfrey given you any of his quelling looks, I wonder? But how long do you stop here?'

'Three or four days only now,' said Harry, 'then I go to the Oxteds' for a week, and come back here by the beginning of November for ten days. After that, London till the fifteenth.'

'Dear fellow, so near as that—so near as that, is it?' said Mr Francis. 'Ah, Harry,' and he held out his hand to him. Then seeing that the serious note was slightly embarrassing to the young man:

'Ah, Templeton has given us the Luck again!' he cried, changing the subject abruptly. 'Upon my word, the thing seems to grow brighter and more dazzling each time I see it. This nephew of mine, I must tell you, my dear Godfrey, is a very foolish fellow in some ways. He almost—I may say almost, Harry?—believes in that old legend; really a remarkable survival of superstition among the educated classes. I shall write to the Psychical Research about it. That amiable society collects nightmares and superstitions, I am told. A quaint hobby.'

'I have drunk obediently to the Luck night after night, have I not, Harry?' said the doctor.

'Of course; it is the rule of the house. By the way, let us set that point at rest. Dr Armytage told me that you believed in the Luck, Uncle Francis. I simply couldn't credit it. You have always ridiculed me for even pretending to.'

Mr Francis laughed.

'Harry, these medical men cannot keep a secret,' he said. 'No, my dear boy, I am only joking; but it is quite true that I have found myself wondering, after your extraordinary series of accidents early in the year, whether it were possible that there could be anything in it.'

He paused a moment, and then went on quite naturally.

'And these last three horrible escapes of yours,' he said. 'How strange! The ice-house—frost; the gun—fire; the sluice—rain. "There are more things in heaven and earth—" Well, well!'

Here was proof at any rate that Mr Francis knew how entirely Harry trusted him, and though, at the thought of that awful scene between Geoffrey and his uncle, the lad was startled at so direct a mention of that which had caused it, it was something of a relief to know that the subject did not cause Mr Francis pain.

'Yes, taken all round, it would be sufficient to convince the most hardened sceptic,' said Harry. 'Poor old Luck! what an abominably futile business it has made of it all!'

Mr Francis suddenly covered his face with his hand.

'Ah, it won't do to jest about,' he said. 'I spoke lightly, without thinking; but I find I cannot quite stand it, dear Harry. It is too recent, too terrible!'

At this the talk veered to less intimate subjects, and before a couple of minutes had passed, Mr Francis was again in that exuberance of spirits which had made him play 'See the conquering hero comes'. He had always some contribution, apposite and gay, to make to the conversation, capable of fantastic development and garnished with pleasant conceits. But for him the meal would have somewhat languished; for whether it was that Harry's old habit of reserve had returned to him, or that his thoughts were again a prey to the perplexities which his uncle's words might have recalled, he was unwontedly silent, while on the part of the doctor it seemed that a somewhat absent assent or dissent, and that only when directly appealed to, was all he had to give. But Mr Francis was the man for the moment; he rose to the social emergency, and he told a hundred little anecdotes, diversified and amusing, and the growing silence of the other two was but a foil to the amazing agility of his tongue. But the most capacious mill is emptied at last, and about the time of dessert spent and dropping shots without effect were the only remnant of that loquacious artillery. And it was in silence that the first glasses of port were poured out, and to break a notable hush that Harry rose.

'The Luck!' he said. 'I drink to the Luck!'

The doctor and Mr Francis rose to the toast, the latter with too eager alacrity. His napkin, which he flung on the table, caught his glass, and the wine was spilled.

On the Saturday that the doctor and Mr Francis were travelling up from Vail, Geoffrey was also going to London, in consequence of a strangely unexpected summons. He had duly received the doctor's letter a week ago, and this had been followed three days later by a shorter note, informing him that he and Mr Francis were leaving Vail for London on the Saturday following, and asking if Geoffrey would give the writer an opportunity of seeing him on a matter the importance of which could not be estimated. Dr Armytage would be at his house that evening between five and seven, and if these hours would not suit, he asked Geoffrey to name any time which was convenient to him after their arrival in London, and he would make a point of being in then, laying any other engagement he might have aside. Then followed a notable sentence.

'It occurs to me,' wrote the doctor, 'that you, following the thread of the suspicions of which Lord Vail has spoken to me, may see in this request a deep-laid scheme for ensuring your presence in London on a given day and hour, and your certain absence from any other place. But I beg you to ask yourself why, if such was the case. I should have written to you at all. I may add that Mr Francis Vail and I reach Paddington at 12.37 (mid-day) on Saturday. Be at the station, if you will, and assure yourself that we have left Vail.'

So far the letter ran with the precision and orderliness of a dispatch. Then followed the signature, and after the signature a strange postscript.

'I must see you, I must see you!' read Geoffrey, and the writer's pen had spluttered with the underlining of the words.

No very long consideration was necessary, but knowing from Lady Oxted what he did of the doctor's antecedents, it was clearly possible that he might be placing himself in a position of some personal danger. To attempt to form any accurate idea of the scheme which might conceivably lie latent behind this letter was an idle task; but what he saw, and that without shadow of doubt, but with a certain exultation, was that it was he above all men whom Mr Francis had most reason to fear, and as long as he went at large, with all the circumstantial evidence that he held, it was clearly very unlikely that any further attempt would be immediately contemplated against Harry, for the risk would be prodigious. So far, then, it looked that this letter might be a bold and cunning scheme to get him, too, into the power of this hellish man. On the other hand, he could not neglect this possible chance: the letter might conceivably be genuinely inspired. Looking at it coolly, as was his habit of mind, he thought that this balance of probability dipped to the sinister side; this Dr Armytage was far more likely to be Mr Francis's confederate than a disinterested doctor, or a foe. Yet there was a certain touch of truth about the spluttering pen of the postscript, and Geoffrey's debate was but of short duration.

Then, with wonderment at his own slowness of wit, next moment the obvious safeguard struck him, and he telegraphed to the doctor at 32, Wimpole Street, that he would meet him at five o'clock at the junction of Orchard Street with Oxford Street. This was conveniently near to his own lodgings, where they could retire to hold conference if it appeared that there was reason for it, while it would be scarcely possible for anyone, even with the legions of hell to back him, to spirit away an active young man from that populous thoroughfare without attracting public attention.

Geoffrey arrived in London late in the forenoon, and spent a couple of hours in writing out, with the most minute particulars, the account of all those incidents on which his suspicions were founded, and which had led to his scene with Mr Francis. This he sealed up in an envelope, and with directions on the outside that, in case nothing more was heard of him till Monday mid-day, it was to be opened.

He put this into a large envelope, addressed it, with a short note, to his father, and posted it. Finally, before he set out for his rendezvous at the corner of Orchard Street, he slipped a loaded revolver into his breast-pocket to guard against the very remote possibility of his being attacked in his own rooms. Its presence there, though not unattended with qualms—for he was something of a stranger to this branch of firearms—yet filled him with a secret glee of adventure.

Punctually at five he arrived at the appointed corner, and a few moments' observation of the shifting and changing crowd was enough to enable him to single out a man, spare and dark, who also lingered there. It was evident, too, that he had observed Geoffrey, no less than Geoffrey had observed him, and on the third or fourth occasion that their eyes met, the man crossed the street to him.

'Mr Geoffrey Langham?' he asked, and to Geoffrey's silent gesture of assent: 'I am Dr Armytage.'

They turned and walked a little way down Oxford Street before either spoke again. Then said the doctor:

'Your plan was reasonable, that we should meet in some public place; it was natural that you should not wish to trust yourself to my house. But I would suggest, if we are to talk in public, that we get into a hansom, or I should prefer a four-wheeler.'

'Why?' asked Geoffrey.

'Because we are dealing, or I hope shall soon be

dealing, with a very subtle man, who, for aught I know, may be watching either you or me.'

Geoffrey wheeled round quickly.

'Come to my rooms in Orchard Street,' he said—'No. 12; I will walk on the other side of the road.'

The distance was but a few dozen yards, and three minutes later the two men were in the sitting-room, which overlooked the street. Geoffrey pointed to a seat, and waited for the other to open the conversation.

'I repeat,' said the doctor, 'that your amendment of my plan was reasonable, for you have little reason to trust me.'

'It seemed to me so,' said Geoffrey. 'I thought it wise to take that and other precautions. But it was you who asked for this interview; kindly tell me what you have to say.'

'It is told in two words,' said Amytage. 'Your friend Lord Vail has, by almost a miracle of luck, escaped from three well-devised schemes against his life. Thrice has Mr Francis failed. We cannot expect such luck to continue.'

Not a muscle of Geoffrey's face moved.

'You mean he will make another attempt?' he said.

'He will certainly make another attempt.'

Geoffrey's hands were playing with a box of cigarettes on the table, opening and shutting the lid in a careful and purposeless manner.

'Here, smoke,' he said, 'and give me a minute to think.'

The doctor took a cigarette, lit it, and waited. He had smoked it half down before Geoffrey spoke again.

'You see my position,' he said at length. 'There is no harm that I can see in my telling you that I know how intimate you are with Mr Francis. I am wondering whether possibly I may be aiding him and you by seeing you; for your intimacy with Mr Francis was very close as much as three-and-twenty years ago, at the time, let us say, of the violent death of George Houldsworth. That is so, I believe?'

'Certainly,' said the doctor. 'I received, I may tell you, two thousand pounds for the service I did Mr Francis at the corner's inquest.'

Geoffrey looked up quickly.

'Ah! that sounds genuine,' he said.

'About that you must decide for yourself,' said the doctor.

Geoffrey snapped down the lid of the cigarette-box, took out of his coat-pocket the revolver he had placed there, and laid it on the table close to the doctor's hand.

'I have decided, you see, to trust you,' he said.

'Perhaps my parting with that revolver is an unconvincing proof, for it would certainly be incautious of you to shoot me here and now, but I can think of nothing better. There it is, anyhow.'

Dr Armytage took up the revolver and opened it.

'Six chambers—all loaded, I perceive,' he said.

'Let me return it you as I received it. I have no use for it.'

Geoffrey took it from his hand, and put it back in the table-drawer.

'And now let us talk,' he said.

An extraordinary look of relief crossed the doctor's face; the whole man seemed to brighten to the eye.

'I hardly dared hope you would trust me,' he said, 'and your affection for your friend must have been strong. But let us waste no more time. Yes, your suspicions were quite correct. Harry Vail has no bitterer enemy than his uncle. He has made no less than three attempts to put him out of the way.'

'You speak as if you were sure of it,' said Geoffrey.

'I am; but what evidence have we? It would not take a lawyer ten minutes to tear it to shreds; for it is entirely circumstantial, and weak at that. There is the devilish cunning of the man. Again, if we are to save Harry, we must save him in spite of himself, for he believes not a word of it and we deal with a man who is cunning and utterly unscrupulous, far more cunning probably than you and I put together. But we have one great advantage over him.'

What is that?' asked Geoffrey.

'The fact that he counts on me to be his accomplice. If we succeed I am to have ten thousand pounds.'

At these words distrust again flared high in Geoffrey's mind, refusing to keep silence.

'God give you your portion in hell,' he cried, 'if you are playing a double game!'

The doctor showed no sign of resentment, but he did not immediately reply.

'This will not do at all,' he said at length. 'Either you trust me or you do not. If you do not, I will go; we are but wasting words. I may remind you, however, that if I am playing a double game, my conduct in wishing to see you is utterly unaccountable, but if not, that it will be barely possible for me alone to save your friend; for it is my strong impression that Mr Francis's man—Sanders, is it not?—will help his master. Come, which is it to be?'

'Yes, yes, I trust you,' said Geoffrey in great agitation. 'I ought never to have said that. Please go on.'

'I can give you no certain details yet,' said the doctor; 'but the attempt will be made between Harry's return to Vail from Lady Oxted's, where he goes in a few days, and his moving to London before the marriage. So much I have gathered from Mr Francis. It is, you will understand, of the utmost importance to him that the marriage should never be consummated. More exactly than that I cannot tell you, but I want you in any case to hold yourself in readiness to come to Vail or anywhere else at a moment's notice, and at a word from me.'

'Yes, I promise that,' said Geoffrey.

'The particulars I cannot give you,' continued the doctor, 'for I do not yet know them; indeed, I doubt whether Mr Francis has yet worked them out himself. But today, as we were coming up in the train, he blew on his flute a long time, and then said suddenly to me: "I have a new hobby, the properties of certain powerful drugs. We will have some great talks about drugs when we are in London." From this I gathered that he means to poison Harry.'

'The damned old man!' exclaimed Geoffrey.

'Precisely. Now, his motive, you know, is plain. He is heir; but from what I have seen of him lately he sets less store by that than on the fact that Harry's death will give him the Luck.'

'But he doesn't believe in the Luck,' said Geoffrey. 'I have heard him laugh at Harry a hundred times for pretending to believe in it.'

'There you are wrong,' said the doctor. 'I should be rather tempted to say that the Luck is the only thing in the world he does believe in. I tell you this for an obvious reason: he is not sane on the point. We are dealing with a monomaniac, and he is more to be feared than a sane man—he will run greater risks to secure his end. But it is late; I must go. During the next week I shall certainly have the whole of Mr Francis's plans, for I shall refuse to help him in any way unless I know all. Good-bye; you will please stop in London till you hear from me.'

Geoffrey got up.

'Tell me,' he said, 'when did you determine to help Harry?'

'I do not think that if I told you you would trust me the more,' said the doctor.

'I assure you I shall not trust you less.'

Dr Armytage took his umbrella from the corner.

'A fortnight ago only,' he said, 'on the day I first saw Harry. Think of me as you will, so long as you do what I tell you: I really care very little about anything else, even whether you trust or mistrust me, provided only you behave as if you trusted me. Yes, till I saw him, and spent the evening with him on the day you left, prescribed for his agitated nerves, and gave him a sleeping-draught——'

'I'm glad I didn't know that before,' said Geoffrey frankly.

'It might certainly have caused you some uneasiness. But not till then did I decide to save him if I could, and not to do—the other thing. And every day strengthened my decision, and the thought of the ten thousand pounds grew less attractive. My reason is hard to give you—convincingly at any rate. It was due perhaps to a great charm and attractiveness which Lord Vail possesses; it was due perhaps to an idea in my own mind that I would not commit murder. That sounds a little crude, does it not? Good-bye, again.'

Geoffrey held out his hand.

'I trust you,' he said, 'quite completely, and so, it seems, does Harry. I do not believe that we are both wrong.'

Dr Armytage turned quickly away without a word. A moment afterwards the street-door banged behind him.

Chapter 22

Lady Oxted Has a Bad Night

HARRY was sitting cross-legged on the hearthrug after dinner, poking the fire in an idiotic manner with the tongs. Gun-cotton would have smouldered out under so illiterate a stroke. He was also talking with about equal vivacity and vacuity to Lady Oxted and Evie; but while his conversation was not more than difficult to bear, his poking of the fire was quite intolerable. Lady Oxted got swiftly and silently up from her chair, and, in the manner of a stooping hawk, took the instrument from him.

'We can attend better, dear Harry,' she said, 'to your most interesting conversation if you do not distract our minds by making a bayonet of improper fire-irons. You can do that after we have gone to bed.'

'They are improper,' said Harry; 'but my sense of delicacy forbade my telling you so. How a respectable woman like you could tolerate their presence in the house has been more than I was able to imagine. 'But now the ice is broken—oh, I never told you about the ice-house—no more I did.'

Lord Oxted looked up from the evening paper which he was reading distractedly but diligently, and made a bee-line for the door. His exit, though made without protest, was somewhat marked. He had no manners, as his wife often told him.

'The ice-house,' said Harry, as if he was giving out a text to a diminishing congregation, and a spicy emphasis was required to retain the rest, 'and the gun and the sluice.'

The shadow of Lord Oxted lingered a moment in the doorway at this alluring selection, but immediately disappeared on the next words—'I'll make your blood run cold.'

'Has the Luck been singing its nursery rhymes?' asked Lady Oxted, uncertain what to do with that white elephant the tongs.

'Singing?' cried Harry, digging the shovel into the fire—'singing, quo' she! My good woman, I can and will a tale unfold, which, if you have tears, prepare to shed them now,' said he with a felicitous air.

Lady Oxted annexed the shovel also. Thus there were two white elephants.

'I am not the washerwoman, Harry,' she remarked with reason.

'No, dear aunt,' said he, growing suddenly grave; 'and if I hadn't been so absurdly happy tonight, I shouldn't have made a joke of it; for, indeed, it was no joke. Anyhow, the doctor congratulated me on my admirable nerves.'

'Some people, when they prepare to tell a story,' said Lady Oxted, 'begin at the beginning. Others—this is without prejudice—begin at the end, and work laboriously and slowly backwards. Let me at least ask you, Harry, not to be slow. Tell me about this doctor, as we are to go backwards. Did his name begin with an A?'

'Quite right,' said Harry; 'and it went on with an R.'

Lady Oxted dropped her white elephants on the carpet, and sat down by Evie.

'Armytage?' she asked; and the fooling was gone from her voice.

'Right again. You had much better tell the whole story for yourself, hadn't you?'

'No; when other people begin to talk about the Luck, I take no part in the conversation,' said she, 'except, at least, when Geoffrey is here, and then I talk of Bears and Bulls.'

The Harry who had played bayonet with the tongs had by this time vanished; vanished also were the flying skirts of farce, and in absolute silence on the part of his audience, and in gravity on his own, he told them the three adventures, narrating only the salient facts, and alluding neither directly nor otherwise to Geoffrey or his uncle. But while his tale was yet young Evie crossed from the sofa where she had been sitting with Lady Oxted, and joined Harry on the hearthrug. One hand held her fan, the other was on her lap. Of the latter Harry easily possessed himself, and the tale of the gun was told with it in his. But as he spoke of the raking gash that riddled the cornice and ceiling of the gun-room, it was suddenly withdrawn and laid on his shoulder.

'Oh, Harry, Harry!' she murmured.

He turned and stopped, spontaneously responsive.

'My darling,' he said, 'I ought never to have told you; only I could not help telling you some time, and why not now? Was it not better to tell you like this, making no confidence of it?'

If ever a word ought to have carried the weight of a hint, the word was here. But Lady Oxted showed not the slightest sign of following her husband, or saying she must write two notes.

'Go on, Harry,' she said. 'We are waiting. So the gun went off?'

But Harry turned to the girl.

'It is with you,' he said. 'Will you have the third adventure? Simply as you wish. Here am I, anyhow.'

'Yes, tell us,' she said.

At the end Lady Oxted rose crisply.

'I never heard of such impotent magic in all my life,' she said. 'Really, Harry, if you must tell us supernatural experiences in the evening, we have a right to expect to be pleasantly frightened. But I have never been less frightened. You whistled your way into an ice-house, you took up a gun carelessly, you stood on a piece of unsafe stonework. If I were you, Evie, I should buy him a nice leading-rein.'

These brutalities were effective, and banished the subject, and, without pausing to comment or let others comment, Lady Oxted sent for her husband, and they sat down to a table of bridge.

'The only thing I insist on,' he said, 'is that my wife shall be my partner. Her curious processes of thought, when she is engaged in this kind of brain-work, are a shade less disconcerting and obscure to me than they would be to others. *Aimer c'est tout comprendre.* And if I do not quite understand them all,' he added, as he cut for deal, 'I understand more than anyone else. Eh, dear Violet?'

Lady Oxted's brow was always clouded when she played bridge, and tonight the blackness of the thunderstorm that sat there was not appreciably denser than usual. She played with a curious and unfortunate mixture of timorousness when the declaration was with her, and a lively confidence in the unparalleled strength of her partner's hand when the declaration was passed to her. Thus, at the end of two hours, as these methods tonight were more marked than usual, the house of Oxted was sensibly impoverished. But with the rising from the card-table her disquieted looks showed no betterment, and her husband offered consolation.

'We can easily sell the Grosvenor Square house,' he said, 'if that is what is bothering you, Violet, and if that is not enough we can give up coffee after dinner, and have no parties. The world is too much with us.'

'And with the proceeds we can buy a hand-book

on bridge,' said she with spirit. 'I will give it you for a present at Christmas, Bob. Let us go to bed.'

Lady Oxted employed in the almost daily conduct of her life methods which she characterized as diplomatic. A less indulgent critic than herself might have labelled them with a shorter and directer word, yet not have felt that he was harsh, for the diplomatic methods did not exclude what we may elegantly term evasions of the truth. Tonight, for instance, she talked with Evie for a few minutes only in her bedroom, and exacted a promise that she would go to bed at once, for she looked very tired. For herself, she would have it known that her head was splitting and that if she got influenza again she would turn atheist. With these immoderate statements she secured herself from interruption, and went, not to bed, but to the smoking-room, where she found Harry alone. The rustling of her dress made him look up quickly, and the most undiplomatic disappointment was evident on his face.

'No, I am not Evie,' remarked this clear-sighted lady. 'She is tired and has gone to bed, so I came for a chat with you. Dear Harry, it is so nice to see you again. But what terrible adventures you have been through! I want to hear of them more particularly, but I thought it would frighten Evie to talk of them longer. That is why I was abrupt to you.'

'And so she is tired. Diplomacy,' said Harry.

'Yes, just a touch of diplomacy,' assented Lady Oxted, 'for she looked scared and frightened. Now, were you alone when all these things happened, or was Dr Armytage there? And how did Dr Armytage come to be at Vail at all?'

'He came to Vail,' said Harry, 'on the evening of the third affair, the breaking of the sluice. I telegraphed for him because I was frightened about my uncle. He is liable, you know, to cardiac attacks, and I was afraid of one coming on.'

'He was naturally agitated at your series of escapes,' said Lady Oxted.

'Naturally,' said Harry.

Lady Oxted rose with some impatience, and threw diplomacy aside.

'Your efforts at dissimulation are pitiable, Harry,' said she. 'If you won't tell me what happened, say so; I am going to fish no more.'

Harry did not immediately reply, and Lady Oxted continued.

'Seriously speaking,' she said, 'I think I ought to know. If there is nothing more, if your conscience allows you to say that there is nothing to tell, I am content. If you cannot say that, I think you ought to tell me.'

'Do you not think that you are putting an unfair pressure on me?' asked Harry.

'No; for you are no longer only your own master. You must consider not only yourself, but Evie. In her mother's absence, I have a certain duty towards her. I do not ask you from curiosity, but because of the relations in which both you and I stand to her. You have within the last few weeks been in three positions of extreme danger. Can you, however vaguely, account for this? Have there been no suspicious circumstances of any kind which might lead anyone to think that these were not entirely accidents? You say that Geoffrey was in the house on all these occasions. Did he take it all as lightly as you seem to?'

'I would rather not bring Geoffrey into it,' said Harry.

'Have you quarrelled?'

'Yes; I suppose that you may say that we have quarrelled,' he replied.

'Harry, why will you not tell me, and save my asking you all these questions? I intend to go on asking them. Was your quarrel with Geoffrey connected in any way with these accidents?'

'Oh, give me a minute,' cried Harry. 'I want to make up my mind whether I am going to tell you or not. I suppose if I did not, you would go to Geoff?'

'Certainly I should,' said Lady Oxted promptly, although this had not occurred to her.

'Well, it is better that I should tell you than he,' said Harry, and without more words he told her all that he had purposely left unsaid, from the mistaken direction which had sent him to the ice-house instead of the summer-house, down to the scene in the smoking-room when he had parted with Geoffrey. She heard him in silence without question or interruption, and when he had finished, still she said nothing. Apt and ready as she was for the ordinary social emergency, she could frame nothing for this. She could not say what she thought, outspokenly like Geoffrey, for Harry's sake. She would not say what she did not think, in spite of her diplomatic tendencies, for her own.

At last the silence became portentous, and Harry broke it.

'Have I, then, lost another friend in addition to Geoffrey?' he said, in a voice that was not very steady.

He could not have given her a better lead.

'Ah, do not say things like that, Harry,' she said. 'You do not think it possible, in the first place, and even if you did it would be no part of wisdom to say it. But I tell you frankly that, though Geoffrey seems to me to have spoken most hastily and unwisely, yet I can understand what he felt. There are, I don't deny that I see it, many curious circumstances about all these adventures which lend reasonableness—pardon me—to his suspicions.'

'I know—I know all that,' said Harry; 'but I find it a sheer impossibility to believe them in any degree at all. Geoffrey's suspicions are out of the question. That being so, I cannot away with what he has done, with the speaking of my uncle like that; I cannot away with that condition of mind to which, however plausible the idea, the idea was possible.'

Lady Oxted was a quick thinker. She knew, moreover, that to decide wrong was better than not to decide at all, and before Harry had finished speaking she was determined on her line of action. Geoffrey, she rightly guessed, had at least as much influence with Harry as herself; yet Geoffrey, in all the heat and horror of these adventures, had been powerless to move him. Her chance, then, speaking at this cooler distance, had scarcely the slightest prospect of success, and secret coalition with Geoffrey was evidently preferable to open collision with Harry.

'I see—I quite see,' she said; 'but, oh, Harry, do not throw away a friend lightly. Geoff is a good fellow, and you must remember that it was for your sake that he risked and suffered a quarrel with you. Friends are not so common as sparrows. You will not find them under every house-roof. Don't do anything in a hurry—wait. No situation is hopeless until you have given time a chance to work. Don't write—if you have not already done so—any angry letter, or, worse, any dignified, calm, world-without-end letter. It is so easy to make an estrangement permanent; you can always do that.'

'I haven't written at all,' said Harry. 'I tried to, but I could not do it. There is no hurry; besides, Geoffrey will not expect to hear from me. Dr Armytage wrote to tell him not to.'

Lady Oxted just succeeded in suppressing the exclamation of surprise that was on her lips.

'That was very kind of him, and wise as well,' she said.

'He is both the one and the other,' said Harry. 'He was down at Vail a week; I liked him immensely. But I don't mind telling you that I was glad to get away—to part with him, with Uncle Francis, with the Luck for a time. I felt as if there was some occult conjunction against me, and I didn't like it. I had continually to keep a hold on myself, to make an effort not to be scared. But here I am being beautifully relaxed; I feel secure. Yes, that's the word.'

Lady Oxted continued her diplomatic course.

'There is nothing so catching as superstitition,' she said, 'and all the evening, since you told Evie and me about it, I have been wondering—— Oh, it must be all nonsense!' she cried.

'You mean the Luck?' asked Harry. 'Is Saul also among the prophets?'

'Yes, I mean the Luck. How does the nursery rhyme go? Fire and frost and rain, isn't it? Well, there they all were, and it is no use denying it.'

'Not the slightest,' said Harry.

'Certainly it is very strange. Harry, I don't like the Luck at all; it's uncanny. I wish you would smash it, or throw it into the sea. Yet somehow I feel as if you are safe as long as you are here, away from it. I wish you would stop here till your marriage. Then you go away, you see, for six weeks, and in the meantime some burglar might be kind enough to steal it.'

Harry shook his head.

'No; I put the good things it has brought me much higher than the evil,' he said. 'And it is going to bring me another very good thing—the best. After that, if you like, I will smash it.'

'Well, stay here till your marriage, anyhow.'

'I must go down to Vail once to see that they have finished up; the house was upside down when

I was there. But, barring a couple of days then, there is nothing I should like better. You will have nearly a month of me, though. Consider well.'

'Then stop till I tell you I cannot bear you any longer. I am a candid woman, and fond of giving pain, and I promise to speak out. Dear me, it is nearly one! I must go to bed, and if I dream of the Luck it will be your fault.'

Lady Oxted did not dream at all for a very long time that night. She was at her wits' end what to do. All Scotland Yard, with all the detectives of improbable fiction thrown in to aid, were powerless to help; for the evidence against Mr Francis in Harry's story, though conclusive to her own mind, would weigh lighter than chaff in cross-examination, and no further evidence was procurable until Mr Francis made another attempt, and at the thought she shuddered. What, too, was that sinister doctor doing at Vail? What was the meaning of the seeming friendliness in averting a final rupture between Harry and Geoffrey? He had written, according to his own account, a letter to Geoffrey which should avoid this; but what did his letter really contain? It was far more likely that he had told him that the rupture was final, for clearly he and Mr Francis would not want to risk the possibility of Geoffrey, who knew all, and whose attitude was so avowedly hostile, coming down to Vail again. The only consolation was that Harry for the present was safe, and that she could go up to London next day and see Geoffrey. But what could they do even together? What defence was possible when the blow might fall at any moment from any unsuspected quarter?

By degrees, as she paced her room, a kind of clearness came to her. Mr Francis's design was evident; he had shown his hand by the nature of his earlier attempts in which he had tried to stop Harry's marriage. Then, in the miscarriage of that, he had turned to directer deeds—fouler they could scarcely be, but of more violent sort. There had been a species of awful art in his doings; he had taken, with a fiend's gusto and pleasure in the ingenuity of it (so she pictured), Harry's avowed superstition in the power of the Luck to compass his ends. As a musician takes a subject, and on this theme works out a fugue, as an artist paints a portrait in a definite preconceived scheme of colour, so had Mr Francis taken the Luck, and the dangers it was thought to bring to its possessor; these he had elaborated, put into practical shape. It must have dwelt in his mind like a lunatic's idea; not only, as in the case of the gun, did he make his opportunity, but, as in the affair of the ice-house, he must have been alert, receptive, instinctively and instantaneously turning to his ends whatever chance put in his way.

This thought brought her a certain feeling of relief on the one hand, but on the other it added an indefinite terror. No man morally sane could devise and steadily prosecute so finished a scheme; the very thoroughness and consistency of the three attempts stamped them as the work of a madman. Nine-tenths of the blood murderously shed on the earth was to be put down to a spasm of ungovernable anger and hate which at the moment possessed the murderer; this long premeditation, this careful following of one idea by which frost, fire and rain should be the direct causes of Harry's death, was not to be attributed—so devilish and so finished was the application—to a sane author. Here lay the consolation: her shuddering horror of the white-haired old gentleman, with his flute-playing and his boyish yet courtly manner, was a little assuaged, and gave way to mere human pity for a mind deranged. But simultaneously, as if with a clash of cymbals, her fear of him clanged in her breast; that cunning of a madman was far more formidable than the schemings of a sane man. He would soon, maddened by failure, reck nothing of what happened to him so that he attained his object.

What, then, looking at it thus, was his object? The mere death of Harry, merely the lust for blood? That seemed hardly possible; she could not put him down as a homicidal maniac, since it seemed that he had no desire to kill for killing's sake, and the world was not yet staggered with a catalogue of subtle undetected murders. Nor was the explanation that he wished to inherit Vail and its somewhat insufficient revenues more satisfactory. He was old, he had, so far as anyone could guess, no wish for more of this world's goods than he possessed under Harry's generosity; the motive could scarcely be here. Then, in a flash, a more likely solution struck her. The Luck—perhaps he wanted the Luck! A year of ownership, so she told herself, had already affected even Harry's sanity in this regard. What if here was a man, old and already poised on the edge of his dug grave, who all his life long had dreamed of and itched for it, believing God knew what was in store for its possessor? This, she guessed, was the taint of blood, the same that so mysteriously, though uncriminally, possessed Harry. Here, perhaps, was the cause—not the fire and the frost and the rain, but the belief in their perils, coupled with the belief in great and unwonted good fortune which the possession of it gave. Mr Francis had more than once in her hearing laughed at Harry for his fantastic allegiance to the heirloom, but this, if anything, confirmed Lady Oxted in her theory; this cunning was of consistency with the rest.

Long since she had dismissed her maid, and, tired with fruitless thought and baffled with but dimly cipherable perils, she finished her undressing and blew out the lights. But through all the dark hours she was clutched by the night-hag; now the Luck appeared to her like the Grail in 'Parsifal,' emitting an unearthly radiance; but even as she gazed, she would suddenly be stricken with the knowledge that the brightness of it was not of heavenly but of diabolic birth. A piercing light emanated therefrom, but of infernal red, and voices from the pit moaned round it. Then it would be gone, and for a little while a wriggling darkness succeeded; but slowly the break in the blackness which heralded its coming would begin to shine again and grow intolerably bright; faint lines where it would shortly appear stretched themselves upon the field of vision, growing momentarily more distinct; but, instead of the Luck, there came first in outline, then in awful and indelible vividness, the features of Mr Francis, now very kind and gentle, now a mask of tormented fury.

Next morning she found that her resolve to see Geoffrey without delay had not been diminished by the shattered phantoms of the night, and some lame toothache excuse served her end. She did not certainly know whether he was in London or not, and, for safety's sake, she sent him two telegrams, the one to his father's house in Kent, the second to his lodgings in Orchard Street, both bidding him come to lunch that day in Grosvenor Square without fail. The one addressed to London found him first, since, after his interview with Dr Armytage, he had stayed on there, and this, followed after an hour's interval by the other, sent on from his father's house, constituted a call of urgency. He, therefore, obeyed the summons, leaving a note for Dr Armytage, as had been agreed between them, to say when he should be in again and where he had gone.

The conference began after lunch. Each found it in a measure a relief to be able to confide the secret haunting sense of peril to another. Each, on the other hand, was horrified to find that someone else shared the apprehensions each still hoped might be phantasmal. Geoffrey, on his part, had his account of his dealings with Dr Armytage to add to Lady Oxted's information, she her own conviction that they were dealing with a man not morally sane, whose one desire was to have and to hold the Luck. To her this alliance with Dr Armytage, of which Geoffrey told her, seemed but a doubtful gain.

'What does one know of him?' she asked. 'Nothing that is not bad. Mr Francis could not have chosen a more apt or a more unscrupulous tool. He got two thousand pounds, you tell me, for his services in connection with the Houldsworth case. What will he not do for ten? Oh, we may be dealing with a cunning of which we have no conception! What if all this was told you simply to blind you? Nothing can be more probable, and how admirably it has succeeded! Already you trust the man—their object, as far as you are concerned, is gained.'

'I had to trust him or distrust him,' said Geoffrey, 'and I chose to do the former. If I had chosen the latter the door would have closed on it, and I do not see that we should be any better off than we are now. If he is dealing straight with us, we have an immense advantage in knowing all he knows of Mr Francis's plans; if he is not, he can at the most give us misleading information, which is not worse than none at all.'

Lady Oxted considered this in silence a moment.

'Yes, that is true,' she said; 'yet somehow my flesh misgives me to be allied with that man. Oh, Geoffrey, is it because this awful Luck has cast a spell on us that we imagine Harry surrounded by these intimate and immediate perils? Are our fears

real? Let us tell ourselves that we are ordinary
people, living in an age of prose and policemen;
we are not under the Doges! This is the nineteenth
century,' she said, rising, 'or the twentieth, if you
will. We look out on Grosvenor Square; a hansom
is driving by.'

She stopped suddenly.

'I am wrong,' she said, 'it is not driving by. It
has stopped at the door, and Dr Armytage has rung
the bell. Oh, what shall I do?' she cried. 'God in
heaven, what are we to do? What has he come
to tell us?'

Geoffrey got up.

'Now quietly, quietly, Lady Oxted,' he said. 'He
has come on a matter of importance, or he would
have waited till I returned to Orchard Street. I have
decided to trust him, and I suggest, therefore, that
we see him together. It is our best chance; it may
be our only one.'

'But I don't trust him,' said Lady Oxted. 'I distrust
him from head to heels.' And she bit her finger-
nails, a thing she had not done since the days of
the schoolroom.

'Very well, then, I shall run on my own lines,'
and he got up to leave the room.

'Wait, Geoffrey,' she said. 'You are absolutely
determined?'

'Absolutely.'

'I yield, then. You, at any rate, have some plan,
and I have none. Yes, show Dr Armytage in,' she
said to the man who had brought his card.

Chapter 23

The Meeting in Grosvenor Square

THE doctor entered with the brusqueness of a man who had no knowledge of, or, at any rate, no regard for, the usages of polite society. He treated Lady Oxted to little more than his profile and an imperceptible pause, which indulgence might construe into a bow, then walked straight up to Geoffrey, with face businesslike, concentrated.

'I had important information,' he said, 'which I was desirous of telling you without delay. My hansom is waiting.'

Geoffrey felt his heart thump riotously, a heavy, repeated blow.

'We have to act immediately, you mean?' he asked.

'No, not that,' said the doctor. 'I only thought——' and he looked for a brief moment at Lady Oxted. She rose.

'How do you do, Dr Armytage?' she said. 'Mr Langham and I were, when you entered, talking about the same business as that on which you have come. Harry Vail, I must tell you, is a great friend of mine; he is staying with me now. Last night he told me the history of the past fortnight very fully. It will not therefore surprise you to learn that I came up to London today to see Mr Langham.'

'It does not surprise me in the least,' he said. 'I take it, then, that you wish me to speak before you? If that is so, I will send my hansom away.'

He was back again immediately, and waited till the others sat down, warming his hands at the fire, with his back turned to them. The silence, so to speak, was of his own making, and neither thought to interrupt it. Then, facing them, he spoke.

'There is no need, therefore,' he began, as if continuing his private train of thought, 'that I should speak at any length of what has already happened. Harry, I gather, has told you, Lady Oxted, of his three escapes; he has told you also of his quarrel with his friend here, and the reason of it?'

There was something in his bald abruptness which pleased Lady Oxted; it looked genuine, but at the same time she made to herself the conscious reservation that it might be a piece of acting. If acting, it was a very decent performance. She gave a silent assent.

'You have asked me to speak before you,' he went on, 'but in doing so I am somewhat at a personal disadvantage. I have no reason to suppose that you trust me; indeed, there is no reason why you should. You know of me probably as an intimate friend of Mr Francis, and when it appears that I am a traitor to him, you naturally ask yourself if I am really so. But'—and he paused a moment—'but I do not think that this need much concern me. I am here to tell you in what way Mr Francis hopes to kill his nephew. It is our object, I take it, to prevent that.'

There was something in his tone that smacked of the lecture, so dry and precise was it; but a clearer observer of him than either of his present audience, to whom the words he said were so much more just now than the man who said them, would have seen that an intense agitation quivered beneath the surface. The man was desperately in earnest about something.

'There is one more preliminary word,' he went on. 'We are dealing, so far as my observations go, with a man who is scarcely sane. In the psychology of crime we find that such patient, calculated attempts to take life are usually associated with something else that indicates cerebral disorder, some fixed idea, in short, of an insane character, which is usually the motive for the homicidal desire. That symptom is present here.'

'The Luck!' exclaimed Lady Oxted.

'Precisely. The idea of owning the Luck possesses our—our patient. He believes that it brings its owner dangers, possibly, and risks, but compensations of an overwhelming weight. He believes, I may tell you, that it will keep off death, perhaps indefinitely; and to an old man that is a consideration of some importance, especially if he has such an exuberant love of life as Mr Francis has. On the other hand, we must remember that before the last outbreak, if we may call it such, Mr Francis procured the death of a man who stood in no relation to the Luck. Yes, he shot young Houldsworth,' he said slowly, looking at Lady Oxted, 'for nothing more or less than the insurance money. One may have doubts whether all crime of a violent kind is not a mere form of insanity; but that particular form of insanity is punished with hanging.'

It is by strange pathways that a woman's mind sometimes moves. She, may take short-cuts of the most dubious and fallacious kind to avoid a minute's traversing of the safe road, or walk a mile round in order to avoid a puddle over which she could easily step, but she at any rate knows when she has arrived, and at this juncture Lady Oxted got up and held out her hand to the doctor.

'I entreat your pardon,' she said, 'and in any case I trust you now.'

A certain brightness shone in those dark, sad eyes as he took her hand.

'I am glad to know that,' he said, 'and I advise you, if possible, to continue trusting me. You will have a trial of faith before long.'

Geoffrey moved impatiently. All three seemed to have forgotten their manners.

'Oh, go on, man, go on!' he exclaimed.

'Bear in mind, then,' said the doctor, 'that we may be dealing with a lunatic. This fixed idea inclines me to that belief; the murder of young Houldsworth pulls the other way. But Mr Francis has made his plans; he told me them this morning—for I, as you will see, am to figure in them—and what he will do is this.'

The doctor again paused, and adjusted his finger-tips together.

'He expects Harry,' he said, 'to return to Vail before the end of the month, He and his servant will return about the same time, or perhaps a day or two earlier, for there will be a few arrangements to make. I shall also accompany Mr Francis, so he tells me, on the ground of his continued ill-health.'

'Ah! those heart attacks,' said Lady Oxted; 'are they genuine?'

'Perfectly; they are also dangerous. To continue: On the night appointed—that is to say, as soon as we are all there—I am to administer to Harry a drug called metholycine. In all respects it is suitable for Mr Francis's purpose, and a small dose produces within a very few minutes complete unconsciousness, to which, if no antidote or restorative is applied, succeeds death. It also is extremely volatile, more so even than aconite, and a very few hours after death no trace of it would be found in the stomach or other parts of the body. The drug, however, is exceedingly hard to get. No chemist would conceivably give it to any unauthorized person; but a few years ago I was experimenting with it, and it so happens that I still have some in my possession. Mr Francis has a most retentive memory, and though I have no recollection of ever having mentioned this fact to him, he asked me this morning if I had any left. He did so in so quiet and normal a voice that for the moment I was off my guard, and told him I had.

But perhaps, after all, it was a lucky occurrence, for he seemed much pleased, and played on his flute for a time. Then he came back to me, and told me what I have already told you, and what I shall now tell you.'

There was something strangely grim about the composure of the doctor's manner. You would have said he spoke of Danish politics. More grim, perhaps, was this mention of the flute-playing. Certainly, it added an extreme vividness to his narrative, and the flute-player was more horrible than the man who planned death.

'In this respect, then, first of all,' continued the icy voice, 'I am useful to him. In the second place, Mr Francis seems to have a singular horror of doing himself, actually and with his hands, this deed. In another way, also, I shall be of service to him; and here I must touch on things more gruesome, but it is best that you should know all. The drug is to be administered late at night, after the servants are out of the way. It is almost completely without taste or odour, and Mr Francis's suggestion is that a whisky-and-soda, which he tells me Harry always takes before going to bed, should be the vehicle. Ten minutes after he has taken it he will be unconscious, but he will live for another half-hour. During that time we shall carry him down to the plate-closet, where the Luck is kept with the rest of the plate. There Sanders will be. That part will be in Sanders' hands, but he will not use firearms for fear of the noise of the report reaching the servants, and the blow that kills him, you understand, looking at the occurrence from the point of view of the coroner, must be dealt while he is still alive; otherwise the absence of effusion of blood and other details would show a doctor that he was already dead when his skull was broken—this is the idea—by a battering blow. Here again Mr Francis anticipates that I shall be of use to him in determining when unconsciousness is quite complete and death not yet immediate. He has a curiously strong desire that Harry should feel no pain, for he is very fond of him.'

Lady Oxted and Geoffrey alike were glued to his words, both paler than their wont. As the doctor paused they sought each other's eyes, and found there horror beyond all speech.

'Some of the most valuable of the plate,' continued the doctor, 'will be taken, and, of course, the Luck. The plate will be the perquisite of Sanders; the Luck Mr Francis will keep secretly, the presumption being that it was stolen also. Why, then, you may ask, should not Mr Francis simply steal the Luck? For this reason: that as long as Harry lives it is his; on his death it becomes Mr Francis's. Thus, morning will show the plate-closet rifled and Harry clubbed to death on the floor. The plan is complete and ingenious; indeed, it has no weak point. It will appear that Harry, after the servants had gone to bed, drank his whisky-and-soda, and hearing something stirring, went downstairs. Finding the door of the plate-closet open, he entered, and was instantly felled by a blow on the side of the head, which killed him. The burglars did not rouse anyone else in the house, and escaped—even the details are arranged—by the same way as they entered, through the window of the gun-room, which looks out, you are aware, on to the garden-beds which adjoin the sweep of the carriage-drive. Footprints of large, heavy boots will be found there; Mr Francis bought a pair today at some cheap, ready-made shop.'

Again a horror palpable as a draught of cold air passed through the auditors, seeming to each to lift the hair from the scalp. These trivial details of boots and flute-playing were of almost more intimate touch than the crime itself; they brought it, at any rate, into the range of realities, to the time of today or next week, to a familiar setting. Again the doctor spoke.

'I have already taken one precaution,' he said. 'I have emptied from its bottle the real metholycine, and substituted common salt. I went to my house hurriedly after seeing Mr Francis to get it, and I brought it away in my pocket. I shall be glad to dispose of it; it is not a thing to carry about.'

He drew out a small packet, folded up with the precision of a dispensing chemist, and opened it. It contained an ounce or two of white, coarse-grained powder, very like to ordinary salt, and, without more words, he emptied it on the fire. The red-hot coal blackened where he poured, then grew red again, and for a moment an aura of yellow flame flickered over the place.

'And Mr Francis will not find it easy to get more,' said the doctor.

The effect of this was great and immediate. Both Lady Oxted and Geoffrey felt as much relieved as if an imminent danger had been removed, though the logic of their relief, seeing that they both trusted Dr Armytage, in whose domain the poison lay, was not capable of bearing examination. At any rate, Lady Oxted sat briskly up from the cramped huddling of the position in which she had listened to the doctor's story, and clapped her hands.

'Ha! check number one,' she said. 'And what next, Dr Armytage?'

'That depends on what end you have in view,' said he. 'Is Harry's safety all?'

'Yes, but his safety must be certain,' she said. 'I must see that man in a criminal lunatic asylum or in penal servitude. Harry will never be safe till he is behind bars.'

'I agree with you,' said Geoffrey.

Dr Armytage left the fireplace, where he had been standing since the beginning of the interview, and sat down.

'Do you realize what that demands?' he said. 'It means that Mr Francis must be allowed to make the attempt.'

'Which we have already frustrated,' said Lady Oxted, pointing to the fireplace.

Dr Armytage shook his head.

'If the idea is to catch him red-handed, that is not sufficient,' he said. 'Harry takes whisky-and-soda and salt one night, very little salt, for the drug is potent. He may or may not notice the salt. What then? Sanders, meantime, is waiting in the plate-closet. No doubt we can thus catch Sanders. But that is all.'

Lady Oxted rang the bell.

'We can do nothing,' she said, 'except go straight to Scotland Yard and put the whole matter in the hands of the police. You will please come with me, Dr Armytage, Geoffrey too. To us, of course, the evidence is overwhelming; look at it, from the Houldsworth case onwards——' And she stopped suddenly and looked at the doctor. 'Good heavens, I never thought of that!' she said.

The doctor rose.

'I, as you may imagine, have thought a good deal of that,' he said.

'Is it possible by any means to get hold of this man Sanders?' asked Lady Oxted at length. 'Get me a hansom,' she said to the man who answered the bell.

'I should prefer to try that first,' said the doctor, 'and I will see what I can do. It may be possible to buy the man; he may be scamp enough to be venal. But if we have to go to Scotland Yard, we have to go to Scotland Yard, but for the moment we need not; Harry is safe with you for ten days more, and Mr Francis is not thinking of leaving London for ten days. Something, perhaps, may turn up in the interval. If not, I am ready.'

Lady Oxted felt that no words could meet the situation, and did not make the attempt.

'Then the hansom shall take me to the station instead,' she said. 'I have just time to catch my train. Drive with me there, Geoffrey.' She stood up, drawing on her gloves. 'Please let me hear from you, Dr Armytage,' she said; 'or if you have any communication to make which had better not be written, come down to Oxted, or wire for me to come up. At present, then, there is nothing more to be said?'

She shook hands, and the three went out through the hall and across the broad pavement to where the hansom was waiting. Lady Oxted got in first, and Geoffrey was already on the step to follow, when a man crossing the road came from behind the hansom, and stepped on to the pavement close to where the doctor was standing.

'Dear fellow,' said a very familiar voice, 'what a glorious afternoon!'

The thing was so sudden that the doctor had literally no time to lose his nerve.

'Get in and don't look round,' he said, very low, to Geoffrey.

But he was too late; at the sound of that voice Geoffrey had already looked round, and he and Mr Francis for one stricken moment stared at each other. But the pleasant smile did not fade from the old man's face; rather, it seemed fixed there.

Simultaneously from inside the hansom came Lady Oxted's voice.

'Get in, Geoff,' she said; 'we haven't too much time.'

Mr Francis advanced a step, so that he could see into the hansom.

'Ah, and Lady Oxted, too,' he remarked gently. 'Drive on, cabman.'

The horse broke into a rapid trot, and he and the doctor were left standing together.

Mr Francis stood looking after the diminishing vehicle for a moment, still smiling.

'And Lady Oxted, and Lady Oxted,' he continued to murmur to himself. Then he turned briskly to his companion, and in gentle, modulated tones, and without haste: 'A charming woman, one whom one is delighted to call friend,' he said. 'And dear Geoffrey, too, dear Geoffrey, Harry's great friend. How nice to have even so short a glimpse of him! What good fortune to meet you all together like this! Well, well, I must go on. Good-bye for the present, my dear man.'

He turned from him, walked three paces away, then stopped and faced round again. For the moment the doctor thought his eye or his brain had played him some inexplicable trick; he could barely credit that the face now looking at him was the same as that which two seconds ago had been so smiling a show of sunlit urbanity. Now it was scarce human; a fiend or a wild beast, mad with passion and hate, glared at him. The iris of the eyes seemed to have swelled till the white was invisible; from each a pin-point of a pupil was focused on him. Great veins stood out on his forehead and neck, blue and dilated, the lips were drawn back from the mouth till the gums appeared, showing two rows of white and very even teeth. The pleasant rosiness of the face was blotched and mottled with patches of white and purple, the forehead and the corners of the quivering mouth were streaked with corrugations so deeply cut that the dividing ridges of flesh cast shadows therein. The stamp of humanity was obliterated.

He stood there for perhaps five seconds, his lower jaw working gently up and down as if chewing, and a little foam gathered on his lips. Each moment the doctor expected him either to fall senseless on the pavement or to spring upon him; for it seemed impossible that any human frame could contain so raging an energy of emotion and yet neither break nor give it outlet. Then the horrible chewing of the jaw ceased, and the man, or beast, wiped the froth from his lips.

'You black, treacherous scoundrel!' he said, very softly. 'Do you think I am the sort of man to be thwarted by a faithless subordinate?'

He came a step nearer; his mouth still seemed to be forming words; but it was as if the human nature of the man had been so effaced as to preclude speech, and he stood chattering and gesticulating like some angry ape. Yet the resemblance roused in the doctor no sense of the ludicrous, but only a deep-seated horror at this thing which had doffed its humanity like a cloak, and become part of the brute creation. He summoned all his courage to his aid—an empty effort, for he knew within himself that if this travesty of a man came but one step nearer, he would, in spite of himself, simply turn tail and run from it.

But Mr Francis came no nearer, nor did he speak again, and before the lapse of another five seconds he turned away, and walked quickly down towards the corner of the square without looking back. The doctor followed him with his eye, and saw him hail a hansom at the end of Upper Grosvenor Street, and then get in and drive northwards. He himself stood there, his brain a tumult of bewildered conjecture, and did not see who it was rapidly approaching him till the figure was by him, and he heard his own name called.

'I got down as soon as I could stop the cab,' said Geoffrey. 'He has gone? Where? What has happened?'

'He knows I have betrayed him,' said the doctor, 'that is all, and for the moment he was no longer human. In this mood he will not stop to weigh risks or consequences. Before anything else we must find out where he is going. Probably to his own flat, where we must watch him, possibly first to my house—ah, yes, for the metholycine. Thank God that is harmless!'

There were no cabs about, so they started to walk northwards in the direction Mr Francis had taken. At the corner of Green Street they found a disengaged hansom, and drove to 32, Wimpole Street. Here the doctor got out.

'Drive on to his flat in Wigmore Street,' he said to Geoffrey, 'and ask the porter if he has come in; then come back here.'

Three minutes later Geoffrey returned.

'He came in a minute or two before me,' he said. 'He has kept his cab.'

The doctor pointed to a row of bottles on a shelf in his cabinet.

'The metholycine is missing,' he said. 'He came here, where he is known to the servants, told the man he had instructions from me to take a certain bottle from my cases and was allowed. I asked if he appeared in any way strange or excited. Not a bit of it. He had a smile and a joke, as usual. Come on.'

'Where?' asked. Geoffrey.

'To see where his cab goes. By the way, what of Lady Oxted?'

'She went on to catch her train. It is far better she should be with Harry. I told her I would telegraph all that happened.'

'Quite so. Here is Wigmore Street. We will wait in this entry. There is his cab still at the door. Ah! we must have a cab waiting, too.'

He stepped out of the entry, hailed a cab from a rank a little way down the street, and said a few words to the cabman, pointing out to him the hansom he was to keep in sight. He drew up at the curb opposite their place of observation. Not forty yards in front was Mr Francis's hansom.

The sober, respectable street dozed in the haze of the afternoon sun with the air of a professional man resting for a little from his work. Vehicles were but few, the pavements only sparsely populous, and the roadway nearly empty. The driver of Mr Francis's cab got down from his perch, and was talking to the hall-porter of the house of flats and pulling at a laggard pipe. Then suddenly both porter and cabman looked up as if they had been called from within, and disappeared into the entry, to come back with various small pieces of luggage. Then the cabman mounted his box, and, with the other's assistance, drew up a portmanteau on to the roof. At that moment Mr Francis stepped across the pavement and entered the cab. He had on a straw hat. In his hand was the morocco flute-case, on his mouth a smile and thanks to the porter. Sanders followed, and, after a word, got in after him. At that same instant of time the doctor and Geoffrey had sprung into their places, and the two cabs started together.

The passage of half a dozen streets was sufficient to make their destination tolerably certain, and when Mr Francis's cab turned into the steep decline leading to the departure platform at Paddington, the matter was practically beyond doubt. Here the doctor stopped the cab, and they got out.

'It is certain,' said Geoffrey, though no word had passed between them. 'Look, it is ten minutes past five. The fast train to Vail will start in seven minutes. Now, what are we to do?'

'Harry is at Oxted,' said the doctor, as if speaking to himself. 'Yes, we only want to be perfectly certain that Mr Francis goes to Vail.'

'I will find that out,' said Geoffrey.

He walked down the incline past Sanders, who was busy with the luggage, and into the booking office. There were a considerable number of passengers waiting, but Mr Francis was already high up in the queue. Geoffrey waited with his back turned till he heard him speak to the clerk.

'One first and one second single to Vail,' he said.

With this their information was complete, and he rejoined the doctor.

Harry at Oxted; Mr Francis; with luggage for a prolonged stay, at Vail—here was the sum of it, and the movements were duly telegraphed to Lady Oxted. So far all was well, in such a degree as anything could be well in this dark business, and by mutual consent they determined to leave all further deliberations till the morrow. They were fully informed, prepared for all moves. Tomorrow, it might be, Mr Francis would show for what reason he had gone to Vail.

Chapter 24

Jim Goes to Bed

GEOFFREY, in spite of, or perhaps owing to, his anxieties, slept long and late, and it was already past ten when he came half-dressed from his bedroom to the adjoining sitting-room in quest of letters.

But there was no word either from Dr Armytage or Lady Oxted, and here no news was distinctly good news. No fresh complication had arisen. Harry, it might be safely assumed, was safe at Oxted, Mr Francis as certainly at Vail, though his safety was a matter of infinitesimal moment. Yet, in spite of this, Geoffrey had no morning face; an intolerable presage of disaster sat heavy on him, and he brooded sombrely over his meal, reading the paper, yet not noting its contents, and the paragraphs were Dutch to him. Even here in London, the fog-centre, one must believe, of created things, the morning was one of fine and exquisite beauty. Primrose-coloured sunshine flooded the town, the air was brisk with the cleanly smell of autumnal frost. How clearly could he picture to himself what this same hour was like at Vail! How familiar and intimate was the memory of such mornings when he and Harry had stepped after breakfast into the sparkling coolness of the young day, and the sunshine from without met with a glad thrill of welcome the sunshine from within. The lake lay level and shining—the brain picture had the vividness of authentic hallucination—a wisp of mist still hanging in places over it; level and shining, too, were the lawns; a pearly mysterious halo moved with the moving shadow of the head. Blackbirds scurried and chuckled over the grass, the beeches were golden in their autumn liveries, a solemn glee even smiled in the grey and toned red of the square house. At that, regret as bitter as tears surged up within him. Never again, so he thought, could the particular happiness of those unreflecting days be his; tragedy, like drops from some corroding drug, had fallen in sting and smoke upon him; over that fair scene slept on the wing the destroying angel; between himself and Harry had arisen the barrier of irreconcilable estrangement; and, like a monstrous spider spinning threads, God knew where, or to catch what heedless footstep, Mr Francis stretched his web over every outlet from that house, and sat in each, malign and poisonous.

These vague forebodings and the mordancy of regret grew to be unbearable, and, taking his hat, Geoffrey walked out westward, aimlessly enough, only seeking to dull misgivings by the sight of many human faces. The crowd had for him an absorbing fascination, and to be in the midst of folk was to put the rein on private fancies, for the spectacle of life claimed all the attention. But this morning this healthful prescription seemed to have lost its efficacy, or the drugs were stale and impotent, and the air was dark with winged fears that came to roost within him, chattering evilly together. Yet the streets were better than his own room, and for near two hours he wandered up and down the jostling pavements; then, returning to Orchard Street, he entered his weary room, and his heart stood suddenly still, for on the table was lying a telegram.

For a moment he stood by the door, as if fearing even to go near it; then, with a stride and an inserted finger, the pink sheet was before his eye.

'Harry has just left for Vail,' it ran, 'passing through London. Sanders has telegraphed that his master is dangerously ill, and he must come at once to see him alive. Take this direct to Dr Armytage.'

The shock was as of fire or cold water, disabling for the moment, but bracing beyond words. All the brooding, the regret, the dull, vague aches of the morning had passed as completely as a blink of summer lightning, and Geoffrey knew himself to be strung up again to the level of intelligent activity. As he drove to Wimpole Street he examined the chronology of the message. It had been sent off from Oxted, it appeared, three hours ago; it was likely that even now Harry was passing through London. A cab was standing at the doctor's door, which was open, a servant by it. At the same moment of receiving these impressions, he was aware of two figures in the hall beyond, and he stopped. One was with its back to him, but on the sound of his step it turned round.

'Oh, Geoff,' said Harry, holding out his hand, 'Uncle Francis is ill—very dangerously ill. I am going to Vail at once, and was just coming to see you first. But now you are here.'

By a flash of intuition, unerring and instantaneous, Geoffrey saw precisely what was in Harry's mind, and knew that next moment an opportunity so vitally desirable, yet vitally dishonourable to accept, would be given him, that he had no idea whether in his nature there was that which should be strong enough to resist it.

'Won't you come with me?' asked Harry, low and almost timidly. 'Can't you, in case we are in time, just ask his forgiveness for the wrong you did him? He is very ill, perhaps dying—dying, Geoff!'

At this moment the doctor stepped forward, Bradshaw in hand, to the brighter light by the open door. In passing Geoffrey he made a faint but unmistakable command of assent. His finger was on the open page, and he spoke immediately.

'We can catch the 3.15, Harry,' he said. 'Shall I telegraph to them to meet it?'

'Please,' said Harry, still looking at the other. 'Geoffrey!' he said again, and touched him on the arm.

Geoffrey heard the leaf of the Bradshaw flutter, and the sound of his name lingered in his ears.

Much perhaps was to be gained by going; and the price? The price was just deliberate deception on a solemn matter. To say 'Yes' was to declare to his friend that he desired the forgiveness of that horrible man whom he soberly believed to be guilty of the most monstrous designs. But the momentous debate was but momentary.

'No, Harry, I cannot,' he said.

The two turned from each other without further words, and Geoffrey took a step to where the doctor stood.

'I came to have a word with you,' he said; and together they went into the consulting-room.

Scarcely had the door closed behind them when Geoffrey drew the telegram from his pocket.

'I have just had this from Lady Oxted,' he said. 'Probably she has telegraphed the same to you. Now, how did Harry come here, and what has passed between you?'

The doctor glanced at the sheet.

'Yes, she telegraphed to me also,' he said. 'Harry's coming was pure luck. He wanted me to go with him down to Vail to see if anything can be done for Mr Francis. I hope,' he added, with a humour too grim for smiles, 'to be able to do a great deal for Mr Francis.'

'So you are going—thank the Lord!' said Geoffrey. 'And do you believe in this illness?'

'He may have had another attack,' said the doctor, with a shrug; 'indeed, it is not improbable after the agitation of yesterday. Again, he may not, and he is a subtle man.'

'It is a trap, you mean, to get Harry there?'

'Possibly, and if so, a trap laid in a hurry, else he would never have telegraphed to Harry at Lady Oxted's; he might have guessed it would be passed on to us. I am sorry, by the way, that you could not manage to say "Yes" to his wish that you should go with him. But I respect you for saying "No".'

'I couldn't do otherwise,' said Geoffrey. 'All the same if it appears desirable, I shall come to Vail.'

'Ah! you will come secretly, on your own account, just as you would have if you had not seen Harry. That will do just as well. Now, I can give you three minutes. I shall be in the house; you, I suppose, will not. How can I communicate with you?'

Geoffrey thought a moment, and his eye brightened.

'In two ways; no less,' he said. 'Listen carefully, please. At any appointed time tap at the portrait of old Francis in the hall. I shall be just behind it, and will open it; or, secondly, go to the window of the gun-room, open it, and call me very gently. I shall be within three yards of you, in the centre of the box-hedge just outside. I will do whichever seems to you best.'

'Does Mr Francis know of either?' asked the doctor, after a pause.

'He knows of the passage inside the house: of that I am sure. I don't know that he knows of the box-hedge.'

'Then we will choose that. Now, how will you get to Vail? You must not go by the same train as we. You must not run the risk of Harry seeing you.'

'Then I shall go by the next—5.17, same as Mr Francis went by yesterday. It gets in at half-past six. I will be at the box-hedge soon after seven.'

'Very good,' said' the doctor. 'Now in turn listen to me. Mr Francis believes he has the metholycine with him; he has also Sanders. It seems to me, therefore, probable that he will attempt to carry the thing out in the way he indicated to me, which I told you and Lady Oxted.'

Geoffrey shook his head.

'Not likely,' he said. 'You hold the evidence of the metholycine he has taken from your cabinet.'

'Yes, but he is desperate, and the drug almost untraceable. Also the fact that he has the metholycine from my cabinet may be supposed to shut my mouth. It looks very much as if I was his accomplice, does it not? He will guess that this is awkward for me, as indeed it would be, were not the metholycine common salt.'

'Ha!' said Geoffrey. 'Go on.'

'I expect—I feel sure, then, that his plans are more or less the same as before, only he and Sanders will have to carry them through alone. I see no reason why they should alter the idea of the supposed burglary. It is simple and convincing, and my mouth is sealed in two ways.'

'How two?' asked Geoffrey.

'Two, so Mr Francis thinks. Houldsworth and metholycine. Now, the metholycine will fail, and they will have to get Harry into their power some other way. Also, Mr Francis will be very

anxious, as I told you, that he should not suffer
pain. Of that I am certain; it is a fixed idea with
him. Probably also the attempt will be made
as planned, late, when the servants are in bed.
Now, is there not a groom in the stables very like
Harry?'

Geoffrey stared.

'Yes, the image of him,' he said. 'And what
about him?'

'Go down to the stables as soon as you get to
Vail, and tell him he is wanted at the house. He
knows you, I suppose. Walk up with him yourself,
and let him be in the box-hedge with you.'

For a moment the excitement of adventure
overpowered all else in Geoffrey's mind.

'Ah! you, have some idea?' he said.

'Nothing, except that it may be useful to have
two Harrys in the house. Allowing time for this,
you should be at the box-hedge by eight. That shall
be the appointed hour.'

'But what shall I tell Jim?'

'Jim is the name of the groom? Tell him that
it may be in his power to save his master from
great peril. Harry is liked by the servants, is
he not? All that we know at present is that he
must wait in the box-hedge with you in case
we need him. But supposing he is swiftly and
secretly needed, how are we to get him into
the house?'

'By the secret passage within,' said Geoffrey,
quick as an echo.

'Good again. It looks as if the Luck was with

us. And this passage comes out at the back of old Francis's portrait? Bad place.'

'Yes, but also at the bottom of the main stairs, through a panel between them and the hall.'

'That is better. There, then—O God, help us all! And now you must go. Harry is waiting for me. I dare not risk trying to convince him. He quarrelled with you, his best friend, for the suspicion; I can serve him better by going with him.'

They went out together, and found Harry in the hall. He detained Geoffrey with his hand, and the doctor passed on into the dining-room.

'You will lunch here, Harry,' he said. 'It is ready.'

From outside the lad closed the door. Geoffrey knew that a bad moment was coming, and set his teeth. But the moment was worse than he had anticipated, for Harry's voice, when he spoke, was broken and his eyes moist.

'Oh, Geoffrey,' he said, 'cannot you do what I asked? If you knew what it means to me! There are two men in the world whom I love. There, you understand—and I cannot bear it, simply I cannot bear it.'

The temptation had been severe before; it was a trifle to this.

'No, I can't,' cried Geoffrey, eager to get the words spoken, for each moment made them harder to speak. 'Oh, Harry, some day you will understand! Before your marriage—I give it a date—I swear to you in God's name that you will understand

how it is that I cannot come with you to ask Mr
Francis's forgiveness.'

Disappointment deepened on Harry's face, and
a gleam of anger shone there.

'I will not ask you a third time,' he said, and
went into the dining-room.

Geoffrey had still three hours to wait in London
before the starting of his train, and these were
chequered with an incredible crowd of various
hopes and fears. At one time he hugged himself
on the obvious superiority of their dispositions
against Mr Francis—he would even smile to think
of the toils enveloping that evil schemer; again mere
exhilaration at the unknown and the violent would
boil up in effervescence; another moment, and an
anguish of distrust would seize him. What if, after
all, Dr Armytage had been playing with him?—how
completely and how successfully he writhed to
think. A week ago the sweat would have broken
out on him to picture Harry travelling to Vail with
that man of sinister repute, to be alone in the house
with him, Mr Francis, and the fox-like servant. Had
he been hoodwinked throughout? Was the doctor
even now smiling to himself behind his paper at the
facility of his victim! At the thought London turned
hell; he had taken the bait like a silly, staring fish;
even now he was already hauled, as it were, on
to dry land, there to gasp innocuously, impotent
to stir or warn, while who knew what ghastly
subaqueous drama might even now be going on?
He had trusted the doctor on evidence of the most
diaphanous kind, unsupported by any testimony

of another. The sleeping-draught given to Harry, the brushing aside of the revolver he had passed to him when to shoot was impossible, these, with a calculated gravity of face, and an assumption of anxious sincerity, had been enough to convince him of the man's honesty. He could have screamed aloud at the thought, and every moment whirled Harry nearer, helpless and unsuspecting, to that house of death.

Meantime, the journey of the two had been for the most part a silent passage. Each was absorbed in his own thoughts and anxieties—Harry restless, impatient, eager for the quicker falling behind of wayside stations, while the doctor brooded with half-closed eyelids, intent, it would seem, on the pattern of the carriage-mat, his thoughts unconjecturable. Once only as the train yelled through Slough did he speak, but then with earnestness.

'Don't let your uncle know I have come, Harry,' he said. 'It may be that Sanders has unnecessarily alarmed you; so see him first yourself, and if this has been a heart attack like to what he had before, and he seems now to be quietly recuperating, do not let him know I am here. It may only alarm him for his condition.'

'Pray God it may be so!' said Harry.

The doctor looked steadfastly at the carriage-mat.

'Medically speaking,' he said, 'I insist on this. I should also wish that you would guard against all possibility of his knowing I am here. Sanders, I suppose, looks after him. I should therefore not wish Sanders to know.'

'Oh, he can keep a secret,' said Harry.

'Very likely, but I would rather he had no secret to keep. I am not speaking without reason. If, as you fear, and as the telegram seems to indicate, this attack has been unusually severe, I must assure you that it is essential that no agitating influence of any kind should come near him. If he is in real danger, of course, I will see him.'

'Would it not be likely to reassure him to know you are here?' asked Harry.

'I have told you that I think not,' said the doctor, 'unless there is absolute need of me. I hope'—and the word did not stick in his throat—'that quiet will again restore him.'

A trap was waiting for him at the station, driven by Jim, and the doctor had an opportunity of judging how far the likeness between the two might be hoped to deceive one who knew them both. Even now with the one in livery, the other in ordinary dress, it was extraordinary, not only in superficialities, but somehow essentially, and he felt that it was worth while to have arranged to profit by it, should opportunity occur. The groom had a note for Harry, which he tore open hastily.

'Ah, that is good!' he said, and handed it to the doctor.

It was but a matter of a couple of lines, signed by Templeton, saying merely that the severity of the attack was past, and at the time of writing Mr Francis was sleeping, being looked after by Sanders, who had not left him since the seizure. And to the one reader this account brought an upspringing of hope, to the other the conviction that his estimate of Mr Francis's illness was correct.

Harry went upstairs immediately on his arrival, leaving the doctor in the hall. Templeton, usually a man of wood, had perceptibly started when he opened the door to them and saw the doctor, and now, instead of discreetly retiring on the removal of their luggage, he hung about, aimlessly poking the fire, putting a crooked chair straight and a straight chair crooked, and fidgeting with the blinds. All at once the strangeness of his manner struck the doctor.

'What have you got to tell me?' he said suddenly.

The blind crashed down its full length, as the butler's hand dropped the retaining string. The rigid control of domestic service was snapped; he was a frightened man speaking to his equal.

'This is a strange illness of Mr Francis's,' he said.

The doctor was alive to seize every chance.

'How strange?' he asked. 'Mr Francis has had these attacks before.'

'I sent for the doctor from Didcot as soon as it occurred, unknown to him or Sanders,' said Templeton, 'but he was not allowed to see him. Why is that, sir? There was Sanders telegraphing for his lordship, and saying that Mr Francis was dying, yet refusing to let the doctor see him. But perhaps he was expecting you, sir?'

'He does not know I am here, Templeton, nor must he know. Look to that; see that the servants do not tell Sanders I am here. Now, what do you mean? You think Mr Francis is not ill at all?'

'Does a man in the jaws of death, I may say, play the flute?' asked the butler.

'Play the flute?'

'Yes, sir. It was during the servants' dinner-hour, but I had no stomach for my meat today, and went upstairs, when we might have been at dinner perhaps five minutes, and along the top passage to his lordship's room to see if they had it ready. Well, sir, I heard coming from Mr Francis's room, very low and guarded, so that I should have heard nothing had I not stood outside a moment listening, you may say, but I did not know for what, a little lively tune I have heard him play a score of times. But in a minute it ceased, and then I heard two voices talking, and after that Mr Francis laughed—that from a man who was sleeping, so Sanders told us.'

'This is all very strange,' said the doctor.

'Ah, and then the door opened, and out came that man Sanders; black as hell he looked when he saw me! But little I cared for his black looks, and I just asked him how his master was. Very bad, he told me, and wandering, and he wondered whether his lordship would be here in time.'

The doctor came a step nearer.

'Templeton,' he said, 'I rely on you to obey me implicitly. It is necessary that neither Mr Francis nor Sanders knows I am here. Things which I cannot yet tell you may depend on this. And see to this: let me have the room I had before, and put his lordship into the room opening from it. Lock the door of it which leads into the passage, and lose the key, so that the only entrance is through my room. If he asks why his room is changed, make any paltry excuse. Say the electric light in his room is gone wrong—anything. But make his usual room look as if it was occupied; go up there during dinner, turn down the bed, put a nightshirt on it, and leave a sponge, brushes, and so on.'

'Master Harry?' gasped the butler, his mind suddenly reverting to old days.

The doctor frowned.

'Come,' he said, 'do not get out of hand like that. Do as I bid you, and try to look yourself. I can tell you no more.'

Harry came down from the sick-room a few minutes later with a brow markedly clearer.

'He is much better—ever so much better, Sanders thinks,' he said. 'He was sleeping, but when he wakes he will be told I have come.'

'Ah, that is good!' said the doctor. 'Did Sanders tell you about the attack?'

'Yes; it came on while he was dressing this morning. Luckily Sanders was with him, but for an hour, he tells me, he thought that every breath might be his last. He's a trump, that man, and there's a head on his shoulders, too. He has hardly left him for five minutes.'

'Will Sanders sleep in his room tonight?' asked the doctor.

'Yes; he has his meals brought to him there, too, so that it will be easy for you not to be seen by him, since you make such a point of it. Oh, thank God, he is so much better! Ah, look! we are going to have one of those curious low mists tonight.'

The doctor followed Harry to one of the windows which Templeton had left unshuttered and looked out.

The autumn twilight was fast closing in, and, after the hot sun of the day, the mist, in the sudden coolness of its withdrawal, was forming very quickly and rapidly over the lake. There was a little draught of wind towards the house, not sufficient to disperse it, but only to slide it gently, like a sheet over the lawns. It lay very low, in thickness not, perhaps, exceeding five feet over the higher stretches of the lawn, but, as the surface of it was level, it must have been some few feet thicker where the ground declined towards the lake. It appeared to be of extraordinary density, and spread very swiftly and steadily, so that even while they watched, it had pushed on till, like flood-water, it struck the wall of the house, and presently lawn and lake had both entirely vanished, and they looked out, as from a mountain-top, over a level sea of cloud, pricked here and there by plantations and the higher shrubs. Above, the night was clear, and a young moon rode high in a heaven that silently filled with stars.

Geoffrey, meantime, had followed two hours behind them; his train was punctual, and it was only a little after seven when he found himself, having walked from the station, at the edge of the woods, looking down on to this same curious sea of mist. The monstrous birds of the box-hedge stood out upon it, like great aquatic creatures swimming there, for the hedge itself was submerged, and the descent into it was like a plunge into a bath. Not wishing to risk being seen from the house, he made a wide circuit round it towards the lake. Here the mist rose above his head, baffling and blinding; but striking the edge of the lake, he followed it, guided as much by the sobbing of the ripples against the bank as by the vague muffled outline, till he reached the inlet of the stream which fed it. From this point the ground rose rapidly, and in a few minutes he could look over the mist again and see the house already twinkling with scattered lights, moored like some great ship in that white sea. A few hundred yards more brought him to the stables, and, conveniently for his purpose, at the gate stood Jim and a helper, their work over, smoking and chatting. Geoffrey approached till it was certain they could see who he was.

'Is that you, Jim?' he said. 'They want you at the house.'

Jim knocked out his pipe and followed; his clothes had 'evening out' stamped upon them, and there seemed to be an unpleasant curtailment of his liberty in prospect.

'Come round by the lake,' said Geoffrey in a low voice when the groom had joined him. 'I have something to tell you.'

He waited till they were certainly out of earshot.

'Now, Jim,' he said, 'it's just this: We believe that

an attempt will be made tonight to murder Lord Vail. I want your help, though I can't tell you in what way you can help, because I don't know. But will you do all you can or are told to do?'

'Gawd bless my soul!' said Jim; then, with a return to his ordinary impassivity: 'Yes, sir, I'll do anything you tell me to help.'

'Come on, then. You can trust me that you shall run no unreasonable risks.'

'I'm not thinking you'll let them murder me instead, sir,' said Jim, 'And may I ask who is going to do the murdering?'

Geoffrey hesitated a moment; but, on reflection, there seemed to him to be no reason for concealing anything.

'We believe—Dr Armytage and I, that is—that Sanders, Mr Francis's man, will attempt it.'

Jim whistled under his breath.

'Bring him on,' he said. 'Lord, I should like to have a go at that Sanders, sir! He walks into the stable-yard as if every horse in the place belonged to him.'

They had by this time skirted the lake again, and the booming of the sluice sounded near at hand; then, striking for higher ground, they saw they had already passed the house, and close in front of them swam the birds of the box-hedge.

'The mist had sunk back a little, and now they sat, as if in a receding tide, on the long peninsula of the hedge itself, visible above the drift, and black in the moonlight.

'This way,' said Geoffrey.

And, groping round to the back of it, they found the overgrown door and entered. Thence, going cautiously and feeling their way, they passed down the length of it, and soon saw in front of them, like a blurred moon, the light from the gun-room windows. The time had been calculated to a nicety, for they had been there scarcely five minutes when a shadow moved across the blind, which was then rolled up, and the window then silently lifted a crack. The figure, owing to the density of the mist, was indistinguishable, but Geoffrey recognised the doctor's voice when it whispered his name. He touched Jim to make him follow, and together they stood close by the window.

'Good! you have Jim with you,' said the doctor, 'and you have told him we may need him? I want him inside the house, so go with him through the secret passage, and open the panel by the stair which you told me of. I shall be there, and I will tell you what we are going to do. Harry has gone to dress, and the house is quiet. Wait, Geoffrey; take this', and he handed him out a rook-rifle and eight or ten cartridges. 'Put these inside the hedge,' he whispered, 'and come round at once with Jim.'

Five minutes later Geoffrey gently opened the panel of the door, and the doctor glided in like a ghost, latching it noiselessly behind him. His face brooded and gloomed no longer; it was alert and active.

'There is very little time,' he said, 'so first for you, Geoffrey. Go back for the rifle and cartridges, and get somewhere in cover where you can command the front of the house. What course events will take outside I cannot say, but the Luck and the plate will be stolen, and they will have to get them away somehow. You must stop that. Sanders, I expect, will try to remove them.'

'Beg your pardon, sir,' put in Jim, 'but Sanders was down at the stable this afternoon, and said that the door of the coachhouse and one of the loose-boxes was to be left unlocked tonight, in case a doctor was wanted for Mr Francis. He said he could put-to himself, sir, so that none of us need sit up.'

The doctor's keen face grew a shade more animated; his mouth bordered on a smile.

'Good lad!' he said. 'Well, that's your job, Geoffrey; you must use your discretion entirely. You may have to deal with a pretty desperate man, and it is possible you will feel safer with that rifle.'

'Where shall I go?' asked Geoffrey.

'I thought the summer-house on the knoll would be a good place; it stands above the mist.'

'Excellent. And for Jim?'

'We must be guided by the course of events. Jim will have to wait here in any case probably till eleven, or even later. Then I expect he will go to bed in Harry's room, where I—I can't tell you; it is all in the clouds at present. I want to spare Harry horror. Anyhow, he will stop here until I tap twice on the panel outside. Now I cannot wait. Harry may be down any minute; we dine at a quarter-past. Ah! this is for you, Geoffrey,' and he handed him a packet of sandwiches, 'and this for you, Jim. Now, you to the summer-house, Geoffrey; Jim waits here; I dine with Harry. Yes, your hand and yours. God help our work!'

Though never a voluminous talker, the doctor was even more silent than usual at dinner that night, and, despite the alertness of his eye, confessed to an extreme fatigue. Thus it was that soon after ten he and Harry went upstairs, he straight to his room, the latter to tap discreetly at the door of the sick-room and learn the latest of the patient.

The change of Harry's room from the one he usually occupied to that communicating with the doctor's caused no comment, either silent or spoken, from him, nor did the loss of the key seem to him in any way remarkable. He came straight from his visit to Mr Francis to give the news to the doctor.

'Still sleeping,' he said, 'and sleeping very quietly, so Sanders tells me. And I—I feel as if I should sleep the clock round. I really think I shall go to bed at once.'

He went through the doctor's room and turned on his light, then appeared again in the doorway.

'Got everything you want?' he asked. 'Have a whisky-and-soda?'

A confused idea of metholycine, a distinct idea that he did not wish Harry to run the risk of being seen by Sanders going to another room than the ordinary, made itself felt in the doctor's reply.

'Not for worlds,' he said—'a poisonous habit.'

'That means I mustn't have any—does it?' asked

Harry from the doorway. 'Now, that is hard lines. I want some, but not enough to go and fetch it from the hall myself. Do have some. Give me an excuse.'

'Not even that,' said the doctor.

'Well, good night,' said Harry, and he closed the door between the two rooms.

For so tired a man, the doctor on the closing of the door exhibited a considerable briskness. Very quickly and quietly he took off dress-coat, shoes and shirt, and buttoning a dark-grey coat over his vest, set his door ajar, and switched off his light. The hour for action, he well realized, might strike any moment; but he was prepared, as far as preparation was possible. Outside there was waiting Geoffrey with the rook-rifle, inside the secret passage the spurious Harry—both, he knew, calm and bland for any emergency. Meanwhile, the real Harry was safe for the present. None but he and Templeton knew of the change of room, and none could reach him but through the chamber he himself occupied. But an intricate and subtle passage was likely to be ahead, and as yet its windings were unconjecturable. As a working hypothesis—for he could find no better—he had assumed that Mr Francis's plans were in the main unaltered. Harry, drugged and unconscious, was to be taken to the plate-closet at some hour in this dead night, where Sanders would be waiting. Yet this conjecture might be utterly at fault; in any case, the drugged whisky, mixed as it was with innocuous salt, could not have the effect desired, and for anything unforeseen—and here was, at least, one step untraceable—he must have every sense alert to interpret to the best of his ability the smallest clue that came from the room opposite. Mr Francis and Sanders were there now; firearms were not to be feared. Here was the sum of his certainties. This also—and this, from his study of Mr Francis, he considered probable to the verge of certainty—Harry would be unconscious when the deathblow was given.

In the dark, time may either fly with swallows' wings or lag with the tortoise, for the watch in a man's brain is an unaccountable mechanism, and the doctor had no idea how long he had sat waiting when he heard the latch of a door open somewhere in the passage outside. Two noiseless steps took him to his own, and through the crack where he had left it ajar he saw a long perpendicular chink of light—bright, it seemed, and near. Without further audible sound this grew gradually fainter, and with the most stealthy precautions he opened his own door and peered out. Some fifteen yards distant, moving very slowly down the passage, were two figures, those of Mr Francis and his valet. The latter was dressed in ordinary clothes, the former, vividly visible by the light of the candle the servant carried, in a light garish dressing-gown and red slippers. At this moment they paused opposite the door of the room Harry usually occupied, and here held a word of inaudible colloquy. There was a table just outside the door fronting the top of the stairs, and a dim lamp on a bracket hung above it. On it Mr Francis put down a small bottle and what looked like an ordinary table napkin, and the two went down the stairs.

It was the time for caution and rapidity. Already, as he knew, luck had favoured him in that neither had entered Harry's room, and, after giving them some ten seconds' law, he went noiselessly over the thick carpet of the passage to the table, and opened the bottle Mr Francis had left there. The unmistakable fumes of chloroform greeted his nostril, and he stood awhile in unutterable perplexity. Fresh and valuable as this evidence was, it was difficult to form any certain conclusions about it. Conceivably, the chloroform was an additional precaution, in case Harry had not drunk the whisky; conceivably also the metholycine idea had been altogether abandoned in the absence of a skilled operator. That, at least, he could easily settle, and turning into the bedroom Harry usually occupied, he switched on the electric light. Templeton had followed his instructions about making the room look habitable, but on the dressing-table stood what was perhaps not the work of Templeton. A cut-glass bottle was there on a tray, with a glass and a syphon. He spilled a teaspoonful of the spirit into the glass and tasted it. Salt.

So much, then, was certain. One or both of the figures he had seen go downstairs would return here with the chloroform. And still cudgelling his brains over the main problem, as to why Mr Francis had gone downstairs at all, he lingered not, but felt his way down to the bottom of the flight. Here he paused, but, hearing nothing, tapped twice at the panel which opened into the secret passage. It was at once withdrawn, and Jim stepped out.

'Come!' he whispered.

With the same rapid stealthiness they ascended again, crossed the landing, and entered Harry's bedroom. The bed stood facing the door, in an angle between the window and the wall, and the doctor drew the curtain across the window, which was deep and with a seat in it.

'Undress at once,' he said to Jim. 'They might notice that your clothes were not lying about if they have a light. Quick! off with them—coat, waistcoat, shirt, trousers, boots—as naked as your mother bore you. There is a nightshirt; put it on. Now get into bed, and lie with your face half covered. Do not stir, or make any sound whatever, till I turn up the light or call to you. I shall be behind the curtain.'

There were two electric lamps in the room, one by the door, the other with its own switch over the bed. The doctor had lit both, and as soon as the groom was in bed, extinguished the one by the door. Then, crossing the room, he got up behind the curtain in the window-seat, and from there turned off the other.

'And when I turn up the light, Jim,' he whispered, 'throw off anything that may have been placed over your face, and spring up in bed. Till then be asleep. You understand?'

'Yes, sir,' said Jim softly.

At that moment, with the suddenness of a long-forgotten memory returned, the doctor guessed why Mr Francis had gone downstairs. The glory of the guess was so great that he could not help speaking.

'He has gone for the Luck,' he said.

'Yes, sir,' said Jim again, and there was darkness and silence.

Interminable aeons passed, or maybe ten minutes, but at the end of infinite time came scarcely sound, but an absence of complete silence from the door. From behind the thick curtains the doctor could see nothing, but a moment later came the sigh of the scraped carpet, and from that or from the infallible sixth sense that wakes only in the dark, he knew that someone had entered. Then from closer at hand he heard the faintest shuffle of movement, and he knew that, whoever this was in the room beside the groom and himself, he was not a couple of yards distant. After another while the least vibration sounded from the glasses in the tray, as if a hand had touched them unwittingly, and again dead silence succeeded, till the doctor's ears sang with it. Then from the bed his ear suddenly focused the breathings of two persons, one very short and quick, the other a steady respiration, and simultaneously with that his nostril caught the whiff of chloroform. Again the rustle of linen sounded, and hearing that, he held his breath, and counted the pulse which throbbed in his own temples. Twenty times it beat, and on the twentieth stroke his finger pressed the switch of the light, and he drew back the curtain.

Already Jim was sitting up in bed, bland and

impassive in face, and his left hand flung the reeking napkin from him. By the bedside crouched a white-haired figure, clad in a blue dressing-gown; close by it on the floor stood the leather case which held the Luck; the right hand was still stretched over the bed, though the napkin which it had held was plucked from it. His face was flushed with colour; the bright blue eyes, a little puckered up in this sudden change from darkness to the glare of the electric light, moved slowly from Jim to the doctor, and back again; but no word passed the thin, compressed lips.

Suddenly the alertness of the face was gone like a burst bubble; the mouth opened and drooped, the eyes grew staring and sightless; the left hand only seemed to retain its vitality, and felt gropingly on the carpet for the Luck. Then, with a slow, supreme effort, the figure half raised itself, drawing the jewel tight to its breast, folding both arms about it, with fingers intertwined in the strap that carried it. Then it collapsed completely, rolled over, and lay face downwards on the floor.

For one moment neither of the others stirred; then, recovering himself, the doctor stepped down from the window-seat.

'Put on your coat and trousers, Jim,' he said, 'and come with me quickly. Yes, leave it there; I will come back presently. We have to catch Sanders now, and must go without a light. You behaved admirably. Now follow me.'

'Is it dead, sir?' whispered Jim.

'I think so. Come!'

In the eagerness of their pursuit they crossed the passage without looking to right hand or left, and felt their way down the many-angled stairs. The hall was faintly lit by the pallor of the moonshine that came through the skylight, and without difficulty they found the baize door leading into the servants' parts. But here with the shuttered windows reigned the darkness of Egypt, and, despairing of finding his way, the doctor lit a match to guide them to the further end of the passage, where was the plate-closet. But when they reached it, it was to find the door open and none within. In all directions stood boxes with forced lids; here a dozen of spoons were scattered on the floor, here a salt-cellar, but the rifling had been fairly complete.

'How long do you suppose we were waiting in the dark?' he asked Jim. 'Anyhow, it was long enough for Sanders and Mr Francis to have taken most of the plate. I had thought they would do that after—afterwards. Now, where is the plate, and where is Sanders?'

'Can't say, sir,' said Jim.

The match, which had showed the disorder of the place, had burned out, and the doctor, still frowning over the next step, had just lit another, when from outside rang out the sharp 'ping' of a rifle-shot.

'That is Geoffrey!' he said; 'and what in God's name is happening? Upstairs again.'

They groped their way back along the basement to the door leading into the hall. Close to this went up the backstairs, forming the servants' communication with the upper story, and seeing these, the doctor clicked his teeth against his tongue.

'That's how we missed him,' he said; 'he went this way up to Mr Francis while we were going down the front stairs.'

'Yes, sir,' said Jim.

They passed through into the hall, and a draught of cold air met them. There was no longer any reason for secret movements, and the doctor turned on the electric light. The front door was open, and wreaths of dense mist streamed in.

'Go and see if you can help Mr Geoffrey, Jim,' he said, 'if you can find him. It is clear that Sanders has left the house; who else could have opened that door? I must see to that which we left upstairs.'

He ran up. The room door, as they had left it, was open; on the floor still lay what they had left there. But it was lying no longer on its face, the sightless eyes were turned to the ceiling, and the Luck was no longer clasped with fingers intertwined in its strap to the breast.

The doctor fought down an immense repugnance against touching the body; but the instinct of saving life, however remote the chance, prevailed, and, taking hold of one of the hands, he felt for the pulse. But as he touched it, two of the fingers fell backwards, dislocated or broken.

Then, with a swift hissing intake of his breath, he pressed his finger on the wrist. But the search for the pulse was vain.

Chapter 25

Mr Francis Sleeps

It was about a quarter-past eight when Geoffrey
left Jim in the secret passage, and, in accordance
with his instructions, went back to the box-hedge
where he had concealed the rifle and cartridges.
With these he skirted wide up the short grassy
slope that led to the summer-house, and trying the
door, found it unlocked. It stood, as he supposed,
some fifteen feet above the level of the mist that
lay round the house below, and was admirably
situated for the observation of any movement or
manoeuvre that might be made, for it commanded
a clear view past the front of the house down to
the lake, while the road from the stables passed
not fifty yards from it, joining the carriage sweep;
from the carriage sweep, at right angles, ran the
drive. Clearly, then, if Jim's account of Sanders's
visit and order to the stables covered a design, the
working out of it must take place before his eyes.

The summer-house stood close to the background

of wood in which last summer Evie and Mr Francis
had once walked, a mere black blot against the
blackness of the trees, and Geoffrey, pulling a chair
to the open door, sat commandingly invisible. His
rifle he leaned against the wall, ready to his hand,
and it was in more than moderate composure that
he ate the sandwiches with which the doctor had
provided him. There was, he expected, a long vigil
in front of him before any active share in the
operations should stand to his name; the first act
would be played in that great square ship of a house
that lay anchored out in the sea of mist. What should
pass there in the next two hours he strenuously
forebore to conjecture, for it was his business to
keep his brain cool, and avoid all thoughts which
might heat that or render his hand unsteady. That
short interview with the doctor had given him a
confidence that made firm the shifting quicksands of
fear which all day had quaked within him, for the
man had spoken to him with authority, masterful
and decided, which had stilled the shudderings and
perplexities of the last twelve hours. He had to see
to it that they should not awake again.

At intervals of seemingly incalculable length the
clock from the stable drowsily told the hour, and
but for that and the slow wheeling of the young
moon, he could have believed that time had ceased.
No breath of wind stirred in the trees behind, or
shredded the opaque levels of the mist in front; a
death and stagnation lay over the world, and no
sound but the muffled murmur of the sluice from
the lake broke the silence. The world spun in space,

and the sound of the invisible outpouring waters might have been the rustle of its passage through interstellar space.

Then the spell and soothing of the stillness laid hold of him; the hour of action was near, the intolerable fret of anxiety nearly over. Inside the house that dark, keen-eyed man was not one whom the prudent would care to see in opposition—and on which side he was Geoffrey no longer entertained a doubt's shadow—nor, for that matter, was his lieutenant, the impassive spurious Harry. By his unwilling means last summer had Mr Francis made the first of his vile attempts; by his means, perhaps, this should be the last. Geoffrey could rest assured that they would do all that lay in the power of two very cool heads; his business was to see that his own part should not be less well done.

Some years ago—or was the stroke still resonant? —half-past ten had struck on the stable clock, and, since eleven had not yet sounded, it was earlier than he expected it, when there came a noise which sent his heart hammering for a moment in his throat. He could not at once localize or identify it, and though still obscure and muffled, he had only just decided that it could not be very far off before he guessed what it was. Its direction and its nature came to him together: some vehicle was being cautiously driven over the grass towards the house from the stables, and on the moment he caught sight of it. It was moving at a very slow pace, more than half drowned in the mist, and all he could see of it was the head and back of a horse, the head and shoulders of the man who led it, and the box seat and rail of some vehicle of the wagonette type. It reached the gravel walk with a crisp, crunching sound, and drew up there. Then he heard the unmistakable rattle of the brake being put hard on, and the man, tying the reins in a knot, looped them round the whip-holder. He then left it, not forty yards from where Geoffrey sat, and was swallowed up in the fog, going towards the house. The curtain was up for the second act. What had the first been?

The thing had passed so quickly and silently that he could almost have believed that his imagination had played him some trick were it not for the sight of that truncated horse and carriage, which testified to its reality. There, without doubt, was the carriage from the stables of which Jim had told them, but he could not have sworn to the identity of the man who led it in the uncertain light. And he picked up his rifle and laid it across his knees, prepared again to wait.

Soon afterwards eleven struck, and while the strokes were still vibrating came the second interruption to his silent waiting. Out of the mist between the wagonette and the house dimly appeared two heads, moving slowly towards the carriage, and rising gradually as they climbed the slope above the level mist till they were distinct and clear as far as the shoulders. They walked about a yard apart, and words low and inaudible to the watcher passed between them. Arrived at the carriage, they seemed to set something down,

and then, with an effort, hoist it into the body of
the vehicle; and, as they again raised themselves,
Geoffrey saw that the one head sparkled whitely
in the moonshine, and he well knew to whom
those venerable locks belonged. Then there came
audible words.

'Come back then, Sanders,' said Mr Francis, 'and
wait at the top of the back-stairs, while I go very
gently to his room to see if it is all right. In any
case, I shall use the chloroform; then, when I call
you, come and help me to carry him down to the
plate-closet. There I shall leave you, and go back
to bed. Afterwards drive hard to the village, leave
the plate at the cottage I told you of, and bring
the doctor back. Are you ready? Where is the—ah,
thank you! No, I prefer to carry it myself. The
Luck! the Luck! At last! at last!'

He raised his hand above his head; it grasped a
case. The man's face was turned upwards towards
the moon, and Geoffrey, looking thereon, could
scarcely stifle an exclamation of horror.

'It is not a man's face,' he said to himself. 'It is
some mad incarnation of Satan himself.'

In another minute all was silent again, the
inhuman figures had vanished; again only the
section of horse and cart appeared above the mist.
For a moment Geoffrey hesitated, unwilling by any
possible risk to lose the ultimate success; but the
chance of being heard or seen by those retreated
figures was infinitesimal, and he crept crouchingly
down the slope to where the wagonctte stood. Then,
opening the door, he lifted out, exerting his whole

strength, the load the two had put there, and, bent double under the ponderous weight, made his way back to the summer-house. The burden chinked and rang as he moved. There could be no doubt what his prize was.

He had not long been back at his post when muffled, rapid footsteps again riveted him, and he saw a moving, dark shape coming with great swiftness up from the house. As before, with the rising of the ground, it grew freer of the mist, till, when it reached the carriage, he could easily recognise the head and shoulders of Sanders. Somehow, and, if possible, without the cost of human life, he must be stopped. He had already swung a small case, easily recognisable by the watcher, on to the box, and he himself was in the act of mounting, when an idea struck Geoffrey. Taking quick but careful aim, he fired at the horse, just below the ear. At so short a range a miss would have been an incredible thing, and with the report of the rifle the head sank out of light into the mist.

Then he stood up.

'If you move, Sanders, I fire!' he cried—'this time at you.'

But, even as he said the words, the box was already empty. The man had slipped down with astonishing rapidity behind the wagonette, and when Geoffrey next saw him dimly through the mist he was already some yards away. Even while he hesitated, with another cartridge yet in his hand, he was gone, and waiting only to put it in, he ran down to the cart. The case, the same beyond a doubt as was in Mr Francis's hand ten minutes ago, which he had seen Sanders swing on to the box before mounting himself, was gone also.

At that he ran down at the top of the speed he dared use after the vanished figure. Once he heard the crunch of gravel to the right, and turned that way, already bewildered by this blind pursuit in the mist; once he thought he heard the rustle of bushes to his left, and turned there. Then beyond any doubt he heard his own name called. At that he stopped.

'Who is it?' he cried.

'Me, sir—Jim,' said an imperturbable voice close to him.

'Ah! is Harry—is his lordship safe?'

'Yes, sir, quite safe. The doctor sent me out to see if I could help you.'

Before Geoffrey could reply, a sudden wild cry rang out into the night, broken short by the sound of a great splash.

'My Gawd! what's that?' cried Jim, startled for once.

'I shouldn't wonder if it was Sanders,' said Geoffrey. 'Come to the lake, Jim. God forgive us for trying to rescue the devil! I wonder if he can swim.'

'Like a stone, sir, I hope,' said Jim cheerfully.

The roar of the sluice was a guide to them, but they had lost each other twenty times before they reached the lake. In that dense and blinding mist, here risen above their heads, even sound came muffled and uncertain, and it was through trampled flower-beds and the swishing of shrubs against their faces that they gained the edge and stood on the foaming sluice. The water was very high, the noise bewildering to the senses, and despite the fact that five minutes ago Geoffrey had been hesitating whether or no to shoot at that vague runner through the fog, caring nothing whether he killed him, yet now he did not hesitate to run a risk himself, in order to save from drowning what had been within an ace of being the mark for his bullet.

'He must be here,' he said to Jim; 'the pull of the water would drag him against the sluice.'

'You're not going in after that vermin, Mr Geoffrey?' asked Jim incredulously.

Geoffrey did not reply, but kicked off his boots and threw his coat on the grass.

'Stand by to give me a hand,' he said, and plunged out of sight.

'Well, I'm damned!' said Jim, and took up his stand close to the edge of the water-gate. The risk he had been willing to run for his master he had faced without question—indeed, with a certain blitheness of spirit; but to bear a toothache for Sanders's life appeared to him a bargain that demanded consideration. But, even as he wondered, a voice from close to his feet called him.

'Give a hand,' bubbled Geoffrey from the water; 'I've got him. I dived straight on to him.'

Jim caught hold of Geoffrey first by the hair, and from that guided his grasp to a dripping shirt-

collar. Then, after Geoffrey had got a foothold on
the steep bank, between them they dragged the
nerveless and empty-handed figure from the water,
and laid it on the grass.

'Dead or alive?—that is the only question,' said
Geoffrey. 'Get back to the house, Jim, and bring
the doctor here. I don't know what to do to a
drowned man.'

Jim made an obvious call on his resolution. To
stay here with that dripping clay at his feet was
a task that demanded more courage than he had
needed to get into Harry's bed.

'No, sir,' he said; 'you run back to the house
and get your wet things off. I'll stay here,' and
he set his teeth.

Geoffrey could not deny the common sense of
this, nor, indeed, had he any wish to, and he
shuffled and groped back to the house. As yet he
knew nothing except that Harry was safe, and
for the present his curiosity was gorged with that
satisfying assurance. The hall-door he found open,
the hall empty and lit, and running upstairs, he
,saw the door of Harry's bedroom open and went
in. The doctor was there; he was just covering
with a sheet that which he had removed from
the floor on to Harry's bed. He turned round as
Geoffrey entered.

'Quick!' said the latter. 'Go down to the
sluice. Sanders lost his way in the fog, and fell
in. We fished him out, alive or dead I don't
know.'

His eye fell on the covered shape on the bed,

with an awful and sudden misgiving, for it was Harry's room.

'Not——' he began.

The doctor turned back the sheet for a moment, and then replaced it quickly.

'Go to my room very quietly, Geoffrey,' he said, 'for Harry is asleep next door, and get your wet things off. Put on blankets or something, or clothes of mine. By the sluice, you say?'

It was some half-hour later that Geoffrey heard slow, stumbling steps on the stairs, and, barefooted and wrapped in blankets, he went out into the passage. Jim and the doctor were carrying what he had found in the ooze of the lake into Harry's room, and they laid it on the floor by the bed.

'It was no use,' said the doctor; 'I could not arouse the least sign of vitality. Cover the face. Let us leave them.' He stood in silence a moment after this was done.

'So they lie together,' he said, 'in obedience to the inscrutable decrees of God. In His just and merciful hands we leave them.'

So the three went out, leaving the two there.

The doctor led the way down into the hall, Geoffrey in his blankets following him. Jim had brought the rest of his clothes out from the chamber of death, and stayed in the passage, dressing himself, for it was better there than in the room. No word passed between the others till he had joined them. Then said the doctor:

'None of us will be able to go to bed till we have

pieced together what has happened in the last two hours. So——'

'Two hours?' interrupted Geoffrey.

'Yes; it is now only a little after twelve. It was soon after ten that Harry went to his uncle's room, before going to bed, and found him sleeping.'

'He sleeps now,' said Geoffrey. Then, in a whisper: 'Tell me, did Sanders kill him?'

'No. Mr Francis, I feel sure, was dead when——when Sanders came. But he took the Luck, so I imagine, from him. I left him clasping the Luck; I returned to find it gone. And two fingers of his hand were broken. But where is the Luck?'

'That I think I can tell you,' said Geoffrey, 'when my turn comes. But begin at the beginning. I left Jim before dinner in the secret passage.'

So in a few words the doctor told all that had happened inside the house, from the moment when he opened his door and saw the two who now lay upstairs talking in the passage down to his return from the plate-closet to find the Luck torn from Mr Francis's death-grip. Then Geoffrey took on the tale to its completion. At the end he laid his hand on the groom's shoulder with the action of a friend and an equal.

'We have done the talking,' he said, 'but here's the fellow who did the hard thing in this night's work. I could no more have borne that—that man creeping across the room to where I lay in bed——'

'Than I could have jumped into the lake in the dark, sir,' said Jim, 'when all that was to be found was—Lord, love us all!'

Then there was silence for awhile, for the events were still too awful and too close for chattering. The doctor broke it.

'There are two more things to be done,' he said; 'one to bring back the plate from the summer-house, the other, Harry. He must be told everything, but tomorrow will be as well as tonight. By the way, Geoffrey, where will you sleep? You, too, Jim? Can you get into the stable so late?'

'Yes, sir; thank you, sir,' said Jim. 'I'll wake the helper. I brought in the rifle, Mr Geoffrey; you left it by the lake. Shall I help bring in the plate, sir?'

'No, we must get Templeton and another man, in any case,' said the doctor. 'It must be stowed somewhere tonight; the lock of the plate-closet is forced. So get you to bed, Jim. Shake hands like a man, for you are one.'

'Jim, you devil, say good night to a man,' said Geoffrey, and pleasure and pride made the groom laugh outright. 'But you won't tell Harry tonight?' said Geoffrey, after a moment. 'Hush, what's that? My God—Harry!'

The gleam of a candle shone through the door leading to the staircase, and Harry advanced two steps into the hall.

'I woke just now,' he said, speaking to the doctor, 'and—Geoffrey!'

'Call Jim back,' said the doctor. 'Steady, Harry. Not a word.'

Geoffrey gathered his blankets round him, and went to the hall-door, which the groom had just closed behind him. He came back at once in answer to the call.

'But what is it—what is it all?' cried Harry. 'Where is my uncle? I woke, as I began to tell you, and thought I heard people moving about, and got uneasy. I thought he might be worse, or something. Then I went into your room, Dr Armytage, but you were not there. His door, too, was open, and there was a light burning, but he was not there. Where is he? What is it?' he cried again. 'Geoffrey, Jim, what are you doing here?'

He looked from one to the other bewildered, but for a moment none could speak.

'Oh, for the love of God, tell me!' he cried again.

Jim's right hand went to his head in salutation.

'Please, my lord, it's late; I'd better go,' he said feebly.

'No, wait,' said Harry. 'Damn it all do what you are told. The doctor wishes you to stop, so stop. But why and how is Geoff here, and Jim? And where is he?'

Both of the other young men looked at the doctor, and without more words he told the story for the second time, with as direct a brevity as was possible. No word of any kind interrupted him, but in Harry's eyes a wondering horror deepened and grew convinced. Once only did any sound come from him, and that when the doctor said that beyond doubt Mr Francis was not sane, but then a long sigh, it would seem of unutterable relief, moaned from his lips. He heard of the plot as orginally told by his uncle to the doctor, of all the business of the metholycine, of all the communications going on between his uncle's supposed accomplice and Geoffrey, of the scene on the pavement of Grosvenor Square. Then came for the second time that evening the events of the last two hours, but Harry's head had sunk on his hands, and the eyes of the others no longer looked at him, for it was not seemly to behold so great an amazement of horror and grief.

At length the words were all spoken, and for a long space there was silence, while the truth, bitter, and burning as vitriol, ate into the poor lad's brain. Then said Harry, his face still buried:

'As God sees you, Dr Armytage, this is true?'

'It is true, Harry,' said he.

'Geoffrey?' asked the same hard, cold voice.

'God help you, yes.'

'And Jim?'

'Yes, my lord, as far as this night's work goes.'

Harry got up from his chair quietly and steadily. He advanced to the groom, and grasped both his hands in his. Still without a word he turned to the doctor, with the same action. Then, still steadily, he walked across the hearthrug to Geoffrey, and the doctor moved from where he stood, touched Jim on the shoulder, and withdrew with him. Not till then did Harry speak, but now his mouth quivered, and the tension grew to snapping-point.

'Geoff, Geoff!' he said, and the blessed relief of tears came to him.

Epilogue

EVIE was sitting in one of the low window-seats in the hall at Vail regarding, with all the gravity due to the subject, her two-months-old baby—that soft little atom round which revolved the world and the stars and all space. Her discoveries about it were in numbers like the sands of the sea, but far more remarkable. This afternoon they had been, and still continued to be, epoch-making.

'His-nose,' she said, after a long pause, to Lady Oxted, who was sitting by the fire, 'is at present like mine—that is to say, it is no particular nose; but it will certainly be like Harry's, which is perpendicular. That's a joke, dear aunt—the sort of thing which people who write society stories think clever. It isn't really.'

Lady Oxted sighed.

'And his brains exactly resemble both yours and Harry's, dear,' she said—'that is to say, they are no particular brains.'

Evie took no notice whatever of this vitriolic comment.

'And his eyes are certainly Harry's eyes,' she went on. 'Oh, I went to see Jim's wife today—you know, the dairymaid whom Harry was supposed—well, I went to see her. Jim was there, too. I love Jim. You know the resemblance to Harry is simply ridiculous. I was in continual fear lest I should forget it was Jim, and say, "Come, darling, it's time to go." And then Harry might have behaved as I once did. Oh, here's nurse! What a bore you are, nurse! Oh, my own angelic!'

Evie gave up a kiss-smothered baby, and went across to where Lady Oxted was sitting.

'And Mrs Jim's baby, I must allow, has its points,' she continued. 'That's why I am sure that Geoff's eyes are like Harry's, because Geoff's eyes are exactly like Jim's baby's eyes, and Jim is Harry. By the way, where is the spurious Geoff—the old one, I mean?'

'The old one went out within five minutes of his arrival here,' said Lady Oxted. 'I tried to make myself agreeable to him, but apparently I failed, for he simply yawned in my face, and said, "Where's Harry?" '

'Yes, Aunt Violet,' said Evie, 'you and I shan't get a look in while those men are here, and we had better resign ourselves to it, and take two nice little back-seats. In fact, I felt a bit neglected this morning. Harry woke with a great stretch, and said, "By Gad! it's Tuesday; Geoff and the beloved doctor come today," and he never even said good morning to the wife of his bosom.'

'He's tiring of you,' remarked Lady Oxted.

'I know; isn't it sad, and we have been married less than a year! As I was saying, he got up at once, instead of going to sleep again, and I heard him singing in his bath. Oh, I just love that husband of mine!' she said.

'So you have told me before,' said Lady Oxted acidly.

'What a prickly aunt!' said Evie. 'Dear Aunt Violet, if Geoffrey and the beloved physician and Jim weren't such darlings, all of them, I should be jealous of them—I should indeed.'

'What a lot of darlings you have, Evie!' said the other.

'I know I have. I wish there were twice as many, for the whole point of the world is the darlings. A person with no darlings is dead—dead and buried; and the more darlings you have, by so much more is the world alive. Isn't it so? I have lots. Oh, and the world is good! All those I have, and you, and Harry even, and I might include my own Geoff, also Uncle Bob—especially when he is rude to you.'

The prickly aunt was tender enough, and Evie knew it.

'Oh, my dear,' she said, 'it makes my old blood skip and sing to see you so happy! And Harry—my goodness, what a happy person Harry is!'

'I trust and believe he is,' she said, 'and my hope and my exceeding reward is that he may always be. But today—today!' she said.

Lady Oxted was silent.

'Just think,' said Evie, 'what was happening a year ago. At this hour, a year ago, Harry was here with the doctor and his uncle, and his uncle's servant, and then evening fell, as it is falling now; later came Geoffrey and Jim. Oh, I can't yet bear to think of it!'

'I think, if I was Harry, I should be rather fond of those three,' said Lady Oxted. 'Being a woman, I am in love with them all, like you.'

'Of course you are,' said Evie. 'Oh yes, Jim was just going out, when I was with his wife, to meet the others.'

'To meet them?' asked Lady Oxted.

'Yes. Harry said it was a secret, but it's such a dear one, I must tell you. They were going together—it was Harry's idea—to the church. The two graves, his uncle's and that other man's, are side by side. I asked if I might come too, but he said certainly not; I was not in that piece.'

'And then?'

Evie got up.

'I think they were just going to say their prayers there,' she said. 'Oh, I love those men! They don't talk and talk, but just go and do simple little things like that.'

'And the women sit at home and do the talking,' said Lady Oxted.

'Yes, you and I, that is. Oh, I dare say we are more subtle and complicated, and who knows or cares what else, but we are not quite so simple. One must weigh the one with the other; and who cares which is the best? To each is a part given.'

'You had a big part given you, Evie,' said the other.

'I knew I had, and feebly was it performed. Ah, that morning! Just the one word from Dr Armytage, "Come!" '

Evie returned to the fire again and sat down.

'If Geoffrey had not been here the night before,' she said—'the night when it took place—I don't know what would have happened to Harry. There would have been a raving lunatic, I think. As it was, he just howled and wept, so he told me, and Geoff sat by him and said, "Damn it all, Harry!"—yes, I don't care—and gave him a whisky-and-soda, and slapped him on the back, and did all the things that men do. They didn't kiss each other and scream, and say that nobody loved them, as we should have done. And, as like as not, they played a game of billiards afterwards, and felt immensely better. I suppose David and Jonathan were like that. Oh, I want Harry always to have a lot of men friends,' she cried. 'How I should hate it if he only went dangling along after his wife! But he loves me best of all, so don't deny it.'

'Oh, I don't anticipate his eloping with the doctor,' said Lady Oxted.

Outside the evening was fast falling. It was now a little after sunset, and, as a year ago, a young moon, silver and slim, was climbing the sky, where still lingered the reflected fire from the west in ribands and feathers of rosy cloud. But tonight no mist, low-lying and opaque, fit cover for crouching danger, hung over lake and lawn. The air was crisp with autumnal frost, the hoarse tumult from the sluice subdued and low, after a long St Martin's summer. The four men—Jim, servant-like and respectful, a little distance from the rest—had left the churchyard, and strolled slowly in the direction of the stable and the house. Opposite the stable-gate Jim would have turned in, but Harry detained him.

'No, Jim,' he said, 'come with us a little further.' And like man and man, not master and groom, he put his arm through that of the other. Then, by an instinctive movement, the doctor and Geoffrey closed up also, and, thus linked, they walked by the edge of the lake and paused together at the sluice.

'And it was here,' said Harry, 'that one day the sluice broke, and down I went. Eh, a bad half-hour.'

'Yes, my lord,' said Jim, grown suddenly bold; 'and here it was that Mr Geoffrey jumped in of a black night after a black villain.'

'And somewhere here it is,' said Geoffrey 'that the Luck lies. How low the lake is! I have never seen it so low.'

They had approached to the very margin of the water, where little ripples, children of the breeze at sunset, broke and laughed on the steep sides of ooze discovered by the drought. Their sharp edges were caught by the fires overhead, and turned to scrolls of liquid flame.

'And that was the end of the Luck,' said the doctor.

'The Luck!' cried Harry. 'It was the curse that

drove us all mad. I would sooner keep a cobra in the house than that thing. Madness and crime and death were its gifts. Ah, if I had guessed—if I had only guessed!'

Even as he spoke, his eye caught a steadfast gleam that shone from the edge of the sunken water. For a moment he thought that it was but one of the runes of flame that played over the reflecting surface of the lake, but this was steady, not suddenly kindled and consumed. Then, in a flash, the truth of the matter was his—the leather case had rotted and fallen away in the water. Here, within a foot of the edge of the lake, lay his Luck.

He disjoined himself from the others, took one step forward, and bent down. With a reluctant cluck the mud gave up the jewel, and he held it up high, growing each moment more resplendent as the ooze dripped sullenly from it. The great diamonds awoke, they winked and blazed, sunset and moon and evening star were reflected there, and who knows what authentic fires of hell? There was a glow of sapphire, a glimmer of pearl, a gleam from the gold. But two steps more took Harry on to the stone slab that covered the sluice, and there, on the scene of one of its crimes, he laid the priceless thing. Then, as a man with his heel crushes the life out of some poisonous creeping horror, he stamped and stamped on it, and stamped yet again. This way and that flew the jewels; diamond and sapphire were dust, the pearls, unbroken, leaped like flicked peas, some into the lake, others into the outflowing thunder of the sluice. Then, taking the crumpled and shapeless remnant, he flung it far into mid-water.

'And the curse is gone from the house!' he cried.

MORE VINTAGE MURDER MYSTERIES

MARGERY ALLINGHAM
Mystery Mile
Police at the Funeral
Sweet Danger
Flowers for the Judge
The Case of the Late Pig
The Fashion in Shrouds
Traitor's Purse
Coroner's Pidgin
More Work for the Undertaker
The Tiger in the Smoke
The Beckoning Lady
Hide My Eyes
The China Governess
The Mind Readers
Cargo of Eagles

E. F. BENSON
The Blotting Book
The Luck of the Vails

NICHOLAS BLAKE
A Question of Proof
Thou Shell of Death
There's Trouble Brewing
The Beast Must Die
The Smiler With the Knife
Malice in Wonderland
*The Case of the Abominable
  Snowman*
Minute for Murder
Head of a Traveller
The Dreadful Hollow
The Whisper in the Gloom
End of Chapter
The Widow's Cruise
The Worm of Death
The Sad Variety
The Morning After Death

EDMUND CRISPIN
Buried for Pleasure
The Case of the Gilded Fly
Holy Disorders
Love Lies Bleeding
The Moving Toyshop
Swan Song

A. A. MILNE
The Red House Mystery

GLADYS MITCHELL
Speedy Death
The Mystery of a Butcher's Shop
The Longer Bodies
The Saltmarsh Murders
Death at the Opera
The Devil at Saxon Wall
Dead Men's Morris
Come Away, Death
St Peter's Finger
Brazen Tongue
Hangman's Curfew
When Last I Died
Laurels Are Poison
Here Comes a Chopper
Death and the Maiden
Tom Brown's Body
Groaning Spinney
The Devil's Elbow
The Echoing Strangers
Watson's Choice
The Twenty-Third Man
Spotted Hemlock
My Bones Will Keep
Three Quick and Five Dead
Dance to Your Daddy
A Hearse on May-Day
Late, Late in the Evening
Fault in the Structure
Nest of Vipers